THE GREATEST ODIA STORIES EVER TOLD

Also translated by Leelawati Mohapatra,
Paul St-Pierre & K. K. Mohapatra

Ants, Ghosts and Whispering Trees: An Anthology of Oriya Short Stories
The HarperCollins Book of Oriya Short Stories
Uncle One Eye (Novel) by Laxmikanta Mahapatra
The Brideprice and Other Stories by Fakir Mohan Senapati
Sundardas (Play) by J. P. Das
The Gravediggers (Play) by Bijay Mishra
Night Dogs (Stories) by Kishoricharan Das
Between Worlds (Stories) by Gopinath Mohanty

The GREATEST ODIA STORIES EVER TOLD

selected and translated by

LEELAWATI MOHAPATRA
PAUL ST-PIERRE
K. K. MOHAPATRA

ALEPH BOOK COMPANY
An independent publishing firm
promoted by *Rupa Publications India*

First published in India in 2019
by Aleph Book Company
7/16 Ansari Road, Daryaganj
New Delhi 110 002

This edition copyright © Aleph Book Company 2019
Copyright for individual stories vests with respective authors/proprietors
English translation and Introduction copyright
© Leelawati Mohapatra, Paul St-Pierre and
K. K. Mohapatra 2019

The note from the translators on pp. 229–30 constitutes an extension of the copyright page.

All rights reserved.

While every effort has been made to trace copyright holders and obtain permission, this has not been possible in all cases; any omissions brought to our attention will be remedied in future editions.

This is a work of fiction. Names, characters, places and incidents are either the product of the authors' imagination or are used fictitiously and any resemblance to any actual persons, living or dead, events or locales is entirely coincidental.

No part of this publication may be reproduced, transmitted, or stored in a retrieval system, in any form or by any means, without permission in writing from Aleph Book Company.

ISBN: 978-93-88292-97-9

3 5 7 9 10 8 6 4

Printed at Parksons Graphics Pvt. Ltd, Mumbai

This book is sold subject to the condition that it shall not, by way of trade or otherwise, be lent, resold, hired out, or otherwise circulated without the publisher's prior consent in any form of binding or cover other than that in which it is published.

*For
all our dead
and
all our living*

CONTENTS

Introduction: Buy 1, Get 2 Free   ix

1. Ananta, the Widow's Boy FAKIR MOHAN SENAPATI   1
2. Maguni's Bullock Cart GODAVARIS MOHAPATRA   16
3. The Solution GOPINATH MOHANTY   20
4. The Holy Banyan BAMACHARAN MITRA   26
5. The Witness SATCHIDANANDA RAUTRAY   35
6. Ghania Celebrates Ganesh Chaturthi SURENDRA MOHANTY   43
7. The Atheist KISHORI CHARAN DAS   51
8. Mother India (The Chronicle of Uddhav Malik) MOHAPATRA NILAMONI SAHOO   60
9. A River Called Democracy AKHIL MOHAN PATTNAIK   72
10. The Tale of the Snake Charmer CHANDRASEKHAR RATH   79
11. Plus Minus Greater than Zero SANTANU KUMAR ACHARYA   91
12. Trojan Horse KRUSHNA PRASAD MISHRA   97
13. Mrs Crocodile MANOJ DAS   104
14. Savitri RABI PATNAIK   113
15. Savara CHAUDHURY HEMAKANTA MISRA   121
16. The Mantra JAGANNATH PRASAD DAS   127
17. Patadei BINAPANI MOHANTY   142
18. Salvation PRATIBHA RAY   151
19. Anatomy of Madness RAMACHANDRA BEHERA   162
20. Longing for Ramakanta Rath NRUSINGHA TRIPATHY   174

21. News of the Day KANHEILAL DAS   187
22. The Whore: A Love Story KAMALAKANTA MOHAPATRA   192

Appendix

Rebati FAKIR MOHAN SENAPATI   204
The Sanyasi REBA RAY   215

Notes on Authors   223
Acknowledgements   227
Note from the Translators   229

INTRODUCTION
BUY 1, GET 2 FREE

This is no gimmicky marketing offer. It is as real as it can get. Here's why: though thick as thieves while translating, we decided, by common consent, to part ways when it came to writing the introduction. So instead of one long, bland piece, the reader can have the opportunity of sampling three different perspectives.

The introduction (being an introduction) is, umm, well, predictably, inevitably, always placed first in any anthology of short stories but usually read last. (Usually, the reader goes straight for the jugular—the stories). Sometimes this preliminary piece is skipped over entirely; sometimes returned to only afterwards as an afterthought, if the stories have had the desired effect. With so much—or so little—riding on it, we thought a bunch of three might be more tempting than one.

I

As I sat agonizing at my desk over my slice of the introduction, my teenage niece wandered in and wondered what I was tearing my hair out over. (For the record, I'm as bald as an egg.) After she had heard me out, she said, airily: 'No sweat. Keep it short, okay? Nobody wants to read a long, ponderous, parochial introduction to a book of stories. Remember, no aperitifs. Just bring on the main course.'

Bring on the main course indeed!

As she turned on her heels after dispensing this piece of unsolicited but sage advice, her eyes alighted on the pata chitra of the navagunjara I keep under the glass on my desk. 'I hope you're aiming at something like that!' she said. 'Good luck with the beast.'

Good luck with the beast indeed!

In the middle of the fifteenth century, Sarala Das, an apparently unlettered but divinely blessed (his own stout claim, so who are we to dispute it?) scribe set out to render the Mahabharata into Odia (previously spelled Oriya; follows from Orissa now being spelled Odisha; a matter of reclaiming one's identity, yes?), which until then was available only in Sanskrit, and while pegging away at it, went overboard and invented a whole slew of stories, episodes, incidents, weaving them all into the fabric of the grand Indian epic. Among others, he visualized a fantastic being having the body parts of nine animals: the navagunjara, the form in which Lord Krishna apparently manifested himself to his favourite Pandava, Arjuna, when the poor fellow was sunk in deep despair. With the head of a rooster, neck of a peacock, waist of a lion, hump of a bull, tail of a snake, a leg each of an elephant, tiger and deer, and a human hand holding out a lotus, the mysterious creature has come to be interpreted in more ways than one. The one that appeals most is that it is a symbolic representation of the nine basic human emotions as defined in the Indian literary tradition: shringar (love, beauty), hasya (laughter, humour), adbhut (wonder, amazement), raudra (anger, resentment), shanta (calmness, tranquility), veera (courage, fearlessness), bhayanaka (fear, trepidation), karuna (compassion, pity) and, finally, vibhatsa (disgust, repulsion).

In our way, we too have tried to fashion a navagunjara of sorts out of the vast riches of the modern Odia short story while putting together this anthology. But instead of keeping it confined to nine parts, we have let it run to twenty-four, the last two being historically quite significant—the very first modern story to appear in the language (which, incidentally, was written by none other than the maestro, Fakir Mohan Senapati, considered the father of modern Odia prose) and the first modern story by a woman writer.

The emergence of the new medium of modern short stories in the different Indian languages goes back to the late nineteenth century, roughly to the same point of time, give or take a decade or, at a pinch, two. It owed its inspiration to: one, the winds of a renaissance blowing over a colonized country that stimulated the creative spirit; two, the influence of the West, where short fiction had made significant strides since the middle of the nineteenth century; three, the felt necessity of reaching out to a larger audience in a way it would better understand; and, four, the growing realization that the complicated truths underlying the mind-boggling human predicament were better purveyed in prose, rather than in poetry.

Like in the other Indian languages, the modern period of Odia literature was a product of the colonial encounter. Until then, poetry dominated and what little prose existed was in the form of myths, legends, tales, fables, parables, anecdotes, sketches and episodes. (There had been sporadic prose writing in the past: notably, *Rudra Sudhanidhi* in the seventeenth century and *Chatura Binoda* by Brajanath Badajena in the eighteenth.) The short story in the modern sense, focusing on only one incident, a single setting, a limited number of characters, and covering a short period of time did not exist.

As a genre, therefore, the modern Odia short story is only a hundred and twenty years old and counting. But one hundred and twenty is a mythic (and magical) number in Indian lore. Anyone, or anything, existing for one hundred and twenty years is considered to have lived a full and purposeful life in the Kaliyug. A decent length of time in which there has been every opportunity to fully express all that has been experienced in life: joy and sorrow, happiness and bitterness, success and failure, hope, love, lust, despair and death (of others), mundanity and spirituality, and so on. The same seems true of the genre under scrutiny.

The genre germinated in 1898, with the publication of Fakir Mohan Senapati's 'Rebati'. (Included in this anthology in the Appendix, not only because it has the honour and distinction of being the first Odia modern story, but because it continues to be read and discussed, admired and anthologized to the present day. The first century of the story was celebrated in 1998 with several celebrated writers of the day reimagining, re-imaging and reworking the story; there was even an anthology of these stories trying to bottle old wine in new containers, appropriately named *Rebati Rebati*, to commemorate the occasion.) No other first modern short story in any other major Indian language is quite as fêted and celebrated as this. And what's more significant, 'Rebati' bears no signs of a tentative beginning, or fumbling for effect in the new medium. It has, besides, all the quintessential features of Senapati's oeuvre: energetic and robust use of colloquial language, humour, lack of heavy-handed didacticism and value judgement.

For a first story, 'Rebati' is a haunting portrayal of a young girl's burning desire for education—almost like aspiring for the moon, in those days—and the price she pays. Of course, the misfortunes that befall the family are not as causally related as the grandmother of the unlucky girl would have us believe. It has come to stand for a harrowing tale of love, loss, and death in the time of cholera in a nineteenth-century Indian village. (Readers and critics have never ceased wondering why, when dealing with a subject dear to his heart, Senapati laid out such a grim scenario: the eponymous heroine, her parents, the young man she falls in love with and who reciprocates her feelings, her carping grandmother who chants curses like mantras—all perish.)

Literary historians have pointed out that Fakir Mohan Senapati was probably the first Indian writer to write a short story in the modern sense of the term with his 'Lachhamania', published in 1868. Sadly, this story, which appeared in a literary journal of the day, remains lost to posterity. (Doubtless, there will be a re-evaluation of the genre of Indian short story, when, if ever, it surfaces.)

In its day, 'Rebati' inspired several fictional forays into the problematic realm of women's education in all its ramifications, including Reba Ray's 'The Sanyasi', which has the distinction of being the first modern short story by a woman writer (included here in the Appendix precisely for that very significant reason). Published in 1899 in the pages of *Utkal Sahitya*, the same literary journal in which 'Rebati' first appeared, Ray's story may seem only marginally less grim. Instead of killing off all the characters as Senapati did, Ray kills only the girl but exiles her husband to sanyasihood.

Senapati also inspired a whole host of Odia writers into trying their hands at short fiction, which, thanks to the burgeoning proliferation of literary monthlies and bi-monthlies, received a huge fillip. The monthly journals encouraged short stories not only because of constraints of space but also as a way of introducing variety into their content.

Senapati's stories and novels marked the emergence of a new literary form out of a long tradition of folklore and orality. The world of swooning princesses and swash-buckling princes living in enchanted castles gave way to an active engagement with the problems and preoccupations of a prosaic everyday world peopled with ordinary beings. The expansive and digressive oral narration of marvellous incidents by a garrulous, avuncular narrator was soon displaced by an authorial presence controlling the economy of the narrative and addressing a literate reading public.

The Odia short story has come a long way since 'Rebati'. It has provided generations of writers with a ground for restless experimentation with techniques of narration. At a rough count, there are over one hundred thousand stories scattered in anthologies, collections and magazines. The short story has never lacked a fascinated and enthusiastic readership. This may be due to the fact that it has remained rooted in tradition while seeking to transform it. It has absorbed alien influences without becoming alienated from its milieu.

The social world which framed the background for Fakir Mohan Senapati's stories has since been transformed. Senapati sought to dramatize the transition from orality to literacy, from the country to the town and the shift from a communitarian way of life to a more individualistic mode of living. The trauma associated with the break-up of a traditional social order gave his stories their poignancy and continued to shape the vision of a large number of his successors. But the pace of change has accelerated since India's independence and the social world of the Odia short-story writer has fragmented under new and irreversible pressures. Modern Odia short stories are not so much preoccupied with articulating nostalgia for a lost order as with giving voice to defining the anxiety of coping with a rapidly changing world, which often appears quite hostile and incomprehensible. In the process the form of the Odia short story has had to be adapted to accommodate the new and unsettling experiences of change.

Senapati's contemporaries were not as technically accomplished as he was and have long dropped out of sight. They not only lacked the maestro's extraordinary energy and narrative power, but his dexterous use of the earthy vernacular too.

It is impossible to convey the richness and variety of a century-old tradition of short-story writing within the compass of a single anthology, let alone select the greatest stories ever told. What we have attempted here is to bring together a handful of representative stories which, we hope, will give the reader not only an idea of the evolution of the form in Odisha, but also its variety and fecundity. Not all of them are shining examples of flawless craftsmanship, but their hold on the Odia mind has not lessened. No wonder most of these find their unerring ways into vernacular anthologies and textbooks. Having been together for over a quarter century at the business of translating Odia literature in English, Leela, Paul and I had a tough responsibility to dispense with a large number of stories we had already put into anthologies in the past. Repetition of those stories would have left a reader with a sense of déjà vu. Therefore, we left the old selections alone and, barring just about two or three, translated new stories by the acclaimed and established short-story writers for this anthology. Our overall aim has been to highlight the range and variety of Odia short stories written over the last one hundred years.

We are aware several serious practitioners of the genre have been left out because of the constraints of space. But then an anthology is like a zoo or an aquarium; at any given point of time it keeps more specimens out than in. Which, however, does not prove that those outside the pale of this anthology—or for that matter any—are any less significant. As we have always held, an anthology is just an anthology and not the end of the world in terms of literary recognition; and a truly great story or a truly good writer will survive the caprices, machinations and meanness of any anthologist or anthologists.

Over to Leela. For her slice of the cake.

K. K. M.

II

Why does a story move us? Young or old, we are drawn to a tale well told; hence our desire to immortalize it in stone, ink, paint, or celluloid. It has the power to lull a child to sleep, or as Scheherazade found out, keep an emperor awake. Alexander the Great was known to have read Homer in bed. Individually, nationally, culturally we are, to a large extent, defined by our stories, the ones we spin about ourselves, our world and our gods.

If the human brain tends to seek patterns, sometimes where none exist, to find meaning in random events which make up existence, then in some way a story is our attempt to impose purpose on chance, sense on senselessness.

In primitive societies where life was brief and hazardous, and scientific discoveries were yet to be made, man relied on stories to explain frightening natural phenomena like earthquakes, floods, eclipses. Each primal force of nature like fire, wind, or water was attributed divine qualities, and stories of these gods and how they could be propitiated were formed.

These myths, spread initially by word of mouth, went on to answer basic existential questions about Creation, man's place in it, and his relation to a higher power. All this became the bedrock of religious beliefs, binding entire communities together.

But stories, unfortunately, can also be a source of discord, whenever people believing one set of narrative have tried to exert their supremacy through war, crusade or bloodshed.

The story has come a long way from its inception. Much has changed, yet remains the same. It still explores man's relationship to his milieu, evokes the same sense of pity, terror or wonder, assures the reader that though time is fleeting and the face he confronts in the mirror changes with each passing day, he remains the same child at heart who can be enthralled by a good story. It is through stories we flow into other people's lives; stories possess the magical key that admits us into worlds not our own.

My own foray into the world of Odia stories has been fortuitous. One evening in the early 1980s, in the midst of one of Kolkata's hot and humid power cuts, K. K. read out Kishori Charan Das's *Wild Peacock* to me in the light of a hurricane lantern, and a desire to translate it took shape. A few years later, Paul joined us and our little team of translators was truly complete.

The stories we have selected for this volume, like entrenched memories, have the ability to claim us back from the solitude of the self into the community of a language. We know that through these stories and the love we bear for them, we remain connected to a whole race who have loved them before and will in the future. They are the invisible, indivisible strings on which whole generations are strung.

Stories can travel from region to region, heart to heart. I invite the readers to draw closer, shut out the turmoil of the outside world for a while, and prepare to be mesmerized by these tales on offer. They are timeless and can be transplanted into any fertile imagination.

Let the magic begin.

L. M.

III

And now for the last little bit before the real stuff.

These stories can only be reduced to their core elements by paring away what is essential to each—their specific anchoring in time and place, their unique ability to transcend particular events, their various ways of telling a story, their own take on reality, and their attempt to present what is particular to any situation. This is what makes it difficult to write about them in any meaningful way as a group, as a 'collection', for to do so is to be unfaithful to what sets each apart from all the others, what makes each an *individual* story, a story of individuals—unless, of course, one simply repeats what the stories themselves have to say, what they are able to say with much greater skill and depth than I can muster. This individuality of each story is, as K. K. has written here, constitutive of short stories in the modern sense, and so any attempt to find, in any detailed and meaningful way, recurrent themes or similarities going beyond what is characteristic of each is bound to betray. But then, as a translator, I know betrayal well.

'I can't go on, I'll go on.' Beckett was a great one for aporias such as these, and that's where I now find myself, faced with these twenty-two Odia stories, plus an additional two 'firsts' in the Appendix. Their tone varies from pathos to irony to satire to humour to righteous and indignant condemnation. They take aim at social conventions, political corruption, religious insincerity, caste restrictions, abuse of power, and hypocrisy in all its forms. Some are quite conventional in the way they tell their story; others consciously experiment with the form they adopt. Life in the villages figures prominently, but so too does the transition, often unsettling, to the city. Many, the later stories especially, give an important place to women, often centered around questions relating to agency—sometimes negatively (in the description of the space accorded to women), but at other times in a positive and hopeful fashion, in stories in which women play a primary and powerful role. All these stories, to quote Leela, 'attempt to impose purpose on chance, sense on senselessness', and none do this more, or more explicitly, or perhaps even better, than the first short story in Odia, included here, 'Rebati', by Fakir Mohan Senapati.

So three for the price of one! A *real* bargain, and not just for this introduction. We three have translated often together, for many years now, and I for one have learned much from the experience—not just about Odisha and Odia literature, though that too, but also about translation and about what it means to truly work in collaboration. I am thankful for that, and happy to now leave you, dear readers, with the results of our work together, hoping you will enjoy 'the main course'.

P. ST-P.

ANANTA, THE WIDOW'S BOY
FAKIR MOHAN SENAPATI

Subal Mahakur spent virtually all his life in the forest near Harishpur, with the herd of buffaloes he had inherited from his father. His visits home were few and far between.

Winter, monsoon, summer were all the same to him; if anything, he liked the season of rains the most, for that was when grass sprouted in abundance and the buffaloes produced more milk. Wearing a palm-leaf hat and carrying a long sturdy bamboo stick on his shoulder, he would untiringly follow his herd, wading through knee-deep, sometimes waist-deep water, bespattered with mud. The only bother during the rainy season was the shelter he had to build every year, to cook and sleep in. Nothing fancy, mind you, just a few twigs and sticks stuck into the mud, with a thin layer of dry grass and leaves for a roof. It was small, and he had to stoop to get inside; there were no walls to block his view of his herd. He slept on the bare ground, resting his head on a pair of thick wooden clogs, his broad-brimmed hat pulled down over his head—as long as the rain didn't patter down on his face! He kept the young calves tethered to the shelter, so whenever it rained the floor swam with dung and urine. He wallowed in the muck like a merry eel.

Every day, in the small hours of the morning, he would wake up to the eager buffaloes straining at their tethers. He would take them into the forest to graze. That was when he had to be more alert than ever; at the slightest opportunity a sly wolf could easily spirit away a calf.

In the forest, the buffaloes' snorting would warn him if a tiger was on the prowl. He could produce yells and howls so terrifying and bloodcurdling that even the biggest and most ferocious tigers panicked. All the big cats in the Harishpur forest knew his mighty voice, and kept away from his herd.

At the crack of dawn he would lead the herd back to the hut, where he would quickly tether and milk them, fill the milk cans, and wait for his wife, Devaki Mahakuranee, to show up with his needs for the day: a big pancake baked from pounded rice not fully husked; five seers of coarse parboiled rice; and a plug of tobacco. He'd promptly devour the pancake, washing it down with big gulps of fresh, frothing milk. Sitting by his side as he ate and smoked, his wife would fill him in on the news of the household and the village, and return home with the milk pots balanced on her head.

Twice a day, Mahakur would build a fire and bring the rice to a quick boil, throwing into the pot the greens, vegetables, or other things he had found in the forest. He was not the kind to put a lot of effort into what he cooked. Plain rice and fresh buffalo milk formed his staple diet.

Summer was more difficult: he had to leave the forest for the lake, where the buffaloes, skittish from the heat, would wallow in the water from sunrise to late afternoon, submerged to their nostrils. He would pitch his palm-frond umbrella at the water's edge and, in its parsimonious shade, cook, eat and sleep at night, curled up like a centipede, his clogs under his head, with a damped-down fire of dry buffalo dung on either side to keep the mosquitoes away. But there were so many mosquitoes—dark, big and long-legged—it was difficult to drive them away with smoke alone. So he would scoop up handfuls of mud from the lakebed, cover himself from waist to toe, and lie down to sleep, muttering under his breath: 'Fuck off, brothers!' When he felt their bites burn on his back and hands, he would kill scores with every sleepy slap. And as his sleep wore thin he would yell at his herd: 'Hey Malati, Sukri and Kali! Are all of you out there?' The buffaloes understood him and would sneak back if they had strayed. The wilder ones had wooden bells around their necks so that Mahakur knew the moment they snapped their tethers.

One year, the goddess of death struck like a lightning bolt and in a week's time his herd was almost wiped out. This broke Mahakur's spirit, but not his wife's. 'My dear,' she urged her husband. 'Stop this brooding! Just look at yourself—bent double with worry! Whatever has happened is done. Don't break your heart over it. I'll go into the milk business. I can raise any money I need on credit from my brother and Burunda Barik. In two years' time I'll get you a herd as large as the one you've lost—you can count the heads and see for yourself.'

Mahakur sold off the surviving buffaloes, all the orphaned calves, and took over as the seth—chief herdsman—for the zamindar, who had four large herds. It was a good opportunity for him, and his wife was thrilled. As the seth's wife, she demanded everyone address her as Sethanee. If anyone—male or female—failed to do so, she'd be so incensed she'd pick a quarrel with the culprit—even rushing out to beat him.

In winter that year, the police commissioner came to Makrampur on inspection, and his tent was pitched in the grove near the police outpost, less than a mile from the lake. It was thick with birds—pelicans, flamingos, hornbills, storks, herons and cormorants—and as soon as the sahib learned this he picked up his gun and set out, followed by a retinue of four constables and eight lathi-wielding chowkidars wearing red and yellow rags for turbans. When the excited sahib fired his gun, thousands of birds rose from the water, squawking wildly, circling the sky, perhaps wondering who the white devil was and what he was up to. A pity their comments in the language of birds should seem nothing more than wild cacophony to human ears!

When the scene had settled a bit, two birds with broken legs and wings were seen plunging into the lake. But who would dare fetch them from the deep waters, where two man-eating crocodiles were rumoured to lurk? The sahib looked at his subordinates, but the constables were wary of wetting their uniforms, and the chowkidars thought it prudent to pretend they didn't know how to swim. The sahib could fine them, even fire them, but death in the jaws of a crocodile was by a long shot worse than either of those.

It so happened that Subal Seth was out inspecting the zamindar's herds and was present at the scene, watching the performance with considerable amusement. Suddenly, without a word, he dived into the water, retrieved the dying birds, and threw them at the sahib's feet. The white man was impressed. He carefully looked the stranger over a couple of times. Subal was a big, burly fellow, his broad shoulders rippling with muscles; he had a large round face with flaring nostrils, and his thighs were straight and strong like young sal tree trunks.

'Who are you?' the sahib enquired.
'Subal, my lord, the zamindar's chief herdsman.'
'Would you like to become a constable?'
For a full minute Subal was silent. 'Not until I discuss it at home.'

Unable to grasp Subal's reply, the sahib turned to the head constable, who was reputed to have mastered the *First English Primer* from cover to cover and to be able to sign his name with a flourish in the alien script.

'This cow-man Mahakur, sir,' the head constable explained. 'He says he go home and ask wife. If she says yes, he will constable.'

A ghost of a smile crossed the sahib's lips, but it was a minute or two later that the implications of the explanation dawned on him. He fished out a notebook and wrote: 'Subal Singh is fit to be a constable. He seems to be a clever man and knows how to show respect to the fairer sex.' He looked at Subal again. 'Present yourself at the camp tomorrow morning.'

That was how Subal Seth became Subal Singh, the sahib's personal attendant and his favourite servant. He was put in charge of the hunting gear, and the sahib never went anywhere without him. Noticing how pleased the sahib was with Subal, favour-seekers cultivated him and greased his palm. Every month he made a tidy sum over and above his salary of nine rupees.

His wife Devaki was strict with him and took him to task for the smallest extravagance. 'Wood-chewer!' she would scold. 'If this is how you're going to blow your hard-earned money, you'll stay a slave all your life. Don't forget that!' Now she was Singhanee, Singh's wife and no longer Sethanee, and she saw to it that people realized this very quickly.

A couple of years after Singh had taken up his police job, the commissioner invited the district magistrate to hunt in the Dompara forest. The magistrate managed to put a slug into a tiger they had been stalking, but only to lodge it in the animal's flank. The tiger crawled into the dense undergrowth, growling murderously. There were about a hundred men with the sahib, but who would go near the wounded animal? As the saying goes, a wounded tiger is the same as Yama, the god of death! The commissioner cast a sidelong glance at Subal Singh, who, without a word, raced into the bush with the stick he had kept from his herding days. He battered the poor tiger to death and dragged it out by the tail. No wonder he received a reward of twenty rupees on the spot and a promotion to the rank of head constable, which brought his salary to fifteen rupees a month.

But even as all these good things were happening to him, his time was quickly running out. When the month of Kartik came around,

Singh quietly succumbed to a brief bout of fever.

Singhanee was not one to crumble under the blow she had been dealt. After carrying out all the funeral rites, she went into business herself. In mental ability as well as in physical strength she was more than a match for her husband. Large, dark-skinned, imperious, she had a belly that bulged out of the sari fastened below her navel. She loved to deck herself out with jewellery, which she had to remove temporarily during the period of mourning: heavy bracelets covering her forearms from wrist to elbow, a massive nose stud weighing not less than twelve grams, a large necklace of gold coins hanging down to her stomach, and eight rings as large as oysters on her fingers.

Her courage was phenomenal. She continued to live on the edge of the village, now alone with her little son, Ananta. One night, three thieves drilled a hole through the wall and got into the house. Before they could pin her down she gave one mighty shake of her arms, and the poor devils landed on their backs four feet away. Two of them managed to run off, but she caught hold of the third by a leg. With a thick rope she tied him to the central pillar of the room and went back to sleep. In the morning the news spread and villagers came flocking, wondering who the thief could be. Imagine their shock when they saw it was Jhapat Singh, the village chowkidar! Singhanee was advised to hand him over to the police, but she scoffed: 'He's not worth the trouble. I can fix him myself.' She did. And how!

Two resounding slaps, and Jhapat Singh had bitten the dust. His cheeks swelled like rising dough; he stayed in bed for a fortnight.

Ananta was four when his father died. An only child, he was the apple of his mother's eye, more precious than a million moons. He took after his parents, in both physique and complexion. In the evenings, her chores completed, Singhanee would set him on her capacious lap and lovingly caress him for an hour, crooning lullabies. The sight was reminiscent of a cow-elephant with her calf. Every morning she rubbed the boy with a quarter-seer of pure mustard oil and turmeric paste, straightened his hair with a wooden comb and tied it in a small knot. At times, catching herself staring dotingly at her son, she would bite her tongue: 'Good Lord, am I a mother or a witch!' She would scrape a little mud from under the tulsi plant in the courtyard and quickly smear it on the boy's forehead, and then sprinkle a little cow dung on his hair to ward off the evil eye. There were all kinds of women in the village, and how could one know who were witches? Singhanee left nothing to chance—around the boy's neck she tied an amulet containing part of a pig's snout, on his arm she tied another containing a wood-apple leaf consecrated in the temple of Lord Siva, a couple of counterfeit coins on a string, and four silver lockets containing herbs. She often dabbed his forehead with dust from her own feet. Once all this had been done, she would give him the pancake baked the night before from a large measure of rice, and then sit down to churn the curd for sale in the village.

People would stop and watch in wonder as she strode down the village path swinging her huge arms, undulating her hips, balancing three vessels of curd—one on top of the other—perfectly on her head. 'The Nandighosh chariot!' they would remark to each other. She had earned for herself a string of epithets: Devaki the Milkmaid, Mahakuranee, Singhanee, Taraka the Demoness—but these were muttered behind her back. She responded with good grace only when addressed as Singhanee. The shrewd ones took advantage of her weakness when buying her curd. If someone said 'Singhanee this' or 'Singhanee that' to her with a little admiration in their voice, she would respond by pouring two or three seers of curd into their bowl for free.

Time and tide wait for no one. Little Ananta was now ten, but looked almost twenty—so big and strong was he. For lunch he could gobble down three large seers of coarse rice—often only half-cooked and unstrained—washed down with four seers of fresh milk. He never made a fuss about food, but sometimes his loving mother's heart ached enough for her to cook him a bowl of dal or boiled vegetables.

As days passed, Singhanee began to have some minor problems on account of her darling boy, though she put it all down to the jealousy of the villagers, ganging up against him for no reason. Complaints poured in every day: Ananta had emptied someone's cucumber patch; he had cleared someone else's stretch of sweet corn; he had stripped every single mango, tamarind, and blackcurrant tree in another's grove, and so on. But Singhanee never reproached her son for any of this; far from it, she fussed twice as much over him. Although he was now a big hulk of a boy, she still sat him on her lap and cuddled him every evening.

One day, on her way home, her eyes lit upon Vaishnav Mohanty's grammar school, conducted under a bakula tree. It struck her that here was the solution: Ananta could get some education and that might put an end to his peccadilloes. Next morning she took him there. 'Teacher,' she said, 'you must teach my child as well as you can.' Ananta sat down with the students, like a good boy, for if there was one person on earth he was mortally afraid of, it was his mother.

The teacher traced the first two letters of the Odia alphabet on the ground and asked Ananta to learn them by moving his finger over them. The boy's fingers moved, but his eyes had begun to search the foliage overhead. And there he spotted a ripe bakula fruit. He climbed up the tree like a nimble monkey, plucked it, put it into his mouth, and slid back down to his lessons—all in the twinkling of an eye. He was so good at climbing trees that he could chase even a monkey up the tamarind tree in their garden, grab the hapless thing by the tail, and beat it to death.

With Ananta around, the teacher soon lost control of his class. He couldn't turn his back even for a moment; given a chance, Ananta would push, prod, pummel, pinch and tickle his classmates. Sometimes he dared them to gang up on him, but no one was that foolish. In the beginning, the teacher hesitated to upbraid him out of fear of his mother. Quite apart from the woman's fiery temper, he had no wish to forego the free curd she dished him out daily. Fear and greed, as the saying goes, prevent many a good deed.

But after a few days the teacher simply could not take it anymore; he picked up his cane and flogged Ananta. That did not seem to deter the boy, however; his eyes were trained on the bakula boughs, and his hands idly smoothed away the sting of the beating. Soon it became a routine. 'Lord Siva may run short of wood-apple leaves,' the students joked, 'but our Ananta will never be lacking our teacher's canes.' Every day a new cane was broken on his back. His mother had absolutely no idea about what was going on, for Ananta never complained to her; the moment he walked out of school he forgot it all.

Four or five months passed. Ananta had mastered the first letter of the alphabet and graduated to the second. The teacher, whose hands were sore from beating the boy, was at the end of his tether, yet he couldn't throw him out. One fine morning, however, he decided he had had enough. He threw away his cane in disgust, grabbed a bunch of nettles, and lashed the boy's legs, arms and back.

That was the first time Ananta felt pain, but he didn't bawl or protest. 'I'll fix that bastard,' was his only remark to his classmates afterwards.

The next morning the teacher was in for a pleasant surprise. Ananta, the very picture of sincerity and concentration, sat practising the alphabet, not looking up at anyone. The teacher glanced at him from time to time out of the corner of his eye, wondering why on earth he hadn't hit upon this wonderful punishment before! After an hour, he felt the urge to go out to the fields to move his bowels and, as usual, shouted to the boys: 'Hey there! Fetch me some tobacco, some embers and the jug.' Five or six boys sprang to their feet to see to the arrangements. They always did the teacher's chores, from washing his clothes to scouring his cooking pots, and no matter how rich a home a student came from, he had to press the teacher's feet. That, the teacher said, ensured faster learning!

The teacher rolled himself a fat cigar. 'Hey, Mukund!' he scowled, exhaling a deep puff of smoke. 'This tobacco's no good, boy.'

'Not my fault, sir,' replied Mukund. 'It's what my father got from the market yesterday.'

'Hmm!' He turned to another boy. 'Binodia, you never brought us the good Baleswari tobacco leaves you said your father got in Cuttack.'

'I tried to, sir,' said Binod. 'My mother has hung them in a sling from the ceiling, and I can't reach that high.'

'Here's what you can do. When your dear mother's away for her bath, get hold of a bamboo basket, turn it upside down, and climb on top of it. See if you can reach the sling. Just pull out a couple of leaves, don't try to take the whole lot in one go. And if you fail to manage this, I suggest you have a good look at what's in my hand.' He twirled his cane.

Then he looked at Ananta. The boy was poring over his lessons, and the teacher was deeply moved. 'Ananta, my boy!' His voice softened. 'Take the jug and get me some water so that I can go for nature's call.'

Obedient pupil that he was on that morning, Ananta got up at once and hurried off to the pond.

The teacher smiled and waited.

Ananta took a long time, and it became sheer torture for the teacher to wait any longer. Casting desperate glances at the pond, he finally rose to his feet.

Ananta was hiding behind the fence and, as soon as the teacher came close to it, he darted out and handed over the jug of water in such a fashion that the teacher had to take it by the rim, without dipping his fingers into the water. Pulling vigorously on his cigar, the teacher ran towards the outlying fields.

About half an hour later he came running back, his clothes in disarray and barely held together by the waist-knot, screaming to high heavens. He'd lost the jug somewhere. 'May he not live long after this—damn him to hell, that young devil, that bloody Ananta! The bugger's just about killed me!' He grabbed his cane and lashed out. 'Where's the bastard?'

Ananta had vanished.

The teacher rolled in agony from one end of the classroom to the other, howling for water. A pupil got some from the kitchen. The teacher took a mouthful, and the next moment the bowl went flying from his hand. 'My God!' he cried, rolling about in redoubled frenzy. 'Oh father, oh mother, I'm done for!' Soon his voice was gone and he could only utter a few groans. His face had swollen so much that his eyes were covered over. He couldn't see a thing.

The villagers came running, carried him to the pond, and dunked him in the water. Towards evening, when the cold got to him, he was given a good massage with linseed oil. Solitary words began to fall from his lips. 'Hungry!' he whimpered. But he was hardly in a position to do justice to anything solid, and was given a big bowl of warm milk, which he drank in slow, painful gulps. The hot drink and the oil massage made him feel better.

The village elders drew out the details. It was all Ananta's doing. The widow's son had nursed a grudge against the teacher for the whipping with the nettles, and when he was sent to fetch water for the teacher Ananta had seized his chance at revenge. The little beast had half-filled the jug with nettles, not forgetting to sprinkle a handful in the teacher's drinking-water pot in the kitchen before running away.

'I swear,' said the teacher, as he rose in anger, swishing his cane through the air. 'I'll deal with the widow's brat this time.'

The villagers tried to stop him, but he rushed off in the direction of Singhanee's house. Anger had blinded him. 'Hey, Devaki, you bloody milkmaid, where's that bastard of yours?' he screamed.

Singhanee had already hidden her son inside the house, and was waiting for the teacher. When she heard his challenge, she hefted her husband's famous buffalo-taming stick and jumped off the veranda. 'Damn you for a rotten teacher!' she roared. 'May the pox take you, you witch's turd, you driftwood, you garbage! You dare call me a milkmaid? You've forgotten, haven't you, that my husband was head constable? And how dare you call my son names! Just wait till I lay my hands on you.'

The teacher's blood ran cold when he saw her. Her sari had slipped from her head; wisps of dishevelled hair tossed in the wind like angry snakes, and the bamboo stick bounced on her shoulders. The woman's physical strength was legendary. The teacher remembered the sight he had once seen with his own eyes: one morning she was walking along the riverbank, three full vessels on her head, on her way to sell her curd, when the huge ill-tempered bull from the Binodbehari temple suddenly charged headlong at her. Singhanee stopped short for a split second, caught the bull by the horns without letting the pots atop her head so much as tilt; steering the struggling animal to the edge of the bank, she pushed it down. The poor bull rolled down the slope like a rag doll onto the riverbed, breaking a hind leg. It was so chastened that it stopped thrusting its angry head for all time to come. No wonder the teacher now turned back and bolted like a doe chased by a tigress—tripping, stumbling, falling, bruised all over.

Singhanee chased him a good distance, brandishing her stick. The ground trembled, her bouncing belly gave off a strange sound, and the clanging of her brass bangles could be heard a quarter of a mile away. The whole village reverberated with her battle cry: 'Come back here, you straw-chewing slave! Where have you hidden my son? Hand him over, or I'll smash your skull with my bangles.'

The teacher vanished into the darkness; neither hide nor hair was seen of him the following morning.

Five or six years passed. The villagers' despair grew and grew; Ananta had become the scourge of their gardens and orchards, going after the fruit and vegetables. Not a single cucumber, mango, wood apple, cob of corn, or berry was spared, but he would never have bothered to even look at gold or silver, even if a garden had been strewn with precious metals.

Moreover, he had grown up to be as helpful as he was destructive; it was only when rubbed the wrong way that he had it in for the offenders. The first thing he did was break down their door and windows, though mercifully out of respect for his mother he never roughed up the culprits. But if one knew how to handle him, he was ready to wipe the shit off their bottom, and the clever ones in the village made him do a good bit for them free of charge, almost every day. If someone was digging up their backyard and he passed by, and they asked him politely: 'Anta my friend, what'd we do in this village without you?' Then he'd grab a hoe without another word and in an hour dig up the whole patch to a depth of one foot—a job that would have taken four farmhands one full day. If someone's house remained unthatched because there were no workers available, and they caught hold of Ananta and cajoled him, he would do it for them single-handed, even if it took him a whole day or two.

When Rama Bhina's father died of cholera, not one of his relatives came forward to help perform the cremation rites, and the corpse was left rotting in the house until midnight. When Ananta happened to pass by on his way home, Rama poured his heart out to him and, without so much as a word, Ananta rolled up the body in the mat on which it lay, hoisted it onto his shoulder and headed for the cremation grounds through the dark, deserted village. He was afraid of nothing, not tiger, bear, ghost, snake—in a word, he was fearless.

True, he would plunder your garden. If you tried to stop him and give him the fruit instead, things would only get worse. Incensed, he would start tearing down your house.

What he did to Bindia Chand, the weaver, was unforgettable. Bindia was a big moneylender and could advance you eight to ten thousand rupees on the spot; he managed a good trade in clothes, too. Once, Bindia was building a large room for a shop; the foundation had been laid and the corner pillars raised. The workers were having a tough time with the central pillars, each one eighteen hands high and as heavy as the trunk of a sal. It so happened that Ananta was passing by.

'The widow's brat can leave the ten of us standing,' one of the workers commented, puffing and panting with exertion. 'He could have easily raised this pillar all by himself.'

'Hey, Ananta!' Bindia called out, rather thoughtlessly. 'Come give us a hand with this, will you? I'll give you two rupees to buy yourself some sweets.' Who could have saved the unfortunate weaver after this slip? 'Bloody weaver!' Ananta lunged at him. 'Bastard, am I your servant? Am I going to work for you for money? How dare you ask me to?' It was lucky indeed for the weaver that he managed to hide from the boy that day. Ananta set himself to the task of systematic demolition. In an hour's time he had undone what had taken ten workers twenty days to complete—the pillars and posts lay uprooted and the foundation was dug up. Bindia complained to the village council, but all he got was a sound scolding. Didn't he know the widow's brat better?

In the end, only the clever ones in the village could take full advantage of Ananta, and get him to do their chores.

The village of Binodrayapur was on ground only slightly higher than the bed of the Bhargavi, which ran north of it. It was protected from flooding, thanks to the government's foresight, by a mud embankment, twenty hands wide and half as high, running eighteen miles from Gopalpur to Ramnagar. The village of some two hundred households was quite prosperous. The land was fertile, and many of the inhabitants were engaged in government service or in trade.

Came the month of Ashwin, and people living away from their native village were back home for the festival of Durga Puja. As always at this time of year, the village was awash with joy, feasting and merrymaking.

On the sixth day of the full moon, an ugly patch of cloud loomed over the northern corner of the morning sky. The sun rose and quickly ducked behind it. It was not long before the whole sky was blotted out. A wild breeze sprang up.

Seeing the ominous signs, the old priest, Govind Panda, repeated the saying:

A sunrise you can't see, like red sky at night,
Foretells disastrous rain, that's exact and right.

Barely had the words passed his lips when the lower depths of the cloud broke open and the drumming of the rains started. It poured endlessly without a moment's letup, right through the sixth, seventh, eighth and ninth day. People could not step out of their homes, and the oldest inhabitants admitted that even they had never seen anything quite like this. Several houses, soaked through by the rains and constantly buffeted by the wind, collapsed.

On the morning of the tenth day, the village was seized with panic; the river had risen to its brim and the banks were all but overrun. The men—old and young, high-caste and low—swarmed out of their homes with shovels, hoes and baskets. The river resembled an ocean; angry waves, five hands high, dashed remorselessly against the mud-bank. The people kept watch over it: whenever the water washed over, hundreds of buckets of mud were thrown onto the spot, instantly raising the height of the bank. So much mud was scooped out from the foot of the embankment that it looked like a lagoon.

Meanwhile, eight miles downstream, the river did overflow at Rampur, and the waters reached the outskirts of Binodrayapur by the evening. The submerged fields looked like a sea, and now the threat to the village came from these eddying backwaters, which kept rising steadily.

The women, clutching babies to their breasts, spilled out of their homes, abandoning their chores. They ululated, blew conch shells, prayed and wailed. The world was coming to an end; the sun had set. The water had already entered the village through the bathing ghat, eroding it by some five hands, and widening it by almost as much. Jets of water shot into the village as though from a huge hand pump.

'O Hari,' the people cried. 'Please help us now!' Soon the sea would swallow them all. Yet no effort was being spared; hundreds of thousands of buckets of mud were being piled up to stem the tide, to block the onrushing water. But the current was so strong that not even a handful remained in place.

The world was no doubt coming to an end, but what did that matter to Ananta? The hulk was busy making sorties into the village, in the drenching rain, collecting cobs of corn and cucumbers. The rising commotion from the bathing ghat finally got the better of him, and he thought he might as well go and watch the fun. He witnessed a strong current racing into the village and heard people wailing that this was perhaps the end. He stopped to gather his wits about him, then ran back to the Binodbehari temple and took the heavy lion-door, five hands by four, off its hinges. Balancing it on his head, he ran to the bathing ghat, collecting Parvati's mother's rice-husking paddle from her front room on the way.

Back at the ghat, he thrust the door into the swell of the tide, using the husking paddle as a support. Pressing himself against the door for good measure, he began urging the villagers: 'Come on, folks, throw mud! Mud, mud, and more mud! Hurry up!'

From both sides came flying baskets of mud—mud, stones and sand. One moment it was up to his waist, and the next to his chest. 'Come on,' Ananta exhorted, as it rose up to his neck. 'Don't slow down now!' He was buried up to his lips. 'Praise God and throw on more mud,' he kept shouting. 'Mud!'

The frenzied activity stopped only after the torrent had been stemmed. The day had been won; the world had not come to an end after all. It was time to catch one's breath and thank the widow's brat. But where was that fine fellow?

'The blessed soul!' the crowd cried in unison. 'Blessed is the widow's boy.' As if God had been watching it all, the rains let up abruptly, and the water began to recede.

Sitting on her veranda, Singhanee wondered what the delirious loud chanting from the bathing ghat might mean. Her son had been absent since morning; time she went to look for him. She picked up her husband's bamboo stick, bolted the door, and strode out.

As she passed through the village, she heard people singing her son's praises. Men and women came rushing to her, throwing themselves at her feet. 'Blessed is your son! Glory to your Ananta!'

She marched on to the ghat, taking in the whole story without a word. Her eyes were riveted on the centre of the newly-raised mudbank. Pacing back and forth, her glance swept over the sheet of water. How deep was the river here—five, ten, or twenty hands?

She spun sharply on her heels.

A sudden splash...

The sound made the villagers cry out. They trained their flaming torches on the river. Five hands off the bank there was a frothing eddy, and a little farther away a bamboo stick could be seen moving downstream, bobbing up and down in the current.

MAGUNI'S BULLOCK CART
GODAVARIS MOHAPATRA

Births and deaths: Khalikote, with about two hundred thousand people, had its inevitable share of both. Reports of either, however, never travelled beyond the confines of families and neighbourhoods. But when Maguni died, the news spread throughout the town and beyond. Whoever heard it, exclaimed, after a stunned silence, 'So the poor fellow's gone! How sad!'

Who was Maguni? The ruler of Khalikote? The king of a neighbouring state? A major figure in the administration? A big taxpayer, a rich moneylender? A Congress leader spearheading the Satyagraha movement for independence, delivering stirring speeches to delirious crowds? An acclaimed patriot? Or a prominent citizen who was always chosen to receive visiting dignitaries? Who was he? Why did everyone in the town as well as in the far-flung villages on the forest's edge know who he was?

Maguni was not an important man. All he ever did to eke out a living was drive a bullock cart. He had struggled throughout his life, not for his country or countrymen, but simply for himself, for his own survival. Yet the bond he had forged with his pair of bullocks left a lasting impression on people's minds.

Every day Maguni made his trip to the railway station, as regular as the sun that rose and set over the fort town. He was as punctual as a clock, people said. In the rainy months, when the sun remained hidden behind clouds, his passage announced the time of day. The seasons could be irregular, the monsoons delayed, or the summer not hot enough, but never did a day go by without Maguni's cart rumbling along the road. Even on bitterly-cold winter mornings, when people sat on their verandas wrapped in blankets, Maguni drove his cart along the serpentine road beneath the hills with a song on his lips.

So what if the king of Khalikote had two motorcars, Maguni sometimes joked, did the king have a driver like him? His bullock cart was far better than any motorcar. He just had to gently pat Kalia and Kasara on their rumps to rev up the engine and belt out snatches of the popular ballad 'Rama and Laeekhana followed the trail of the magic deer...' to make the bullocks fly. The song echoed through the hills, waking up the birds and animals. Forest pheasants called, stray village dogs howled as his cart inexorably rolled by.

Criss-crossing the entire length and breadth of the town and beyond, he kept people hooked on the stories of his life, which flowed from his mouth in an endless stream. Raised with love and care by doting parents, his had been a wonderful childhood: a comfortable bed, copious meals, not having to do a day's work. Life continued to treat him well even after both his parents died and he grew into manhood. He married a beautiful girl, whose words were as sweet as her lips. Her breath was fragrance itself and flowers bloomed where she walked. Life was a dream, a glorious riot of happiness and joy. Only this didn't last long. His young wife departed for the other world, where he hoped to join her when his days were done.

These poignant stories brought tears not only to the eyes of listeners, but to his as well. Discreetly wiping away his tears, he would change the subject and talk of something else. The journey would come to an end, but not his stories. With the solitary exception of the king of Khalikote, everyone, from the dewan to the managers, from lawyers and moneylenders to the followers of Mahatma Gandhi, had boarded his cart at one time or another. His cart had witnessed so much: young widows on their heartbreaking journeys from their in-laws back to their parents; merry brides riding joyously from their parents' home to their husbands'; Gada Raul of Mandal village, jailed for failure to pay his taxes, and whose worldly possessions, down to his last broom, were transported to the king's court in this cart; or Madhu Rath of Bendalia, sent to prison for committing a murder; prosecution lawyers; handcuffed peasant leaders courting arrest with a smile on their faces. Maguni's cart had seen sorrow, it had seen joy. Torrents of tears had drenched its straw seats just as bursts of laughter had rattled its bamboo ribcage. So when Maguni spoke, a legend spoke, the living voice of Khalikote's history spoke. He brought so much gusto and excitement to his stories that even the bullocks at times slowed down and stopped. 'Look how these animals love to listen to my stories,' he'd chuckle. He never used the goad on them.

But the day came when Maguni learnt that people were to have another means of transport. The wealthy Singhs were planning to put a bus on the road. He broke into uproarious laughter. A bus to beat his well-nourished Kalia-Kasara team? Would people ever desert his cart for a god-forsaken bus?

Everyone laughed at him, but he was unfazed.

A few days later a monster of a motorbus rolled into town.

Poor Maguni's done for, people remarked. Now his business will fold. How can a bullock cart ever match a bus that can carry twenty people at a time and cover forty miles in an hour?

Maguni's heart sank and panic seized him. True, he did not break down and cry, but he came close to tears. He remembered the public meeting at Kodola he had once driven past. A speaker there had asserted that machines were no match for human hands. If that was true, then wasn't his bullock cart better than a motorbus? He'd go and appeal to all those people who had attended the meeting and listened to the speech. Would they turn a deaf ear to him? If they did, then he'd go to their leader, Mahatma Gandhi. Everyone said he was a great friend of the poor and the wretched of the earth. Would he too turn Maguni away? Would he say let Maguni perish and the Singhs prosper?

The bus plied the same route as Maguni's cart. Day after day after day the bus went full, the cart empty.

Maguni rose at midnight to go and park his cart in front of the railway station before daybreak, but the passengers chose to wait for the bus, which arrived late in the morning.

Maguni changed the old upholstery of his straw seats for new jute sacking, but people still headed for the bus.

Maguni took passengers by the hand, to lead them to his cart, but they all headed for the bus.

Days passed, and then some more.

Maguni stuck it out. He cut down his meals from two to one a day.

A few days more and Maguni switched from hot, freshly-cooked rice to watered rice.

More days passed, and Maguni went from a single helping of watered rice a day to one every two days.

Still more days; he did not light his hearth for days on end, as there was nothing to cook.

Kalia and Kasara became dreadfully thin. Their ribs jutted out. Often Maguni put his arms around their necks and the three of them wept silent tears.

Gone off his hinges, people commented, crazy from hunger and grief. More days went by.

Then came the morning when people had to break down the door of Maguni's house to get to his body. He lay lifeless on a tattered mattress, his goad beneath it.

A pyre was lit for him. Thick black smoke billowed into the sky, and countless birds, flapping their wings in anguish, flew by. The news swept the town, and nearly two hundred thousand people lamented, 'So poor Maguni's gone! What a pity!'

THE SOLUTION
GOPINATH MOHANTY

Dadhibaman stared off into the darkening horizon, eyes dilated, face crushed by humiliation as he recalled the turbulent day at the office. He felt angry, hot, tired and worried. Night was falling and he had just got home. A dog's day, toiling from ten to five, practically the whole time, unrelenting pressure at work, file upon file, no end in sight. And on top of all that, calls for explanations, reprimands, insults.

All for a measly salary of seventy-five rupees a month—not even the cost of three large sacks of rice in these hard times. Out of that, the house rent, the doctor's fees... Laundry alone came to seven rupees, and firewood to fifteen, and so much else too. It was tough to make ends meet. Delicious food was only a dream; patched rags worn at home; skimp and save, skimp and save. How he and his family managed to hang on was a mystery. Ten years in the job, yet nothing more to show for it. His debts had only grown larger and the sheer pressure of work was nearly splitting his skull. The insults, the reprimands, the threats were only the final straw.

There—that was his life. Looking at the sahada tree at the back of the house he mulled things over. What more was there than work and reprimands? The future seemed as bleak as the past. They were his life; nothing more.

'Mein...mein...mein...' A tug at the hem of the rag wrapped around his waist and Dadhibaman came out of his reverie. His pet goat was demanding attention, producing a sound closely resembling 'I' in the national language: 'Mein...mein...mein...'

Dadhibaman bent over and patted the animal on the back. The soothing contact reduced his bitterness by half. His voice dripped with affection as he murmured his name: 'Betu! Betu!'

Betu twitched his tail, raised himself up on his forelegs, shoved his nose into his master's face, and expressed himself in his native tongue. Then he moved away and scampered around a bit, the bells around his neck tinkling. He circled Dadhibaman, rubbed against him and bleated: 'Mein...mein...mein...'

Just one year old, but how he had grown! Dadhibaman hadn't been able to put off his young son when he had asked for a kid goat as a pet. In the twelve months since then, Betu had grown a goatee, while Dadhibaman wondered whether or not to have him castrated.

Dadhibaman touched the goat. He ought to get a she-goat so they could raise some kids. The price of goat meat had soared; already three rupees a seer! Meat—curried, roasted, fried! The intimate relationship between the eater and the eaten always came to Dadhibaman as a revelation, increasing his desire to stroke the goat.

Dadhibaman continued to pet him.

As Dadhibaman's three young children came bounding out of the house, Betu began to prance around again, his bells tinkling. 'Betu!' The children chanted. 'Betu!'

Dadhibaman stood watching his life's main achievements. He had stuck to his damned job for the sake of his children. Why else would he have done it? Even a cobbler made five rupees a day, and a rickshaw puller, three—the coolie carrying sand and bricks made a rupee and a half. If he had had a paan shop he could have built a house for himself! Feyda Miyan, who had just a bicycle repair shop, had managed to buy four houses in just twelve years, with still enough money to lend out at a high interest rate. Couldn't Dadhibaman have done the same?

He was afraid on account of his children, he realized as he watched them. What if a business took two years to take off? How would he manage during that time? How would he earn at least a steady seventy-five a month? And if he didn't, what then?

No friend in the future, and none in the past! If he were about to starve to death, no one would come to his rescue. This is what made him hesitant. Shutting the unfulfilled dreams out of his mind, he sighed—business wasn't for him, it was not his destiny! Though those who succeeded in business weren't necessarily better than him. Many a time he had been about to give up his job, only to back out at the last moment—what would his children live on the first few years?

If not for this fear he'd gladly have left his bloody job—today, this very moment. The insults, reprimands and jibes were becoming intolerable. Just today the big boss had clucked and tut-tutted for an hour, as if Dadhibaman had set fire to his house or something. And as if that weren't enough, the boss had then demanded a written explanation why Dadhibaman hadn't attended to such-and-such files.

Dadhibaman fished the boss's letter out of his pocket. The overpowering urge to read it yet again was like trying to find out if a wound had healed by picking its scab. He had almost learned the words by heart. What thundering language—demeaning, insulting, soul-killing! How would he reply? What reply would work? The pressure of work? No one would buy that. That he didn't get two square meals a day? That he didn't get enough sleep on account of his children constantly falling ill? No one would buy these either. If Lord Brahma had to work as hard as Dadhibaman, even he would make mistakes! Would anyone accept such an explanation? No one was willing to recognize the truth, but the same people would be content with clever lies! But what clever lies could Dadhibaman cook up? He was sadly lacking in imagination.

Dadhibaman smoothed the boss's letter out on the ground and went through it once again. Tears welled up in his eyes. What a life, what a wretched life!

'Mein...mein...mein...'

Dadhibaman lowered his head and gently pressed his eyelids to Betu's lips. The goat turned away, shook his ears, rubbed his head against his master's knees, and looked up at him in bewilderment.

A goat's life was fine, Dadhibaman reflected. Everyone's life was fine. Everyone's except his.

All of a sudden Betu snatched the letter from Dadhibaman's hand, and the folds of skin over his jaws started moving up and down furiously. Before Dadhibaman could stop him, the piece of paper was already inside his tummy.

'What—you gobbled it up, Betu? Now what explanation will I give?'

'Mein...mein...mein...' bleated Betu, shaking his beard. 'Don't worry,' he seemed to be reassuring him. 'I'm here for you.'

All this took some time to sink in, but when it did Dadhibaman was dumbstruck. This was the last straw. Instead of providing an explanation he would have to ask the head clerk for another copy of the boss's letter—an unpleasant prospect, at the very least. He thought he knew the letter verbatim, but now that it was gone, so was his memory of it.

The words seemed to have faded into oblivion, even as he wondered what is remembered and what is quickly forgotten.

Damn it, what's gone is gone! Suddenly resolute, Dadhibaman stood up. Betu's round eyes seemed to have become bloodshot. Dadhibaman suddenly remembered the enormity of the problem, and smoke seemed to come out of his eyes. When people had made up their minds not to be convinced by a genuine explanation, why provide any? No, he wouldn't bother; let them do as they pleased. Dadhibaman's self-control had crumbled. He was on fire.

He strode inside, Betu in tow. Heaped on the table were some office files. Picking up Betu he brought him near the table. Betu seemed to show great interest. All worked up, Dadhibaman pushed a file towards Betu's mouth. The goat wagged its short tail and gratefully fell on the task of disposing of the file at hand. The taste of the local newspapers and the papers the children did their homework on was familiar, but office work clearly had a distinct flavour! He placed his forelegs on the edge of the table and propped himself up. 'These files are so delicious,' he bleated from time to time, 'but there's so little to sate my hunger.'

Dadhibaman gently nudged another fat file towards Betu.

The next day, at around ten o'clock, the office watchman saw Dadhibaman coming from his house, just a stone's throw from the office, followed by a goat. There was a red ribbon with bells tied around the animal's neck. The bells were tinkling.

'Shoo! Scram! Beat it!' the watchman yelled at the goat. 'Look at the damned goat, it's trying to get in!'

'Stop, don't do that,' Dadhibaman said. 'He's a pet; he won't do any harm: he's just like a person.' Dadhibaman turned to the goat. 'Come on, Betu. Follow me.' Betu did, most obediently.

'So well-trained!' commented the watchman.

'Yes, just like a human; understands everything. Goats are like that. Haven't you seen how well they perform in circuses?'

In the office, Betu was introduced around.

'Well, well, a damn healthy specimen,' commented Ram. 'About ten seers of quality meat, don't you think?'

'But what's the use?' remarked Gopal. 'The meat would have a god-awful stink. Pity, Betu wasn't castrated when he was a kid.'

'Mein?' bleated Betu, looking askance.

'There'd be no foul smell to the meat, I tell you,' said Feyda Miyan, 'if, as I do, you knew the secret of how to slit its throat!'

A lively discussion ensued about various meat dishes and their preparation. Betu took a leisurely stroll around the office and came back to his master. Butting his feet with his head, he seemed to ask, 'Mein?'

Dadhibaman turned over the wastepaper basket for Betu. The goat settled down at his feet and set about disposing of the scraps of paper.

Betu went about his job at a lively pace. Hour after hour passed. Done with all the wastepaper baskets, Betu turned his attention to the files sitting on the shelves. It didn't take him long to go through one. Once he'd caught hold of it, he was finished in minutes. Sometimes he pulled down eight or ten at a time. After a little rest, he'd reach for someone else's. It was a feast day.

Finally he reached the head clerk's table, loaded with piles of papers and files all marked 'urgent'. The head clerk had gone to see the big boss, and Betu set to lightening the poor fellow's load. After a bit of good work he ambled off, but not before depositing by the table a few precious droppings—a particularly good fertilizer.

'Betu,' Dadhibaman called out.

The goat came running back, his bells ringing.

'Come, lie down here.'

Betu wedged himself between Dadhibaman's legs.

The head clerk returned. 'You all have so many pending files that the boss is boiling. Now, tell me frankly—and I want your word on this—are you going to dispose of the files before the end of the day? What about you, Dadhibaman?'

'All done, sir.'

'Really? That's very good.'

'Mein?' Betu bleated, getting up. 'Mein?'

'Hey look, look, a bloody goat has strayed inside,' the head clerk shouted. 'Watchman!'

'The goat's my pet, sir,' Dadhibaman said. 'He's followed me to the office. He's no nuisance, sir; just let him be. The smell of a goat fights tuberculosis, you must know that, sir. At least that's what doctors say. And considering the dark, dingy halls in which we work...'

'Oh yes,' answered the head clerk, seeming to think out loud, his eyes riveted on the goat. 'Could easily make eight or ten seers of lovely meat. But why on earth didn't you get it castrated, Dadhibaman?'

'Mein!' Betu shook his beard, nimbly stepping up to the head clerk's table, with still a large stack of 'urgent' files on it. Betu's work was far from finished: there were plenty of disposals pending.

THE HOLY BANYAN
BAMACHARAN MITRA

If you've ever passed through Naripur, you would've sat and rested for a while in the shade of the holy banyan. (The tree is no longer, alas; bedevilled by humans, it gave up the ghost leaf by leaf—branches, roots and all.)

For a long time, the holy banyan was a well-known landmark. Spreading well over an acre, it once stood at the edge of the village; its hanging roots had become mighty trunks. The ground underneath it was clean, polished like a cement floor. The roads connecting Naripur to the surrounding villages—Dihasahi, Daitapur, Dhanua and Gamara to the east, and Nuagaon, Nuapatna and Ahmedpur to the west—all passed the tree.

To the north lay the village cremation grounds, littered with human skulls big and small, discarded torn mats, mattresses and pillows of the dead. It resounded now and then with cries of Haribol, and the sobbing and wailing of women. They threw their clay cooking pots and pans into the growing heap of rubbish, took a dip in the pond, and returned home. The blazing cremation fires died down, silence and darkness surged back in again. After the period of mourning, everything returned to normal; life went on as before. But the dead remained dead, their flesh and bones enriching the soil, nourishing the grass and the weeds. What became of their souls? Christians believe they wait until Judgement Day and then, according to their karma, are sent either to heaven or to hell. Hindus believe in rebirth, the day after someone dies or two hundred years later. Atheists, of course, dismiss everything: once dead and turned to ashes, all is over! But doesn't the Bhagavad Gita say the soul endures forever? But no matter what the pandits say, the people of Naripur believed—and had reason to believe—that when a rebirth was delayed, many a soul, unable to get over their attachment to their former homes and families, chose to take shelter under the holy banyan. Even those who'd normally have found a place in heaven. Only the other day, Anta, a robust young man in the prime of life, passed away after an attack of cholera. His young widow cried so bitterly she fainted on the cremation ground. As Anta's relatives were returning home after the cremation, a fat branch of the holy banyan broke off and crashed to the ground. No whiff of a breeze, let alone of a hurricane or whirlwind. Unable to get over his love for his young wife, Anta's ghost had obviously settled in the big tree. No matter that within a month the young widow eloped with Ram Pradhan to Calcutta. This led to tongues wagging, and it came to light the young woman had poisoned her husband at the instigation of her lover. Anta's ghost was often sighted; it never left the tree.

No one could keep count of all the ghosts inhabiting it. Not only those of Naripur but the ghosts of several surrounding villages had chosen the tree as their nesting place. People claimed to have seen them climbing up and down the tree and roaming the roads.

Not a drop of rain nor a ray of sunshine could penetrate the holy tree's foliage. The ground beneath it stayed warm in winter, like a mother's lap, and dry in the monsoons. When it threatened to rain, cowherds would shelter their cattle, goats and sheep under it. The animals would sprawl on the smooth surface and chew their cuds in peace. The boys would climb up and prance about on branches as wide as roads, while some stretched out on their backs belting out snatches of a song: 'Tell me, oh sweet damsel, whose daughter or wife are you, and who has reduced you to tears?' Others swung from the hanging roots.

A weary traveller, longing for a short rest on a hot summer day, would choose the shade of the mighty tree. Some said it gave forth a cool breeze to welcome visitors as soon as they came near. The traveller would take off his turban, wipe away his sweat and lean back against the trunk to catch his breath. A while later he'd swig a bellyful of cool rice water, delicious with salt and crushed chillies, lie at the foot of the tree and pass into deep, contented sleep. He'd awaken by late afternoon, when the shadows had grown long and, with a reverential bow to the tree, resume his journey. In winter, merchants would stop there for the night, accompanied by thirty or forty bullock carts piled high with merchandise. With the bullocks fed after being unyoked and tethered to the hanging roots, dinner cooked and eaten, everyone would drop off to sleep. The place, snug and warm as if under a blanket, kept the biting cold at bay. In the morning, after paying their respects to His Holiness, they'd go on their way.

The holy banyan had been planted by Banabehari some four generations ago. A quiet, honest and truthful man, he felt disturbed by the bad blood between the two villages and went away to the high Himalayas to pray and meditate. In those days, community leaders did not have recourse to politics to solve problems; no, they considered all discord their personal failure and would undertake fasts and meditations, after which they would try with redoubled ardour to establish the rule of virtue. Quite unlike the leaders of today who advocate the rejection of religion and spirituality. There's apparently no place in modern, scientific society for such concepts, considered figments of the imagination. The only true aim of life these days is making money, creating wealth, through industry, through commerce; money alone matters. Well, time will tell who is right. Maybe imagination makes a god out of a human being, while science turns him into a demon.

A year of penance and meditation in the Himalayas later, Banabehari returned with a tiny banyan sapling and planted it at the edge of the village in a ceremony enthusiastically attended by people from nearly twenty-five nearby villages. The feasting went on for seven long days.

The sapling grew into a gigantic tree. Burying their differences, the villagers met and mingled in peace, harmony and brotherhood under its vast canopy.

When Banabehari died, his ghost settled on its branches, instead of pushing off to heaven. Until recently, generations of his descendants had distributed rice water to thirsty passers-by under the tree during the summer. Whenever Batasundar, a descendant of Banabehari, recited the Sivastaka or the Siva-tandav stotra by Ravana, not only the temple in which the mantras were chanted but the mighty tree too seemed to vibrate. Batasundar could not get over his attachment to Naripur, and when his mortal remains returned to the dust of the cremation ground, his ghost too decided to nest in the holy tree.

Every year, on the occasion of the dwitiya-osha, the tree was given a ceremonial bath. This was an important occasion, marked by the sound of drums, conch shells and ululation. The tree was draped in new clothes, the main and the larger trunks were dabbed with vermilion. Incense sticks were lighted, their fragrance enveloping the place, and the feasting began. The Hindus from twenty-five villages even sat and ate with the Muslims of Ahmedpur. Shops sprung up, folk opera and pala troupes performed day and night.

Apart from this great annual celebration, there were smaller functions all round the year: offerings made when a wish came true—whether it was a child begotten, or that child getting a job. The tree had brought together people over a vast area. For four generations, it had been the centre of their existence.

The village of Haldia was to the north, bordering the Naripur cremation grounds. A large village, its inhabitants were richer and more educated. The children of Naripur went to work in the fields from an early age, minded cattle and picked up swear words instead of learning nursery rhymes like 'There goes Kanhai, the dark-complexioned, with Rohini's son...' No wonder the Naripur upper-primary school never grew into a middle school, while the middle school of Haldia had long since blossomed into a high school, and was all set to become a college. Haldia villagers were in business and government service, quite a few in high positions too; the local MLA came from the village, as did the panchayat chairman. While Naripur was full of dingy little houses—its cowsheds bigger than its living rooms—Haldia had many brick-and-mortar buildings.

But Naripur's greatest pride was its mighty banyan tree, before which, no matter how big or important the other villages were, all had to bow their heads. It was the Kalpataru, the wish-fulfilling tree, a living god.

But times began to change. The Panchayati Raj came to stay. More and more people became educated. The economy changed. Like Bhagiratha bringing the Ganga to earth from the heavens, the architects of the country's destiny got funds from abroad, which then flowed from the centre to the states to the panchayats. These modern-day Bhagirathas even tried to direct the flow directly to their own states. Some funds disappeared in transit, just as the waters of the Ganga had—a crafty Lord Siva or a Jahnu Muni could reroute the stream in their matted locks! But that made little difference. As long as the torrents jetted in full force, a little stealing here, a little pilfering there made no difference, did it? Well, who cared!

But the trouble started when those who had been deprived awoke and suddenly turned patriotic. Their attire changed overnight: white cap on the head, cloth bag slung from the shoulder and coarse white dhoti down to the knees.

Naripur's Batakrishna was seen dressed like this one fine day. He had been working in a jute mill in Calcutta, but once he got the scent of what was cooking in the village he rushed there like a vulture to a carcass. It took him less than a moment to figure out how to divert the flow of funds from Haldia. The first thing he did was set up the Divine Banyan Development Committee and call for a meeting. People from the twenty-five villages attended. They decided that henceforth every village would contribute an anna a month to the Development Committee. Individuals wanting special services would have to cough up two rupees. The washerwomen could no longer carry away for free the mountains of dry leaves and twigs they swept up from under the tree; they'd have to pay a paisa for every bundle; and so on and so forth.

Batakrishna became the secretary of the committee. Funds were collected, and quite a handsome amount they added up to. Around the principal trunk of the tree a huge cement platform was built; smaller platforms came up around lesser trunks. A brick ashram was put up for Batakrishna, and he came up with ever new ideas to increase collections.

He recognized a brilliant opportunity in the poetic excellence of Jaan Mohammed of Ahmedpur. Jaan, a popular bard, wrote slim books of verses on subjects like 'The Quarrel between Mother and Daughter-in-law' and 'The City-smart Daughter-in-law from Cuttack' and sold them out of his bag, trudging from village to village. It was he who had earlier versified the story of Anta's wife poisoning him and then eloping with Ram Pradhan to Calcutta. That book had done quite well; the village women had snapped up copies. Batakrishna commissioned Jaan to pen 'Miracles of His Holiness the Sacred Banyan'. When the book was ready, the name of Batakrishna appeared as its humble author. The stories of miracles spread, the number of pilgrims grew. Not only did the fame of the holy tree grow, but so did Batakrishna's too. More and more money flowed into the committee's coffers, and some of it found its way into Batakrishna's.

Batakrishna then made a foray into the village panchayat committee, becoming an ordinary member. Shortly afterwards a rumour began to circulate that a no-confidence motion against the president of the panchayat committee—Batuk from Haldia—was in the offing.

The roof on Batuk's second floor remained to be cast. He saw trouble approaching, but he wasn't one to take it lying down. A compulsive litigant, he always wreaked vengeance through the law courts. On his payroll could be found a phalanx of witnesses swearing to speak nothing but the truth and then proceeding to speak anything but. For just two rupees and a free meal, they could casually tell the most outrageous lies, even as they tripped miserably during cross-examination. Poor judge! What could he be thinking while reading the transcripts? The truth completely eclipsed by lies, like the moon by dark clouds?

Batuk was naturally much feared. Before the panchayat meeting convened to push through the no-confidence motion against him, he slapped four or five false cases on Batakrishna, with charges ranging from molestation and rape to cheating and committing burglary—involving all the important sections of the Indian Penal Code.

Batakrishna appealed to His Holiness and went on a fast, stepping up the sales of 'Miracles of His Holiness the Sacred Banyan'. The cases were fought using the Banyan's funds, the false witnesses were bought off. Batuk lost the presidency. Batakrishna took his place, but he claimed it was a victory for His Holiness, not for himself.

As the flames of fights between Naripur and Haldia leaped higher, the cracks between Naripur and the other villages surfaced too.

But Batuk became more determined than ever, hatching plans to bring a non-confidence motion against Batakrishna. He bribed the members, piled them into a truck and drove them to Bhubaneswar, where they were made to swear their loyalty and allegiance not only in the presence of the minister but before Lord Lingaraj in his temple over consecrated mahaprasad, before returning to their homes. All this before the night was over. The whole operation was carried out as stealthily as the silent movements of the sly murrel fish; not even their next-door neighbours got whiff of it.

But Lord Lingaraj's influence apparently did not extend as far as Naripur, which was under only the fiat of the holy Banyan. Groups of pala singers, daskathia and jatra troupes, in addition to Jaan Mohmmed, fanned out to the villages to spread the gospel of His Holiness and, in the process, the stories of Batakrishna's greatness. Neither Lord Lingaraj nor the minister was enough to pierce the wall of propaganda. Batakrishna eyed the position of the chairman of the panchayats, and seemed to inch closer to his goal by the day. He adopted the banyan tree as his election symbol.

It was then that it struck Batuk that the myth of the sacred Banyan had to be shattered once and for all.

A couple of days afterwards, an ascetic was found in the cremation grounds of Haldia deep in meditation. His name was Batia Baba. The news eddied around that he was a worshipper of Goddess Kali, that he honed his spiritual powers on corpses at the dead of every new moon night. He had harnessed evil spirits and could destroy anyone by letting them loose, or just as easily could rid anyone of a chronic disease, or dogged ill luck, with a pinch of ash from his sacrificial firepit. Like lightning the news spread and soon there started an unending stream of people to the Baba.

A few days later, a new panic gripped the villagers all around: their homes were being bombarded with stones and excrement at midnight. No one could figure out what was happening. Terrified, people went to Batia Baba to find out the cause and the cure. So Batia Baba went into a trance, and what he revealed after his puja stunned everybody. The issue was the ghosts of all twenty-five villages, who until now had lived in perfect peace and harmony in the branches of the sacred Banyan, like the members of a large joint family, were having problems. The ghosts of Naripur, cussed as always, were suddenly trying to evict all others to have full run of the tree, and their evil designs were being supported by the Muslim ghosts of Ahmedpur. So, naturally, the homeless ghosts of the other villages were up to all sorts of mischief, including pelting homes with stones and faeces. What was the remedy? Let every village plant a banyan tree of its own to shelter its own ghostly population. A bright idea, it appealed to all. Dhulia, the chief of Batuk's lackeys, accosted him in private and suggested: 'Sir, why not slap the Naripur ghosts with Sections 17, 447, 426, 323, 500, 504, 325, 354 and 379 of the Indian Penal Code? We have a doctor who can issue medical certificates to order, though his graphic account of bruises can be misleading. And witnesses? Not only am I myself available, I can easily round up several others.' For once, Batuk was supposed to have lost his cool and told the lackey to bugger off.

The decision was taken that Batia Baba would plant the first banyan sapling in the Haldia cremation grounds and name it His Majesty the Mighty Banyan. The preparations afoot, Batuk left for Gaya to bring back a sapling of an ancient holy tree.

Batakrishna caught on to Batuk's plans and swung into action. It didn't take a lot of work. He caught hold of Naripur's Widow Bati. Although no great beauty, she had felled many a mighty man, just as she had saved some from doing time. She did not tolerate any opposition, if she was properly cajoled and appealed to.

Three or four days after she paid nocturnal visits to Batia Baba's ashram, the Baba left Haldia to set up an ashram in Naripur.

When Batuk returned from Gaya, he found his wits deserting him. He had been outsmarted and was left gnashing his teeth. Asked why he had returned empty-handed, he spoke of the dream he had on the way. It was revealed to him that if the new banyan trees were not the offshoots of the holy banyan, the homeless ghosts would refuse to roost in them. Every village had equal rights over the banyan, and was free to break off branches and grow them into new trees. 'Besides,' he added, 'to tell the truth, the holy banyan is really my property. I own the land he stands on; I bought it from Sapani for five hundred rupees. I have paid the land rent for the last five years and have the receipts to show for it. But I'm donating the holy tree to the people of all twenty-five villages. You all are welcome to cut a branch, take it to your village, and grow your own holy banyan trees to save yourselves from the menace of your brood of ghosts.' Batuk Pradhan's generosity surprised everyone; they were in a hurry to act upon his suggestion. But the whole thing was kept under wraps for some time.

One day, at midnight or thereabouts, Batakrishna awoke to the sound of axes falling on the banyan tree. People from Haldia and a few from other villages were hacking off branches. It took minutes for the news to swirl through Naripur. Armed with knives, axes, sickles, spears and sticks, its denizens came rushing out. A mighty branch came crashing down. It echoed eerily in the temple of Bateswar, sounding like the last gasp of Time Eternal.

The two sides promptly came to blows. The holy tree trembled. Volleys of deafening laughter issued from the temple. Doomsday had arrived. Into the fray jumped the Muslims of Ahmedpur, brandishing swords. Batuk had kept them on standby. The Muslims had borne a grudge against Naripur people, ever since Batakrishna had banished them from the communal worship of the holy tree.

The combatants scattered at the sight of the naked swords. Before running for his life, Dhulia buried, as instructed by Batuk, a large quantity of the deadliest poison under the main trunk of the sacred Banyan.

The next morning the bodies of eight men and fifteen severely wounded were found at the foot of His Holiness. The ones who had sustained minor injuries had managed to crawl away.

The police arrived on the scene. Section 144 was imposed on and around the holy banyan. About a hundred arrests were made. Both Batuk and Batakrishna were handcuffed and taken into custody. All the sections of the IPC Dhulia had once suggested using against the ghosts were now cited against the two, with Section 302 for murder thrown in for good measure. Just as vultures and dogs arrive in droves to clean up carrion, touts and lawyers descended upon the villagers to make money. The wealth Batuk and Batakrishna had amassed seemed to vanish in a bonfire.

A few days afterwards, the holy banyan began to droop and wilt. The mighty tree seemed sunk in sorrowful meditation. Thinking about the past? Worrying about the future? Lord Siva, the embodiment of eternal Time, had swallowed poison during the churning of the oceans to save mankind. Perhaps the sacred tree had decided to give up the ghost to save the people of Naripur?

But of course it was a plain case of murder. But could a tree file a case against its assassins under Section 302? If you are a tree you have no recourse, and nobody laments your passing.

The government auctioned off the wood. The people of Naripur and Haldia, their resources burnt up in court cases, didn't have money enough to bid. The ones who did were the Muslims of Ahmedpur. They logged away the big trunks and branches. The Naripur folks bribed them to leave a little something behind—the smaller branches and twigs. In two days flat, the holy tree had completely vanished; not a vestige remained.

A civilization had come to an end. Another had begun. Nothing to worry about of course. Nothing remained forever, except eternal Time.

Even to this day many people swear to have seen the ghost of Banabehari wandering about, lost, and to have heard the sound of his sighs and his wooden clogs slapping against the ground.

THE WITNESS
SATCHIDANANDA RAUTRAY

'I, Jintan Sahu, the son of late Salagram Sahu, aged fifty-three, resident of Alisha Bazaar, Cuttack, under the jurisdiction of Lalbag police station, swear that I shall speak the truth and nothing but the truth.'

The lawyer began his examination.

'What is your occupation?'

'I run a paan shop.'

'And what do you sell?'

'Nehru brand tobacco, Gandhi brand areca nut, spices for paan, biscuits, lozenges and chocolates, Lux body soap, Sunlight laundry soap, et cetera, et cetera.'

The judge was curious about the witness's name. 'What does Jintan mean?' he wanted to know.

'Your Honour, my father also sold paan. In his day there was this Jintan brand paan masala. It came in little red pellets packed in beautiful tin boxes, shipped all the way from England. A small rectangular box contained fifty good-smelling pellets. The box was nicely painted too. The price wasn't high, only three annas. The white sahibs came on their horses all the way to father's shop. Even Commissioner Jefferson Sahib would stop by...'

'Enough.' The judge stopped him.

The lawyer resumed his examination.

'How long have you been in business?'

'Ever since I finished class four, some forty-five years ago. I've been in business long enough. You can see two of my fingers are worn to the bone from dabbing slaked lime on the leaves.' The witness held his right hand high enough for everyone to see.

'It started,' the witness continued, 'as an hour or two here and there, but very soon my father told me to quit school and take charge of the shop full-time. Since then folding paans has been my business.'

'Do you know Baraju Samal, the accused?'

'I do.'

'For how long?'

'Close to two years.'

'How did you make his acquaintance?'

'He'd cycle down to my shop every so often, order a paan, smoke a cigarette, munch a biscuit sometimes, and hang around for an hour or two.'

'An hour or two? What did he do all that time?'

'He'd stand with his hands in his pockets and take in the street scene, whistling. He'd ogle the college girls as they passed by on rickshaws.'

The public prosecutor rose to his feet. 'This may be noted, Your Honour. The accused ogled college girls as they passed by on rickshaws.'

The defendant's lawyer spun on his heels. 'Your Honour, that is irrelevant.'

'It is not, Your Honour,' shot back the public prosecutor. 'It speaks volumes about the moral character of the accused.'

'Not at all,' the lawyer argued. 'If anything, it's only proof the accused appreciates beauty. All Odias love beauty. To love beauty is no crime.'

Jintan was hugely enjoying it all. He did not know sparks could fly so thick and fast on the simplest of matters. He wasn't as nervous as when he'd first taken the witness box, and he felt his self-confidence returning.

The lawyer turned to him. 'Don't go beyond what's being asked. Answer directly.'

Jintan nodded.

'Do you know where Baraju lives?'

'No, but I once heard him say he lived somewhere near Khan Nagar.'

'How did you notice his bicycle?'

'I told you, he rode it to my shop. He'd lean it against the lamppost while he had a smoke.'

'How did you know it was his bicycle?'

'I saw him using it for well-nigh two years. Once when I asked him about it, he said he'd bought it from someone from Mahanga.'

'Did he tell you the seller's name?'

'That was none of my business. Baraju was a good customer, and I didn't want to put him off by asking questions.'

'The court isn't interested in your opinions.' The lawyer looked at him sharply. 'Did you have any idea what Baraju's occupation was?'

'No. But I do remember him once mentioning he wanted to hire the sports-stadium cycle stand on lease. I never enquired whether the deal came through. It was none of my business to quiz a customer, and Baraju was as good as any. After all, I'm just a paan seller and know to keep out of personal matters.'

The lawyer indicated he had finished.

The public prosecutor took over. His voice was strident.

'So you admit Baraju Samal came to your shop to have paan?'

'Yes, sir.'

'Did you ever notice if he had stolen goods with him?'

'No, sir.'

'For example, a watch, or a fountain pen, or a bicycle?'

'Never.'

'How did he arrive at your shop?'

'On his own two legs.'

The public prosecutor grimaced in irritation. 'Of course he'd use his legs and not his arms to reach your shop. What I wanted to know is his form of transportation—a rickshaw, bicycle, motorcar?'

'A bicycle, sir.'

'Would you be able to identify the bicycle?' He pointed at a bicycle in the dim, ill-lit corner of the courtroom. 'Whose is that?'

Jintan hesitated, never having seen either Baraju or his bicycle before. He looked furtively at the lawyer. The lawyer winked at him.

'It's Baraju's.'

'Are you telling the truth?'

'Yes, sir.'

'You might be lying.'

'No, sir.'

The public prosecutor suddenly seemed tired. He rested for a minute and began again.

'Tell the court what Baraju does and where he goes after leaving your shop.'

'No idea, sir. But more than once I heard him say he was headed for Barabati Fort.'

'Did he ever say why?'

'He said it was refreshing to sit by the moat around the fort.'

'Objection, Your Honour.' The defence lawyer stood up. 'This line of cross-examination has nothing to do with the issue. It is totally irrelevant.'

The public prosecutor brushed him aside. 'Your Honour, it has a crucial bearing on the case. The point is the accused is a loafer, a vagabond, given to roaming all over town aimlessly. It's people like him who take to stealing.'

'On the contrary,' retorted the lawyer. 'It just shows the accused is a peace-loving man given to observing nature. His visits to Barabati Fort underline his great love and respect for the history and heritage of Kalinga. Every true son of Kalinga should be proud of my client.'

The court adjourned.

The police witnesses—two constables—had already been examined and cross-examined. They had confirmed the person they had seized the bicycle from was Baraju Samal, but their testimony did not prove it was stolen. There were no other witnesses. Even though some people knew Baraju was using stolen bicycles they wouldn't have dared testify against him in open court. The man had been tried twice before and released.

When the hearing resumed in the afternoon, the public prosecutor took the floor.

'Did Baraju go to the cinema?' he asked the witness.

'Yes, sir,' Jintan attested without batting an eyelid. 'Sometimes he'd come back and tell me the story.' He paused and added, 'But he wasn't into selling cinema tickets on the black market.'

The courtroom broke into titters.

'How did you know he went to see films?'

'I told you just now. He'd come back and tell me the story.'

'And what kinds of scenes did he like best—stealing, fighting, committing burglary?'

'No, none of those.'

'Which ones then?'

'Romance, love scenes.'

'Who's his favorite hero?'

'Dharmendra.'

'Why Dharmendra?'

'He said that Dharmendra was the only superhero, that he knew how to woo a woman.'

'Objection, Your Honour.' The lawyer was on his feet. 'All irrelevant questions.'

'On the contrary, Your Honour,' the public prosecutor protested. 'These are highly relevant. They demonstrate the accused's lack of moral fibre, his lack of values, his mental imbalance.'

'Far from it, Your Honour,' refuted the lawyer. 'They only show hero worship on his part. Baraju Samal is simply an inveterate hero-worshipper, if anything.'

Jintan was enjoying the trial. He felt a sharp thrill. His simplest answers seemed to trigger jousting between the two lawyers and bring up layers of meanings he'd never suspected existed. He was beginning to believe he had a great future as a professional witness.

The judge smiled.

The court rose for the day.

Jintan had enjoyed his first session as a witness. It had been a lark. All one needed to do was get to the courtroom, stand in the dock, swear to speak the truth and nothing but the truth, and proceed to answer exactly as the lawyer said, and the matter was over. The whole thing was thrilling as well. Before this he'd only posted bail bonds. His ancestral house was in town—so what if it was a thatched little run-down place—and that was the most important qualification for posting a bond. Few people in Cuttack owned property, and fewer still could claim they'd been settled there a long time. Most were first-generation residents, but he could trace his ancestors back to the times of the Mughals and the Marathas. Not only his father's forefathers but his mother's too were from Cuttack. Her people still lived in Bhula Mian Bazaar, a stone's throw away. As Jintan's father used to say, Commissioner Jefferson had stopped by their shop. The sahib would ask his coachman to pull up in front of the shop and fetch him a few paans. They so satisfied him he once exclaimed: 'Fantastic!' Those days the shop was at Chandini Chowk bus stand, close to the Commissioner's bungalow. When the bus stand was shifted, the business fell on hard days, and Jintan's father was forced to move to Cuttack Chandi Square, cabin and all. Initially, business was pretty good. A women's college had come up nearby and for a large population of the town's young men the paan shop was a popular hangout. They were all avid smokers and paan-chewers, and they hung around for hours on end. After some time, though, the police came into the picture and didn't let the loafers hang around. To make matters worse, new paan shops cropped up. Business went downhill. Besides, there were too many holidays—summer holidays, puja holidays, winter holidays and what not. Naturally, business suffered. Wasn't one holiday too many bad for studies as well? Jintan was in a spot. He had five people to look after. His eldest daughter, Malati, was in class six and needed books and clothes. His little son needed shoes. His wife's asthma was getting worse. He was in no great shape either, suffering from one ailment or the other year-round and high blood sugar on top of everything. Making ends meet was getting more and more difficult. This was when the lawyer had caught hold of him and given him the idea of making some money by posting bonds. As a result, he was in the courthouse almost every day of the week, from ten to five. At the lawyer's insistence he had posted bail bonds for all sorts of people: pickpockets, thieves, fake doctors, cheats. The lawyer had taken care of everything, and the business wasn't bad at all. He made forty or fifty rupees for posting a bond, of which the lawyer's commission was ten or twelve. The amount remaining was not inconsequential. But then he had a big scare. He posted bond for Yerraiah, a rickshaw-puller, who had already cooled his heels in prison for two months with no rescuer in sight. The lawyer had persuaded Jintan: 'Do it and you'll make a killing. Sixty rupees!' Yerraiah was set free on bail, but the fellow vanished shortly afterwards. Twice the case came up for hearing, and since Jintan had posted the bond he was on the verge of losing his ancestral home. It would have to be put up to auction to recover the amount. Luckily, the lawyer was able to get the police to trace the fugitive to his native village and bring him back. The scare, however, had been enough to make Jintan lay off for a while. Months later the lawyer had sought him out again: 'Jintan, how're you doing, man? How about appearing in court as a witness? You can make up to twenty-five rupees per appearance. Give it a thought.' Jintan gave it a thought. This was a whole new ball game. Two new shops selling cold drinks had sprung up under the big banyan tree near the court. Thank God, Kathjodi River was still the same as before, its stream rippling in the sun. The mohul tree on the riverbank had grown and nesting birds twittered in its branches. Two stray cows had gotten into the habit of hanging around the old tea shops. Attending court daily from ten to five was no joke. In the past, the strain had been considerably less because he had had his bicycle, but it had been stolen about two months back. He had left it unlocked in front of the general post office and in the few minutes it had taken him to run in and buy a postcard it was gone. He rushed to the police station to file a complaint, but he couldn't give the number of the bicycle. It'd never occurred to him to note it down. It was an old Hero, was all he could say, and it had been stolen from the general post office. Nothing came of his complaint. He'd expected nothing would. Every day hundreds of people reported missing bicycles and their reports gathered dust on the police tables before being tipped into the dustbin. Whenever there was criticism in the press citing police inefficiency and ineffectiveness, the police would wake up, make themselves visible for a few days, and then relapse into somnolence.

On the last date of the hearing both sides made cogent summations of their arguments.
 The public prosecutor was the first to take the floor. 'Your Honour, the accused is a loafer and a person of proven bad character. He's been arrested twice already on charges of stealing bicycles, though released on both occasions for want of proof. He must not be allowed to get away scot-free this time too. He should be handed a stiff sentence. The spirit behind Section 379 of the Indian Penal Code, and not just its literal meaning, should be kept in mind while pronouncing judgement. After all, stealing and thievery are caused by, among other things, loafing around and ogling women. It is these that give rise to the impulse to steal...'
 The defence lawyer's arguments were no less strong and impressive: 'Your Honour, the accused is completely innocent. He's a nature-loving, peace-loving young man, with respect for history and heritage. He's given to hero worship too. It's a pity the police should catch hold of an innocent man instead of the real culprit. In my opinion, the police are after Baraju simply to cover up their own inefficiency. A malicious claim is being made against my client that a few days ago he stole the very bicycle he's been using for close to two years. There's no proof to back this up; the police have failed to produce a shred of evidence. There're no witnesses either. On the other hand, the defendant's witness has already testified that the bicycle belonged to Baraju and that he had

seen Baraju use it for two years. The accused therefore deserves to be acquitted and the case filed against him under Section 379 of the IPC thrown out. The court may be pleased to give direction to the police to forthwith restore the seized bicycle to my client.'

The judge handed down his verdict: Baraju Samal was innocent. The police had not proved their case; it was dismissed and the man acquitted. His bicycle was to be returned to him without the slightest delay.

Exultant, Baraju, Jintan and the lawyer trooped out of the courtroom, and while the lawyer and the witness waited under the banyan tree Baraju went back to retrieve his bicycle. After twenty or twenty-five minutes he came back pushing it and handed them their money: fifty rupees to the lawyer and thirty to the witness.

Jintan took a good look at the bicycle. Until now he'd only seen it from far off, in a dark corner of the courtroom. It dawned on him in a flash the Hero cycle Baraju was holding on to was his own, Jintan's, which had been stolen two months ago when he'd left it in front of the general post office for less than a minute. It was his and now he was face-to-face with the man who had stolen it!

'Hey!' Jintan put his hand on the bicycle seat. 'This is mine.'

Baraju brushed away his hand, jumped on the bicycle, and pedalled off, triumphantly fluttering his handkerchief.

Under the banyan tree, the lawyer's face split into a wide grin.

GHANIA CELEBRATES GANESH CHATURTHI
SURENDRA MOHANTY

The sun that rose that morning over the untouchables' colony at the edge of the village was unique yet familiar. It turned the clouds gold and grey; the dappled sky looked like the coat of a leopard. In all his fifteen years Ghania had never seen anything so enchanting. He was an orphan brought up by his grandmother after his mother died of cholera three years ago.

He stretched and yawned, sitting on the veranda. The goats were bleating in the shed and his grandmother was coughing her lungs out in bed. The old woman was racked by a persistent cough in the mornings that eased up only when the sun had been up for an hour or two.

Looking up at the sky, he wondered where the leopard's coat had gone. Millions of tiny, golden fish scales had taken their place. He looked around. Bula, the old mangy dog with no fur on one flank, was still asleep, his stump of a tail twitching occasionally to drive off the swarms of flies. 'Bula!' Ghania shouted. 'Hey, lazy dog.'

The dog opened its eyes a slit, looked at him for a moment, and closed them again. He wasn't a bloody crow or a magpie that he'd wake up this early and scrounge for food. No chance he'd get up until the morning was a solid hour or two old. Often it took a beating with a broom from Grandmother to spur the dog on: he'd totter to his legs, stretch and yawn, and take the first few steps of the new day. Then slowly he'd set out on his daily visit, entering all the colonies in the village, all the houses, sniffing at the drains for a morsel. Sometimes he'd be beaten with a stick, sometimes someone would throw a stone at him; he was used to all that. Only if the blow hit hard did he let out a yelp and stare at the offender with sad, unblinking eyes, as if to say: 'Go ahead and hit me some more if that's your thing, but remember he who gives a beating isn't as great as he who receives one.' Once, in a Mohanty household, when he had dipped his snout into a pot placed near a drain, somebody had scalded him with boiling rice water, peeling off half his fur. Yet he didn't die. Here he was, alive and kicking, and getting on famously with the small naked children of the village. They often tied a rope around his neck, rode his back and fed him puffed rice and rice cakes.

Ghania had found him as a helpless little black puppy three years ago and brought him home. His mother had christened him Bula—the vagabond. He became a loyal member of the family and guarded the house at night. If a cat passed by, he'd jump up and down in full fury and bark his head off; it was quite another matter that he shrank back and hid in the hedge if the cat bristled.

Shivering from the morning breeze, Ghania looked away from Bula, wrapping the end of his dhoti around himself and leaned against the wall. A crow flew into the drumstick tree and started cawing. The distant sound of children's voices reached his ears. He looked up expectantly. It was a little too early for children. A minute or two later he saw a noisy bunch with flower baskets, hooks and sticks. They were all from the respectable parts of the village.

'How are you all today?' he asked. 'Where are you headed so early in the morning?'

'Don't you know today is Ganesh Chaturthi? We're collecting flowers for the rituals. Do you have any around here?'

They left without waiting for an answer.

Ghania looked at the two night-jasmine trees in his courtyard. Hundreds of flowers had dropped from them and the morning air was sweet with their fragrance. But these flowers were never used for worship, nobody ever picked them; they bloomed, withered and died, unwanted. Ghania scooped up a handful, brought them to his nose, and inhaled deeply.

The front yard was now filled with the sun's slanting rays. He heard the loud bleating of goats and got up to open the door to the shed and let the animals out. He could hear his grandmother sweeping the inner courtyard in between bouts of coughing.

A group of untouchable young boys passed by. 'Hey,' one of them asked Ghania, 'aren't you coming to Mahanpur? There's work there. The wages are good too. The Pradhans are laying the foundation for a new house. Hurry up if you want to join us. It's a good two-mile walk to get there.'

There had been no rain, and the land was parched and cracked; the cattle had nothing but dry earth to sniff at; if somebody offered wages, takers came running from far-off places. No wonder the lads from the untouchables' colony didn't want to miss out on it. First, a quick dip in the dark, dank, weed-choked water of Dark Pond, and then they'd rush to Mahanpur.

'Damn,' Ghania said. 'Who works on Ganesh Chaturthi?'

'What the hell's Ganesh Chaturthi to you, boy?' Kanhu said.

'Isn't he aiming to grow into a big bloody pandit!' laughed Birju.

'Oh, our Ghania is like the sacred bull of Lord Mahadev,' added Mahna, a distant uncle. 'Untamed, unfettered.'

Ghania was incensed, but he had no one to vent his anger on save the dog. 'Look at this bloody leper! It's late in the morning, but he's still sleeping. Get up, get up, you lazy bum.' He chucked a stone at the sleeping dog.

The dog limped off with a howl.

Ghania stormed into the house and sat down on the floor with a thud.

'What's up with you?' his grandmother asked. 'Aren't you going to Mahanpur to look for work? The sun's so hot already. Have a bath before you go.'

'Surely,' he flared up, 'I'm not going to go anywhere to work on Ganesh Chaturthi!'

'What's Ganesh Chaturthi to you? It's for schoolchildren.'

He was suddenly so angry he could have whacked her. 'Grandmother, don't start yakking right from morning. I'm not going anywhere today. That's it!'

'Up to you, boy,' she said, sweeping the goat droppings into a heap. 'But don't bare your teeth at me like a monkey.' She began to lament aloud: 'God, you snatched away a son like Barju, leaving me alive only to be tortured!' She broke into a fit of coughing; it became so bad she had to sit down to catch her breath.

Ghania stormed out of the house. Memories of his schooldays came flooding back to him.

Ghania's father, Barju Malik, had had high hopes his son would study and make something of himself. The boy had gone to school, when his friends, at the age of six or seven, had begun doing chores: taking the cattle out to graze, collecting greens from the fields, gathering firewood, and working in the fields. His father had bought him a red dhoti, slate, some pieces of chalk and a book with the alphabet. Ghania wore brass bangles and a black thread around his wrist, and followed his father to the village school, carrying a good measure of puffed rice and rice flakes in the waist fold of his dhoti. The teacher, Bai Mohanty, seated on a torn blanket with his back against the wall, was dozing with his mouth open. He was addicted to opium. Beside him, on the floor, lay two canes, one as thin as a wire, the other as fat as his finger. The pupils were loudly chanting the multiplication tables. Suddenly, two flies flew into the teacher's mouth, making him sneeze, cough, spit and sit up with a start. The boys shook with suppressed laughter; even Ghania and his father broke into a chuckle. That was too much for the teacher. Straightening up, he picked up a cane and swished it through the air. 'All right, what's seven times twenty-five?' he asked. The cane danced. 'And thirteen times fourteen?' The blows rained down so torrentially that the pupils forgot the questions as well as the answers. The teacher hit whoever caught his fancy; the cane moved furiously as if possessed. The boys lifted up their voices in unison; the chanting of the multiplication tables resumed.

'Respectful greetings, teacher,' Barju Malik said, placing the bundle he was carrying on the floor.

'Who—Barju?' The teacher's eyes rested on the bundle. 'Is that your boy with you? All right, ask him to sit on the veranda out there. Today's Wednesday, an auspicious day for getting started with lessons. What've you got in that bundle?'

'I'm a poor man,' Barju said, opening the knot. 'What do I have to offer you?' The bundle held a seer of fine rice, two wads of tobacco leaves, betel leaves and areca nuts, four aubergines, a coconut, some turmeric powder and a bunch of holy duba grass.

The teacher's eyes widened with greed. 'Hey, Nathia,' he called out to a pupil. 'Take all these things to my home. And look sharp. Don't walk, run. But first spit here.'

The boy called Nathia sprang up from his seat and swooped down on the bundle. He was about to fly off when the teacher stopped him with a sharp blow on his back. 'This bugger's supposed to be from a Mohanty family!' he shrieked. 'Scoundrel! Ghost! You touch an untouchable's cloth and then go pollute my household, do you? First throw off your clothes, boy!'

Chastened, Nathia untied the knot of his dhoti and it fell to his feet. Buck naked, he picked up the bundle Barju had brought.

'Before you leave, spit here,' said the teacher. 'If you don't get back before the spit has dried, I'll cane you seven times.'

The boy shot off like an arrow.

The teacher looked at Barju. 'Where's the fee?'

Barju produced four annas and placed the money at the teacher's feet. The fellow counted the coins and tucked them into his dhoti.

'I have to go to work,' Barju said. 'Ghania'll collect my cloth when he goes home after school.'

After Barju left, the teacher asked a boy called Sania. 'Go draw Brahma, Vishnu and Maheswar on the floor and show the boy how to move his finger over them.' He turned to the boy. 'What's your name, boy?'

Ghania gulped nervously before replying.

'You'll sit out there on the veranda for your lessons,' the teacher added. 'Don't ever step inside the classroom.'

Sania drew three crude circles.

A year passed. Then another. Every month Barju dutifully turned up to pay up his respects along with the fees. After every market day, Ghania brought the teacher some tobacco leaves and a handful of green chillies. But his lessons did not progress beyond the alphabet and the first of the multiplication tables. When the sun fell directly on the school's east-facing veranda, the teacher asked him to move to the veranda in the rear. Banished out of sight, the boy had a rollicking time, catching dragonflies, running after goats and sheep, looking for birds in the trees. Occasionally, he'd run into the teacher, when the latter, clad in a towel and pulling on a homemade cigar, happened to go out to move his bowels in the bamboo grove behind the school.

'What's two times seven, boy?' the teacher would ask.

The boy would stare at him like a little dumb animal. Much as the teacher longed to thrash him, the fear of pollution would stop him and he'd engage Sania or Nathia or somebody else to carry out the task. 'Give him four resounding blows on his back,' he'd order. 'And a slap on each cheek.' The student would promptly take off his clothes to avoid pollution, and rain down blows on poor Ghania. Before a more severe form of punishment was recommended, Ghania would, just to save his skin, promise to bring the teacher one more wad of tobacco leaves.

After two years of this, the boy was taken out of school. 'We're poor untouchables,' his father said. 'What's the point of wasting time in school? It's time the boy worked for a living.'

And so, Ghania began to take the goats and cattle out to graze.

In the two years he had been at school there had been yearly worship of Ganesh and Saraswati, the god and goddess of learning, and Ghania, along with the others, had been made to bring the teacher a monetary contribution as well as cucumbers from his garden and a coconut from the market. But being an untouchable, he wasn't allowed to participate in the ceremony; he couldn't even offer a handful of flowers to the deities.

'Ghania bhai!'

Ghania started, his reverie broken. A bunch of boys from his colony carrying baskets and sticks were approaching him. 'What are you boys up to?'

'We're celebrating Ganesh Chaturthi in school today. The upper-caste boys from the Brahmin and the Mohanty quarters have collected a load of flowers already. They were up early and have beaten us to it. Come help us gather some flowers.'

'But what does Ganesh Chaturthi matter to you?' Ghania couldn't hide his surprise. 'It's for boys from the upper castes.'

'It's as much for us as for them,' the boys replied. 'We're a free country now, and the new teacher said we too can offer flowers to Lord Ganesh.'

A surge of pride passed through Ghania. 'Come on, then. I'll get you loads of lilies and lotuses from Dark Pond, so many you won't be able to carry them all to the school. I'll get you champaks too. Short of flowers, are you? Have the upper-caste boys collected more? We've got to show them!'

The boys and their excited chatter followed Ghania.

That day there was no dearth of lilies and lotuses, but Ghania was still not satisfied. He clambered up a deodar tree and plucked enough leaves and branches to fill a bullock cart. Arches and festoons were put up in front of the school.

The new teacher praised the efforts of the untouchable boys. The boys from the Brahmin and the Mohanty quarters wore long faces. Ghania sat below the school veranda, overwhelmed by his own effort. The smiles of the boys from his part of the village applauded his heroic efforts; when they offered flowers to Lord Ganesh, they offered what Ghania had picked.

The ceremony came to an end. Coconuts had to be smashed against a grinding stone. The boys from the untouchable colony split theirs in the very first attempt, while it took the upper-caste boys two tries or more; some didn't succeed at all. 'Maybe these guys failed to observe the strict fast!' Ghania joked. 'Maybe they tucked in on the sly!'

When the prasad was being distributed, the teacher spotted Ghania. 'Come on up, dear child, and have some.'

Ghania hesitated. 'I'm no longer a child, sir.'

'So what? You must have some prasad. Look at what you've done today.'

Ghania spread the end of his dhoti and the teacher filled it with puffed rice, flakes of rice sweetened with jaggery, sesame laddus, pieces of coconut, cucumbers and bananas.

It was late when Ghania returned home. Bula accosted him along the way and gleefully wove in and out of his legs. On another day Ghania would've unceremoniously kicked him, but today the dog got a generous handful of puffed rice and a sesame ball. 'Come on, Bula. This is Lord Ganesh's prasad.' The dog lapped up the food. 'Want another sesame laddu?' Bula went wild. What good fortune, what joy!

As he approached home, he overheard his grandmother shouting: 'Ghania! Aye, Ghania, where are you? Damn you, Lord Yama, god of death! How could you spirit away my Barju, the light of my eyes, and leave me with this boy? Ghania... Hey, boy!'

'Where were you?' she screamed when she saw him sauntering up with leisurely steps, with an excited Bula at his heels. 'Where were you? It's so late and you're roaming around God-knows-where on an empty stomach!'

'Today's Ganesh Chaturthi, Grandmother. Don't you remember?'

'What's that to you, boy? It's for the upper-caste boys at the school.'

'Here,' he offered her some prasad. 'Eat and enjoy. I got it for you from the school. And for heaven's sake don't go on grumbling the rest of the day.'

The old woman popped a sesame laddu into her toothless mouth. 'Why, this is hard as a stone. If only I had my teeth...'

Bula wagged his tail and danced. Ghania threw him some more puffed rice. 'I swear there's a bloody witch inside this little bugger's belly!'

Bits and pieces of the sesame laddu dribbled out of the old woman's mouth. Looking at her fondly, Ghania burst out laughing.

THE ATHEIST

KISHORI CHARAN DAS

I'm not an atheist; anyone who knows me will testify to that. Even Abhiram has said as much. No matter what, he said, since your heart is pure you can bring yourself to love God. Yes, maybe I can, if only He is like Abhiram. What a pity He's not; He's like no one for that matter. He's a lie, I'm sure of that. That has long been my conviction; don't expect me to change it overnight.

Yet I'm not an atheist, far from it. And, if you must know, I'm more inclined to love than hate. I can't wish anyone dead, let alone kill. I admire the quiet manifestations of nature, the small felicities of Creation: a puddle of water in the courtyard breaking into shadowy ripples; a kitten huddled inside a wicker basket licking its fur; the tender leaf of a sapling growing out of a crack in a wall, trembling in a gentle breeze; small sparrows pecking at each other… All the little things you wouldn't expect an atheist to bother about. Above all, I love children. Indeed, I suffer because I love too much. Now, could anyone still insist I'm an atheist?

Abhiram and I haven't met for quite some time. Doesn't he want to look me up? No, not likely. Come to think of it, I haven't been to meet him all this time, either. Well, I hardly get any time off work. I suppose I should go to his place this Sunday. Indeed, I must. No putting it off this time. And I mustn't forget to take my son along.

My son's red rubber ball has rolled out the door into the pouring rain. He's been watching it getting soaked. He must be mulling something over. I know what. But surely he can't have figured everything out, right? Of course, he wouldn't understand how sad I feel about it all. Maybe one of these days I'll tell him what happened. I suppose he alone would shed a tear for me—he's so young and innocent, uncontaminated by religion and all the claptrap.

I met Abhiram about a year ago, when I was transferred to Calcutta.

Although we worked in different organizations, our offices were in adjoining blocks. One day, for the first time, I went to the canteen. The place was dirty, overcrowded and full of smoke. The grimy food-stained marble-topped tables and wobbly chairs made me so nauseous I had half a mind to run away. Then I caught sight of this fellow. He sat there with his eyes closed, like a praying mantis, a plate of food sat untouched before him. Presently, he offered it to some invisible—non-existent perhaps—God. He beamed when his eyes met mine. 'Oh, please come and join me,' he said.

More curious than friendly, I took a chair next to him. So here's one of those creatures crazy about God and stuff, I thought. I have to admit I have a strong prejudice against such people. Generally, I avoid them at all costs. But in spite of myself I felt a strange attraction towards this fellow. He had such a disarming smile. The funny thing was I found myself agreeing to his suggestion we meet more often for lunch. The fellow won't be bad company in any case, I thought to myself, for an occasional half-hour. Even if he talks nonsense, that's not long enough to bore the life out of me.

Eventually, I realized that not only was he deeply religious but also an ardent believer. I found him growing numb with ecstasy at the strains of *Ramdhun* on the radio. At such moments he would become totally oblivious to his surroundings and get covered in goose pimples. Afterwards, when he came back to himself, he would blush profusely and look down in embarrassment at having made such a public spectacle.

Abhiram wasn't ugly; there weren't any conspicuous blemishes in his features. Fair, short, slightly—but becomingly—bald, like any other executive he wore a bush shirt with dark trousers or a staid suit, his clothes always impeccably clean and well ironed. He had no distinct mannerisms, and never jabbered on about himself. The only peculiar thing about him was that he worshipped God with all his heart, and this sole weakness the poor fellow could never conceal. Effectively, that is.

I often wondered what could be the source of his intense piety. While for most people religion was an expedient, Abhiram's devotion was something rare. Only yogis and countryfolk, untainted by sophistication, could sustain such fervour. But Abhiram didn't belong to either category. In fact, he formed a category apart.

One day, as we waited at the Chowringhee Maidan to catch a tram home, he looked at the sky, smiled, and predicted a shower in the offing.

'Say, what's He like, your God?' I charged at him suddenly, knowing fully well his polite nature wouldn't permit retaliation.

He looked surprised.

'In what form do you perceive your God?' I harangued him. 'Father, mother, lover, friend, child, what?'

I was now being openly sardonic, but he chose to ignore that. 'I never see God,' he replied, his voice as placid and matter-of-fact as ever. 'I feel Him.'

Just then the long-awaited tram pulled in, and there weren't many passengers on the footboard. We made a dash to reserve some space for ourselves.

'Do you understand what I mean?' he continued, as we manoeuvred to stand inside the crowded carriage, gripping the rails overhead with one hand and the briefcase with the other. 'When I say I sense Him, what I mean is I simply sense myself. Myself. You know, I understand myself. I feel emptied of all desires and wants.'

The conductor came jostling through the mass of faces to collect the fare. I performed the acrobatics of fishing out the fare with my free hand. Abhiram stood like one possessed, oblivious to everything.

'I'm reminded of a funny incident,' he chuckled. 'One day I was saying my prayers, and of course I had my eyes closed. When I finished, I found my daughter, Indu, sitting cross-legged in front of me. She, too, had her eyes shut. She opened them after a while and gave me a quick little smile, showing her chipped front tooth. That was all, we didn't say or do anything, but I felt like we had shared a marvellous secret that belonged to nobody else, not even her mother.'

He laughed heartily and added, 'She's an imp, my Indu. She loves to tease me. She loves me very much.'

He suddenly realized he hadn't paid his fare and had gone on about himself more than what was decent. Painfully embarrassed, he apologized, offered to pay and clammed up for the rest of the journey.

Bullshit, I thought to myself. Your philosophy is unclear and I don't believe a word of it. But I forgive you because you love your daughter so much; after all, she's a creature of flesh and blood and not a celestial being!

'I look forward to meeting your little girl someday,' I said.

A chipped front tooth, a slightly upturned nose, large nostrils, thick raven hair soaked with oil and combed back severely like a village girl's, with a wilting marigold in a red-ribboned plait. She was around ten and her name was Chandrika.

She and my son became friends right away. So much so that my son had the audacity to pluck the flower from her plait, and she, half-crying and half-laughing, chased him all over the place. Abhiram had come to visit with his wife and daughter.

'Her name's Chandrika, isn't it?' I said. 'Why do you call her Indu?'

From the way he puffed up, Abhiram seemed to relish the chance to explain. 'The thing is,' he began, 'she was born with such a round face and chubby cheeks, you know, that her mother and I felt that her name ought to match her moon-like face. She chose Chandrika and I Indumati...'

The rest was easy to guess, but he went on with great gusto, as if it were a mysterious episode needing elaborate explanation.

Afterwards, as we went on to other things, he returned to his usual reticent, amiable self: everything's fine with the world; people are basically nice; the government's policies aren't all that harsh; popular anger isn't totally unjustified; have patience, things will look up; such and such fellow isn't really bad, he merely seems to be; and so on and so forth. Mild protests, faint smiles, reassuring words all the way—poor, dear Abhiram.

Damn it, I thought, doesn't anything ruffle this man? Doesn't he ever suffer? I could hardly believe it. A stab of jealousy shot through me. I suddenly cursed him with all the vehemence I could muster: may he suffer, may something happen to make him beg and plead before his God—that'll teach him.

Mercifully, this ugly mood passed, and I began to feel ashamed. Here's a poor god-loving fellow, I reasoned with myself, a witless, pitiable creature. Why should I wish him ill?

Meanwhile, the children carried on with their games, which showed no signs of ending. My son lent Indu a hand in building a mud house, temporarily setting aside his scorn for such feminine preoccupations. Then they started playing football. Indu seemed to love the red rubber ball. 'Goal!' she would shriek joyfully, kicking the ball with abandon.

Their game ended as abruptly as a clap of thunder. A stinging shot from Indu hit my son bang on the nose. Indu broke into a fit of laughter. Smarting from the humiliation, my boy razed the toy house to the ground. They both rushed to their fathers in a huff, pouting in anger. Inevitably, a predictable measure of consolation and scolding had to be doled out, which I did. But Abhiram didn't scold Indu at all. 'All right, it's okay, it's okay,' he murmured, petting her.

The crisis showed no signs of abating. Abhiram stole surreptitious glances at his watch; I fidgeted in my chair.

Just then a street-peddler passed, calling down the lane: 'The boy will play...the girl will play...the boy will...' A strange cacophony of squeaks and squeals followed his chant. My son pricked up his ears. The toy seller was a regular fixture in our locality, but I had always managed to talk my son out of buying anything. Look, I'd tell him, these are cheap Japanese toys and toys are for girls. Today, his eyes shone with hope. He looked from my face to Indu's. The boy's here, he seemed to tell me, and the girl's here too, you can't refuse today; you won't have the heart to.

At the faintest nod from Indu he rushed to the door; she excitedly followed on his heels. She had forgotten her anger immediately. 'Want to have this horse? See how it's shaking its tail?'

'No, I don't want the horse. I'll have that little birdie with the red beak.'

'Look at this froggy here!'

'Oh, no.'

Presently, a veritable menagerie poured into the drawing room, creating an uproar. My son and Abhiram's daughter beamed with joy.

'When will you visit us again?' I asked Indu, while seeing them off.

'Not until he pays us a visit,' smiled the proud little lady, looking at my son.

He gave a chivalrous nod.

But they would never meet again.

I kept meeting Abhiram on and off, but could never get down to visiting him with my wife and son. In the beginning it was plain laziness on my part, but then he went away to his village on a long summer holiday.

Ten or fifteen days before his holiday was supposed to end, I received a call from him. 'Namaskar,' he said most unhurriedly. 'I've come back.' After a little chat he casually mentioned that Indu wasn't well and that he'd had to cut short their holiday.

I went to his house that evening directly from the office. He and his wife received me warmly. They treated me to the special sweets they had brought from the village and chided me for not having brought along my wife and son.

I looked for Indu. Abhiram said she was in bed with a slight temperature. She was having fever intermittently and had lost a lot of weight, her mother worriedly added.

Abhiram seemed embarrassed by this mention of Indu's illness, as though it would burden me with the obligation to sympathize. I didn't like this attitude. Why did he treat me as an outsider? Wasn't Indu like a daughter to me? I insisted on checking in on her before leaving.

She was fast asleep. She had become woefully emaciated. I ran my palm over her forehead, wishing her a speedy recovery.

The fever never abated. It was typhoid, with a number of other complications as well. But nothing to be alarmed about, the doctor reassured professionally.

I didn't see any change in Abhiram. He reached his office right on time. He continued to have his lunch in the canteen and went on with his wishy-washy discussions on national and international affairs. Only occasionally did he lapse into brief spells of distraction. On the whole, however, nothing seemed to ruffle him. While his wife frequently broke down at Indu's sickbed, he simply watched Indu and smiled like a child. And the poor girl, whose cheeks had surprisingly retained their chubbiness, would smile back at him. It seemed as if father and daughter were playing a very secret, a very private game of their own, perhaps as they had during their prayers.

There was a deep core of anguish to the whole situation. Every time I witnessed this strange pair of father and daughter, I sensed a nobility and depth in their sorrow that transcended any worldly experience. It was as profound as a motionless ocean that knows neither joy nor grief. No wonder, the ominous portent of events had escaped Abhiram.

'The doctor,' said his wife one day, 'says there's a seventy-five per cent chance Indu will recover.'

'Of course, she will,' I answered. "The other twenty-five per cent will depend on our prayers.'

Abhiram stared at me.

I felt awkward. I couldn't tell him I wasn't alluding to any god, but to human wishes, yearnings and hopes. Didn't they count for anything?

My son suddenly upset everything. He came down with a fever. Two days later, blisters erupted all over his body. Smallpox, the doctor pronounced without the slightest hesitation, an epidemic had broken out in many parts of the city.

A perverse pride came over me when I informed Abhiram. Well, I thought, tragedy has struck me, too. Come, show me your respect, offer me your sympathy.

I excused myself from going to his place and forbade him from coming to ours.

Soon, however, I had to cast aside the frills and facade of my sense of tragedy. My son grew worse. It was numbing to see him suffer. His entire body was riddled with sores. He howled all the time. The monstrous beast of the deadly disease was torturing him, pricking needles into his flesh, roasting him over a blazing fire. I wanted to sit beside him and make him feel better, as Abhiram would to Indu. I consoled my wife, but I failed to conceal my own restlessness and agitation. I longed to do something—something outlandish and impossible—to break or build something, something that would restore my self-confidence and yet act as a soothing balm on my son's feverish skin.

Then, one evening, I noticed the shadow of death creeping up his pale forehead. It was useless to call the doctor, for like a wise old owl he would cock his damned head and advise us to wait and watch. I couldn't stand the glare of the lights, the many medicine bottles rolling all over the place, the crushed orange peel and scattered pomegranate seeds, the bitter smell of neem leaves, and the sound of my wife perpetually crying—anything at all. All the efforts to prolong his life suddenly seemed detestable. Why this unnecessary cruelty? I wondered. Why this protracted suffering? Why should someone destined to die be kept alive, why should someone destined to live suffer the pains of death?

I sneaked out onto the rooftop, wanting to be alone. I looked at the sky. There were stars. Down below, human beings bustled about.

Someone shone a light on his car in the garage—doing some precious investigation, eh? Does he know about my son—does he even care? Behind their closed glass windows people were talking and laughing. Two workers pulled in a loaded cart down the road. The solitary sentry at the gate of the police barracks stood staring moodily at the sky.

I wondered, what should I do? What the hell should I do? Pray? Give in like a spineless creature? Oh goodness, is this where it always ends up? Am I one of those hypocrites who deny Him in cold logic but in the throes of misfortune seek Him out?

I pulled myself together; Abhiram came to mind. Can he be suffering as much as I am, I thought. How could he be, he who's so blissfully immersed in an illusion?

Suddenly I knew that one of the two children would die. And I knew which one.

I didn't wish or pray for such an outcome, and I certainly bore no ill will towards Abhiram. Besides, didn't I love Indu like a daughter? Yet I felt in my bones my son would pull through and Indu wouldn't. Logically, I hastened to justify my reaction, that's the way it ought to be. Abhiram is so bloody religious it wouldn't hurt him as much.

I felt strange. Had the people behind the glass windows burst into laughter? Were the people in the street smirking and winking? What grudge did the speeding cars and the lonely sentry hold against me? They all seemed to have ganged up on me—the outsider, the atheist.

I fled from the roof and rushed down the flight of dark stairs to my apartment. I sat down at my son's bedside.

My wife raised her head; her eyes were swollen. 'Where were you?' she whined. 'Abhiram babu called.'

'Did he?' My voice shook, but my anxiety didn't reach her. 'What did he want?'

'Nothing much,' she replied irritably. 'He asked after our son. Oh yes, he said Indu's getting worse…'

There's not much more to add. I couldn't make it to Abhiram's place the day Indu died. My wife went by herself. It seems nobody could make out if Abhiram cried at all. He shut himself inside a room for a long time, but there was no sign of tears when he came out; he looked about as serene and unruffled as usual.

I was right, wasn't I? Of course, I haven't any regrets. Why should I? But does anyone suspect that my sorrow about Indu's death is not truly sorrow but a mere facade to camouflage my happiness? Look here, right now the toyseller will come along calling down our lane. Or maybe he won't come today. But his singsong chant rings in my ears: 'The boy will play...the girl will play...the boy will...'

His voice haunts me. It sets me trembling.

I have never bought anything from him, nor will I ever.

MOTHER INDIA
(The Chronicle of Uddhav Malik)

MOHAPATRA NILAMONI SAHOO

What I'm going to talk about goes back some forty years at least, or even a couple of years more, when I was just a child of eight or nine, in a rundown village fifty or fifty-five kilometres from Cuttack, with only a mud road built by the district board connecting the two. The road turned into a quagmire of mud and muck four months a year—all through the monsoons. Dense groves and patches of deep forest bordered it on either side, with the holy river Prachi running next to it, its riverbank dotted with shrines and temples—all places of pilgrimage. Five or six miles before it met the sea, the river took one last lap through the dense forest. Among its denizens were a few panthers and leopards, wolves and wild boars, hyenas and a large number of deer. Our village at the time seemed no more than an afterthought to the forest. Things now have changed, and how! The tall trees have all been cut down and the place is as barren as a desert. The rains have steadily decreased too. Quite a change from the magical days of my childhood, when it didn't rain but poured, often without a moment's pause. For days on end, maybe fifteen at a stretch, the sun was nowhere to be seen. The village was overrun with grass, bushes, weeds and creepers. New trees grew from seed, and the bigger and older trees—the banyan, peepul, mango and jackfruit, gamhari, tamarind, chakunda, coconut and palm, bamboo, chhatiana and polang—closed in on our village from all sides, together with trees bearing nuts and berries—bar, nar, sahada, satyamba, jeuta, ambada, mihinga and ashadhia. The grazing grounds near the riverbank were also dotted with bushes that produced nuts—kantei, beta, bhainchi, khir, sagadapatua—to say nothing of clumps of screw pine, ketaki and bhutiari. And in those bushes, chirped and twittered, called and cawed all day long birds of all kinds—crows, cuckoos, magpies, orioles, mynahs, chaffinches, morning-heralds, honeyeaters, birds with pointed crests, white-breasted and brown-backed kites, snow white herons, glossy green parrots and many others. In the middle of the outlying paddy fields were two large ponds—Khajuria and Sickle-face—overrun with lilies, lotuses and nettles and home to a whole host of water-birds—kingfishers, cormorants, ducks, swans and more. During the holidays, as kids we roamed these places, gorged on nuts and berries, and trapped birds. The village had its fair share of snakes, from the deadly poisonous cobras and vipers, to harmless water snakes, and of course pythons. We ran into them every now and then. Then there were the entertaining creatures like monitor lizards, mongooses, otters and wild cats. And finally, there were ghosts and spirits, witches, gnomes and goblins, who inhabited particular trees in specific parts of the village. And these were of all faiths—Hindu, Muslim and Christian. The Hindus included Brahmin ghosts—the Brahmadaityas. But only the faint-hearted were afraid of them and met their end, every once in a while, smitten with loose motions or vomiting blood. Nor should the thieves, bandits, highwaymen and cutthroats lurking on the outskirts of the village go unmentioned; they struck more at pilgrims and wayfarers.

There was a pond between our village and the market. A gloomy grove of mango and jackfruit trees grew on one side and a dense bamboo thicket on the other. On the banks of the pond lived an old man in a mud hut, all by himself. An untouchable, his name was Uddhav Malik. He didn't have any children; his wife had died long ago. He was tall and thin, his back straight, and people speculated he was already over sixty. His head was small and smooth, like a coconut without its fibre; a grey pigtail five or six inches long grew at the back; when unknotted, it flew in the breeze. Around his neck he wore two strands of thick tulsi beads, a sign he had been initiated as a Vaisnav. Inside the hut was a picture of Radha and Krishna that he worshipped.

Those were the days of the British. Since he was the village chowkidar, he put on his uniform whenever on duty, or when the police sergeant paid a visit: a blue sleeveless coat on top of a dirty linen dhoti barely reaching down to his knees, a blue cloth bag dangling from his shoulder, a stout stick in hand, and most conspicuously a blue turban on his head. We saw him in his uniform quite often when we were young. At all other times, he wore only a towel around his middle as he sat on the bank angling. When not so engaged, he'd be making the rounds of bushes and groves to gather nuts, berries, mangoes, guavas, sour wood-apples and apricots, which he kept in his hut for us. The moment school was out we children would descend on him in droves. I, for one, avidly looked forward to our visits, and he seemed to have grown fond of me too. He'd have us sit around him, offering us fruits and nuts, and plying us with stories of ghosts and spirits, bandits and burglars, as engrossing as they were hair-raising. His teeth had all fallen out, with maybe just a couple of molars left behind, but as a raconteur, aided and embellished by wild gestures and gesticulations, his style of narration was bathed in drama. One new moon night of the Savitri festival he'd run into the ghost of a cow while trudging back from the police station fifteen kilometres away. The ghost had blocked his path, snorting and stamping on the ground, digging up clumps of mud with its long horns, swishing its tail and weaving rings around him, provoking him. Shivers of fear and excitement would run through us as he recounted how he escaped this badly-behaved horned demon. Another time, he ran full tilt into two dacoits trying to bore a hole through someone's mud wall. He pounced on them, managing to cuff them after a brief struggle. In the outfields behind the colony of the Brahmins, which they used for defecation, he had run into not one but four Brahmin witches shortly before the crack of dawn. These witches were buck naked and feasting on night soil, their heads down and naked legs thrust into the air. He sneaked up on them and made off with their clothes. They had been unmasked, for all to see. Our excited ears drank up his stories more quickly than they could run off his excited tongue.

But when I visited him alone, all by myself, he never brought up these stories, despite my open interest in them. God knows what he saw in me, but all his stories for me were mythological and spiritual. How Lord Krishna sucked the life out of demoness Putana, how he neatly split the demon Baka in two, yanking his beak apart, subdued the malevolent serpent king Kaliya, uprooted and lifted the Govardhan hill and balanced it atop his little finger for seven days. Uddhav seemed to speak from the deep recesses of his heart. Of all the people who'd done their best to enshrine Lord Krishna in my heart as the living embodiment of God, Uddhav Malik stood out. Mind you, I'm not belittling the contributions of ardent Vaisnav Bhaigi Mishra of Gopinathpur, just beyond our village, or those of dedicated Vaisnav Bhajani Das, from the untouchables' colony, nor of Sadhu Nayak, the police duffadar in our village; the same goes for Nrusingha Barik, from the barbers' colony too. During the kirtans, especially while celebrating the spring romance of Radha and Krishna, Uddhav would beat his chest calling out to Krishna and fall down in an ecstatic faint every so often. I saw it with my own eyes more than once. I was also hugely swayed by my father's friends Loknath Mohapatra and Dinabandhu Sahoo, the oil presser, in the roles of Krishna and Yashoda on stage, bathed in tears the whole time. There were others too, but more of that later. Uddhav Malik is our subject at the moment, and let me take you through the chronicle of this great man.

Vaisnavs are meant to abstain from fish and meat, so the sight of Uddhav Malik catching fish didn't seem quite right. 'Grandfather Uddhav,' I confronted him one day. 'How come, as a Vaisnav, you catch and eat fish?' He didn't bristle the slightest; on the contrary, he proceeded to answer with a big beaming smile. 'Grandson, you've asked a very pertinent question. You might not be aware that fish and meat have not been denied us. Sri Chaitanya himself wrote that staying away from fish and meat does not apply to the lower castes and untouchables. We can eat all the fish and meat we want; all our sins will be wiped away if we take the Lord's name just once. But all the upper castes—the Brahmins, the Kshyatriyas and the Vaishyas—they'll go to hell if they succumb to the temptation.' Then he sang a ditty I remember very well to this day: 'Catfish curry and the warm lap of a young wife—damn it, praise Hari, praise Him for the twin pleasures!' Only the other day, I heard an important wise man putting a spin on this: apparently, the fish curry stands for the unceasing flow of tears down a seeker's cheeks; the young woman's lap symbolizes Mother Earth, forever in the flush of youth; to seek salvation all you need to do is roll on the ground crying Hari's name! I have no stomach for such convoluted explanations; to me, the one offered by Uddhav Malik, whose love of fish was as intense as his love of Krishna, made more sense. It was simpler, better.

Grandfather Uddhav had built a raised mud platform for the holy tulsi plant in front of his hut on the bank of pond. We sat there whenever we met. He spoke of the deepest spiritual matters—the universe of the physical Self, the six enemies, Heaven–Hell–Earth, the journey to the Land of the Dead, the heavenly accountant named Chitragupta—as if I were an adult and his equal in the study of the scriptures and the

Vedas. He never treated me like a child, a mindless oaf, and I felt all grown up around him. I felt like I was able to make sense of things, as if I was George, the hero of Santanu Kumar Acharya's novel *Narakinnar*, inexorably drawn to the real gurus of my life, and whom the gurus instantly recognized.

As far as I can recollect, Uddhav was unlettered. So how had he acquired all that knowledge of the scriptures? Hundreds of hymns, prayers and kirtans were at the tip of his tongue. One of his favourites was: 'A strange child is he, that little one who split the demon Baka in two.' He'd howl with laughter and roll on the ground whenever he sang it—so mystifying to someone like me who couldn't make head or tail of it. 'A little child, eh?' he'd want to know. 'A tiny tot, huh? Pray, says who? The demon Baka is to him what a pond heron is to us humans, isn't that right, grandson? But all very strange, if you ask me. What say you? You go to school, don't you? Explain it to me, then.' I could make out what he was driving at, but I couldn't unravel for the life of me why he laughed so uproariously.

Sometimes, up on his perch on the pond bank fishing, he'd start gabbing. Once I tried to nail him down: 'Tell me, Grandfather, you go out on your beat at night, not only around our village but the surrounding ones too. Aren't you scared?'

'Scared? Never. 'Cause we're never alone. Mother India's always by our side, keeping us company. Ghosts and evil spirits, witches and demons daren't do us any harm. Even ferocious beasts like man-eating tigers keep out of our way.' He closed his eyes and raised his hands to the heavens above.

On more nights than one we'd suddenly be awakened by his robust chowkidarish calls. Three times, at set places in the village—the two ends and the middle—he'd stop and belt out at the top of his voice:

> Mother India's awake and stirring,
> Beware, brother. Beware!

We could make out the words echoing distinctly through the village.

I loved the lonesome rainy nights, that's when things would happen. Someone would strangle someone else and dump the body in the narrow alley leading to the village deity's temple; cholera would break out in some colony or the other; the daughter-in-law of some family somewhere would get possessed by a spirit. People claimed to hear doomsday threats issuing from the heavens in the middle of the night. Owls hooted from the impenetrable foliage of tamarind trees in someone's backyard; male jackals let out three staccato barks before falling ominously silent. God, the chill of fright could get into one's heart. The only reassuring thing was Grandfather Uddhav's battle cry, his words of warning and caution: Mother India's awake and stirring, Beware, brother. Beware!

Who was this Mother India—a flesh-and-blood being, an idea, a concept? Who knew! But at the mention of these magic words the image of a sublime lady making protective gestures would appear in my mind. And in the deep booming voice of Uddhav Malik the lady flooded my heart with confidence.

Those were the days of the British, as I have already said. The silver jubilee of the coronation of Emperor George the Fifth had just been celebrated across the length and breadth of the country. We schoolchildren went out in a procession waving the Union Jack, singing a song poet-saint Madhusudan Rao had especially penned for the occasion, and had our share of free sweets. I still remember snatches of Madhu Rao's song: 'Sing, sing with gusto/ Beat the drums lustily/ Sri George the Fifth/ Among men the greatest/ Rules the land and the seas visible and beyond...'

But they were also the days when the Congress leaders were descending on our village every now and then to hold meetings. In emotionally-charged voices they listed the atrocities the British government had committed on the hapless Indians. I kept hearing that someday soon India would become free and independent, that the colonial government was nothing but an instrument of oppression. I went to a couple of the meetings, where I heard the names of Gandhi and Nehru often invoked. Tiny portraits of Gandhi were on sale too. Straddling the map of India was the image of Mother India on a lion, sitting up, back straight, much like Goddess Durga, with a diminutive Gandhi at her feet. He sat with his left leg folded under him. This picture had become a hit with the masses. As far as I was concerned, the picture of Mother India bore a strong similarity to the image of her I had enshrined in my heart. Not only that, the faces of Mahatma Gandhi and Uddhav Malik resembled each other uncannily. No wonder Gandhi's portrait appealed to me so greatly. He didn't seem remote; he seemed like someone near and dear, though I hadn't any notion at all about this great man. All I needed to know was he was our leader, the leader of Congress, and was fighting against the British with nothing but non-violence, and the war he was fighting was called Satyagraha. I once saw some Congress followers observing Satyagraha in front of the village opium and hashish shop. They threw themselves on the ground in front of the shop door to prevent people from entering and advised them against deadly intoxicants.

Whenever there was a Congress meeting, I found Uddhav Malik hovering on the fringes, dressed in his blue uniform, stick in hand, intently listening to every word, along with his superior, Birabar Mishra, the duffadar of the village, darting around. As government servants they were required to keep tabs on the goings-on against the Raj.

There was no one in the village who could enlighten me about these things, and the teachers in the school were very tight-lipped. Once I asked one of them, 'Sir, who's Gandhi?' his response was: 'Hush! You're just a child. Why do you want to know who Gandhi is? Go do your work.' There was, of course, Nilamoni Pradhan of Baharana, a village some distance from ours, who I could have asked. Enormously popular, he spearheaded the Satyagraha movement in our area; he'd been in and out of jail and badly beaten up by the police. Later, he became chairman of the district board and then an MLA. Somehow a ministerial berth eluded him, but people loved and respected him more than any minister. It was he who had brought the flame of freedom to our area; it was he who had led us to rediscover our age-old culture and values. Since his first name and mine were the same, I developed an obsession with him and was dying to follow him around. A short man in a khadi dhoti and a loose shirt, his thick lips were always ready to speak the truth without fear or favour. Behind the lenses of his spectacles his eyes shone with love and kindness. He was mobbed wherever he went. I followed him like a puppy when he came to our village, listened to him with rapt attention, washed over by waves of love, respect and loyalty. I think I'll have to speak of him at length some other time.

Once I saw Uddhav Malik respectfully offering him some kau fish.

'How's it going, Uddhav?' Pradhan asked.

Uddhav gave a brilliant smile, cheeks sunken, teeth all gone. 'Sir, everything's as Mother India wishes. And these few kau fish I've got you—I seem to have had some fantastic luck with my fishing rod!'

'But first tell me, have you given up opium?'

'Thanks to Mother India's grace, I'm totally off that terrible addiction, sir. Mother India's kindness has been most palpable.'

Their conversation intrigued me, and I gradually grew to love and cherish the words 'Mother India'. The Bengali settlers in our village made beautiful images of Goddess Durga during the puja festival. How lovely she looked! A lot like Mother India I would have guessed.

One late afternoon, on my way to the market, I made a detour to Uddhav Malik's hut. Outside, he had a fire going to cook his dinner, and was sitting beside it drawing on a hand-rolled cigar. The moment his eyes lit upon me, he beckoned: 'Come, come, my dear. I've got some berries for you from Cuttack. I was there yesterday.' I sat down beside him and started munching the oh-so-sweet berries. Meanwhile Grandfather Uddhav was full throttle into his story of the salt disobedience movement, describing the incidents more vividly than any participant could. Soon he was bringing in allusions from the Mahabharata: Yudhishthira, the son of Dharma, had incarnated as Gandhi, choosing India as the place of action this time—to round off the half-day battle leftover from the original war. This time around he'd fully exterminate the Kaurava army masquerading as white imperialists. Empress Victoria was Queen Gandhari; Mother India, Queen Kunti. Grandfather Uddhav didn't know that Victoria was long dead and gone. But I swallowed every word he said. 'So, Grandfather,' I wanted to know, 'who's this George the Fifth?' He didn't bat an eyelid: 'Dhritarashtra!' Then he became cryptic once again. 'Just wait and watch. Deadly battles will be fought in this land of Bharat, rivers of blood will flow, but Lord Krishna will shield it from utter destruction with his mighty Sudarshan Chakra.' 'Where is he right now?' I asked. He pointed towards the south with a broad smile: 'There. There. And see how serenely he sits pretending to be a dumb wood gnome! He's in camouflage as the Buddha and hiding in his Big Temple by the sea. But he'll emerge when the time is right.' 'Grandfather, have you seen Lord Jagannath?' 'Only once. But that was enough to get a picture of him.

'I'd been to the annual chariot festival that year—the year of the deadly cholera epidemic, when thousands of people dropped dead like flies. And the chariot of the Lord? Well, take a good look at the palm tree over there. You see how tall it is? The Lord's chariot was four times taller. And the idol was nearly the same height as the chariot. And he was four times as rotund as the Brahma banyan tree in our village. His round eyes shone brighter than the sun. I couldn't keep my eyes open. One look at him and the next moment I was rolling in the dust of the Big Path chanting "Krishna, Hare Krishna." Then I fainted, and people sprinkled water on my face and revived me. I am telling you, you can't sustain the sight of him! No wonder half the people who try to look upon him full in the face come down with cholera. Do mere mortals have eyes strong enough? Most pilgrims, I found, had their eyes shut, with just the words "Oh, Lord, oh Emperor of the World" on their lips. Only the great saints, sanyasis, vaisnavs, vedantists and masters could rise to the occasion. Son, I am telling you, I've never been to Puri again; once was enough. Now I've got a picture of the Lord on a wooden pedestal, to which I offer holy tulsi leaves and water daily.'

I knew a little something about Lord Jagannath. My father was a devotee of him and of his abode at Puri. All through my childhood, he made frequent trips there, and returned with baskets of consecrated savoury sweets. We had an image of the Lord in our home too, and my father could hold forth on him. Lord Jagannath was Lord Vishnu himself. I also heard the words 'Daru Brahma'—the divine spirit manifested in a log of wood—and several other names He was known by: Patitapabana, Jagabandhu, Deenabandhu. Puri was a town by the sea, and night didn't exist there. My father was an ardent worshipper, and I was deeply moved by the prayers and hymns he and his friend, Uncle Bali, sang so soulfully together. So every tale of the Lord from Grandfather Uddhav's lips meant a great deal to me.

After he had finished talking about his pilgrimage to Puri, I suddenly asked him, apropos of nothing, 'Grandfather, I heard your policewallahs at Cuttack gave the Congress folks absolute bloody hell the other day. Beat the life out of them. And went and threw the Mahatma in the clink too.'

'True, son,' Grandfather Uddhav replied. 'Who did you hear all that from? Don't noise it around, keep it to yourself.'

'I overheard Teacher Raghu and the headmaster discussing it. They read the paper together.'

Uddhav Malik fell silent for a long moment, as if shell-shocked. Then he blew on the embers and, in the sliver of a flickering flame relit his cigar, took a vigorous puff as one does on a hashish pipe, exhaled slowly throwing his head back, and said in a strained voice, 'The British government is no small beast. It makes the tiger and the goat drink together at the same waterhole. The sun and the moon do not set on their empire. But then the Mahatma is no small opponent, either; he's Yudhishthira, the incarnation of Dharma himself. Something's got to give. Just wait and watch. The British government might put him behind bars, lock the building and set a day-and-night watch outside, but Goddess Jogmaya will cast her spell: she'll put the guards to sleep—into a deep, dark slumber—and the Mahatma will steal through the bars, in a breeze. He'll come and hide under the bejewelled throne of Lord Jagannath for three months, three fortnights, and three days. That's where all our thirty-three crore gods and goddesses are hiding. No one will ever divine where the Mahatma is, not even the sun and the moon will be any the wiser. Then, when the time is ripe, lords Jagannath and Balabhadra will set out to war on their white-and-black steeds—with their weapons of choice, the Sudarshan Chakra for Jagannath, and the ploughshare and mace for Balabhadra. Just wait and watch. The earth will tremble, but eventually evil would be put to the sword. Have a little patience, son. Just wait awhile. Do you have any idea what the charkha actually is? Nothing other than the Sudarshan Chakra!'

I drank in his words, my faith redoubled. Could there be any doubt the British would bite the dust this time?

But still the thought of Gandhi in jail rankled. I was as angry as I was upset. So I went back to Uddhav Malik. 'How come, Grandfather, being a chowkidar, and as someone living off the salt of the British, you're taking the side of the Mahatma and Congress?'

'And thereby hangs a mystery!' Uddhav smiled. 'That's the crux of the matter. Whose salt am I consuming, huh? The coming war will be fought on the issue of salt. The Mahatma is on an all-out war for salt. Salt will decide everything. Who does the salt belong to? Who owns it? Therein lies the difficulty. Didn't Bhishma and Drona live on the salt of Duryodhana? To such an extent they never deserted the

Kauravas until they perished. But who were they in truth? These are deep matters, son, and you can begin to make sense of them only when you're sufficiently grown up.'

But of course I didn't have to wait until I had sufficiently grown up. I was already beginning to understand such matters; deep mysteries were making themselves explicit, beginning to make sense to me. A truth-loving man ate somebody's salt but sang the praises of some other. The determination of the true ownership of salt was all that mattered. The question was whose salt it was. It didn't belong to the person we got it from, not always.

Uddhav Malik lived a long life. He retired when India became independent. He was still around when the Mahatma fell to Nathuram's bullets. By then, I had left the village for college, and lost touch with him. Occasionally, when I went back for the holidays, I would visit him. Wrapped in a dhoti, he was always to be found sitting quietly on the mud platform he had built around the sacred tulsi plant on the pond bank. He had gone completely silent, save for spells of coughing. One time I got him some oranges from Sylhet. He had cataracts in both his eyes and could hardly see. His gout made it painful for him to walk. Only once did he break his silence, after I'd jabbered on and on about this and that. 'The earth,' he said, 'has been taken over by darkness since the Mahatma left. I can't imagine plodding on anymore, can't take so much suffering.'

'The Mahatma might be gone, Grandfather, but Nehru's still around.'

He joined his palms and touched them to his forehead. 'Yes, Parikshit has succeeded Yudhishthira; he's the one ruling now, and that's how it goes, always did, down the aeons. Remember, when Parikshit was in his mother's womb, Ashwatthama, the wily, crafty, mean and mighty Brahmin, dispatched his most powerful weapon, the Brahma arrow, to destroy him? But did he succeed? Lord Krishna dispatched his Sudarshan; the Chakra whirled over the mother's womb and protected the embryo. It was the Lord's deed, his leela. So fond of leela is he! One moment he's out performing his miracles, and the next he's back in his sanctum sanctorum in the Big Temple pretending to be a wood gnome incapable of the slightest movement! But who can plumb the depths of his doings, who?'

Now, at this point of my life, I realize that the millions of India's illiterate rural folk aren't fools; on the contrary, they have in their genes the wisdom passed on by sages like Vyasa and Valmiki. The events of history make no difference to their understanding of the eternal Truth—of the meaning of life and of its mysteries. Their mythologies are enough for them to unravel the deepest secrets and help simplify arcane issues and matters. They do not need to pore over the tomes of history, geography, economics, psychology, physics, chemistry or biology.

On the other hand, we who are educated tend to dismiss mythological stories as tall tales, reading the newspapers with far greater respect than the Vedas and Upanishads. We are cut off from the stream of universal consciousness. Our lives, circumscribed by petty political and economic considerations, are highly dissatisfying. We vent our discontent through complaints and laments. We do not seek or find the timeless epic figures of a Duryodhana, Yudhishthira, Rama or Ravana in the pages of our newspapers. We fail to see that the battles between Rama and Ravana, the Kauravas and the Pandavas are still raging on everyday in the world. We neither take sides, nor remain completely impartial. Confined within an empty, solitary existence, we bemoan our fate and blame others.

Within a year of that last meeting of ours, I received the news of Uddhav Malik's passing. A most tragic incident—he drowned in the pond on the Janmashtami festival in the month of Bhadrav; it took the police of independent India two whole days to fish him out. In his hut was found a sandal paste-smeared picture of Lord Jagannath, a picture of Lord Krishna holding Govardhan hill atop his little finger, and two fishing rods; his blue chowkidar's bag held a half-torn wrinkled picture of Mahatma Gandhi sitting at the feet of Mother India.

Today, in 1979, there's no trace of his hut on the bank of his pond, but his image shines brightly in my mind. Whenever I face a moment of crisis or turmoil, I hear Uddhav Malik's night cry reverberating in the recesses of my heart:

> Mother India's awake and stirring,
> Beware, brother. Beware.

And slowly but steadily hope, faith, and strength flow back into my weary heart.

A RIVER CALLED DEMOCRACY
AKHIL MOHAN PATTNAIK

It was unmissable. I drove by it twice a day, but became curious only four or five months after the shelter came up. One afternoon, on my way home from the office, my car unexpectedly ran out of petrol, stalling close by. My driver went to the nearest station to buy a container of petrol, and I, with nothing to do, lit a cigarette and got out of the car to explore the surrounding area.

It was on the opposite side of the road, in front of the Accountant General's office. This was the heart of Bhubaneswar, next to the city bus stand, bustling with the roar of buses and taxis, hawkers and lottery-ticket sellers ceaselessly making their sales pitches. The din was constant. A little ahead from there was the club where the top bureaucrats and business executives—the movers and shakers, the wheelers and dealers—hobnobbed in the evening. The road to the west led to the ministers' bungalows, easily recognized by the powerful lights on the front gates.

Strange that a shelter should have come up here of all places; twelve feet by fourteen, tarpaulin thrown over a bamboo lattice, a knee-deep layer of hay and a thick cotton mattress covering the floor.

I saw four people sitting inside engrossed in a game of cards, keenly watched by a number of onlookers, all unmindful of the world flowing past them. Nothing seemed to distract them—the crowd, the revving buses, the raucous urchins engaged by private busowners to shout out the destinations. Nothing. Who were these people? Why had they put up the hut? Who had let them?

My curiosity was so strong I forgot the cigarette between my fingers until it began to scorch my skin. I flicked it away with a start and took another look at the shelter. It was festooned with two large red banners, one proclaiming 'Vande Mataram' and the other 'Inquilab Zindabad'. There was a smaller one, but I couldn't make out the writing from where I stood. Whoever they were, there was no doubt they were votaries of democracy, protesting some gross miscarriage of justice.

I beckoned to the fellow who stood drinking from an open pipe next to the shelter. The tap was missing and water was gushing out.

'What's going on?'

He looked at me with surprise, as if I was from a different planet. 'Don't you know? Dhanu Nayak is on a dharna. Protest. For quite a few months already. He was a peon in the A. G.'s office before his sacking.'

How had I missed such a momentous event?

My informant seemed keen to fill me in further, but I didn't show much enthusiasm. My driver was taking a long time.

The card players and onlookers took no notice of me.

The sun began to set and its slanting rays fell directly into the shelter, heating it up. Two players got up and hung a towel strategically to block them out. Then they went back to their seats and were quickly caught up in the game once again.

Meanwhile I was thinking of the dharna, a perfectly democratic act of protest, with its origin in Satyagraha. Picketing. An excellent example of the middle path; it didn't disrupt anything but definitely registered disagreement and protest. Live and let live.

My driver came back with the petrol, and as he drove me home I burst into sudden gales of laughter, which took not only my driver by surprise (he craned his neck more than once to see if I was alright), but also the pedestrians we drove past on a particularly crowded part of the road.

The incident remained in my mind; I thought about it a lot. On the day Dhanu Nayak was sacked he must have reached the protest venue with his neck garlanded with strings of marigolds and surrounded by quite a few well-wishers. He must have sat down on dharna, his democratic right of protest, with his legs crossed in the lotus pose. How long did it take to put up the shelter—the bamboo, the tarpaulin, the bales of hay, a bucket and a bowl, and the rest? Maybe the first day there was a relay fast: Ram Nayak from breakfast hour to lunchtime, Dam Nayak from lunchtime until six in the evening, then the baton must have passed from one hand to another to keep the fast going around the clock. Dam must have bequeathed the responsibility to some Sam Nayak, like handing over the torch of the Olympic Games. Slogans must have been raised in support of Dhanu Nayak, loud enough to rise above the noise of the traffic. Things must have cooled down after a few days. His supporters must have gone home to take care of their own problems, after making promises to drop in at night to see how he was faring. Dhanu Nayak couldn't have stayed in the venue twenty-four hours a day, day after day. At least twice daily he'd have to leave to relieve himself. No matter how strong his determination, he couldn't have stuck it out like Bhishma on his bed of nails. As days passed, he must have found time to go around to a few places in town. Perhaps a trip to his village; then probably several, every fortnight.

Who knew whether Dhanu Nayak was actually in the hut the day I stopped by. Maybe after a couple of months he had stopped going there altogether. It was this thought which had made me laugh out loud, oblivious to my surroundings.

I couldn't get it out of my head, and would look for the spot without fail on my way to and from the office. I began to watch the protesters closely. Sometimes I saw them quickly fold their bedrolls, stand up in front of the shelter like disciplined soldiers, and shout slogans of 'Inquilab Zindabad' for three or four minutes. The whole operation reminded me of the way jackals howl every hour during the night. By and by I was able to understand what was happening: whenever a minister's car passed by, Dhanu's supporters registered their protest.

It became a pleasurable pastime to park my car a little distance from the venue and hit the nearby tea stalls. I could watch the hut—the temple rather—of democracy and pump people to find out what was going on.

Sometimes the radio was on in the hut and I could overhear songs aired by Vividh Bharti or Radio Ceylon. Sometimes I was intrigued to see a middle-aged woman among those present. Who was she? What was she doing in the company of men, in a place that looked more like a bivouac for soldiers? I began making enquiries. Not out of idle curiosity but of a sense of duty; I was a police officer after all, and maintaining law and order in the city was my concern. The woman turned out to be Dhanu Nayak's second wife; she came to cook her husband's meals in a recently-added makeshift kitchen. The arrangement was justified. Dhanu Nayak was in for the long haul and needed to have regular home-cooked food if he hoped to stick it out until the end.

The days flowed by, like the water from the pipe. Occasionally slogans would be raised, but they'd evaporate into the empty air. Sometimes the shelter became raucous, the card players animated, like the traffic signal, green one minute and red the next. Sometimes it lay shrouded in complete darkness, with only a slow classical song playing on the radio, as a meagre wisp of smoke rose into the night sky.

Some years—maybe three or four—passed. One day, among the regulars, I noticed a couple of kids, helplessly blinking in the sunlight. Was Dhanu Nayak present? I wouldn't have recognized him even if he were. I had never made an effort to find out which one he was.

Over the years the shelter had changed shape. A mud and brick wall now enclosed it; in place of the tarpaulin there was a thatched roof, the lean-to kitchen had been roofed over with flattened tin drums.

Since I was interested, news of Dhanu Nayak reached me through the grapevine; interesting tidbits which amused me no end. Dhanu had first lived in a slum on the edge of the city; a Harijan minister had given him his first job out of love and concern for people of his own caste. Dhanu had been shunted from department to department and had finally reached the A. G.'s office. He had been allotted government quarters, which he had rented out for one hundred and fifty rupees a month. He began to make more and more trips to his village, his unauthorized absences becoming not only frequent but longer lasting. He stole office stationery, abused his official position. He was once arrested on charges of stealing four typewriters, but was acquitted by the court. Dhanu Nayak, emboldened, became a scourge. His supervisors were driven to distraction. In desperation, they initiated disciplinary proceedings and dismissed him. But he was a citizen of a free country, the land of 'Vande Mataram' and 'Inquilab Zindabad', so he decided to wade into the ever-flowing waters of democracy and protest his removal from service. To protest peacefully was his democratic right; nobody could deprive him of it.

But it'd be wrong to presume that all he did was protest. In the early morning he would begin his rounds of the homes of elected representatives, first members of the legislature, then ministers. Each had something or the other on the side, for which they wanted help. Some legislators, for example, had opened liquor shops under false names and were on the lookout for security guards. A minister's wife wanted pure cow-ghee to fulfil the concluding ceremony of the vow she was keeping. Another minister's personal assistant wanted oil from a rare kochila khai bird as medicine for his daughter's arthritis. These were not available off the shelf in any shop; someone had to be pressed into service. Who better than Dhanu Nayak? Over time the man made himself not only useful but indispensable. Did he do all this without an ulterior motive? What about his dismissal, which was still on the books? His job as a peon might have been lowly, but a job was a job. The poor man was mired in court cases; he had to hire lawyers and pay them using his hard-earned money. No, he deserved a better deal. Justice was, after all, the bedrock of democracy. Justice for all.

Dhanu Nayak's file moved up and down faster than ever before. But no matter how fast it moved, justice was not within the purview of bureaucrats. So the poor man was compelled to ring the bells of the High Court. But those bells, unlike that of a telephone or a bicycle, couldn't simply be rung. Those bells took time, but when they jangled they did so as resoundingly as they might have done in front of a Mughal emperor's palace! The law above everything! The law above everyone!

When Dhanu Nayak's petition came up for hearing, a notice was issued to the government to file within fifteen days the reason for his dismissal and whether it was constitutional. But justice didn't come without a price. The gods and godlings in the corridors, and in the lanes and by-lanes behind the august court had to be appropriately propitiated. Dhanu Nayak had learnt the lesson of give and take. He didn't have to do it himself; he had his friends. But friends also had to be taken care of. Why else would they pitch in? So Dhanu Nayak kept himself free of all domestic entanglements. He packed off his wife and children to his village; besides, he needed people to keep an eye on his land and property.

Meanwhile, in the evening the hut was lit by an electric bulb—albeit of low voltage. Dhanu Nayak had obtained an illegal connection from a nearby paan shop. A curtain was added on the front door too. There was a steady stream of people until midnight. Through the grapevine I learned that Dhanu Nayak had started selling liquor from the protest camp. He wouldn't put up with any dry-day restrictions. Not for any Thursdays, or the second day of every month, Gandhi's birthday or other national holidays. And why should he, for heaven's sake, when licenced vendors didn't observe them either? As a police officer I could have taken suitable steps, but by then Dhanu Nayak was beyond my reach. He was no longer a mere individual, he had become an institution—a blossoming symbol of democratic protest in the face of injustice!

The court hearings continued, and I received news of them. The government counsel sought one adjournment after another; Dhanu Nayak's lawyer kept pounding the table, claiming the dismissal was vindictive, in bad faith, and against all the canons of natural justice. Sometimes the government counsel was so flustered his black gown slipped off his shoulders causing much tittering and laughter in the courtroom, making the judge bang his gavel and cry for order.

Dhanu Nayak's camp became livelier by the day. He diversified. He got two tribal beauties from Phulbani, who stayed in the shelter the whole night. Their presence attracted a large number of people after nightfall. Even in summer the visitors covered their faces as if to keep out a chill in the air. I kept tab on the visitors, and my worst fears were confirmed. I checked and double-checked. Some nights Dhanu Nayak took the girls to the bungalows of some big sorts; I collected their names and addresses.

The court gave its verdict: Dhanu Nayak's dismissal was unconstitutional, and null and void as a result. He had to be reinstated immediately and paid the arrears of salaries and increments for the past seven years.

Dhanu Nayak pocketed thirty thousand rupees and resigned the day after. His businesses had proliferated and he didn't have enough people to look after the operations. Besides, he was now eligible for a lifelong pension of seventy rupees a month. But what really mattered was that his democratic protest had paid off, justice had been done. The banners were taken down, but not the hut. Who would have dared dismantle it? Dhanu Nayak had become a symbol. He himself was a Harijan, he had under his protection two tribal women. He had become an asset. His camp was a safe haven for liquor and the immoral trafficking of women. One couldn't simply requisition a bulldozer and raze it. Whatever had to be done had to conform to rules and regulations and follow due process.

The legal process was put in place. A file on the demolition of an illegal construction on public property was opened; it began to move from the executive officer to the land officer to the estate officer-cum-deputy secretary of the political and services department. Everyone swore by the due process of the law. The file moved back and forth, up and down.

Meanwhile there were political storms too. The Opposition raised the issue on the floor of the House. Dhanu Nayak was a burning example of the ruling party's apathy to the plight of people belonging to the scheduled castes and scheduled tribes. Most were being thrown out of the places they had lived in for years and rendered homeless. A tabloid published an interview with Dhanu Nayak. The government of the day had become vindictive towards him after losing the court case, it had even become undemocratic. If eviction proceedings continued to carry on, Dhanu Nayak would be forced to reveal the names of the legislators and ministers who had exploited tribal girls. That would have been catastrophic. So an unstated go-slow was put in place. There were hundreds and thousands of more important files to attend to.

Dhanu Nayak's file now remains in the custody of a lower division clerk—a rickety baby wrapped in red tape and placed in a cradle on the lowest rung of the secretariat. Who knows when the issue of his eviction will be taken up? Who knows when the slender file will put on weight, or how long it will take to traverse the miles and miles between the first floor of the secretariat and the fourth? But no matter. The river of democracy is flowing, that's all that matters. And on its cool, calm, clear waters are swimming three beautiful black swans—Dhanu Nayak and his two tribal beauties, craning their beautiful long necks.

THE TALE OF THE SNAKE CHARMER
CHANDRASEKHAR RATH

His art was arcane, mysterious, unrevealed to ordinary people; indeed, very few snake charmers were able to master it. Only those like Jhampura, who possessed the knowledge of charming snakes, could manage these miraculous feats. One had to either be very naive or a man of firm convictions to believe in God or in such a snake charmer.

But no one in those ten or twenty villages at the foot of Elephant Head Hill doubted in the least the truth of all they'd heard about Jhampura. The other day, in the bright morning light, he transformed into a great black snake and crawled into a crevice. Gone. Vanished forever. Even his body, which he cast off on the sandy bed of the river, was never to be found again.

Did anyone know his real name? Did he even have one? Because of his thick, unruly, overgrown mop of hair—more like a knee-high bush—he was called Jhampura. His skin was pitch black, his thin pointy moustache curled up at the tips, his roundish eyes—like Lord Balabhadra's—were slightly elongated at the corners, his tight set of teeth were white and shining, his arms muscular and legs sculpted. He wore just a traditional cotton towel around his waist—it barely reached his knees—with two strands of gada herb, an antidote to snakebite, around his neck.

Wicker baskets with snakes hung from either ends of a stout bamboo stick balanced across one shoulder, the biggest at the bottom. Placed on the baskets in front were his stock of antivenom herbs and his snake charmer's flute, hollowed out of a dry gourd. Lying atop the baskets at back were a sharp pointed knife, a long supple stick, and a handheld drum he'd sound before entering a village.

If during the show somebody offered him an egg, he'd save it for his biggest snake. If he was given a second, then he'd help himself. The smaller snakes were fed on frogs and mice he caught while on his wanders. He lived on what he made from his shows. Each day he'd slip the money he'd collected into the basket with his biggest snake; no one would dare touch, let alone steal, it. If he received rice, vegetables and fruit instead of cash, he'd put them in a bundle with his bag of herbs.

The affectionate way he spoke to his snakes, each by name, was unique. He'd gently tap on the basket, blow on it, open the lid just a crack, and out would crawl a full five-foot-long reptile ready to raise its hood, flick its forked tongue and sway. 'There you are, my lord,' he'd begin his spiel. 'My king! Just notice his majestic posture, ladies and gentlemen, masters and mistresses. Watch how he moves and sways. Look, look—ah, devil take you—how badly he wants to bite!' With every strand of hair standing on end, he'd pass his left fist perilously close to the reptile's fangs, holding the lid of the basket as a shield in his right.

'Masters and mistresses, this snake is called a sankhachud. Note the mark of the sankha conch on its hood. A single bite can fell a full-grown elephant! Lift it and you'll see how much it weighs—as heavy as a five-year-old child!' He'd gently slap the snake on the tip of its tail to make it rear up with a hiss.

Snakes like the spectacled cobra, the spitting cobra, the yellow cobra—all highly venomous—darted about like lightning, but he was quicker than them all. He could catch them just as they were about to shoot like an arrow into the wilds, open the lid just a crack and slip their heads in, and in they'd slither. Then he'd clamp the lid firmly down, to the enormous relief of spectators.

People loved to watch him play his snake charmer's flute, especially when he showed off his golden yellow cobra. He'd kneel on one knee and gently move the other around in the air and play a slow tune that rose and fell in waves. It could make the spectators sway too; the snake and the spectators suspended in time, unblinking. The yellow cobra always attracted a shower of coins. The women prayed with folded hands for wealth and prosperity, barren women prayed for children. Jhampura would weave through the crowd like Lord Siva, with the snake swinging from his neck. If someone offered him a coin after touching it to the snake, he accepted it gratefully with outstretched hands. Sometimes an elderly woman would drag a younger woman from behind the door of a house and thrust her in front of him. 'She's borne no fruit although it's been over a year and a half since she came to my house. Touch her with the holy snake, son. May her tree bear fruit.' Jhampura would study the blanched face of a cowering young woman and, firmly holding the snake by its head and tail, put it around the young woman's neck for a few seconds. The more the poor thing struggled to escape, the more the old woman pushed her forward. Drenched in a cold sweat, eyes shut tightly, bones trembling like a handheld drum, she'd imagine the yellow cobra coiling around her neck. Jhampura would take it back before she fainted, returning it to his own neck. 'Mistress,' he'd tell the old woman. 'Don't worry. By this time next year, you'll be kissing and petting your grandchild.'

A snake has venom in its fangs but nectar in its tail—or so people believed. The touch of a snake's tail could heal chronic sores. If an ear was oozing pus, the tip of the tail was inserted into it. People besieged Jhampura to treat all sorts of problems. Their faith was the most important healer, and they had as much faith in the snake charmer as in the snake. That man could work miracles—he had nectar on his fingertips. His touch could make an old gnarled tree break into bloom, a barren woman bear a brood of children. No one knew how to control snakes better than him. At his call, they swarmed out of the cracks and hollows in trees and stones; if he cast a spell they couldn't move an inch; no matter how deadly their venom was, his antivenom herb was even more powerful. If the herb didn't work, he could summon the snake to suck its venom back in. People who witnessed this couldn't believe their eyes. Some called it a hoax, claiming the snake was tame and that they'd just seen a trick. But many didn't agree. After all they'd seen the snake slither out from nowhere and put its mouth on the bite to draw in the poison. But disbelievers would never believe anyway!

After the show, Jhampura would sometimes sit on someone's veranda to catch his breath, smoke a hand-rolled cigar, while men and women crowded around and bombarded him with questions. The women seemed utterly transfixed by his looks: shiny black with a sculpted physique, he was sleek like a black cobra himself! They just couldn't take their eyes off him, though shivers ran down their spine. Beware women, this was no ordinary snake charmer; he possessed knowledge of how to control snakes of all kinds! At times you couldn't tell him from a snake!

'How do you tame these slimy slitherers?' someone asked once.

He gave a toothy smile and continued to smoke in silence, while another answered on his behalf, 'He belongs to the tribe of snake charmers, after all. What harm can the snakes cause him? They are his family!'

'Besides, he has the gada herb in his blood,' someone else added. 'And that is deadlier than snake venom. If a snake bites him it'll drop dead.'

The corners of Jhampura's eyes would wrinkle, the tips of his moustache would twirl upwards, but he would neither laugh nor utter a word. His faster-than-lightning gaze would simply scan the audience: a straight stare at the men, a sidelong glance at the women.

'Why won't you say something, Jhampura? Say something. We'd love to listen to you.'

Once, after being badgered, he pursed his lips and gave a long, low whistle. Instantly, a similar whistling sound came from the basket holding the sankhachud cobra, petrifying the audience. 'You hear that? We spoke to each other just now.' A wink, a smile. 'In the language of snakes. Each has its own. I've lived long enough with them to learn them all.' His voice dropped. 'All of God's creatures have arms and legs. Just as trees have branches. If you take away the arms and legs and branches, you have a snake. No creature is as beautiful. It's like a baby when it sleeps, but a tongue of fire when awake. Usually soft to the touch, it can be harder than steel when roused to anger.'

His mesmerized audience swallowed hard and wondered what he was talking about.

'It sleeps, it turns and twists when it wakes, it eats and drinks and flies into a temper, it responds to love and affection, it's warm to the touch, it weighs as much as a human baby. One summer night...' He stopped, trying perhaps to recollect that summer ten years ago, when he was in his prime. 'The river beside Pitapur had dried up, and I had taken to sleeping on the soft sands under the open sky. Couldn't possibly sleep beneath a tree, because trees, especially tamarinds, give off poison at night that's so strong even the herb isn't of much help. So sleeping in the open, with the dew falling, was better. I woke up one night with a start. The snakes in my baskets were greatly agitated and calling out to me. In the wan moonlight I saw a young yellow male cobra circling one of the smaller baskets, trying to lift the lid and get inside.'

Jhampura's eyes narrowed. He seemed to smile, his gaze on the ground. 'I had captured a female cobra just five or six days earlier and the young male had come looking for her. He had caught her scent, just as the others in the baskets had caught his. My snakes were telling me to chase him away.'

The listeners waited with bated breath. What did Jhampura do?

'I made no effort to chase him away, nor did I try to catch him. I simply opened the basket and let out the female. They slithered off to the riverbank for their tryst.'

The first person to come out of the spell was the elderly head of the family, who at his age, was all heat but no flame. 'Didn't the male realize he could be captured? Had the female called to him? Why did you let them escape?'

Jhampura looked at him with pity, as if he were a dimwit or an innocent babe with clearly no knowledge of snakes. 'When the juices rise within a cobra, it looks for a mate. If you trap it then, the gods get upset. Even animals and plants and trees get upset; the air and water turn to poison. Besides, cobras don't mate within the confines of a basket, only in the open, wherever they choose, in their own sweet time. It's auspicious to come upon them mating. And if someone throws a new cloth on them while they are, the person comes into great wealth. Not just him, but also his family.'

'True,' clucked an old woman. 'True.'

'So what do you do when your snakes want to breed?' the old man persisted.

'I milk them. They get angry, they struggle, but in the end they go to sleep out of pure relief.'

'Is that what makes a cobra so ferocious?'

This incensed Jhampura. He bristled; his face, distorted by a frown, swayed like the hood of a serpent. 'A cobra's not ferocious! It's as peace-loving as any of God's creatures. It lives in its own world, in its own fashion. It strikes only if frustrated, challenged, threatened. But so do all animals including humans, when provoked.

'Venom and nectar are two sides of the same coin. Every living being produces venom. We all have it—humans, animals, birds, trees. The sap of a tree contains venom, as does the honey collected by bees. Human saliva contains venom, as does the saliva of tigers and birds. Look at the different fruits around you—some are good, some poisonous. What's poisonous to humans may not be to other living creatures. The same is true of snake venom: it's both poison and nectar.'

Everyone listened raptly. Half of what he was saying didn't make sense, but the way he talked made everything sound magical, out of this world.

The snake charmer had fallen under his own spell, and spoke mostly to himself. 'There's venom, and there's charred embers. Both are poisonous. The air rising off embers can be deadly. Even the sun rains down venom: it can burn to cinders, turn bodies black, fill beings with unquenchable thirst. The moon too can be venomous; moonlight can rob humans of their sleep, curdle their blood. The clouds can rain down venom that raises blisters.

'There're venoms of all sorts—masters and mistresses. Fresh and old, male and female. One will set you on fire, the other will asphyxiate you. A king cobra's venom spreads through the human body like fire through a haystack. But just as a good downpour can put out a raging fire, the gada herb can counter any snake venom, and lead to rejuvenation, make burnt grass grow. There you are—now you know what poison and nectar are—two sides of the same coin.'

He sat still for a long while. His snakes were inside the baskets, which were stacked below the veranda, on top of each other. Then his body jerked. He leaned towards his transfixed audience, breaking the spell he had cast on them and himself. Was this man an ordinary snake charmer getting by on meagre takings? Or was he something else? Did he really possess oracular knowledge about snakes?

The old man was pleased. He had seen Jhampura perform many times before but had never heard him speak so much, reveal so many secrets. He gave him all the coins he had; others followed. The women ran home and came back with rice flakes and jaggery—only raw food because he wouldn't touch anything cooked.

Then a girl of ten or twelve, with a mass of unkempt hair and eyes shining like stars, came with six freshly-laid eggs in the hollow of her pink palms. With beads of sweat on her face, her mouth open and panting from the exertion, she made her offering, as if to a god.

Jhampura was enthralled. He held her hands in his and looked deep into her eyes. He took the eggs and put them carefully on the veranda, as if they were precious gemstones. Then he continued to caress her hands, completely bewitched. It seemed at long last he'd got what he desired: his gnarled tree suddenly burst into leaves and buds. Could a seasoned snake charmer experience such wild happiness over half-a-dozen eggs? Not coins, not rice flakes, not jaggery—just eggs? True, eggs were always welcome. He loved them as much as his snakes did, as much as his black cobra, which he resembled, did. He loved their smell. But did he love the smell of the dark young girl even more? The women wondered. It wasn't lost on them how long and lovingly he caressed her hands.

'This is Marua,' said someone. 'Nidhi Bhoi and Dhani's daughter. Nidhi died of snakebite five years ago and now Dhani has a hard time making ends meet. She has a few hens...'

Jhampura looked into the eyes of the fatherless girl, stretched out his left hand, and caressed her cheek. Everyone who watched thought the girl was about to turn into a snake, raise her hood and seek shelter in one of his baskets. It wouldn't have been surprising if she had. After all, the man had mastered the knowledge of snakes.

But nothing of the sort came to pass. Jhampura picked up his baskets and walked to the grove at the edge of the village under the relentless midday sun.

That evening Marua reached puberty.

For the next seven days she didn't stir out of her house. The knowledgeable among the village women exchanged knowing looks. 'That wandering snake charmer works miracles. At his touch even a dead and dry branch of a tree like her can bear flowers.'

The rains came. Clouds massed and hung over the hills. It poured. The fields and meadows flooded. Water got into the snake holes, and the snakes crawled out and scattered. Frogs spawned, magpies laid eggs, field rats ran helter-skelter. The snake charmers caught big cobras and put them in baskets. But Jhampura huddled in his hut in Pitapur, the hill on one side and the river on the other, withdrawing completely. Some of his tribesmen switched to other shows to make ends meet: burying their heads in the soil, spinning on top of bamboo poles, selling snakes. Snakeskin was in great demand; snake venom too. Uncle Jambu, nearly the same age as Jhampura's deceased father, was the only other exception. He was stuck with an old python that no longer fit into the biggest basket he had, its tail beginning to curl in the narrow confines. Every ten or fifteen days the old man had to steal a hen to feed it. He could have sold it for a handsome amount, but he flew into a temper if anyone suggested that. He was drawn to tears at the thought of parting with his pet. The only person he could share his grief with was Jhampura, who was also having a hard time and making do with the crabs and snails he caught in the fields. He roasted them over a low fire, mashed them with salt and chillies, and ate them with rice. The rats and frogs he caught were reserved for his snakes.

Even in his own community he was the odd man out. He loved being alone. He kept away from women. Binda, an acrobat who could turn on top of a bamboo pole, had set her eyes on him. Every once in a while she descended on him in all her finery to try and work her charms. One midnight, she came to his hut and saw him swaying like a cobra. Terrified, she ran away. From then on, whenever the topic cropped up, she'd simply say: 'That man's rightful place is in the cremation grounds. He's impotent, a piece of stone.'

'He isn't like any of us,' said the other snake charmers. 'He has entered dense forests where no one has ever set foot; he has his own guru; he possesses the full knowledge of snakes—he has mastered the art of controlling them. He can raise fire and wind; he can make you vanish into thin air.'

Still, old Mangu was keen to fix up his daughter Jhuli with Jhampura. The girl was in full bloom. When she danced on the tightrope, balancing with nothing but a bamboo stick, all eyes stayed glued to her. Coins rained down on father and daughter. But when a rich zamindar's son began to give the girl the eye, Mangu's only wish was she fill the emptiness of Jhampura's hut. He uttered a mantra and blew a little dust into the rich boy's eyes, hissing like a snake. The boy's eyes started itching. No amount of medicine or magic helped. The poor fellow became blind in one eye.

Mangu dragged Jhuli to Jhampura and told him: 'Keep her.'

Jhampura took a long look at the girl. 'Uncle,' he said, taking her measure. 'She has better things in store. Why should she live with a man like me and give birth to a litter of snakes? She'll have nothing but venom to share. My life is uncertain. I'm living on the edge, playing with fate; things may snap at any moment.' He added in an undertone, 'Besides, my guru hasn't given me permission.'

Mangu, a gypsy himself, realized Jhampura wasn't telling lies. A few days later, Jhuli disappeared while on her way to the weekly market. She had eloped with a Santali boy and gone off to Assam.

Since then no girl had tried to ensnare Jhampura.

The rains lessened. Winter was still some months away. It was time for the snakes to slough off their skin. Thrashing about, they emerged out of their old skin like newborn babies from their mothers' wombs, head first, lying helpless until their bodies hardened in the breeze. A cobra, after shedding its skin, could be faster than lightning; its teeth were at their sharpest, its venom at its deadliest, its colour at its shiny best.

When Jhampura's snakes were shedding, he took good care of them. He made no noise. The snakes hissed, moved about lethargically, stayed away from food. But once they had discarded their old skin they were overtaken by a great hunger. Jhampura kept eggs, mice and frogs handy. He gave them time to recover before taking them for shows.

Spring came. It was time to visit Marua's village.

One afternoon, the sun directly overhead, he entered the village beating his drum. Even before reaching the centre he had collected quite a crowd of young children. This time he had brought only four baskets. The yellow cobra was too auspicious to be left behind. The sankhachud cobra was a showstopper. The new black spitting cobra, far from fully trained, was lively. The king cobra—another new catch—was magnificent: grey with black bands, and all of eight hands long already. When it rose up on the tip of its tail it towered over an average man. Jhampura could not sit down when he let it out of the basket. People wondered how he had been able to capture it in the first place. 'This is a child,' he told them. 'It'll reach fifteen hands when fully grown. Its hood will be totally out of reach. It's the king of all snakes.' The show was very different this time—an awe-inspiring tiger of a show. Even the adults were petrified. But the women seemed to hate it: 'How can one play with a reptile as big as an elephant!' Jhampura could read their minds. So he took out the yellow cobra and put it around his neck, and his female spectators were flooded with relief. The other three snakes were safely back in their baskets, thank God. Still he seemed a changed man this time around, although his black skin was as shiny as before, his physique just as sculpted. The shadow of the new king cobra seemed to have come over him and he had an aura which kept people away.

After the show was over, he sat on the same veranda for a smoke, just as he had before. But this time people didn't ply him with questions. He looked around quizzically, his eyes searching for someone.

'Boy,' said an elderly woman. 'My daughter-in-law, whom you touched with your yellow cobra, will soon give birth. You've magic in your fingers, son. The moon becomes full at your touch... There was another snake charmer called Mania, who visited sometime back. He too had his snake draped around his neck, but his knowledge of snakes was nowhere near yours.'

Jhampura bared his teeth and gave a wan smile, looking over the throng.

'And you remember the girl who gave you eggs last time?'

Jhampura looked up with an interest that was not lost on the audience.

'She got her period the same day. Now she sticks to home at her mother's insistence.'

Jhampura lowered his eyes, a huge sigh escaping him. He was clutching at the memories of the fatherless girl. Why did such a sweet little girl have to lose her father? Why did a snake have to bite the man? What kind of snake was it? Where did it bite him? Reptiles were strange sometimes; they did foolish things that gave them a bad name. But most were shy and afraid. They bit out of fear. What did they have besides their hood, mouth, tongue and teeth? They could only open their mouths and flick their forked tongues—whether out of anger or love, whether in fright or in danger. They could only hiss. Poor things—being blamed through no fault of their own. Jhampura got up, picked up his baskets and, with one last look at the crowd, got going. The bamboo pole across his shoulder was bent under their weight. The village women watched him avidly, holding their faces until he vanished from sight around a bend in the path. He was a sight to drink in—a lithe cobra in motion.

As he passed by where the Bhois had their homes, he wanted to stop. Maybe there'd be that little dark face peering from behind a door. When he reached the edge of the village, his head in a whirl, his feet slowed down on their own. Maybe Marua wouldn't have looked half as forlorn had her father Nidhi not died of snakebite!

He stopped at the grove and looked back. The Bhoi colony was no longer visible. He lighted a coarse cigar, took a few quick drags and, picking up his load, broke into a brisk trot. The sunlight was fading.

For a whole year he roamed around. People in his own colony believed he was looking for the cobra with a jewel on its hood—not just any old cobra, but the greatest among them all, the emperor. No ordinary snake charmer had ever caught one. A great snake charmer had caught one long, long ago. But he was so overcome by greed that he tore open the snake's hood and wrested out the jewel, which he then presented to the king, who, in turn, rewarded him with gold earrings and bracelets as a token of royal appreciation. The king put the jewel on a pedestal and worshipped it daily and received whatever he desired. The old snake charmer perished inside of a week—of snakebite! He had betrayed the snakes and his knowledge of how to control them had deserted him. No one could have saved him.

Why then was Jhampura looking for this cobra like a mad man? To take the jewel from its hood? For whom? Was he set to commit the same mistake and sin as the older snake charmer? Did he wish to die of snakebite too?

His king cobra had reached a length of ten hands, his spitting cobra had become stronger than before, his conch cobra more experienced; only his yellow cobra was beginning to lose its shine.

The news spread that Jhampura had finally captured a jewel-head in the depths of the forest two hundred miles from the Mahanadi. And the first thing he had done afterwards was release all his old snakes. He had thrown away the baskets too.

Not only had he caught the cobra, but he'd dragged it two hundred miles. While he trudged the distance like any ordinary human being, the great snake flew from bush to bush, from tree to tree, not touching the ground below.

When Jhampura reached Pitapur, he found his village empty; everyone had left to perform their shows and make some money. Uncle Jambu's old python was the only living thing left behind.

When Uncle Jambu returned, he took one look at his nephew and was convinced the man had indeed achieved the impossible. Jhampura's eyes were gleaming, his body vibrating under high tension.

'So you finally caught it?' he asked.

Jhampura gave him a glance and looked away. Then he went to his hut and locked himself in.

When Jambu told the others of Jhampura's return, nobody dared meet and speak with him. The jewel-headed snake might materialize out of nowhere!

The next morning Jhampura was found sleeping on his back on the sands of the riverbed. Was that to enjoy the falling dew?

By the time the news spread and people gathered, the body was no longer there. The young boy who had first discovered him in the morning led them to the spot. Jambu knelt down and inspected the ground. 'Yes, Jhampura was lying here, but he's no longer human. His knowledge of snakes was ultimately no match for the jewel-headed snake. They fought all night, and clearly he met defeat. If the snake had lost, it'd have had to take on a human form. Now it's poor Jhampura who has become a snake. When morning dawned his human body must have vanished. That takes but a moment. And the jewel-headed cobra has flown back through the air to its abode. I once heard some very old and wise men speak of these matters. But today we have seen them with our own eyes.'

The crowd stared at the impression of a human body on the sand, stealing an occasional look at the hills beyond.

Before the sun went down the story had spread everywhere.

Marua's mother awoke from her late afternoon siesta with a start and saw a huge black cobra, as tall as a man, with its hood outspread, slipping out through the back door. There was no one around. Marua was trembling like someone bitten by a snake.

'It was Jhampura,' the villagers said. 'He came to protect the family.'

'True,' chimed the knowledgeable among the women. 'True.'

PLUS MINUS GREATER THAN ZERO
SANTANU KUMAR ACHARYA

They tore on ahead, skidding, skipping, surging forth like a bubbling dark-green mountain stream. The stones underfoot wobbled like an excited throng of homing pigeons. 'You know, my dad was saying...' Chirping, chattering, twittering, they rushed along the path, satchels, haversacks, lunch boxes and water bottles hanging from their shoulders. A day for nature study, and a holiday to boot. 'Good luck, buddy-o, arm yourselves with butterfly nets, cameras and guns...' The right kind of equipment for studying nature. 'Not only butterflies; there might be grasshoppers, giant spiders, dragonflies, queen bees, snakes and mongooses to catch. Who knows, maybe a penguin or a pelican into the bargain. Whee...!'

Stopping by a clump of overgrown bushes, one boy picked a leaf and sniffed it; another pulled at a spindly branch, scrutinized it and scribbled something in his notebook; yet another leafed through his textbook, cracking his head over the botanical name of a plant he thought he had succeeded in identifying. In the midst of it all, an oafish brute landed a heavy blow out of nowhere on a bush; withered leaves, dry seeds, and flakes of mud drifted down.

Startled butterflies flitted up from the bushes. Swooping down on them with his silken net, someone trapped a flutter of them. 'Ah, excellent! Lovely!' the boy cried excitedly. From inside the net the quivering butterflies were struck with wonder by the swirling gaudy colours of the clothes the boys were wearing. While the boys observed nature, nature observed them.

'Hey, man!' A daredevil piped up. 'Forget the poor butterflies. Let's catch a snake.'

'A snake?' A small, reedy voice quivered like a hairspring.

'Yeah, a snake. Real adventure, man. For adults only, I say. Got a camera, anyone?'

'A camera?'

'Yeah, a camera, you fathead. For God's sake, don't tell me you don't know what a camera is! You know, westerners, especially Americans, they don't worry a bit about snakes. Unlike you chicken guts, they don't ever clobber them to death with sticks, they don't even bother shooting them. They simply catch 'em.'

'Catch them? Don't pull a fast one, man!'

'Catch them, I'm telling you, they grab them. And that too with their bare hands. Also with their cameras. How, huh? Okay, listen you bumpkin...'

'Aw, shut up!' Hairspring raised his voice. 'Don't give me that bull.' Waving his butterfly net, he advanced towards Snakecatcher. The forgotten butterflies, pale and distraught, flapped their wings frantically.

Snakecatcher coolly sauntered off towards an enormous anthill beyond the bushes and leaned against it. As though the proverbial throne of King Vikramaditya was buried inside it, the contact made him spin his yarn—possibly for the benefit of Hairspring—his voice, not far different from an adult's, alternating between a whispery hoarseness and a harsh stridency. Carried away with excitement, his exploring fingers strayed all over his clothes, twisting a button, fiddling with a hole... 'They travel in pairs,' he droned on. 'Yeah, strictly in pairs. Two is ideal: a man and his wife, or better still, a guy and his gal. Yankee gals are some gals, man! Excellent specimens! And you know what they do? The gal loads the camera and the guy goes to the anthill...'

'Where there might be a snake?'

'Yeah. It's the den of the king of the snakes—the king cobra. The vicious reptile lies in its lair, all coiled up, snug and sleepy. The guy sneaks up. On tiptoe. Then he goes down on his knees and starts crawling. Finally, he creeps along on his belly—why, man, just like a snake!'

'Then?'

'Then? Well, the guy reaches the anthill and signals to the gal. She's ready to click the photograph. Meanwhile the snake's still dozing, blissfully unaware of anything unusual. Maybe it's enjoying the morning breeze, or digesting its dinner from the night before. The guy furtively moves his hand forward. The gal watches with bated breath. Loads of suspense. The snake begins to twitch the tip of its tail; the dumb bastard still hasn't caught on. Suddenly in a flash the guy's hand closes firmly around its smooth, slithery tail.'

'Then?'

'Then a loud hiss, you dunderhead.'
'The snake's?'
'Of course the snake's! Real adventure, man, not any silly old stuff. My dad was saying... C'mon, let's catch a bloody snake...'
'The snake doesn't strike the guy?'
'No, the son-of-a-bitch snake can't. When it raises its hood to strike, the guy deftly moves his hand away. The angry fangs hit the ground and venom gushes out, flooding the place. Meanwhile the gal keeps clicking. The guy slowly walks back to her, beaming with pride. The adventure's over.'
'Then?'
'The end. The adventure's over, you idiot. Of course sometimes, my dad was saying, the whole damn thing misfires and the snarling fangs land on the guy's head—a lethal strike, the full burden of it. The poor sod crumples on the spot. But the gal—well, she gets the biggest thrill. The action snaps of her dying boyfriend and the killer cobra could fetch a thousand dollars, if not more. My dad was saying...' His voice trailed off.

The conversation wore thin and the tumult died down. The sun became hotter, fiercer. They unstrapped their water bottles and, gulping down mouthfuls, stretched out in the shade. For a while there was a lull: the ripples in the fierce dark-green stream subsided. The butterflies trapped in the net watched with growing despair. Some had already perished, and the ones that hadn't were too tired to flutter their mournful wings. A boy yawned noisily; another echoed him, mockingly.

The wriggling butterflies formed an inchoate mass. A mass of what? Hairspring wondered. Of emotions? Of cheap, irrelevant, gratuitous, unwarranted feelings? His ready foot suddenly rose menacingly. The whole company winced. Shrieks, screams and futile attempts to stave off the massacre. Bang! Hairspring's foot came down, shoes and all. 'Stuff and nonsense!' he said, smacking his lips, extricating his foot from the mess. 'They must die if they must!' His vulnerable voice shook. His furrowed brows, poised like supercilious question marks over his big brooding eyes, looked as black as the bruised skin of a green banana.

'You brute!' Snakecatcher cried. 'It's you who must die if anyone must. My dad was saying...'
'Aw, c'mon, you cry baby!'

'Shut your mouth, you sissy. Only a minute ago you nearly messed your pants and now you're putting on airs! Hell, who taught you all about adventure, you sissy?'

'Sissy, me?'

'Who'd ever dream of killing some poor butterflies? Only a weakling—someone suffering from a real inferiority complex. My dad was saying...'

'Hang your dad, you bastard!' His voice went berserk like the taut strings of a violin plucked violently. 'Don't ever mention your bloody daddy.'

Bang! Action! Snakecatcher—Superiority Complex—threw his hat in. Bang! Reaction! Hairspring—Inferiority Complex—responded. They looked like two ominous clouds racing towards each other, equally dark and desperate. Lightning split the sky as they collided. They grappled and tried to throttle each other; they hit the dust in turn, rose to their feet quickly, fell and rose, started all over again. Action. Reaction.

The company, the silent spectators, stood huddled together at a distance. (What else could they do? Don't they always stand apart and gawk like this at all times, these ordinary, common folk? Not for them moral qualms, not for them the desire to become the extraordinary, the uncommon; they know pretty well that none but the ordinary will inherit the earth. The extraordinary, the uncommon, they always carry within them the seeds of their own destruction: a Ram for a Ravana, communism for capitalism, minus for plus, and vice versa. If one is present, the other isn't far behind.)

The battle raged on. Neither gave in. Contrary to expectations, Hairspring rallied well to the challenge, parrying the blows with skill and aplomb. They stalked, jumped, whirled, swung around, trampling more butterflies to death. The tension mounted by the second. 'They must die if they must!' Hairspring hissed. 'It must be you if anyone must!' shouted Snakecatcher. The stones scrunched under their warring feet.

A little way from where they were a stretch of roadwork was in progress, with a huge barrel of molten tar. The workers had gone off for midday lunch. Suddenly out of nowhere a little sparrow fell into the barrel, hitting the surface of the tar with a dull thud.

The boys were aghast.

'Oh God!' cried someone. 'Oh God, such a tiny little thing! Save it! Somebody, please! Please save the little bird!'

They milled around the barrel, leaning over the rim and stretching out their hands.

The first to respond was Snakecatcher. 'Wait,' he spluttered, placing his hands on his heaving chest. 'Let's spit on the ground and stop fighting! Can't you hear the poor little birdie screeching for help? We've got to save it.'

'Save the poor little birdie, huh? Save your ass first.' Anger was still blazing in Hairspring's bosom. 'I wouldn't agree to an interruption even if it was a human being. No spit on the ground trick, you sissy!'

Bang.

Action.

Bang.

Reaction.

To every action an equal and opposite reaction.

'Save him!' the boys screamed in panic. 'Oh, save John! He's drowning.'

'John's drowning?' Gautam's hairspring voice trembled. 'Drowning—John, my opponent, my friend?'

John sank slowly like a torpedoed ship. Resolute and unflinching, he raised his hands over his head. In the hollow of his palms fluttered a tar-smeared little bird: a torn flag on the masthead of a sinking ship.

Gautam leaned over the side of the barrel and watched. The boys had fled the gruesome sight. He stood rooted to the ground as if he and John were the two poles of a magnet. The tar reached John's neck. Gautam clambered over the narrow rim of the barrel and stretched out his hand to him. As their hands touched, a shudder shot through them, an electric current flowed. The sparks fused them, blending together their separate identities. Gautam gave John a tug. Then John gave Gautam one. Gautam swayed, lost his slim toehold on the rim of the barrel and tumbled into the simmering pool of tar.

When the warm tar reached Gautam's lips, John was already out of sight. Past all human struggles now, he looked around and found the little bird, which had dropped from John's hands. His final, fully conscious act was to pick up the bird and settle down by John's side to be entombed for eternity.

Late in the afternoon when the road gang returned to resume their work, they found a human hand sprouting from the grimy pool of tar like a tender branch. And the branch was bearing an exotic fruit: a little bird fluttering its wings.

TROJAN HORSE

KRUSHNA PRASAD MISHRA

When I went to take my shower, I found Bobby sitting in the bathtub, his eyes on his Tyco machine gun. He was too taken up with it to notice me.

'Good morning, Bobby. How're you today?'

He greeted me absent-mindedly. His tiny toothbrush was balanced precariously on the edge of the tub. He had forgotten to put the cap back on the tube, and an inch of toothpaste had curled out of it.

'Aren't you done? Come on, hurry up. I've to run to the lab.'

But the only son of my landlady didn't budge. A four-year-old, with chubby cheeks, a small sharp nose, a mass of blond hair and cherry-red lips, he continued to play with his toy gun mounted on wheels until it slipped out of his hands and rolled round in the slippery womb of the tub like a fish.

'Where did you buy it? At Macy's?' I asked. 'Must have cost quite a bit.'

'Six bucks,' Bobby replied.

'Looks great.'

'Thanks,' he said, pushing back the hair falling over his eyes.

As I was wondering how to get him out of the bathroom, his mother, Mrs Cartwright, walked in. 'Oh no, not that gun again!' she yelled. 'Not that horrible thing!' She turned to me. 'I begged John not to buy it. But the doting father wouldn't listen. This is the child's eleventh gun.' She rolled her eyes. 'And he hardly slept a wink last night. He slipped the gun under his pillow and was blabbering all night. What'd you expect, anyway? And this morning he's up here with this horrible toy. God knows what kind of monsters American children are going to grow up into.'

The tirade didn't seem to ruffle Bobby one bit.

'You're making a big thing out of nothing, Mrs Cartwright,' I said. 'Once the novelty's worn off, the toy'll end up in the trash within a week.'

'Maybe. But then he'll ask for another—a Batmobile or a Bat ring or something else. The point is whether kids should be given such horrible toys to play with at all. Won't there be an impact on their psyche, make them used to violence, killing, bloodshed and war? My husband always gets Bobby these weapons; he never listens.'

'Come on, you're working yourself into a fine froth over nothing. Millions of American children play with these weapons, as you call them, and no one feels they're a bad influence. Quite the opposite. Sociologists, psychologists and academics all think early exposure to these toys might purge children of the impulse to violence and bloodletting.'

'They're all kidding themselves,' Mrs Cartwright said, with a sad little sigh, as I headed down to the unheated basement bathroom, which was a torture to use in the November cold. Mr Cartwright had consistently brushed aside my request to do something about it.

I remembered my first meeting with Bobby. Having trudged around Davisville without success, I had stopped at Mrs Cartwright's place. Muttering a quick little prayer under my breath I was on the verge of hopping up the three steps to her front door, when someone barked: 'Stick 'em up!' I nearly jumped out of my skin. I turned around, but couldn't see anyone. Hesitantly, I reached for the bell once again.

'Stick 'em up!' A little child lunged at me from behind the garbage cans and started shooting. 'Bang! Bang! Bang!'

Instinctively, I ducked behind the bag I was carrying, only to realize the next moment what a fool I'd made of myself. This was no real hold-up, just a child with a toy. The door opened right then and a woman came out. 'Bobby!' she yelled. 'Have you been harassing this gentleman? Come on, apologize.' The child muttered a half-hearted apology. Looking into his deep blue eyes, I was moved to give him a hug. He looked the same age as the son I had left behind in India. And what might my little boy be doing right now—dreaming of kites and marbles?

Bobby and I soon became friends. I was impressed by his intelligence, presence of mind, energy and vitality. Sometimes I felt a twinge of regret that Indian children were so unlike him. I was fed up with Mrs Cartwright for scolding the boy. As a Quaker, she was opposed to arms and war, and couldn't stand the sight of toys related to combat, violence and destruction. She often locked horns with her husband—Christian by birth but not by conviction, as he always added with a chuckle—on how to bring up their son. John Cartwright never missed a chance to tease his wife. Quakers aren't Christians, he'd joke, they're Gandhians. Imagine Americans trying to send medicine to the Vietcong their country is fighting. Only Gandhians could throw the law of the land to the wind. Come on, John, Mrs Cartwright argued back, you're getting it backwards. Quakers go back a long way. It was Gandhi who was influenced by the Quakers, not the other way around.

I enjoyed the couple's arguments and banter, never taking sides, but my sympathies were quite openly with the husband. I told them about India, where millions of children went through their childhood without seeing a single toy, let alone being able to play with one. They made do with mud, sand, stone, wood, discarded utensils, rags, and other junk. A burp gun or a Tyco machine gun was only a dream. If an airplane flew past, not only children but even grown-ups rushed out of their homes to watch. Could one expect Indian children to grow up to build sophisticated weapons and planes to fight the enemies of their country? 'Hear! Hear!' Mr Cartwright would applaud; Mrs Cartwright would keep quiet, hurt I hadn't taken her side. At the slightest opportunity she'd buttonhole me and try to win me over to her point of view.

Sometimes, in the evening, as we sat watching the news on the television, she'd start railing against America. Bobby would rush in from playing to watch his favourite show. As soon as she heard his footsteps, the mother would start shouting instructions: 'Leave your snow boots outside, they're too dirty. Take off your jacket and hang it in the closet in the corridor.' The boy would do everything she asked but with the speed of a whirlwind. Then he'd furiously flip the channels until he got Channel 7, brushing aside his mother's protests.

'Hey, what're you doing? What do you want to watch? Just don't break the set.'

'Oh, mother, I'm late for the seven-thirty Batman show.'

Mrs Cartwright would give me a despairing glance. 'See! What can we do? All American children are crazy about trigger-happy Batman. Walk into any American home now and you'll find televisions tuned in to this show. This country's heading towards disaster, if you ask me.

What kind of civilization thinks nothing of putting toy weapons in the hands of little children, and exposing them to violence at an early age?'

Meanwhile, impervious to his mother's words, the boy would be screaming his head off: 'Boom! Pow! Zing!' Yelling and punching the sofa; mimicking every move of mighty Batman battling the enemies of America, matching him in speed.

'Careful, boy,' Mrs Cartwright would warn him. 'Don't hurt yourself.'

'I'm Batman, mother. What can happen to me?'

Another volley of lusty war whoops and the boy'd jump, skip and run around the room. I was delighted with his energy and liveliness. But Mrs Cartwright would find the disturbance too much, and we'd go up to my room to resume our conversation in peace. Mr Cartwright held a senior position in the accounts division of Sears and was never home before eight o'clock.

In the beginning Mrs Cartwright had been quite aloof. Then one day she saw on my table the picture of Gandhi my father had sent me.

'You didn't tell me you're a follower of Gandhi!' she said, visibly pleased.

'No, not me,' I said. 'My father is. He still wears hand-spun clothes and believes Gandhi was an avatar of God. He also believes Gandhi's picture will bring me good luck. I believed that once, but no longer. Not after the 1962 aggression by the Chinese. China still illegally occupies a large chunk of our territory, you know. I strongly feel this non-violence mumbo-jumbo of Gandhi's and Nehru's has held India back.'

'How can you say that? You must be out of your mind. Gandhi was a great man.'

'It's okay for you people in the West to say so. If we had your houses, big cars, wealth, maybe I'd agree with you. But Mrs Cartwright, Gandhi's philosophy is okay for America, not for India. What India badly needs is this.' I picked up one of Bobby's toy guns from the floor. 'This.'

'Oh, dear, you're upset. Cool down. When you're calmer you'll understand Gandhian philosophy is the best.'

We would discuss Gandhian philosophy some more over coffee, arguing back and forth without agreeing. After Batman was over, Bobby would go on to watch Tarzan or Superman.

It was already ten. After my bath and breakfast, I was just stepping out of the house when I saw a bunch of children half-carrying, half-dragging Bobby. My heart skipped a beat. What had happened? Only an hour ago he had been playing with his new toy in the bathtub. When did he steal out, what kind of a scrape did he get into? As they came nearer I noticed Bobby's pale face was contorted in pain. One side of his trousers was soaked with blood. 'I'm gonna fix him!' he was hissing through clenched teeth. 'He just can't get away with it. Today he got the better of me because my gun was a toy and his knife was real. Tomorrow I'll get hold of a real gun and fix him.'

I turned to the boys in bewilderment. 'What happened?'

They all started blabbing together. They'd met in Paul's backyard and Bobby and Paul had got into a fight over who was greater—Batman or Superman. Batman had bit the dust because he had only a toy gun. But Superman's penknife was for real.

I made Bobby stand up straight, rolled up his trouser legs and tied my handkerchief around the half-inch deep gash in his thigh.

'I'm gonna find a real gun.' He muttered the words like an incantation. 'Just wait and see. I'll get even with Paul.'

'But right now we've got to get you to the hospital.'

'Hospital?' His voice broke. 'Injections? Stitches?'

'Maybe.' I carried him into the house.

Her morning chores over, Mrs Cartwright was settling down to coffee and the newspaper. She nearly spilled her drink when she saw her son. 'What's happened to my child?' She sprang up from the sofa, trembling. 'Oh, my God, what's wrong with him?'

I asked her not to panic and to call the hospital. She wanted to call her husband, but I talked her out of it. All through the drive to the hospital Bobby prattled on, cheering up his mother and then lapsing into a tirade against Paul. It must have been an accident, I tried to explain to him. Surely a friend like Paul hadn't stabbed him intentionally. It must have been a huge mistake. Just wait and see, Paul'd come right along tomorrow morning to say 'sorry' and make up, and the good little fella that he was, Bobby shouldn't hold a grudge against him. But Bobby wasn't buying any of this. Brandishing a knife is one thing, but stabbing him with it quite another. Paul had broken the rules of the game and would have to pay for that.

Mrs Cartwright sat like a block of wood, stunned as much by the sight of blood as by her boy's desire for revenge. As I drove her Volkswagen, I could imagine what was passing through her mind. Luckily, getting him fixed up at the hospital didn't take long.

My whole morning was gone. There was no point in going to the laboratory; I knew I wouldn't be able to focus on my experiment. But I didn't want to stay home and read. As I aimlessly walked towards the campus, I couldn't help but think about Bobby. His patience, courage and energy had been exemplary. He hadn't let out a single whimper while his wound was being dressed, or when he was being given the shots. Bravo, children like him would build a strong nation; when they grew up children like him wouldn't hesitate to lay down their lives for their country. Mrs Cartwright was so wrong. Since people had to bear arms and fight wars, there was surely no harm playing with war toys, was there? If human civilization had come to such a pass that the use of napalm and atom bombs was inevitable, why not expose children to imitations and toys? Mrs Cartwright was stuck in her groove: these horrible toys only aggravated the temperament of children; a child lunging at you with a toy gun today wouldn't think twice tomorrow before using a real one; carrying a gun would get into their blood. Oh Mrs Cartwright, she could bore the hell out of anyone.

All of a sudden, a frantic young woman in tears rushed at me from nowhere and grabbed me by the arm. 'Everything's over!' she sobbed hysterically. 'It's all over.'

'What's over?' I stared at her uncomprehendingly.

'President Kennedy's been shot in Dallas.'

'No!' I was stunned. 'No!' I muttered idiotically, as if the universe revolved around my monosyllabic response. 'That can't be true!'

I didn't want to see the woman again. As she released my arm and lurched unsteadily towards another passer-by, I looked around the university campus. A little way ahead was the women's dormitory, then the Arts Faculty building, beyond that the vast green and the drugstore. But everyone was in an awful hurry, as if they were seeking a safe haven. Why did they all look so grim, their eyes swimming in tears? Like a demented child, I stared at them, trying to glean something from their faces. Why were they crying?

I ran up to a young man ahead of me. 'Hey,' I asked, 'is it true President John F. Kennedy has been assassinated?'

'Yes,' he answered in a small voice. 'True. Absolutely true.'

MRS CROCODILE

MANOJ DAS

Miles and miles of swamps; vast stretches of sand, mudflats, and backwaters—none of this seemed to have fazed pre-eminent anthropologist Dr Batstone. He took a train, a jeep and a bullock cart before trudging over a mile on foot to finally arrive at our village in the middle of nowhere, in the back of beyond.

A man who had lived all his life in western cities amid high-rises, Dr Batstone's first wish when he touched down on Indian soil was to visit a truly primitive village.

In those days, when we were still in school, the gulf between towns and villages hadn't shrunk as much as now. The villages were yet to become the distorted shadows of towns. Huge red triangles, those ubiquitous symbols of the government's family planning programme, the election slogans of political parties, advertisements of small-saving schemes or brands of cigarettes had not yet made their appearance on village walls; microphones hadn't yet arrived.

'Wonderful! Amazing!' Sprawled in a wooden armchair on the veranda of our house, Dr Batstone erupted into delighted exclamations every five minutes: 'Wonderful! Amazing!'

His sense of wonder and heightened feelings was understandable. Wasn't it awe-inspiring to be able to survey, without interruption, the full horizon of the clear uncluttered sky to one's heart's content? To see a young cowherd boy controlling a large herd of perhaps a hundred head or more, across unending pastures? Watching the cattle following peaceably without breaking ranks, Dr Batstone experienced the same heady feeling he had while reading 'The Pied Piper' for the first time as a child. Wasn't it wonderful that ninety per cent of village folk could live in perfect harmony and happiness, without any regrets whatsoever, without ever having seen a train or a cinema!

But more than anything else, it was the interview with Maku Mishra, the venerable headmaster of the village lower-primary school that stoked the distinguished visitor's sense of wonder and awe. In all his forty years of imparting precious education to the village ragamuffins, Mishra hadn't heard of Darwin, Marx, Freud, Einstein, or Bernard Shaw—not even one of the illustrious five!

That a white man would one day make a trip to our village was beyond the wildest imagination of the local inhabitants. Even *Malika*, the Book of Predictions, which had unerringly predicted the devastating mid-century cyclone, the sudden collapse of the local temple, and the emergence of Mohandas Karamchand Gandhi on the political firmament of India, had remained pointedly silent about this eventuality. No wonder, then, that at any given point of time about twenty or two-dozen villagers sat cross-legged around the visiting sahib, gaping and gawking.

The sahib too caught on that the villagers meant no harm, that their behaviour was driven by simple curiosity. Bemused, he told me more than once with a smile: 'Where else could I have experienced anything of this kind? If I'd known how to dance I'd have danced up a whirlwind to entertain these God's good people sitting in front of me.'

As he was getting emotionally entangled in the lives of the villagers, he once asked me, out of the blue: 'Well, my dear boy, do these people believe in ghosts and spirits?'

Over the days I had proven to be his most reliable interpreter. As soon as I translated his question for the benefit of the crowd, they all answered loudly in the negative, which made the sahib sit up straight. It was his turn to be amazed. After a long silence he turned to me: 'You know something, babu! These people are more modern and progressive than my countrymen. Believe me, more than fifty per cent of our people believe in ghosts and spirits, whether they admit it or not. Just go on and ask these good people—do they believe in God?'

I translated his question. There was an uneasy silence.

'What's the matter—aren't they sure?' asked the sahib, trying to interpret their silence. 'They're having doubts, right?' His voice was deep with respect. 'Believe me, no matter how rational the people of my country may outwardly seem, they...'

Then there was an uproar as one villager after another began to respond excitedly: 'Never trust ghosts or spirits, sahib! They've no conscience at all.'

'Would you believe it, sahib,' said another. 'My cousin—actually my father's uncle's son-in-law's own nephew—what haven't I done for him, beginning with sharing my pillow to doing his wedding shopping! What haven't I done for the bastard! Who'd believe that once dead he'd zero in on me, of all the people in this village and beyond, to scare the living daylights out of! Who doesn't know I footed half the expenses for his funeral rituals, which were observed in great style? Who doesn't know I couldn't stir out at night to my own backyard to piss or shit, until his spirit was properly appeased.'

'Sahib,' said yet another. 'You're a foreigner. You shouldn't believe in the ghosts and spirits of our country. They're so nasty that given half a chance they'll twist the neck of the exorcist who tries to keep them on a leash.'

'Of course,' added a fourth, 'there are kind and helpful spirits too—nobody can deny that. As a child I've seen the Languli Baba with my own eyes.' Turning to me, he pleaded: 'Explain to the sahib who Languli Baba is, will you? The great naked seer. When I saw him he was already over two hundred years old.' The villager turned to the white man and went on excitedly: 'The circumstances of his auspicious birth are shrouded in mystery. There was once a great epidemic of cholera sweeping the land. His mother, then pregnant with him, was taken for dead and hauled off to the cremation grounds by her relations. It was there the holy man tumbled out of his mother's womb. He lay there crying helplessly for one whole night and a day before another group of mourners reached the cremation grounds. They picked him up from between his dead mother's legs. Tell us, sahib, who looked after the mahatma during those crucial twenty-four hours?'

The compulsively argumentative villager who had asked the question inched closer to the white man and offered the answer himself. 'The spirits and ghosts, of course. No wonder the mahatma neither wore clothes nor spoke to a living being. Whenever an intense desire for conversation came over him he'd hold parleys only with those invisible souls.

'As to your question about believing in God, sahib—is he some kind of a moneylender and we his debtors, or vice versa, that the question of trusting or not would arise at all? He created everything and put us at the heart of it. Now, he might choose to get rid of us, or then again he might decide to keep us...'

The way the crowd nodded it seemed everyone wholeheartedly agreed with him.

I translated as best I could. The sahib listened intently and leaned back in the armchair. 'Fabulous!' he gurgled. 'Amazing!'

'Sahib,' said another villager. 'Do you see the cremation grounds beyond the river? That was where the great naked baba was born. If you have no faith in us, or if you disbelieve us even the tiniest bit, you can go there and check it out for yourself.'

As soon as the river was mentioned, the sahib sat bolt upright once again. 'I don't need hot water for my bath tomorrow. The river seems clean enough. So tomorrow I'll bathe in the river. I only hope there aren't any crocodiles.'

I didn't know many things about the village since I'd been away most of the time, so I asked the villagers about crocodiles. They seemed mighty insulted and protested vociferously. 'Young man, you may be well educated because you've been up to a lot of school learning, but more than anyone you should know crocodiles live in water and not on the top of mountains. Has a crocodile ever harmed a single person from this village? As long as the crocodile's wife is alive and in our midst...' The villagers all pointed their fingers in a particular direction.

I had no intention of making a full and faithful translation of all they'd said. So I simply allayed the sahib's fears: there was absolutely no reason to worry about crocodiles.

But, in the meantime, the white man had become quite eager to follow the entire conversation. The pointed fingers had piqued his curiosity too.

'Dr Batstone,' I tried to paraphrase. 'The tales are quite ridiculous for one thing. By now you must have realized that these villagers are rather simple-minded, inclined to believe anything and everything they get to hear. Anyway, it all goes back a long time. There lived a poor couple by the river. They had only one child, a daughter. She was married off when she was three years old, became a widow at the age of five, and after that lived with her parents.

'The child grew into a beautiful young woman. One day, when she went to the river to bathe, the villagers saw her being dragged into the deep waters by a crocodile. They thought that was the end of her. But miracle of miracles, she resurfaced ten years later. By then her father was long dead and her mother nearing her end, and their small hut on the river bank dilapidated and ready to cave in.

'The girl looked after her mother as well as she could, but wasn't able to save her. When she passed away a few days later, the girl could do nothing but cry her heart out, alone in that ramshackle hut.

'Two days later, an old male crocodile was bludgeoned to death as it was trying to climb up the embankment behind the hut.

'The girl kept on crying, without uttering a word. God alone knows how a strange, jumbled story began to do the rounds of the village: after being dragged away by the crocodile the girl had lived with him as his wife all these years, and her poor husband had lost his life while trying to do what any good son-in-law would have done—look up his wife when she was visiting her parents.

'In the course of time the young woman became old. She's still alive and well, pushing ninety, and is referred to as Mrs Crocodile by everyone. It's firmly believed that, in deference to her, the entire tribe of crocodiles living in the river has not harmed the villagers. In response, the villagers have taken to providing the old woman with her morning and evening meals.'

'Wonderful!' the sahib exclaimed. 'Amazing. Fantastic. But where did she live those ten years she was gone from the village?'

'I don't know. I don't think anyone really does. Because the villagers simply swallowed a story as outlandish as this they never felt the need to cross-check it with the old woman.'

'My dear boy,' the sahib begged. 'Let's get the story of those ten years of her life. I'll regret it if I leave without knowing.'

The moonrise was some hours away; it was still very dark. I switched on the flashlight and walked in front, the sahib following behind. On the way to the old woman's hut he stumbled twice: first over a silent and self-effacing pye-dog, then over a perambulating turtle, perhaps out on a village visit. Each time he just barely managed to avoid falling. But every experience, good or bad, thrilled him no end.

The old woman was sitting by herself, her chin on her knees, beside a lamp burning weakly in her hut. She gave us a warm smile when we entered. The sahib and I poured into her stone bowl the milk, rice and mashed bananas we'd brought with us as offerings. She rewarded us with another beaming smile.

'Grandmother,' I began. 'We're here to ask you a few questions. This gentleman you see with me—he's a true sahib from beyond the seven seas. It's his deepest wish to hear your story from your mouth.'

Not a hint of surprise or hesitation flickered across her wrinkled, weather-beaten face. She seemed to have been expecting our visit. 'Son, I'll tell you the story of a wandering prince and a fairy princess,' she promptly began.

'No, Grandmother, not just any old story. He wants your story, the story of your life. You must know everyone refers to you as Mrs Crocodile. That's plain rubbish. But it's also a matter of record you went missing for ten long years. Where were you all those years, where did you live and how? What did you do? Tell us about it.'

The old woman's hearing didn't seem impaired. Neither did she slur when she began to speak, even though she had not a tooth left in her mouth. And what a raconteur she turned out to be. After every three or four sentences, I had to stop her so I could translate word for word for the sahib. He told me not to leave out a single syllable.

'No sooner did I step into the water than a crocodile dragged me off into the deepest part of the river. God knows how deep it was, probably seven cubits or more. I don't know how...but when I...'

'No embroidery, Grandmother, just give us the hard facts. How did you escape from the jaws of the crocodile? Where did you end up when he set you free? How did life treat you...?'

All these questions didn't seem to make any impact on the old woman. She went on unperturbed: 'Son, when I regained consciousness I found myself under water seven cubits deep, with a large male crocodile in front of me, contemplating me with unblinking eyes. As he stared at me, God knows what happened, but I couldn't take my eyes off him either...'

'Grandmother, if you don't remember how you escaped from the jaws of the crocodile, at least tell us how you lived afterwards and where...'

'Son, did I ever try to escape from the crocodile's den? I told you I found it impossible to avert my eyes from him. There, in the deep waters there was no sun, no moon; it was neither day nor night. I don't know how many days or years passed.'

I thought better of interrupting the old woman once again. Not only did she herself believe her own yarn, but the sahib seemed to hang on to her every word. In the dim light of the lamp I watched our shadows fluttering on the wall. I continued to translate, but now with a certain detachment. Sometimes, when the sound of a boat pushing off the bank reached us, the old woman would pause, as if the call of the river had revived old memories.

The old woman spoke for an hour and a half, recounting the tale of a young woman setting up home with a crocodile in the awe-inspiring depths of the river eighteen miles from the village. During the first few days she hadn't the slightest desire to live with him and had every intention of running away at the first opportunity. But when she came up from the deep and began to float on the water, she found herself turned into a crocodile. When had her husband worked this magic on her? When he was dragging her to his underwater lair, or when he sat staring into her eyes? She felt utterly miserable and began to cry. The crocodile did everything he could to divert her and keep her amused, but she couldn't—and wouldn't—forget her past life. So her husband finally gave in: 'All right. Listen carefully to this mantra and learn it by heart. If you recite it you'll be able to return to your former self whenever you wish. But only not when I'm around, because, you see, no matter how hard I might try to hold back the counter-mantra—and keep you in the form of a crocodile—it'll slip out of my mouth.'

That day as he was preparing to leave his lair for his constitutional, the poor crocodile couldn't help shedding tears. 'I know you'll be gone by the time I return,' he said. 'But take care not to recite the mantra midstream—you'll turn into a human being and drown immediately. Make sure you're safely ashore before you say the mantra.'

When he returned home in the evening he found her still there. Needless to add, he was thrilled.

The young woman didn't leave the next day, nor the day after.

Weeks and months passed.

The crocodile couple began to swim together, delighting in each other's company, roaming far and wide, from one bathing ghat to another.

Once they travelled from their river to another and stopped close to a shrine. She said to her partner: 'Husband, you stay in the water. I'm going to crawl up the bank, assume my human form, and go have a darshan of the deity.' He agreed.

After this, she went on to visit a large number of temples and shrines. She'd swim to the riverbank at night, say her mantra, assume her human form and spend the whole day in pilgrimage, and at night jump back into the river, where her husband would be waiting to transform her back.

But during all this time she took great care to stay away from her own village; she had this fear that, once there, she might not feel like going back to her husband.

After ten years had passed she was seized with a deep desire to look up her parents and, with her husband's consent, returned to her village for a day. What she saw there filled her with dismay. The old way of life had been completely destroyed. Her father was dead and her mother lay dying; in fact, the old lady would die inside of a couple of days. Those two days were all the time she got to spend with her mother.

She remained in the deserted hut brooding about her life, her parents, and their love for her, and yet another day passed. Meanwhile her husband's patience was running out and he was beginning to panic. He wanted to find out what had happened to her, and so he came out of the water. While he was trying to climb up the bank he was spotted and clubbed to death.

Sixty years had passed since then. The old woman had continued to live by the river, all alone.

A pack of jackals began to howl in front of the old woman's hut. The sahib started. As we took leave of her, she gave us a big smile.

The moon had risen. The smoke swirling up from the thatched roofs of the village homes made the moon look bluer and softer than ever.

We walked back in silence. The sahib, wrapped in his thoughts, stumbled twice: first over the turtle—this time it was journeying back to the river—and then over the dog, who remained as silent and motionless as before.

He stopped on the riverbank. 'How far from here is the deepest part of the river she spoke of? Is it upstream or down?'

'What deepest part?'

'The deep waters in which the crocodile couple lived.'

'Wonderful! Amazing!' I laughed. The two words the sahib was so fond of had involuntarily slipped out of my mouth.

Dr Batstone became grave.

We walked back to the village in total silence.

Some years later I received a letter from Dr Batstone. 'Even now, when I think of the time I spent in your village, I feel I metamorphosed into some other being for the entire duration of that night the old woman told us her story—just as she herself had once changed into a crocodile. And I treasure the sensation of my metamorphosis as true and real.'

SAVITRI

RABI PATNAIK

Only eight in the morning, and already the town was steaming under the harsh April sun. Wisps of white and ochre smoke belching from the ferro-manganese factories hung over the hills like clouds. An hour after the siren, the streets, filled earlier with the cacophony of men and women on their way to the mines, fell silent at last but for the occasional angry roar of trucks and dumpers.

Joda: an undulating expanse of hills denuded of trees except for a few sparse patches of jungle. The hollows in the earth looked like yawning wounds on the flanks of a green monster.

In the heart of Jamda-Koira Valley, with over two hundred big and small mines, Joda was neither a town nor a village. The houses and settlements built by the government and Tata Iron and Steel Company gave it the appearance of a town, but from a distance it seemed no more than a forest village. The Bhubaneswar-Rourkela highway dissected it in two. To the east lay the residential quarters of the government and the company officials, all in a line stretching from one end of the town to the other, dominated by the company guest house, Joda View. Well-appointed with manicured lawns and flower beds, it made a visitor wonder whether he was still in the middle of a tiny mining town, or if a magician hadn't waved his magic wand. The architecture, furniture, carpets, and objets d'art chosen with utmost care and taste, could have put a five-star hotel to shame.

This particular morning, the seldom-used guest house was the venue for an important meeting. Cordoned off by armed police, it was in the grip of subdued excitement. The miners and workers were planning to strike beginning the following day; the top bureaucrats and company high-ups were in a huddle to foil this. Labour unrest and strikes never passed off peacefully, and the district collector, police superintendent, and other senior officers were discussing with the mine owners ways to handle the crisis.

The workers were protesting against automation, which would put hundreds out of jobs. Where would they then go, how would they live, on what? The workers' survival was at issue. The mine owners had to be taught a lesson, and all two hundred or so mines brought to a grinding halt. They were led by Sadhan Chatterjee, a former Naxalite, from Calcutta, assisted by local trade-union leaders Ismail Ahmed, Santosh Prusty, Bulu Patnaik, Manmohan Panda, and others, backed by the Communist Party of India (Marxist). Violence was very much in the cards.

Management decided to arrest them by midnight and take them to Keonjhar before daybreak. Their current whereabouts had to be immediately determined; police informers fanned out in all directions.

Like all mining towns, Joda came alive at night. After a hard day's work, men hit the hooch dens and drinking holes to put the dust and grime, the fatigue and conflicts, the anger and altercations behind them, the darkness of day dissolving in the light of night. Strong odours of local brew—handia and mahuli, and the like—seasoned with the smell of boiled and salted gram, roasted dry-fish and diced onions, wafted from the street corners of the slums, where people gathered in knots. The costliest scotch flowed in the officer's club. In the evening Joda lived down its reputation for disparity—all differences between workers and officers washed away by the democracy of inebriation. It mattered little who drank what or where—the officers in their swanky clubhouses, the workers in the dim-lit huts or under the open sky. All were equally soused until morning, when everyone would be ready for another day of hard work, fortified by the overnight binge.

It was in the drinking holes of the workers that one could tap into the grapevine. But only up to ten o'clock, after which the town went to sleep and there was nothing but utter silence, broken occasionally by a sleepless drunk slurring a song or laughing his heart out for no reason.

The police spies headed for the hooch dens and huts, plied their contacts with free drinks and collected information.

Then the police, armed with ammunition and information, struck at midnight, rounding up the union leaders and carting them off to the lock-up before they were fully awake. All except the top brass, like Sadhan Chatterjee, Santosh Prusty, Bulu Patnaik and Manmohan Panda. They seemed to have vanished into thin air and could not be found even during the house-to-house searches that lasted until seven in the morning.

It was at Salkhu Munda's house that Sadhan Chatterjee and Bulu Patnaik had last been seen.

Salkhu was in his mother's womb when she and his father had moved here from the town. He had been born and brought up here, breathing its air and drinking its water. He had dropped out of school after class three to work in the mines. After his parents' death, when his older brother and sister had married and moved out, his house became a hub where people dropped in at all odd hours. But all that had changed when he married a couple of months ago. Now it was rare for someone to visit with a bottle of liquor.

About fifty people were taken into custody for questioning. Forty-nine were released by evening after being roughed up a little—the usual threats, slaps, blows and kicks. Only one was held back—Salkhu Munda.

'Bastard,' the police inspector screamed at Salkhu. 'You know things, but don't want to talk, right? Never mind. We know how to wrench it out of your bloody guts, don't we?'

Around eight o'clock, tired of waiting, the inspector barked at Constable Shambhu: 'Go open the lock-up. See if that bastard is ready to tell us anything yet.'

Two burly constables rose to their feet to open the holding pen. There rose the sounds of slaps, blows and kicks, and screams piercing the silence of the night.

'Shut his bloody mouth,' the inspector barked. 'Stuff his mouth with a towel or something. Tie him up.'

But nothing came out of Salkhu's mouth, despite all the efforts of the police, which lasted until eleven o'clock. All he revealed was that the two leaders had left his house at ten last night and that he had no idea where they were headed, or what they might be up to.

The cell was stinking to high heavens of Salkhu's piss and shit.

'Let the bastard rot in his own filth!' the exasperated inspector ordered.

On the second day of the strike, though the processions hadn't hit the streets yet, people were frightened, expecting the worst. News of skirmishes trickled in from here and there. Who knew when full-scale violence would flare up?

A constable kicked Salkhu awake at daybreak. 'Wake up, son of a whore. Get up, and go fetch some water to clean up your mess.'

Salkhu hadn't eaten at all the previous day. His body ached from the beatings. There were swellings and bruises on his face; his eyelids drooped; his bloodied knuckles and knees were stiff.

He dragged himself to fetch buckets of water and cleaned the cell. Then he swept the floor of the entire police station and swabbed it with water. Before the deputy superintendent arrived at seven the whole place was spick and span, and he was handed two stale vadas and a cup of tea for breakfast.

'Did he say anything?' the deputy superintendent demanded.

'No sir,' the inspector replied. 'He says he knows nothing. Give it a day or two more, sir. He'll sing all right.'

All those who had been rounded up had been let out. All except Salkhu.

Mulgi, his wife, had gone around to the homes of the returnees. What had happened to her husband? Why hadn't he been let out?

All she got were reassurances: Don't worry, he'll be back soon.

She was worried sick, she hadn't slept a wink the previous night.

When the clock struck eight there was still no sign of Salkhu.

'Go ask at the police station,' she was advised. But nobody would volunteer to accompany her. As a young woman of the Kolha tribe, she was used to roaming the forests unafraid of bears and tigers, but she cowered at the sight of a non-tribal man. The townspeople were worse than wild animals, and the police the worst of them all. All tribal men and women were in awe of the police; it was a kind of primordial fear that ran in their blood.

Mulgi gathered her courage about her. Surely the police couldn't gobble her up? Expecially in broad daylight! After all, it was her husband she wanted to see to find out what had happened to him.

She reached the police station and waited below the veranda.

'Who the hell are you?' a constable asked. 'Why are you here?'

Mulgi's mouth went dry and words refused to come out. She had left her little village in the depths of the forest only a couple of months ago and hadn't picked up the language of the townspeople.

'Salkhu,' she mumbled with a lot of effort.

'You're his woman?'

She nodded.

'Come on up and wait in that corner. The inspector isn't here. You'll need his permission to see your man.'

Salkhu lay in the dark, dank corner of the lock-up. He could hardly see or hear.

'A fine piece of goods, man!' Constable Shambhu commented to Constable Shyam, eyeing Mulgi.

'Why, the bitch is like a crunchy little cucumber!' agreed Shyam.

There followed a string of unprintable obscenities.

Mulgi, leaning helplessly against the wall, started when a motorcycle revved into the compound.

The inspector sprang off his mount, kicked down the stand, and strode up the steps. 'Hey Shambhu, who's that little young thing there? Why's she here so early in the morning?'

'That's Salkhu's wife, sir,' Shambhu reported. 'She's here to see her man.'

'So take her to him. Let her see him. Maybe the sight of her will bring the secret out of his innards!'

Mulgi peered through the bars of the lock-up. Salkhu lay in a heap in a corner. Her heart skipped a beat. Was he dead? He didn't stir even a little.

She felt the eyes of the constables on her. They were eating her up.

'Hey, Salkhu,' Shambhu barked. 'Get up. Your woman's here to see you.'

Salkhu stirred. He recognized the voice. It was its owner who had dished out the most blows and kicks last night. He sat up painfully. His swollen eyelids made it difficult to see; his split lips, swollen like frogs, made it difficult to speak. Like a helpless victim staring at the hunter he tried to focus his eyes first on the constable, and then on his wife.

'Why have you come?' he hissed, his words coming in angry, broken sobs in his Kolha dialect. 'Go away. Run. And don't ever come again.' He slumped down, his face between his hands.

Mulgi was struck dumb. A vast grief overwhelmed her. What had they done to her man, who was like a young sal tree trunk with rippling muscles, and in his prime too? He seemed to have turned into a decrepit old man overnight. And he lay like a fallen log, leaves, bark, and branches dried up.

She remained rooted to the spot, her eyes on Salkhu. It dawned on her that if she left she'd never get him back alive. Her chest constricted, her heart clogged up, her eyes became sightless. She ran and threw herself at the feet of the inspector, a torrent of incomprehensible Kolha words pouring out of her mouth.

'Get up, woman,' the inspector said. 'I can't make out a word you're babbling. Why don't you people learn to speak Odia?'

Mulgi was raving like a mad woman.

'Sir,' Shyam explained. 'She's begging you to release her man.'

The inspector reached down and pulled her to her feet, his hands digging deep into her armpits. 'All right, I'll see what I can do. Tell your man to tell us where the union leaders are hiding.'

Mulgi hardly registered the roving hands of the policeman. 'I'm telling the truth, sahib,' she said in broken Odia. 'My husband knows nothing. Neither do I. All those leaders did come to our place in the evening, but they didn't tell us where they were going afterward.'

The touch of her body seemed to have softened the inspector. 'All right. But the matter's not in my hands. I'll have to talk to the higher-ups before I can release your man. You've got to wait.'

He took Constable Shambhu aside and whispered something in his ears, and Shambhu turned to Mulgi. 'Come here, I'll explain it to you.' He knew a smattering of the Kolha dialect.

Around eight o'clock that evening, when the shadow of a woman stole into the compound of the police station, Sambhu reported it to the inspector. 'She's here, sir.'

'Take her to your house. You live alone, don't you?'

'But Jagabandhu's house is right next door, sir. His wife and kids might overhear.'

'You're one dimwit, man. Don't you know Jagabandhu's wife and kids have gone with my family to Murga Mahadev Temple to witness the Savitri amabasya puja tonight? They won't be back before ten. So hurry and take her to your place.'

It was the new moon night of the Savitri festival, the darkness deep and impenetrable. Summer was at its height and so were the power cuts. The only lights came from the distant offices of the company, run on generators.

Two hours later, when Mulgi returned to the police station, she was barely able to stand. The scratches and bites on her cheeks and breasts burned from sweat. She had tremendous pain below her waist. Her back ached as if it had been broken in two. How many had there been? She had not bothered to count. All she remembered was that she had lain spread-eagled on the floor and the men had pushed into her, one after another, like relentless dumpers. She didn't know how many minutes, hours, nights had passed. All she knew was that at the end of the ordeal she'd take her husband home. She would keep the vow she had made to herself and snatch him back from the jaws of the tiger, like the mythological Savitri from the very hands of Yama, the god of death.

Unable to remain on her feet, she slumped to the ground with a thud.

Just then the doors of the lock-up turned on their hinges with a grating noise, and the light of a dim lantern fell on the veranda. Someone dragged himself forward, leaning on the wall for support.

Mulgi's ravaged, bedraggled body seemed to come alive, as if a bolt of electricity had passed through her. She sprang to her feet; the pure, uncontaminated Kolha blood coursing in her veins began to sing. A tremendous sense of life seemed to rejuvenate her. The pain and aches were gone; gone too the regrets she had felt since being robbed of her honour and defiled. As her humiliation evaporated, she metamorphosed into a new being—one of immense power and strength.

She broke into a run and held Salkhu from falling to the ground just in time. She wound his limp arms around her own shoulders, half-dragging and half-carrying him towards their home—a blazing, blinding beam of sunlight in the deepest gloom of a moonless night.

SAVARA

CHAUDHURY HEMAKANTA MISRA

Savara travelled from town to town, living by the marvels he presented in his street shows. I remember asking him once who had given him his unusual name. He merely flashed his celebrated smile, revealing a row of shiny gold teeth—a smile he reserved for the finale of his performance, as he pulled metres and metres of multicoloured ribbon out of his mouth. He took delight in speaking of himself in the third person: *Savara will go to bed now... Savara loves to eat pigeon peas... Savara will have some tea.*

The first time he came to our village he was with a big-built woman—Malli, the bamboo-queen. She'd climb to the top of a bamboo pole and spin on her belly, like a wheel. Savara would cut her into pieces and then make her whole again. He'd hypnotize her and ask her what he'd hidden in the pockets of the people in the crowd. She always came up with the right answers. He'd stuff her into a wooden box and push swords into it so forcefully that some would go right through. Then he'd tie a rope around the box and, ignoring the gasps and protests of the audience, throw it into a large tub of water. And, as if all that wasn't enough, he'd place a large stone on the box. You could hear a pin drop while all this was going on. But right afterwards a beaming Malli would spring out of the box, no longer wearing the dirty striped sari she had on before but a gorgeous dress. The applause that followed would be thunderous and coins would rain onto Savara's plate, some falling on the ground. Putting aside his showman airs he'd pick them out of the dust, count them, and put them in a cloth bag hanging from his waist. Then, bowing low to the audience, he'd announce, 'That's all for today, sirs and masters.'

The next time he visited our village, Malli was nowhere to be seen. Eventually, we learned she'd run away. This time there was a boy named Bhagia with him, a chubby fellow with large sleepy eyes and complexion the colour of cow dung. He was by no means half as good looking as Malli, and without her the shows just weren't the same. We had closed our eyes in fear when Malli was hacked to pieces; we'd danced in joy when she emerged from the dreaded black box, her soft belly bobbing up and down and her enormous breasts threatening to escape the confines of her skimpy blouse. But now this smart aleck in blue silk trousers and a knitted red vest would jump out of the box winking broadly at the audience. It simply wasn't as good as before. Unlike Malli, he couldn't lose himself in the performance. In the evening, hovering around Savara's camp, we'd see Bhagia cooking dinner and getting roughed up by the old man. It was apparent he was also going to desert Savara someday.

I can't recall exactly how or when Savara hooked me in. Without Malli, the crowds weren't too big. His business was failing, although his own tricks were a lot better now. In one of them, Savara would hold up a piece of paper to Bhagia sitting a little away with his back to him. On it was scrawled 'Om Sri Hari'. Without looking at Savara, Bhagia would quietly call out, 'Come to me, come to me! Come!' Unbelievably, the paper, as if hypnotized, would slip out of the old man's clenched fist and float towards the boy. Then Savara would take a blank piece of paper, burn it, and ask someone in the crowd to rub the ashes on his bare back. When we leaned forward we'd see, 'Om Sri Hari' written there, while the same words had vanished from the paper Bhagia was holding. It was terrific, and I doubt any of us had ever seen anything like it. But when it came to giving Savara a large round of applause, I was all alone. I guess that was when he decided to work on me. I don't remember what words or tricks he used; all I know is I left my parents, my home and my village to follow him like a puppy.

At the beginning I was what you'd call a greenhorn; I knew as little about the secrets of the show as about keeping house for the troupe. I wondered why Savara had duped me into joining him and Bhagia when, with the pitifully small pickings, it was hard to scrounge enough food for three people.

I got him to teach me the ropes and, once I got over my shyness I gave a much better account of myself. In fact, there was one particular effect you'd have had to see to realize how good I'd become. Dressed in all my finery, I'd spin on top of a bamboo pole. Bhagia would then cut off a section of the pole, and with me still spinning on it Savara would pick it up, balance it on his head, and whirl around like a dust devil.

Savara bought me some lovely saris, fake jewellery, blouses, and also you-know-whats to wear under the blouses. The first time I got myself dolled up I nearly died of shame, but you get used to anything. Moreover, it was a blessing in disguise because no one could recognize me.

Touring my village was great fun; no one figured out who I was! All the more surprising, considering I'd been brought up there. To my horror though, all through our show my childhood friend Mangulia kept leering at me. In the evening he came and hung around the camp and even had the cheek to offer Savara money to spend the night with me. Poor fellow! If it hadn't been for Savara's threats he wouldn't have left us in peace. Next morning Bhagia and I went in to the village to try and raise some money. At each house he'd call out for alms, although we didn't really qualify as beggars. Bhagia would speak so outlandishly that the lady of the house would smile and toss a coin or two into our palms. Then he'd execute a neat somersault, and we were off to the next house, beating the changu drum. I was just an ornamental adjunct. When Malli was still around she used to put in a catchy song or two.

My heart skipped a beat when we reached our house; I was scared out of my wits. You can fool almost anyone but not your own mother: no matter how good your disguise, she can see right through it.

'Oh, mother of sons!' Bhagia called out. 'Oh, mistress of the large house! Give the beggars something, mother!'

I slipped my hand into Bhagia's and leaned against the doorpost, nibbling nervously at the end of my sari, my heart in my mouth.

My oldest brother strode out in a huff. As peevish as ever he was about to toss a coin at us and go back in, when his eyes lighted on me. Had he found me out? He seemed lost in thought for a few moments. He gave us more money than we'd expected, all the time searching my face. I heaved a sigh of relief when he suddenly turned and left.

Not one to waste a double somersault when there was no one to see it, Bhagia was about to move on to the next house.

'Stop, you bugger!' I whispered to him. 'This is my house!'

He gave me a mischievous smile, whistled under his breath, and called out, 'Oh, mother of sons! Oh, mistress of the large house! Give the beggars a drink, mother!'

My poor old mother came out with a jug of water. I couldn't help staring at her from under my veil. My running away must have caused her a lot of grief. After Bhagia had had his fill she turned to me, but I shook my head. A close shave! A single word and the game would have been up. Bhagia, his mouth hanging open, was waiting for me to break into sobs or something; the bugger was always after cheap thrills.

As long as Bhagia was around I had a jolly good time. Savara was never hard on me. He'd pet me, kiss me, and whisper into my ear, 'My darling, I love you. You're my wife, my Malli. This Bhagia is riff-raff, just a servant.' He insisted that I wear the sari, jewellery, and all the works at home. It didn't take long to find out why poor Malli had run off. Savara's old gun wouldn't fire, which didn't mean he fussed any less.

I never learned who spirited Bhagia away; one fine morning he was gone. The bastard cleaned us out—not even one paisa left in the kitty. There wasn't any money for the next meal, and he also stole the deck of magic cards, the spool of invisible wire and the foam-rubber egg Savara would pass off as a real one.

I had to do all the chores, in addition to my bamboo-queen shows. But as the saying goes, a queen doesn't make a good maid, or vice versa. I couldn't ruin my hands scouring the pots and pans and still shine as the bamboo-queen.

A change came over Savara too; he was no longer as loving. He became crabby, throwing pots and pans at me and scolding me on the slightest pretext.

'This bloody bitch is my ruin!' he shouted one day, after giving me a sound thrashing. This time he'd used his hands as well as his feet. I couldn't believe it was because of me his luck had changed. Later though, he started sobbing and pulled me to his chest. 'It's not your fault, my darling,' he said, slobbering all over me. 'It's my fate. But from now on everything will be fine. Just wait and see. We're going to do a roaring business. Goddess Lakshmi looks after those who look out for themselves, doesn't she?' Then he outlined his plan. I was simply bowled over; the old man was nothing short of a genius.

The next day we hit the road before dawn; the town wasn't far off. In the centre square Savara drew a small crowd by performing some of his routine tricks. He knew how to arouse an audience's interest. 'This is nothing,' he'd shout from time to time. 'Gracious sirs and noble masters, this is nothing. The real thing's on its way. Don't miss it, don't leave without seeing it—Savara's Special!' He slashed his tongue in two, put a knife down my throat, did a little tightrope walking, produced four eggs from the pockets of someone in the crowd and gobbled them up raw. The old boy was in his element.

'Come on Savara,' someone said. 'Cut out the appetizers and let's get to the main dish.'

Savara gave a low bow and took off his old red shirt. The large crowd—me included—was surprised to see what he had on underneath: a handsome robe, fit for a king! How had he kept that from me for so long?

He clambered over the wooden box and held up a small bottle of red liquid. 'Now, noble patrons, what can this be?' he asked, shaking the bottle a little. 'What on earth can this be, eh, eh?' Good God, the blood-red liquid turned milky white the next moment. 'This is a wonder drug, masters, thanks to the blessing of Savara's guru!' Pulling a squawking duckling from his bag, he poured a drop of the liquid into its mouth. Instantly it went limp. 'You can see how deadly it is. But there's more to it than meets the eye. Aha! One drop can neutralize a cobra's venom. An antidote, the one and only infallible potion for snakebite. Savara stands before you today, sirs and masters, to demonstrate exactly that.'

He elbowed his way through the ring of onlookers and brought out an earthenware pitcher he had kept hidden. 'Now, masters, what do you think is inside? A cobra, a deadly cobra, the king of snakes! And soon it's going to bite poor old Savara. Masters, fathers and mothers, this is a show of life and death. May Savara's empty plate fill with coins before the snake's taken out.'

The coins poured down. I collected them and put them into an old cigarette tin. Savara handed me the bottle, called out the names of several gods and goddesses, saluted the audience, and took the lid off the pitcher. We could hear the snake hissing. 'Jai Guru,' cried Savara, plunging his hand into the pitcher. You should have seen the crowd! The people in the front recoiled in fear, while those in the rear pressed forwards to see.

Savara provoked the cobra into a towering temper by tugging its tail. It raised its hood and swayed. Savara beat his drum and passed his hand several times under the darting fangs. At last the snake bit him. Savara promptly put it back in the pitcher and tied its mouth with a piece of cloth, smiling all the while. Then he went around, showing the audience where the snake had bitten him. Back in the centre he stood quietly, allowing the poison to work. Soon sweat started to pour down his face and he turned blue all over. He began frothing at the mouth. Suddenly he slumped to the ground and his body stiffened. He seemed about to die. At a signal from him I poured a drop of liquid into his mouth, and the next moment he sprang to his feet, hale and hearty.

A great roar of applause broke out. Coins rained into the ring. I gathered them up.

Savara stood on the wooden box and shouted, 'Sale! Sale! Sale! One rupee a bottle! Come and get it!'

He had hardly finished speaking when the crowd closed in around him. 'Don't push and shove, masters and patrons,' Savara implored. 'There's enough for everyone. Those who miss out today can buy some tomorrow. Same time, same place.'

The bottles sold like hot cakes. We made our way through the milling crowd, which was now running after us. If not for the pitcher with the snake, they'd have trampled us to death.

Back at the camp we gorged on the puri and jalebi Savara had bought in paper packets. He put his arm around me and literally force-fed me. I was ready to burst. 'My dear,' he said, tucking a hundred rupee note into my hand. 'You must go your own way. I suggest you go back home.' I began to wail. But Savara was unmoved. He said he was going to quit the business and clear out of town before the people found out the hoax and came to lynch him.

He changed his clothes, packed his boxes and crates, hired a coolie and left. No one saw him ever after.

THE MANTRA
JAGANNATH PRASAD DAS

Prabhakar was in a flutter when he returned home from the office that evening. 'You know what,' he couldn't wait to tell his wife, 'Swamiji has decided to stay at the chief engineer's in the end.'

'Which swamiji?' Suhasini asked, although she remembered having read in the papers that some holy man had descended on the state capital. Normally, she would have dreaded the idea of having to listen to her husband go on and on about it, but she wanted a diversion. Prabhakar's favourite topic of conversation was his office.

'Look at you! Just because you stay at home you don't have to shut yourself off from the world. The great Swamiji has deigned to leave his Himalayan abode after a long time and come here, of all places, but you're blissfully ignorant of it. Did you know the chief minister himself went to the airport to receive him.'

'Oh.' She was put off by his snide remark. So what if she stayed at home?

'Now the chief engineer's problems will be over,' he went on. 'God knows he's moved heaven and earth to get Swamiji to agree to stay with him.'

Whatever curiosity she had evaporated instantly. The conversation had fallen back into the same old groove: the office; who toadied up to whom; who gave whom hell; who was corrupt to his bones and who was not; who pulled strings to advance his career and who was out to make life difficult for somebody else.

Even after they got into bed at night, Prabhakar kept on. 'If the chief engineer's transfer order is cancelled,' he said, returning to the same subject, 'it will be proof positive of Swamiji's powers.'

She was still in a foul mood and didn't miss the opportunity to needle him. 'So why don't you catch hold of this swamiji too? The vigilance case against you is still on the books.'

'Shhh, not so loud!' he cautioned her. The children were in another room and perhaps fast asleep, but still... His voice dropped. 'Plenty of them buggers do what they want and nothing happens to them, but when it comes to poor me they start a case. The bloody thing's been left dangling on purpose so that they can keep on taking advantage of me. And what a ludicrous charge: materials listed in the inventory not available in the stores. Ha! Within seven days...'

He trotted out the same old explanation he had provided in his official reply, more to comfort himself than to convince Suhasini. He was sure that, like all the other officers into making money, he'd eventually get off the hook, but his one lasting regret was that unlike other wives his own didn't give him any moral support. Not only was she indifferent to his mental agony, but she seemed blatantly disinterested in the progress of the case.

'Are you asleep?' he enquired, cutting short his account.

'Yes.'

Far from it, she was wide awake. His remark about not keeping track of what was going on in the outside world still rankled. And what precious news! Some swamiji or other making a brief sojourn in some corrupt chief engineer's house! She remembered that when she was at university she had been serious not only about what she was studying—political science—but that she had kept up on national and international affairs; she had made a name for herself not only as a good student but as a student leader too; she had participated in all aspects of university life, from sports to drama. She and her friends had once been caught smoking; they had ragged the hell out of a hapless lecturer when he came to take his first class; once they had had to scale the hostel gate after a late night show. She had given up thinking about all that, but tonight the memories seemed to come flooding back: how she had won the annual debating prize; how she and her friends had sung uproariously all the way back in the train; the words of a two-line poem she had composed for a boy she had had a crush on; the exhilaration and shame at someone's hand brushing past her breasts in a darkened movie hall. No point in remembering all that, she sighed. All her hopes and ambitions had been crushed when she had suddenly been married off in the middle of her doctoral work. Friends of hers not half as bright had landed plum jobs and were now on the road to success while she had spent her years moving from one small town to another. Her husband, a junior engineer, had eventually been promoted to executive engineer, but her own promotion had consisted of her two children, accumulating more gadgets and possessions, and a few more servants. She had learnt to banish her discontent and sense of a lack of self-fulfilment by reminding herself her most important job was to bring up her children. And twenty years had passed.

Suhasini had never had a serious disagreement with Prabhakar, but they were not on the same wavelength. He was an unabashed materialist, putting all his time and energy into acquiring more and more things. He had a reputation for being hard-working and was no more corrupt than any of his colleagues; he was diligent at the office, and at home he made endless plans: where to build their next house, what new things to buy, where to invest his black money. She had no interest in any of that. Sometimes he would show her a blueprint for a new house and ask her for suggestions, but all she would do would be to nod her head absent-mindedly in agreement. He felt hurt that whenever he gave her a new piece of jewellery or documents for new investments, she'd indifferently put them into the closet without a glimmer of joy or gratitude. His sole consolation was that despite her utter indifference there had been prosperity at home. Whatever hopes he had she'd have a change of heart and take an active interest in his career and their future after they moved to the state capital had been dashed. She was as indifferent as ever. Their daughter was enrolled in a college and their son was in the final year of school, and Suhasini had ceased worrying about them. She helped them with their lessons, but now she had time to look up old friends and to tend her little garden. It was a source of bewilderment for Prabhakar that she didn't seem to care how hard he worked to make some extra money so their creature comforts were taken care of. Still, despite her clear lack of interest, every evening he would unfailingly give her a blow-by-blow account of office affairs.

A couple of days later he returned home much later than usual.

'I went to see Swamiji,' he said, 'and what a brilliant talk he gave! It was on the Bhagavad Gita. It seems he's writing a book on it.'

'Thousands of books have been written on it already,' she said, 'and there'll be thousands more. No doubt every swamiji-come-lately will take a shot at it.'

'I don't know what the book will be like, but his words were like divine music to my ears. Once he started no one felt like leaving. It's not only the Bhagavad Gita—Swamiji lectures on the Bible and the Quran too. I intend to go to hear him every evening.'

'If the fellow is supposed to work miracles,' she interrupted, 'why don't you tell him about your vigilance case?'

'It's impossible to talk to him alone. You should see the crowd! After his talk, he takes whoever has struck his fancy into the inner sanctum and gives them a mantra. The mantra is a secret; no one knows what it is. You know who he chose this evening? Mr Rao, the filthy rich contractor. Of all people! Mind you, there was a minister in the gathering.'

'When do you think you'll get your turn?'

'Who knows. He meets people the whole day long. It's like a big fair over there at the chief engineer's house. His drawing room has turned into an ashram. That's where Swamiji gives his talks, explains away your doubts, answers all your questions. It's only when he wants to give someone a mantra that he seeks the lucky person out and takes them into the inner sanctum.'

'A good distraction for the time being, anyway. You all were about to expire of boredom, didn't know what to do after office hours. It will be good entertainment now that there's Swamiji to watch.'

'What kind of talk is that?' he snapped. 'If you listened to Swamiji you'd be convinced.'

The following days, Prabhakar religiously went to the evening talks, and Suhasini had to put up with his nightly commentaries. Swamiji was virtually swamped by a crowd that was growing larger and larger and had to move into a much bigger rented place. He had a mission as well: to raise funds for a hospital in his ashram. The politicians, industrialists and bureaucrats had already poured millions of rupees into his coffers, and he looked forward to returning to the Himalayas once he had collected enough.

One day Prabhakar returned home in a state of high excitement. 'The chief engineer's transfer has been cancelled!'

Suhasini showed no interest.

'Who would have dreamt this would be possible!' he nevertheless continued. 'Simply unthinkable!'

'So Swamiji does have the power to work miracles,' she commented dryly.

If he thought she would badger him for details, he had another thing coming. Her lack of interest was monumental. A couple of days later, however, when he came home and said he had caught Swamiji's eye for a mantra, she was curious.

'So what did he give you? How did he give it to you?'

'I'll tell you later,' he said, annoyed at having been cold-shouldered for so long.

He did not show any eagerness to tell her, and she was determined not to ask again. But in bed she couldn't resist any longer.

'You said Swamiji chose you. What mantra did he give you?'

Prabhakar launched into a long, tedious speech. Swamiji had been at his scintillating best that evening; he had given a memorable talk on the *Kathopanishad*, responding to questions and clearing up doubts. Then he had glanced over the audience until his eyes had come to rest on Prabhakar. Swamiji had led him into the inner sanctum, which had been made over into a worship room, and had asked him to sit down, saying, 'Don't worry, that little problem of yours will be sorted out soon.'

Before she could say anything, Prabhakar hastened to add, 'You may wonder why I'm making such a big deal about it, since what Swamiji said could be true of anyone—who on earth doesn't have a problem or two, after all? But when he started talking about the subtle details of my case there was no doubt in my mind whatsoever. He had seen it all with his divine eyes.'

'How could he have come to know about you and your problem? For that matter, how can he possibly know about the problems of each and everyone who's making a beeline for him? Of course, things would be quite different if he collected the information on all of you beforehand.'

'True, he's surrounded by the wife and children of the chief engineer all the time, but why would any of them bother to fill him in on my affairs? Anyway, Swamiji has assured me he'll take care of my problem.'

'What mantra did he give you?'

'He didn't give me one, just a slip of paper with nothing on it and asked me to wait until my turn came again.'

'That's it?' Suhasini sounded as if she had been let down.

'You can't judge Swamiji from my going on about him. You need to listen to his talks yourself. As for me, I haven't seen a greater sage in all my life.'

'I don't need sages. If I want wisdom, I can read the scriptures.' After a pause she enquired, 'Do women go to see him?'

'More than half the crowd are women, and during office hours there are almost only women. Why don't you go once and see for yourself?'

'I can't be bothered.' But she was intrigued, especially after Swamiji picked Prabhakar for the mantra. She wanted to know why people were flocking to him, what was so special about his talks.

A few days later, when the children were out for the evening, she agreed to go with Prabhakar to hear Swamiji.

In spite of her deep-seated prejudice against swamijis of all hues, she had to admit that at first glance this man was something. The room was overflowing with people, and he was seated on a raised platform at the front. He was about her age, if not younger, and impeccably groomed. A five-star swamiji, a designer monk—his hair, his beard, his flowing ochre robe, all seemed to suggest a handsome matinee idol playing the part of a swamiji. His most striking feature were his eyes, which seemed to bore right through you. They might easily have been damned as roving in another situation, but here they were hailed as omniscient, penetrating, mesmerizing. His talk turned out to be even more impressive. Quoting extensively from biographical accounts by both Indians and foreigners, he spoke at length on Ramakrishna Paramhansa, the unlettered saint who had shaken middle-class Calcutta out of its torpor. Clearly, he had a way with words. She had to admit he was well-read. At the end of his talk he chose the wife of an important bureaucrat in the state administration for the mantra.

'Now you believe me, don't you?' remarked Prabhakar on the way home.

'He spoke well, that's all. But find out if the talks he gave earlier have been taped.'

From then on Suhasini went to listen to Swamiji whenever she had a chance. He never repeated himself, and each talk was as profound as it was memorable. During the day he remained surrounded mostly by women followers, since the men were away at their offices. Suhasini began to attend the afternoon sessions as well. She had grown fond of his lectures, but what she couldn't get over was his practice of leading a new person every day into the inner sanctum to impart the mantra. She found the whole thing quite indecent. Others did too, for as soon as Swamiji led the chosen one inside there would be a barely suppressed wave of sniggers and snide remarks all around. What saved appearances was that the door to the inner room was not completely shut and that there were members of the chief engineer's family going in and out.

A few days passed. She began to wonder why Swamiji hadn't yet picked her. Not that she was no longer repelled by what she considered an intrinsically indecent and obscene practice, with a strong sexual undercurrent. Maybe he was above all that. He didn't choose only young and good-looking women. But did he? She couldn't be sure.

Her curiosity grew stronger by the day about how the mantra was given. Her husband had told her something about it. He had gone back to obtain his and Swamiji had asked him to fold the slip of paper he had given him earlier and drop it into an empty bag. Then he was told to pull it out again. He was not to open it until he was back home. Once there, Prabhakar couldn't wait to open it: there was a mantra written on it, but he had been forbidden to share it with anyone, even his wife, and for once Suhasini found herself dying of curiosity.

The day the fat lump of a woman who usually sat beside her was chosen, Suhasini thought it was time for her to do something. Although she was no longer exactly young she had taken such good care of her looks and figure that people found her very attractive. When she set out for the talk the following day she had groomed herself with extra care and put on an eye-catching sari. But Swamiji's eyes simply swept over her, leaving her to curse him in silence. Good enough, she'd been spared the mortification. Nevertheless she began to dress more and more fashionably and sought out positions in the front row, where she would be clearly visible. Her self-image and pride were at stake; Swamiji's attention had to be captured. She began to sharpen her glances until they gleamed like knives.

No wonder Swamiji capitulated, he simply had no other choice. One afternoon he picked her for the mantra. A sense of victory overcame her as she rose from among the others, even as the gentle but suggestive tittering she knew would follow made her feel somewhat ashamed. Her mental preparation to face Swamiji alone began the moment he led her into the inner sanctum, which turned out to be exactly as Prabhakar had described it. On one side of the room were the idols and images of gods and goddesses on a wooden platform, and on the other was a divan with a deerskin across it. The young woman making arrangements for the worship finished and left, pulling the door gently behind her. Suhasini recognized her: the chief engineer's wife's younger sister. Swamiji sat down on the divan, indicating to her a place at his feet. She found that downright insulting, though somehow it hadn't seemed so in the lecture hall.

'Surely you don't expect me to sit on the floor,' she said, 'while you take the divan?'

'Nobody has objected to that before! Even the chief minister sits at my feet.' He moved a little to one side, to make room for her, but it was so cramped that she realized that she'd have been better off on the floor.

'What's your name, Ma?' He looked her up and down with interest, using the pronoun indicating familiarity.

Ma? she wondered. Was he being fresh? But then addressing a married woman as 'Ma' couldn't be taken as exactly disrespectful, and all swamijis had the liberty to speak as familiarly as they pleased. She decided to tell him her name without protest.

'A sweet name indeed,' he said. 'But I'd much rather call you Swaha. That's it. Swaha is the fire god's wife and one among the sixteen hundred divine mothers.'

Fair enough, she responded in silence, wait until I burn you to cinders. She found herself using the familiar form of address just as he had.

'One look at your face and everything becomes transparent,' said Swamiji. 'What is it that makes your conjugal life unhappy, Ma?'

'Whose isn't, at least a little? You could ask that about almost everyone without fear of being contradicted.'

'But does a look at just anyone's face reveal her husband's name to be Prabhakar?'

She felt a stab of defeat: the fellow had turned out to be a deepwater fish; he'd done his homework. She had to be careful how she spoke and what she said. She looked up at him. He was staring at her with supreme self-possession. Was there a hint of sarcasm in his eyes?

'I'll erase all your unhappiness,' he said, his hands on her face gently closing her eyes.

The dim light and aroma of incense and sandalwood lent the room an agreeable atmosphere of peacefulness and lightness. With her eyes closed she experienced a heady feeling of freedom. His hands exerted a gentle pressure, his fingers running playfully through her hair. When he cupped her face she opened her eyes wide and fixed him with a cold stare. Swamiji did not flinch; he did not withdraw his hands. She couldn't recollect a single instance in all her adult life when somebody besides her husband had ever held her like this. Some had touched her on the sly, making it seem like an accident, but Swamiji oozed boldness and confidence. Things seemed to be slipping out of control.

'Will you give me a mantra?' She was a little uneasy.

Swamiji got up and walked across the room to the platform on which the idols had been placed and picked up a slip of paper. Settling back close beside her, he tucked it into her fist. His hand stayed on hers. After a moment of reflection she placed her other hand on top of his.

'I intend to give you a special mantra,' he said, 'but we need to worship first.'

He walked over to the other side of the room again and sat down in front of the idols. She followed him and lowered herself down beside him.

'Take off your things.'

She slowly slipped off her rings and bangles and undid her earrings. Her body felt on fire. She glanced at him. The heat of his eyes was scorching.

'Everything.'

She had half a mind to walk out but instead found herself glancing helplessly at the door.

He got up and bolted it.

When she came back to her senses she realized a tape of mantras was playing. The heat had left her body and there was a calming air of peace and tranquility all around. The slip of paper was still in her clenched fist.

'Is this how you give everyone your special mantra?' she asked.

'Only to those who take my fancy.' He gave a little laugh.

'You're nothing but a con man.'

'In the space of a single day you've done two things nobody else has dared attempt: you've objected to sitting at my feet, and you've used the informal form of address to speak to me.'

'I don't think I was off the mark,' she said, nestling against him and tweaking his cheek. 'You're a fake, a fraud.'

'True, and when are you coming back to be conned again?'

'Maybe I won't. Ever. But that doesn't mean I want to stop listening to your talks. Whatever you may be, you speak very well—your lectures are truly memorable.'

'In that case maybe I have just the job for you. My followers are after me to publish my lectures. Perhaps you could transcribe the tapes? It'll give you the pretext you need to come and see me as often as you want.'

'You truly are a damned con man—a lustful one at that.' She rose to her feet, tucking the slip of paper into her handbag.

Swamiji hugged her. 'Come again. Soon.'

'I'll see.'

On her way out she met the chief engineer's pretty sister-in-law, and a wave of shame and contrition swept over her. But she quickly got over it, deciding to take stock of the situation only once she was home.

Back home, however, she was kept busy, with chores to do and with looking after the children and the guests.

'My vigilance file was closed today,' Prabhakar announced in high excitement, when he arrived home that evening.

'How did that happen?'

'Swamiji must have had a hand in it; I can't think of any other explanation. Think about it—a vigilance file kept alive for ages is suddenly closed! I intend to go to Swamiji right now with some money. Will you accompany me?'

She wanted to but decided against it. 'I was there this afternoon.'

'Two visits a day isn't forbidden. You know something—you're a born sceptic, you've never had respect for self-realized souls. It'd take a miracle to turn you into a believer. Say what you wish, Swamiji works miracles. My own case is proof enough.'

She told Prabhakar about receiving half the mantra that afternoon—she would have to go back for the other half—and about Swamiji's proposal relating to preparing the transcripts for publication. He felt gratified: she had taken to Swamiji, never mind how little.

The following afternoon, as she was debating whether or not to go to see Swamiji, she received the tapes.

Now she didn't have to go to his talks; she could meet him anytime—alone—to discuss progress in transcribing the tapes. He changed his schedule to give her ample time: suddenly the book had become his top priority. The wind had been taken out of the sails of the gossips too. Prabhakar was elated: his wife had been transformed into an ardent follower. Swamiji had found someone to bare his soul to.

'You said you can make the mantra appear on blank paper,' she said one day, taking the slip of paper out of her handbag. 'Do it. I want to see the miracle.'

Swamiji took the cloth bag from the pedestal and guided her hand inside it. There she found the secret pocket and fished out an identical slip of paper. She unfolded it. Across it was written: Om Sri.

'How long can you fool people?' she said. 'Sooner rather than later you'll be found out.'

'People should realize it's impossible to make a mantra appear on blank paper, yet still they want a miracle. What harm is there if I fulfil their childish expectations? Don't doctors sometimes give their patients placebos?'

'But you seem to be doing more than that. You got the chief engineer's transfer cancelled; you got my husband's vigilance file closed and buried.'

'That's nothing; with the kind of followers I have, making such things happen is simple.'

'What about the money you say you're collecting for your hospital?'

'Believe me, that must be the one good thing I've ever set my heart on. Every coin I get goes to it. Thanks to my followers I don't want for anything and don't need more money. So why not do a good deed for once?' He reached for a box under the divan and opened it. It was full of money and jewellery.

'I believe you,' she said, rolling a bangle off her wrist and dropping it in. 'That's my contribution. Tell me, will you invite me when you inaugurate your hospital?'

Swamiji became serious. 'Just when things were going fine, there's been a sudden snag. I don't know what's in store. I'll tell you about it someday.'

Over the following days he hardly had any time for her, and when he did he was never alone; either the publisher or somebody else was always present. At first this put her off and she berated him in her mind, but then it dawned on her that perhaps the problem he had hinted at had caught up with him.

A few days passed, and then one evening Prabhakar came home with the news: Swamiji had bolted town!

'I knew something like this would happen,' he commented.

'You never said so.' She made an effort to hide her irritation.

'These swamijis are all alike—basically after money and women, no matter how holy they pretend to be.'

She didn't respond.

'Take you, for example. You were so contemptuous in the beginning, but what an ardent follower you turned into!'

She didn't want to get into an argument, at least for now. 'When I listened to his talks I realized he was a man of deep knowledge; when I spoke to him I realized he was honest.'

'People are saying nasty things about the women he gave mantras to.'

Suhasini walked off.

It made front-page headlines in the papers the next day: Swamiji had vanished into the blue. Not only had he taken off with the money and jewellery, but he had been able to con people simply because of the political patronage he enjoyed. The hospital project for which many rich ladies had given away their entire cache of gold ornaments didn't exist. The police was preparing a list of all those who had been taken in. A young woman from a well-known family was missing as well.

Prabhakar phoned Suhasini from the office. 'If the police come around to question you, tell them you don't know anything.'

'What about?'

'About Swamiji,' he snapped with evident irritation. 'I'll tell you all about it when I get home.'

The police didn't show up. In the evening, Prabhakar gave her the gossip: in addition to what he had collected, the con man had spirited away the chief engineer's luscious sister-in-law; the officers and businessmen were lying low because they all had given him fat donations of black money; women had complained to the police he had cast spells on them to get them to part with their jewellery. His eyes searched Suhasini's ears and hands. 'I hope he didn't manage to wheedle anything out of you.'

'I gave him a gold bangle.'

Whatever retort he wanted to make, he stopped short because the children returned home just then, but when they were in bed he returned to the matter. 'Did he hypnotize you to make you give him the gold bangle?'

'I gave it willingly, of my own accord.'

'Is there a bigger fool than you? At least the others were under some kind of spell and didn't know what they were doing, but you... How could you, in your right mind, have given him a gold bangle?'

'Don't forget the gold bangle was mine, given to me by my parents.'

He brought home bits of news the following days. A police officer friend of his had shown him the list of women involved with Swamiji. He was relieved to see Suhasini's name didn't figure on it, although everyone knew how close she had been to Swamiji while she was working on the transcriptions. He had a nagging suspicion his friend might have deleted her name out of pity for her. Prabhakar had faith in her, though he didn't take kindly to her giving away a gold bangle.

Some days later the police nabbed Swamiji and laid their hands on everything he'd taken. The chief engineer's pretty sister-in-law was restored to the bosom of her family, and she told all and sundry how she had been drugged and hypnotized. The women who had lost their ornaments thronged the police station, claiming the same thing had happened to them. Prabhakar begged Suhasini to file a claim for her bangle, but she showed no interest in doing that. 'Why would I want to take back something I gave away willingly?' But he couldn't accept this and asked his police officer friend if all the pieces of jewellery had been identified and restored to their rightful owners. Everything, it turned out, had already been claimed.

Following the police investigation, salacious stories of Swamiji's sex escapades with the ladies of the town made the rounds. The publication of his lectures added fuel to the fire. In the preface Swamiji paid Suhasini profuse thanks for her role in bringing out the book. When Prabhakar, with a friend, saw the book, he went red in the face. People gossiping amongst themselves about Swamiji's philandering was one thing, but having his wife's name linked to Swamiji in print was quite another.

'We'll become the subject of gossip in every household now!' he said angrily, flinging a copy of the book at her.

She picked it up and rifled through it. 'Handsome production.'

'You're mentioned in the preface.'

'Swamiji showed it to me before sending it to the publishers. I did actually help him with the transcriptions. You were so encouraging in those days.'

'Things were different then. The fellow hadn't been found out for what he really was—a cad dressed in ochre robes!'

'But does that make his talks any less interesting? They are as fine as any. I think everyone should read the book.'

'You seem to be taking his side. Did you have something going on with him like the other women?'

'Yes.' Her voice was icy cold.

'You didn't tell me about it before!' His voice rose.

'You never asked.'

'He must have put a hex on you.'

'He did nothing of the sort. Whatever I did I did willingly, not without thinking, deliberately.'

Prabhakar walked away.

The next day he returned home late. He didn't speak to her the whole day. But the following day, returning from the office, he found himself alone with her; the children had gone out. While having tea he couldn't help bringing the topic up.

'You might not have been aware you were already under his spell. If the bloody fellow worked it on so many women, I can't believe he spared you.'

Suhasini remained silent.

'The bloody fellow was well up on the art of casting spells. Oh, that reminds me, didn't you tell me that he gave you a mantra? He gave me a slip of paper with a mantra on it and asked me to keep it a secret, saying that sharing it with anyone could bring harm.' He retrieved the paper from the cupboard and unfolded it. 'Harm, my foot! I'm going to show it to the whole world.'

Suhasini remained silent.

'Let's see the mantra he gave you,' he said. 'He must have warned you not to show it to anyone. To hell with that.'

Without a word she got up and produced a slip of paper from her handbag. There was nothing on it.

PATADEI

BINAPANI MOHANTY

Nobody knew how Patadei had been able to slip out in the middle of that Dola Purnima night, with the brightest full moon of the year lighting up the earth. That year too the deities had been enthroned on little wooden chariots and carried on shoulders from door to door. They were offered prasad, and then taken in a procession, accompanied by the beatings of drums and cymbals, to the fair ground crowded with revellers smearing each other with coloured powders, their children falling asleep or waking up to join the fun.

Holi was a festival like no other—only once a year and over all too soon. The rest of the year the memory of it lay hidden under the dust and grime of daily life. The memory of that particular Dola Purnima night remained buried in Patadei's mind for years and years; under her smile regrets lurked like ghosts.

On that fateful night, nearly as bright as day, she had stepped out in the midst of the hustle bustle. After greeting the deities at her doorstep she went off to the fair ground. Earlier in the evening, she had had a large bowl of watered rice with drumstick leaves and had lain tossing and turning on a reed mat on the kitchen veranda feeling a little queasy. Jagu Behera, her father, had gone out to help carry the deities' chariots. He had been gone since the morning, and there was no one—neither a crow, as they say, nor a cuckoo—at home to speak two words to.

Sister-in-law Mani, with a few others from the neighbourhood, had dropped by in the evening asking her to play cards, but she had excused herself. Someone had tittered in derision and commented: 'Look at that cow. She's gone and loaded herself to the brim and is lolling about like a husking paddle. But if you ask her out she says she isn't feeling well enough...' The group had broken into peals of laughter, the echoes of which the naughty vernal wind had scattered to far corners.

Patadei had continued to lie on her back, staring unblinkingly at the fat full moon, as the sights and sounds of the carnival continued to rage outside. No one could have ascertained what was passing through her mind.

The whole village had erupted in a riot of colour. In the frenzy of bhajans, kirtans, the sounds of drums and cymbals, Patadei stole out to witness the festival, unafraid of dogs, jackals, ghosts, witches, vampires and other creatures of the night she might run into along the way.

After celebrating the whole night people dropped off to sleep in the small hours, too tired to find out who was alive or dead, who had eaten and who hadn't, why Jagu Behera's house was locked, and why Patadei was nowhere to be seen. They had to catch up on their sleep as there was something else to look forward to—the competition between two theatre groups the following night.

When Jagu Behera reached home at noon, tired and hungry, he became angry at the sight of the closed door. He yelled and hollered for his daughter, loud enough to wake up the dead, but only to have the words ricochet back to him. He rested a while before shouting for his daughter again and began looking for her in every house in the village.

He had sold his land—all five gunthas—to raise the money for her marriage. The boy was as handsome as a prince, and owned two acres of land, in addition to the gold people deposited with him against loans. But the girl did not stay with him for more than a couple of months. God only knew why. In those two months her fair complexion turned dark. From brooding? From worrying? She never spoke about it. If someone asked her, she simply stared wide-eyed. Jagu thought maybe she had been overwhelmed by the burden of marriage. He had pampered her since her mother died; perhaps she couldn't get used to the inconveniences at her husband's house. But as a man he couldn't divine the source of her unhappiness, which a mother or a sister would have been able to. Nor was he a big shot who could march to her in-laws and tell them off. So he simply worried a lot.

Then, one night, without the least forewarning, someone banged on his front door. Jagu had gone to sleep covered with a sheet to keep out the chill. He awoke with a start and demanded to know who was there. But no answer came. Must be ghosts, he thought to himself, turning on his side to go back to sleep. But whoever it was started tugging at the door rings and banging on the door once again. Angry and irritated, he got up. Holding a holy tulsi leaf offered to the household deity for protection, he opened the door. Something was compelling him, maybe the call of his own blood.

He jumped out of his skin when, even in the dark, he made out the silhouette of his daughter. 'Pata?' He stammered. 'Is that you, my daughter?'

Patadei sidled past him and bolted the door in absolute silence.

'Why're you here in the dead of night? Did you have a row with your in-laws? Have you left their house in a huff?'

She hung her head, leaning against the wall, the expression on her face inscrutable.

Jagu's knees wobbled and he slumped down. 'Why aren't you answering, girl? What's wrong? Did you fight with your husband? Did they hit you? Are you all right? Are you feeling all right?'

She did not answer.

It must be something serious, thought Jagu. But he didn't subject the poor girl to a midnight interrogation. He expected she would pour out everything in the morning, headstrong and obstinate as she was.

'Would you like to eat something, child? There must be some watered rice in the pot.'

Her face between her knees, she broke down in torrents of tears.

Jagu wondered when was the last time he had seen her cry so bitterly; even on the day after her wedding as she was leaving for her in-laws' house she hadn't done so. He wiped her tears with his towel. Let the night pass and the day dawn, and everything would come to light. Her tender heart might have revolted at something horrible done to her by her in-laws. She wasn't mature enough yet to put up with it and move on. Surely either her father-in-law or husband would turn up in the morning to take her back, but he shouldn't miss the chance to give them a dressing-down.

But no one came. Days and months passed, then years. Jagu never found out what had made her run away. Every time he began questioning her, she gave him a blank stare. Her eyes would well up with tears, her lips tremble, but not a word escaped them.

When Jagu's neighbours badgered him for an explanation, he either remained mum or said his son-in-law had gone off to Madras to look for a job and his daughter had come home and would join him as soon as he landed a good one. But neither a letter nor a messenger came from her in-laws. Out of shame Jagu never tried to get in touch with them. True, he was old and weak, but he could still work as a farmhand and look after his daughter on his meagre wages, maybe skipping a meal now and then.

As for Patadei, she did not apologize even once for causing him anguish and hardship.

Still he couldn't be angry with her; one look at her stricken face and his heart melted. Sometimes he feared she might commit suicide or run away from home if he showed even the slightest anger or displeasure. Who else did she have besides him? Who else did he have besides her? No matter how stubborn she was, or how unreasonable, he'd have to look after her. He'd have to ignore whatever remarks people made about her, reigning in his tongue. Some claimed she'd been driven out by her in-laws after a showdown, others that she'd been kicked out by her husband because he couldn't get along with her, still others whispered some infidelity had surfaced.

Jagu took to leaving home as soon as the crow cawed to look for work, returning in the evening, all the while praying for a solution. He knew he wouldn't be around much longer to look after his daughter.

After the two feverish days of Holi, famished, and tired enough to want to lie down and expire, Jagu lost his temper when he saw the locked door. Instead of waiting to greet him with a bowl of watered rice, the girl had probably gone off to play cards with the neighbours, having a good time this very minute, laughing and joking. How long could he take it? Until he was carried off to the cremation grounds? Was it written in his stars he would labour until his last breath looking after a married daughter? Didn't she owe him a little consideration?

'Pata!' he screamed. 'Where the hell are you, girl? Come here at once...'

No answer.

Jagu went from door to door, combing the whole village looking for her. Morning became evening, but still there was no sight of her. The house remained bolted from outside; the brittle weather-beaten flaps of the door clung to each other and mocked him. The sun set and darkness shrouded everything.

Jagu dozed off on his veranda. He slept through the night, and when the first birds called he awoke to find his front door shut as before.

The villagers who witnessed all this said that was the last they'd seen Jagu in his right mind. He became a different man. He took leave of his senses. He'd simply stare uncomprehendingly when the villagers spoke and reasoned with him; his lips would tremble when someone's daughter or daughter-in-law came with a bowl of watered rice. Tears would stream down his face, but not a sound came out of his mouth. People said he'd been struck dumb since his daughter left home to become a whore. Ten days later he was found dead, his dilated eyes fixed on the latch of his front door, droves of flies on his face.

Three years had passed since Patadei left home and Jagu had died. Three times the fair ground had come alive with the deities; mangoes had ripened; much water, in waves and ripples, had flowed down the river to the sea. Sister-in-law Mani had borne a son and become a widow. Many of Patadei's friends and companions had married and left the village. Nobody missed her, nobody bothered to even wonder what had become of her, where she had gone and settled, whom she had remarried, if she had. The sun rose every day, and the seasons rolled on. Patadei's whereabouts were an unresolved mystery.

Jagu Behera's house remained shut; a tiny house, just a room and a half, with a few ragged reed mats, a couple of bedcovers with holes in them, and a tin trunk without a lock. No villager had coveted any of these ill-starred possessions. Besides, the place was close to the cremation grounds and rumoured to be rife with ghosts and spirits. The lemonwood tree bore no flowers; there was nothing to tempt even a person who might have wanted to pluck them to enter the house out of curiosity, and check out what was inside. What had once been a home had turned into the abode of ghosts. People who passed by on dark evenings reported seeing the apparition of Patadei and hearing Jagu shouting and screaming.

Only three years had passed—they seemed more like three aeons—when one morning there was a huge uproar. The villagers who couldn't remember the incident invented outlandish stories, those who did remember it prayed the village would be saved from disaster. Patadei had been found sweeping her house-front, with a two-year-old boy, sucking two of his fingers, toddling behind her. The girl had put on weight around her waist, but otherwise looked the same—pensive eyes swimming with tears.

The news eddied through the village in no time. Jagu Behera's darling daughter, who'd gone missing, had come back; not alone but with a child in tow. Must be her own flesh and blood; she couldn't possibly have picked up an orphan somewhere. This was the girl who had run away from her husband in the middle of the night, and who had run away once again from her father's house. Surely there was a paramour. And now she dared return. Maybe her lover had put her out because she was no longer young. Maybe she could no longer make a living using her body.

But there seemed a world of difference between the Patadei of three years ago and Patadei now. She didn't seem even a little bit abashed.

Whenever elders questioned her, she'd simply pull the end of her sari tightly over her head and turn her face away. When women turned up, she'd roll out the torn reed mats for them but wouldn't answer. They could make as many cutting remarks as they wanted, laugh any amount at her expense; she couldn't have cared less.

She was castigated and denounced as a shameless hussy. And how did she intend to get by? Why was she being so uppity and disrespectful? God wouldn't forgive her. Did she think she was some goddess, who could flout all worldly norms and live in society on her own sweet terms? How could she even dream of such a thing? How shameless could she be? Could she not even find a little poison to put an end to her shameful existence? Did she hope to hide her misdeeds and still live in the village?

The unanimous verdict was she was giving the village a bad name and must leave right away if she cared to live. If she didn't, her house would be set on fire.

Confronted, pressed to make a choice, she finally confessed: 'All right, yes, this child is my son. There. I gave birth to him.

'When my husband went away to Calcutta the day following our wedding, my in-laws shut me in a room without food and water for fifteen days. Then one night I escaped and came back to my father's house. My father was stunned to see me. He was worried. He put up with every snide remark you people made about me; I received many an insult. He went out to work, toiling day after day to put crumbs in my mouth. His bones wore out, but there was no end to our hunger, nor an end to our shame.' She paused to swallow her spit and moisten her throat. 'I could do or say nothing to save my poor father from hard work or myself from further shame... Then I went and got myself this child... Actually, this cruel world forced the child on me...'

An elder, whom Patadei couldn't make out from behind the end of her sari, pushed through the throng, tightening a towel around his waist. 'What did you say, whore?' he demanded. 'Say it again! The cruel world forced the child on you? Shameless hussy, how brazen can you get? Tell us whose child he is, who his father is.'

Patadei slumped to the ground, her boy sobbing convulsively by her side.

Someone landed a kick on her back and she keeled forward. 'Come clean, slut!' It was Mani's mother-in-law.

'Got a frog in your throat, have you? Why don't you answer? We know what you really are. You behaved as if you couldn't hurt a fly, but you could not live with your in-laws. You were the death of your father. And now you dare show up and say this cruel world forced a child on you? Tell us whose child he is, or else I will cut you in two.' The old woman put her foot on Patadei's neck.

The onlookers seemed to be enjoying the scene.

Patadei found herself suffocating, her face pressed to the ground. But her eyes seemed to shine like glow-worms. Enough was enough, she had had enough, she didn't have to take the insults anymore. She didn't want to be cut in half. No god was going to descend from above to protect her, she had to fend for herself, she alone could decide whether she wanted to live or die.

She pushed the old woman's foot away and sprang up, all five feet of her, contempt and anger turning her face purple. Picking up her bawling baby, she set him up on her hip and fixed the onlookers with a defiant stare. 'So you all want to know who the father of the child is, huh? All his fathers are present here, every one of them—Ramu, Bira, Gopi, Maguni, Naria and a few more. How can I say whose baby it is?

'On the full moon night of Dola Purnima three years ago, when the theatre competition was going on, it was Ramu who pressed his towel over my mouth and carried me off on his shoulders when I stepped out of the house to see the deities at the fair ground. By the bushes down at the edge of the cremation grounds he and the rest of them had me, devouring me limb by limb, until there was nothing left but bones. But before I lost consciousness I saw all their faces in the clear light of the full moon... But how could I be sure who among them is the father of this child? Why not ask Haria Bauri, who carted me off to Cuttack in exchange for the few rupees the gang gave him?

'I kept away from here just to spare my poor father further shame. I haven't breathed a word until now...'

She stared at the old woman. 'Oh, Aunt, why don't you ask them? Is there even one among them who is man enough to put his hand on his chest and admit to being the father of my child?'

There was a hush. The old and the elderly looked at one another in confusion, the younger ones smirked, but no one had an answer. The old woman, crushed, stepped down from the veranda. Ramu, Bira, Gopi, Maguni and the rest stood with their heads hung low.

Wiping her eyes, Patadei picked up the broom and went back to sweeping. When her child began to bawl again, she threw down the broom and hurried to wipe the snot from his nose and tears from his eyes. 'Why are you crying, my sweet child?' she said, covering him with kisses. 'Are you scared? Does the crowd scare you? Don't be afraid, my son. I'm with you. Is there anyone man enough to step forward and claim you as his son? Not to worry, my dear. You may not have a father, but you have your mother!'

God knows what the little one made out, but he broke into a delighted chortle and raised his hands as if to reach out to the day moon. He seemed ready to fly up to the clouds. And as he laughed, the assembly of men and women began to thin out; they all turned and crept away, their heads hanging in shame.

The lemonwood tree which had long been barren had borne a couple of flowers since Patadei's return, and now those flowers seemed all smiles.

Mani's old mother-in-law, bent from the waist, leaned heavily on her walking stick as she shuffled off.

Patadei looked around, and when everyone was gone put a gob of spit on her boy's chest to ward off the evil eye. There had been a big crowd; she couldn't take any chances. Already her little prince had turned a shade darker in the last hour. But did she care; she was at no one's mercy. She was the queen of the house her father had left her and her boy, a prince.

The earth and the sky had fallen silent around her. As she looked up, down and around she began laughing and crying at the same time.

SALVATION

PRATIBHA RAY

For forty long years the man and the woman had lived under one roof, sharing joys and sorrows, delight and despair. Yet never once had they stolen a glance at each other, never once had they exchanged a word or a casual touch.

Since becoming part of her household, the very first time Nuri Das had a chance to look upon the face of his wife's elder sister was when her body was lying on the funeral pyre, and his wastrel of a son, Satya, was about to set fire to it. Her face was enveloped in a haze. Or maybe he couldn't see too well because of his cataracts. He was all of fifty-nine, and the dead woman, Soshi, was eleven years his junior.

When Satya bent down to light the pyre, Nuri Das felt as if someone from up above had slipped the boy a sliver of flame. What did Soshi really look like? Nuri couldn't be sure. How could he? A blurry impression was all he had, which was just as well. Didn't society decree that he should not look upon the face of his elder sister-in-law?

Home after the cremation, Nuri found the emptiness of the house overwhelming. It was hard to step into the courtyard, where he had seen Soshi's two little feet flitting about all those years. He couldn't bring himself to sit on the veranda, where Soshi had always served him his meals. So he went and sat under the mango tree in the backyard, as stiff as a log. Why did the home feel so deserted, so empty without Soshi?

Whenever he had seen her feet approaching, he had backed away; whenever he had seen her arms dropping down in front of him to serve him food, he had shrunk back. When he needed to communicate with her, he'd beam his words at the walls, and Soshi would reply not so much in words as in action. She seemed to anticipate every move of his; there was no room for words. At first light he wanted his black tea, sweetened with jaggery, and rice puffs, followed by four paans. After breakfast, he headed to the vegetable patch, and he'd find all the tools neatly laid out on the veranda—shovel, spade, pots and baskets. Sometimes in the middle of his labour Nuri would catch a whiff of the curry being prepared. When the sun climbed to the middle of the sky, and it was time for his bath, he'd find a bottle of oil sitting on the veranda, so he wouldn't have to enter the house. He'd give himself an oil massage and proceed to the pond at the end of the backyard for a dip. On his return, he'd find the prayer mat and rudraksh beads laid out on the inside veranda. He'd sit cross-legged and proceed to draw lines of sandalpaste across his arms and chest, and on his forehead down to the bridge of his nose. Between the twin lines across his forehead, he'd draw a large dot the size of a four-anna coin. Then he'd launch full tilt into the whole routine—japa, tapa, pranam, prayer, meditation and obeisance. By the time he had taken his last bow to the deities, steaming bowls of food would be laid out on the veranda, and, like an obedient child, he'd tuck in, never ever finding fault with the dishes. He never commented if the curry was salty or without salt, if it was too spicy or too bland. Nor did Soshi ask; she'd find out for herself when she ate after him.

But she did cook for him with genuine love and affection. He ate without a word, perhaps purely out of hunger, never letting on if he was upset or angry. Of all persons under the sun it was she, Soshi, who alone knew what a straight and narrow path the poor man trod, the razor's edge he lived on.

If Soshi's appearance remained hidden for Nuri beneath her layers of clothing, or behind the end of the sari veiling her face at all times, she was fully aware how handsome he was. A superb specimen of a man, he hadn't aged much, neither losing nor gaining weight. Though a little stooped, his features hadn't coarsened. In his twilight years he looked almost as good as in his younger days. He always dressed simply, just a clean white dhoti reaching his knees when at home. He added a short white shirt when he went to the market or elsewhere. And of course he was never without the sandalpaste marks on his forehead, nose, arms and earlobes, the two strands of tulsi beads around his neck, and a towel on his shoulder. Full five hands in height—tall by the village standards—his complexion was as fair as his appearance was pleasing: his nose was straight, forehead wide, small eyes bright and piercing, chest wide as a door panel, shoulders strong enough to carry mountains, straight and long like a ploughshare, a flat belly that seemed to touch his back.

The family did not have much land. Their backyard contained a mango tree, and a couple of drumstick and banana trees. There was also a small vegetable patch, where Nuri grew whatever seasonal herbs and greens he could, which he sold in the market to buy rice and other things that were needed. During the mango months their income went up. He did not know where the mango sapling had come from or when it had been planted, but its fruit was a marvel: fully round like a zero, tapering a little towards the stem, fleshy and full of juice, the skin quite thin, its pulp quivering like aloe vera. With hardly any fibre, it was best served in thin slices. The aroma alone could set the body tingling from the belly to the brain. Buyers snapped up the mangoes. Prices shot up at the end of the season; Nuri demanded fancy prices, according to size.

This patch of green was the mainstay of the family of three. The pond at the back was tiny, but it served quite well for bathing and cleaning; it was also used to water the vegetables the year around. But at the height of summer it went dry, and a deep hole had to be dug in the middle to tap the water underground. Just as stars sprouted in the sky, fish, big and small, sprouted in the pond—kerandi, dandikiri, caryfish, eels, creols and sheuls—but they were of no use to Nuri, a devout Vaisnav and strict vegetarian. No fish or meat ever entered his kitchen. For him the fish polluted the water of the pond, and he encouraged his neighbours to rid him of them, for free. But while generous with the fish, he wouldn't let anyone spirit away a single chilli from his garden.

Summer was a trying time: the aubergines dried up before they grew to full size, the chillies shrivelled up too; he could only dream of growing gourds, pumpkins and cucumbers. But while in other homes greens were lacking, in Nuri's there was not enough rice. How did he manage the summer ordeal year after year?

He did have another resource, although not a regular one. Once a hobby, it had now become a means to keep the wolves of hunger from the door. Sometimes the pickings were too good to be true. He played the mridanga in the kirtan troupes whenever they were called upon to perform—at birth, death, or religious ceremonies—and for his labour he received rice, rice flakes, coconuts, sweets, a little cash, and a dhoti and a towel. He had always loved singing kirtans, and now it had become a love affair—since God knows when. From the evening until dinner was ready, he'd sit on the outside veranda drumming his mridanga, eyes shut in the dark. Sometimes he'd go on until midnight. The evening tempo was slow, soft, unhurried; the midnight beats were fast, furious, obviously matching the rumblings of a belly without food.

Hunger on God's good earth has many facets with different tastes—sweet, sour, pungent, salty and bitter. But the four major hungers—of the flesh, belly, mind and soul—were primal, and held all human beings in their thrall. And the hapless victim—so went one of the lines of a kirtan that Nuri sang—was swept up by a stream of lies and deceit. But he himself recognized only two: the hunger of the belly, and the hunger of the soul. The first had to be sated with food, the second with the singing of kirtans. Hare Krishna, Hare Krishna, Krishna, Krishna, Hare, Hare... All other forms of hunger could be ignored.

What kind of hunger did Soshi have? Everything seemed buried behind her covered face. Nuri saw only a pair of hurrying feet and busy hands. She slaved from morning to night: she scooped the dung from the cowshed, made fuel cakes and put them out in the sun to dry, swept the rooms and cleaned the floor, raked dry leaves and twigs and gathered fuelwood, cooked and washed the utensils...not all of it to quench the hunger of her belly. But she had learnt to trample all other hungers underfoot as she stamped on cow dung to make patties before laying them out to dry, as she swabbed the floor with water and fresh cow dung, as she fed leaves and twigs to the fire over which the food was cooked. Who knew whether the hunger of her soul ever yearned to join the rhythm of her brother-in-law's mridanga.

When she was younger, her pale white feet were like steamed rice cakes, puffed up in the middle. But that was just due to the filarial fevers she came down with month after month. She also had a flower tattooed in the middle of each foot. Her hands were slim and shapely, like the succulent centre of a snake gourd, and her palms were soft and as wafer-thin as pancakes. Nuri caught an occasional glimpse of her arms when she served him food—arms covered with intricate blue tattoos. Sometimes there were flashes of her face from behind her veil—a part of her nose resembling the petal of an upside-down kaneear flower, with a tiny shining nose ring. Nobody had ever seen the end of her sari slip off when Nuri was around, nor for that matter did Nuri's gaze stray in her direction. They outdid each other in their respect for what society required. Bound by custom and tradition, all restrictions were carefully observed.

Had Sashi, her younger sister, not died at childbirth, Soshi wouldn't have veiled her face for the rest of her life in her own home. Sashi's son was born in her father's home, as she and her husband, Nuri, both lived there. Nuri had nowhere else to go. Adopted by his maternal uncle and aunt when they were childless, he fell out of favour once their three sons were born. His aunt turned openly hostile. But where could poor Nuri go? Poverty had driven his own father to give him to his maternal uncle; what was due to him had already passed on to his four brothers.

It was around this time that his would-be wife's family was looking for a son-in-law who'd move in with them. Soshi, the elder daughter, was a child widow, and there was no male heir to keep the family line going. Indeed, both the old man and Soshi were in danger of not having a male family member to perform their death rites. So Nuri, who was welcome neither in his own home nor in his uncle's, came to live with his wife's family after marriage.

Everything went all right until Sashi died giving birth to a boy. The grandfather was able to see the newborn and died soon after, a happy man. It was left to Soshi, the widowed aunt, to cut the umbilical cord and raise the child as her own.

So now they were three in the family: twenty-nine-year-old widower Nuri Das; his newborn son, Satya, motherless from the moment of his birth; and widowed aunt Soshi, who was only eighteen.

Despite the gap of eleven years between them—his wife, after all, had been even younger—Nuri could have married Soshi, but only if she had been his wife's younger sister.

The relationship between a man and his wife's elder sister is the most sacred—holy like the water of the Ganga. Even one-and-a-half times more sacrosanct than that with his mother-in-law. Not only can they not look at or touch each other, they cannot speak to one another, let alone joke and laugh. A little slip and the cost is damnation—an eternal sojourn in Hell.

After her sister died, Soshi let Nuri know through a neighbour that he was free to go wherever he liked, marry a second time, have children and settle down. Society didn't ordain that a young man must remain a widower. But she'd keep her nephew; he was needed to perform rites on the anniversary of her death. And, in addition to that, she'd never let even the shadow of a stepmother fall on the child. Nuri was free to come and see him as often as he wished, but he shouldn't dream of taking the boy away.

Nuri didn't relish the prospect of spending the rest of his life without a wife, but he found the idea of leaving his son behind with his aunt utterly unbearable. Besides, he didn't have a home of his own. Soshi was still a helpless young widow, and the child no more than a waif; he couldn't leave them to their fate and make a fresh beginning elsewhere. It wouldn't have been proper for a good man to do so.

'I'm only interested in my son,' Nuri had it conveyed back to Soshi. 'Not in the property of this family or anything else. And do not ever again broach the subject of my remarrying.'

That same evening he took the mridanga off the wall, where he had hung it from a peg. This was his only possession when he had moved in. He had drummed it while practising kirtans with his uncle when he had lived with him, but hadn't touched it since his wedding. Tonight, it seemed his sole companion—true and intimate. He drummed on it late into the night. From then on he played it for an hour or two every evening without fail, wondering how he could have given it up for the past few years.

A cat will do, so goes the saying, if there's no tiger. In the same way, an aunt could fill the role of a mother. Satya hadn't seen a tiger, nor had he seen seen a mother. Maybe he'd get to see a tiger once he grew up—in the circus or in the wild, but a mother he'd never see. His aunt loved him more than would have a mother, but he didn't know the difference between an aunt's love and a mother's; he hadn't seen his mother, he didn't even have a picture of her. He grew up to be a rogue—wicked, wayward, obstinate as a mule, and a liar to the marrow of his bones.

And he couldn't stand his father. When his old man affectionately called him 'mother-killer', he would retaliate by angrily calling his father 'wife-killer'—an expression he had picked up from the neighbours, who didn't miss a chance to castigate Nuri: 'That man is definitely a wife-killer. What else can explain a healthy sixteen-year-old perishing in childbirth, when girls as young as thirteen or fourteen deliver children without a problem?' Apparently, in Nuri's horoscope, death was the ruling planet in his wife's house. But that came to light only after she had passed away.

A well-known high school, established by the British, was right next door—Nuri's walls practically touched it—and Satya could eat at home and rinse his mouth in the school courtyard. Nuri hoped the motherless boy would seize the chance to get a decent education, pass his matriculation, and find himself a government job, so he wouldn't have to eke out as miserable an existence as his father's: banking on mangoes in season and, out of season, on sweet rice puffs at the end of a long kirtan performance.

But Satya turned out to be a disappointment—he stayed as shy of school as a goat does of water. Maybe because he had no love for his father—his father's 'yes' was the son's 'no'; they argued all the time—and he played truant from school. Once in a while a teacher would bring it to the father's notice, and Nuri would take the boy to task. He'd throw him into a room, tie him to a piece of furniture with a rope, and lock the door from outside. 'It's either me,' he'd say as he read the riot act, 'or him. No one should untie him or give him food. Not until he promises to mend his ways, promises not to cut classes and to concentrate on his studies.' The warning was obviously addressed to Soshi. Who else was there who could set the boy free, wipe away his tears, and give him food?

Soshi wouldn't butt in right away. A father had every right to discipline his son. It was even his duty to do so. But the aunt also had a duty towards her nephew, and no one could stop her from doing what she thought was right. So, as soon as Nuri left home, she'd open the room, free the boy from the leg of the cot to which he'd been tied, dry his tears, coax and cajole him to eat. When Nuri returned from wherever he'd gone, he'd find the boy on the veranda poring over a book, the picture of a perfect student. Of course he knew who was behind it all. But by putting a book into the boy's hands she couldn't make a student out of him!

This happened not just once but more than a few times every month. The boy spent two—sometimes three—years in every class. But that didn't worry his aunt. If the boy sat for the exams but didn't pass, she thought the fault lay with the teachers. What good were they if only the better students got through?

Nuri blamed the boy, Soshi blamed the teachers, the boy blamed his father. Satya was determined to take it out on his father. He was intelligent enough to pass his exams, but he wouldn't grant his father that pleasure.

Meanwhile time flew by imperceptibly, regardless of the daily worries the boy caused his father and aunt. Then one fine day, when he was eighteen, he upped and left, got himself a small-time job in town, where he got married and lived with his wife, determined to keep away from the village.

That left only two people at home. Soshi, fair and plump, was still very much a young woman, and Nuri, quite a strong and virile man; both in good health, neither of them sick or in decline. Their only worry was where the next meal would come from. If they had any other thoughts in their minds, it didn't show, drowned out by Nuri's mridanga drumming, absorbed in the darkness under Soshi's veil.

Meanwhile all kinds of scandals broke out around them—in the colonies of milkmen and of washermen, and in the more respectable Mohanty homes. There was no end to the transgressions: affairs between a young woman and her husband's younger brother, between a man and his wife's younger sister, between a man and a woman sworn before God as brother and sister, between a widowed aunt and her nephew. Sometimes affairs took place between daughters-in-law in rich and aristocratic families and their farmhands. Where were the country and society headed?

But these brought a measure of excitement to village life. Townsfolk could get theirs from the cinema, theatre, and folk opera performances, but villagers had nothing but gossip to fall back on. And so they gossiped wherever they could, from the bathing ghats to the panchayat office. The stories got embroidered, enlarged, exaggerated in the telling, like a large fruit emerging from a tiny seed. Reputations were sullied, dragged through the mud. All this led to the imposition of fines, social boycott, ostracism, fights, murders, suicides and black magic to cast an evil eye, a hex, or a spell.

But Nuri's house—strange how nobody ever referred to it as Soshi's—remained untouched. When Satya lived there the villagers' curiosity had centred on his latest scrapes or acts of mischief. But once he left, the house was as silent as a temple that had permanently shut down. No one could find even the smallest misdemeanour, one the size of a mustard seed. What would the gossips do when there wasn't even a kernel to start with? Not that the villagers were full of praise for Nuri and Soshi. They wondered if the two would have been as self-controlled in a different situation. What if instead of the wife's revered elder sister she had been the approachable younger sister? Only then would they have truly been tested: was he indeed a man with absolute self-discipline and she a woman of impeccable virtue and integrity?

Weighed down by the weight of what was expected from them, Nuri and Soshi grew old. Nuri became asthmatic, and Soshi's legs swelled up from her all too frequent bouts of filaria. There was no one to look after them when they were sick, care for them when they took to their beds. Soshi clucked her tongue in despair when Nuri couldn't breathe during an attack of asthma; Nuri took to drumming his mridanga relentlessly when Soshi came down with a fever. Sometimes they both railed against the unjust social system: even when dying, the elder sister of a man's wife couldn't pour a drop of water through his lips. A man could be pardoned for having a child with his wife's younger sister, but he could not run a hand over the pain-wracked body of the elder one.

As years passed and they both became old and gnarled, they loved and cared for each other more and more. The pain of one badly affected the other. They began to fondly refer to each other as 'old man' and 'old woman'. Before her female companions, Soshi would say: 'The old man's having it bad because of his asthma. There's no one at home to massage a drop of mustard oil on the soles of his feet. What high hopes he had pinned on that son of his! Indeed the man stayed on at his in-laws' only because of the boy. But the boy chose to move away. As long as I'm alive, I'll drag myself around, no matter how ill I am, and cook for the old man. But what will happen when I'm gone? How on earth will he manage? And yet he's not willing to swallow his pride and get in touch with his boy and ask him to come home. But I know how much he's missing him. They share the same blood, after all. I can read his mind as clear as daylight.' And before the menfolk Nuri would think aloud: 'The filarial fevers will be the death of the old woman. Six days a month she goes down and lies like a corpse. No one at home to put a drop of water in her mouth when she most needs it. She showered all her love on the nephew, loved him more than a mother would have, but the ungrateful boy never treated her as anything other than an aunt. Who knows whether he'll turn up to light her funeral pyre? That's the old woman's last wish. She might not say so in so many words, but don't I know what's on her mind?'

No one wanted to know just how they knew each other's mind without exchanging a word. But words have a way about them; they might remain unspoken, but they're never unknown. Even legs and hands speak. People betray their feelings through the slightest gestures: how a person walks says volumes about whether he or she likes or dislikes somebody, how food is served shows whether she cares or not. The way a man beats his mridanga reveals whether he's laughing or crying. Forty years of life under the same roof, seasoned by sorrows, hunger, depression and deprivation, worries and anxieties, regrets and anger, understanding and blaming one another had given them insight into each other's minds and hearts, although their lips were sealed, although they behaved as if the other person didn't exist. Words were unnecessary, redundant. Their understanding was as palpable as the fragrance of a flower spreading on the breeze, like the seeping of water into the parched earth, like the notes of the mridanga rising to the moon.

So when Soshi had a particularly terrible attack of fever, Nuri swallowed his pride and wrote to his son: 'Satyananda, may you live long. Your aunt is dying. Although she's not asking for you, her last wish is to see you. And she thinks her soul will have no salvation if you don't light her pyre. Come as soon as you can. Hurry. Treat this letter as a telegram. This will be the last time I will be making a request of you. And you will not have to come home ever again. Ever with good wishes for you, Nuri Das.'

Satya knew his father, proud as ever, had written for the sake of his dying aunt. He hadn't signed the letter 'your father'. Still he made haste to reach home with his wife and children. The salvation of his aunt's soul was more important than the tone and tenor of his father's request.

Soshi had stopped talking by the time Satya arrived; she couldn't move her lips even a little. Her eyes were half open, unblinking. She was breathing, but just barely. Did it register that her nephew had come at last?

But it struck Satya that the old woman had been waiting only for him; she passed away at dawn.

Back from the cremation grounds after Soshi's body had been consumed by the funeral fire, Nuri sat on the veranda into the gathering gloom of the evening, gently drumming his mridanga, softly repeating a kirtan refrain: 'Hare Krishna, Hare Krishna, Krishna, Krishna, Hare, Hare...'

Inside, Satya's wife was loudly sobbing and wailing: 'Where have you gone, Aunt, leaving us forsaken...' The loud wailing was supposedly for the satisfaction of the departed soul.

Satya sat by the oven, in which the fire had long ago died, calling out to his aunt, torrents of tears streaming from his eyes. The tears were for real. Would that help the soul find salvation?

Nuri drummed his mridanga all through the night to mourn the passing of his dead wife's dead elder sister. His fingers, bruised and bleeding, worked up a delirious beat for the salvation of Soshi's soul.

ANATOMY OF MADNESS

RAMACHANDRA BEHERA

Binay knew it would be inconvenient to have his father living with him in his cramped little first-floor flat. Besides, the old man, who had spent all his life in a village, would find it difficult to settle in to alien surroundings. One thing was certain: there'd be plenty of unpleasantness. For everyone. Was it worth the trouble? Did he have to be as dutiful a son as the mythical Sravankumar, who had carried his decrepit parents on his shoulders all over the world? The young man of today was weighed down by troubles of his own. He didn't have the time or inclination to think of his old parents tucked away in a village, let alone worry about them. Did Binay have to prove he was an exception? To make matters worse, his father had reportedly gone half-mad. That was what was hinted at in the letter he had received.

Binay's contact with his roots had become tenuous and could be summed up in a few words. While still a schoolboy, he had lost his mother. A thin, short, high-strung woman of few words, she had carried out all the chores, from tending the cattle to offering evening prayers with a lighted wick to the tulsi plant in the courtyard. She could never stop worrying about Binay. If he caught a cold, she'd go on a fast, which sometimes lasted a whole day, and offer multiple pledges and promises to gods and goddesses. Faith and devotion, she believed, could move mountains. Even a speck of dust on her darling boy caused her pain and suffering. After her death, a distantly-related widowed sister of his father ran the household, and she did her job with such finesse that people joked only government contractors could match her in misappropriating funds. His father was aware of what was going on—the villagers had started telling tales at the first opportunity—but he realized that to send her packing would be far worse. Besides, didn't she steal only to help out her wastrel of a son and a miserable married daughter, who was always in want? How she still managed to keep things going with the little money left after meeting Binay's boarding school expenses remained a mystery. She deserved praise, if anything.

His father was a loner, a recluse, now more than ever, and had not shown even the slightest desire to live with him in the town. For his part, Binay, too, never tried to persuade him. He had serious doubts whether Father would be able to recognize Suni, his daughter-in-law—although it was he who had selected her after a long search—let alone his eight-year-old grandson, Jim, and five-year-old granddaughter, Rosie. For the grandchildren too, the old man had become a remote figure. The family's village visits were infrequent, and the old man was more edgy than happy to have them around. Even his communication with his son remained a desultory affair: Son, your wife looks worn out, has she not been keeping well?... Tell your boy not to climb the guava tree, he won't listen to me... What's that ugly mark on your daughter's cheek, did she have a boil or something?... When will you come again?... Why don't you take a sack of fragrant rice when you leave? The harvest isn't far off... Vegetables and coconuts are being stolen regularly from our garden... There'll be no collection of honey this year... None of this was meant to elicit Binoy's opinion or suggestion, or for that matter his sympathy. The father simply had to go through the motions of making conversation with his visiting son. Left to himself he would have preferred silence. Somehow he was never comfortable in company and grew more diffident and ill at ease if he had to make small talk. Even dealing with the village shopkeeper was an ordeal; if the dhoti he bought had a tear, or the dal had some stones, he never went back to return or exchange them.

A distant uncle, who had retired as a schoolteacher about a year ago, had written to Binay at his office address. Binay found himself going through the letter again and again. The hint that his father had gone soft in the head was loud and clear. There was no cause for alarm yet, the uncle had generously added, though it did seem odd that a lonely old man was being left to languish in the village when his well-heeled son lived with his wife and children in a nearby town.

So what should the well-heeled son do now? Binay thought. Bring his father home? Obviously, yes! Have him see a doctor? Of course! Whether there was room for one more person in his tiny flat was no longer the question. The old father needed looking after, and if the son neglected him, it wouldn't look good. So, in the end, what mattered was what others expected of the son, not what the son wanted. Home from the office, he waited until he had changed and had tea with his children. Then he handed his wife the letter. 'Read this.'

Suni's face fell when she went through it. 'What will you do?' There was a nervous edge to her voice. 'Go see him? Shouldn't we all?'

'Is that enough?' Maybe yes. Just as long as people saw he cared for his old man.

'What else?' What did her voice betray—fear, anger? Or was it just a plaintive cry?

'I must bring him here.' His voice sounded harsh. Perhaps he wanted it to sink in that he would do as he pleased, that he'd brook no dissent. 'I must take him to the best doctor. My next course of action will depend on the medical opinion.' He paused. 'Worrying about the additional burden, are you?'

Suni blanched, feeling naked and exposed. Did he never mince his words? Who would believe he was the son of a shy and diffident man who was forever short of things to say? 'No, no, no trouble at all,' she said. 'Surely we can't sit back doing nothing when Father most needs our help. The question is, will he agree to come? Just think of the number of times we've tried and failed!'

He was pleasantly surprised: never before had his wife shown such spirit.

'Very well, I'll be off to the village early tomorrow morning. I've already applied for a day's leave. There's no need for all of us to make the trip. If I succeed in persuading Father to come with me, we'll be here before evening.' He got up. 'We'll give him the front room.'

Was it a suggestion or a command? She couldn't figure that out. Fear had started gnawing at her mind. With the children and Binay away from the house on weekdays, how would she spend time with a demented man under the same roof? Didn't mad people often turn violent? Why couldn't the old fellow be packed off to an asylum where he belonged instead of being let loose on her? How long would he stay? Suppose he took sick—God forbid, a stroke or something, which left him paralysed? Who would wash him and clean the sheets? She had neither the mind nor the strength to look after someone she was not close to. They had seldom met, and she had never warmed up to the reticent old man. How'd she bring herself to look after him?

She felt terribly apprehensive. It was like bringing home a time bomb. The eventual explosion would pulverize her world. The first casualty would be her children's studies. They would be constantly exposed to a madman's antics that only outsiders might find amusing. As far as she herself was concerned, she would need to lock herself in whenever she was alone; the household gadgets and goods would have to be kept out of the old man's reach. But why, oh dear, why did a man who'd never ever hurt a fly suddenly go mad? Was his tranquillity, his profound silence, no more than a mask, a mere facade? Did the deep-seated human instinct of violence rise up once the surface was scratched? The more she thought about the future the scarier it seemed, and the more she tried not to think about it the more she did. A menace seemed to hang in the air.

The next morning Binay took a taxi to his village and, because he had an early start, he covered the distance of one hundred and fifty kilometres before nine o'clock despite the very bad road. Their village house was a modest affair: four rooms, a tile roof, a small courtyard, and a wide front veranda.

He found his father on the veranda rummaging through an old tin trunk. A sign of his madness?

'So you've come?' his father said.

Binay observed him closely: a short, thin, pale old man, white hair, snow-white eyebrows, face furrowed with wrinkles, toothless gums. When had he last shaven—twenty, twenty-five days ago?

'Yes.' Binay sat down beside him.

'I wasn't expecting you.' He continued to rummage through the papers. 'How are the kids—all well?'

'All well.'

The old man sounded so normal, he seemed so much like his usual self that Binay's anxiety deepened. Nothing he noticed could remotely be considered madness.

'I didn't expect to find you home at this hour,' Binay said. 'What is it you're looking for among these papers?'

'The farm work's over for the time being and I'm free. God knows why I woke up this morning with an urge to reread your old letters. I remember I had stashed them away in this box.'

How normal he seemed! 'What made you stop shaving? It gives you a sickly look.'

The old man looked up with a smile. 'I've taken a leaf from a holy man's book. Whenever he spoke on the scriptures, about gods and goddesses, he got so carried away he shed tears. Watching and listening to him had such a powerful effect on me that I too began to imitate him—cry, laugh, whatever. People said even my gestures began to resemble his. Of course, I didn't do any of this consciously.'

Binay's heart sank, his face twitched. This wasn't the father he had known all along. He wasn't given to speaking so much in one breath, let alone expressing his profound feelings so freely. Could some bearded holy man's religious discourse have brought about such a dramatic transformation?

'Father,' he begged. 'I think you should come and stay with me.'

'Why not?' The old man's face brightened, his voice alive with a rare enthusiasm. 'Now that there's some respite from farm work, I was toying with the idea myself. Haven't seen the children for ages. Tell me, do you all say your evening prayers?'

After he had nodded yes, Binay felt a momentary stab of conscience. Why had he lied? But wasn't Father's eagerness to visit him a symptom of his madness? Never before had he shown the slightest desire to stir out of the village.

That afternoon, Binay dropped in at the retired schoolteacher's. After all, he was the uncle who had taken the trouble to write to him.

'There's this roughneck in the village,' Uncle said, 'a college dropout, who drinks like a fish. He terrorizes people at knifepoint and threatens to kill the villagers first, then the rest of humanity, and finally God Himself, disembowelling Him and plucking out His innards.'

Binay looked up, surprised.

'One afternoon when this hooligan was throwing his tantrum, your father pounced on him, gave him two stinging slaps, one on each cheek, and before the fellow could react, walked away, as if he had done nothing unusual.'

Uncle wiped his face with his towel and added, 'That evening I went to your place to tell your father off. I was blunt. It was not wise for an old man to take on a scoundrel like that, it could have cost him his life. Can you believe, he didn't even bat an eyelid, let alone admit that he had done something stupid? Worse still, the incident had gone clean out of his mind. Now Binay, what does that tell you?'

There was yet another incident the uncle thought was worth mentioning. An extremely poor man had lost his only son, the breadwinner of the family. The boy's death had left his family in dire straits. When Binay's father visited them he broke down and began to rave and rant. With tears streaming down his face, he berated the dead boy, calling him a coward for abandoning his hapless parents and asking if a sensible young man in his place would have done the same.

'Now tell me Binay, does this strike you as normal?'

'I've never known Father to behave like this,' Binay admitted.

'Me neither. I'm convinced the poor man's not in his right mind. Until recently he was the quietest man in the village. Those of us who love and respect him are unable to accept this change that's come over him.'

'Any instances of violent behaviour?' Binay enquired, after a long pause.

'Not so far. But there was this other incident just eight or ten days ago. Somebody was giving a wedding feast, and your father wanted to be among those who served food to the guests. There was absolutely no need for a frail old man like him to exert himself, but he wouldn't listen. You know what his explanation was? He was so happy to see a wedding without a dowry that he wanted to help out. Of course, strictly speaking, this wouldn't qualify as madness.'

What could Binay say? He was happy Father was eager to come home with him. Nothing else mattered. He looked forward to starting back immediately after lunch.

Walking back home, he wondered whether all those incidents added up to anything. Maybe Father, who had never before shown his true feelings, his gut reactions, was now past bothering about people's opinions; maybe he was past being a mere spectator, a shadow; maybe he had decided to give vent to the emotions he had so far reined in. Not one of the incidents showed Father in a poor light; whatever he had done was honourable, even ethical. There was nothing appalling or humiliating.

Instead of anxiety Binay felt an upsurge of respect for his old man.

'You live upstairs?' his father asked when they got off the taxi.

'Yes.'

'I may have trouble climbing the stairs.' But after two steps, he said, 'No problem. I think I can manage. Will the driver bring the bags up?'

Upstairs there was a deathly silence, as if everyone was in a state of shock. Scared, dry-mouthed, the children hung behind the door, watching every move of the old man. Even Suni wouldn't come near; she greeted her father-in-law from a distance, bowing to the ground.

'Good to see you, daughter,' the old man said cheerfully. 'But first I'd like to wash up. Where're the children? I don't see them.'

The children retreated into the darkest corner of the house. As Suni showed the old man the bathroom she found her heart thudding, her mouth as parched as a desert, her blood frozen.

After the bags were put away, the old man was settled in the front room. He seemed perfectly normal.

'People are perverse,' Binay told his wife, trying to allay her fear. 'They've been maligning Father for no reason at all. Can't you see he's perfectly normal?' He discovered his children hiding in the kitchen and wasn't amused. 'What have you told them?' he confronted his wife. 'That their grandfather's a raving lunatic?' He looked at the children. 'Look here, there's nothing the matter with Grandfather. Go and greet him, and better do it properly, touching your head to the ground. He's been asking after you.'

The children traded worried glances. Could they rely on Father's assurances? Mother's face was a blank.

Binay herded them into the front room. They had to be pushed closer to greet the old man and stopped from bolting at the first opportunity. They shrank at the touch of their grandfather's gnarled and trembling fingers.

'Which class are you in, my sweet little mad thing?' the old man beamed at his granddaughter.

Sweet little mad thing? What a curious form of address, Binay thought. But it seemed to exude love and warmth too, and Rosie showed exemplary courage. She had stopped cringing, and put her arms around the old man, her pale pink cheek against his bristles.

'Still in nursery school,' Binay answered for her.
'And the little imp?'
'Standard Three.'

The beaming old man hugged his grandchildren and then held them at a distance so he could feast his eyes on them. His crumpled, corrugated face glowed with pride and joy.

Binay could feel the atmosphere growing less oppressive.

By ten o'clock next morning—the children at school and Binay in his office—the house seemed to resonate with emptiness. Suni was in the kitchen and the old man out on the balcony; ten feet by four, leading on to both the front room and the bedroom, it overlooked a picture-perfect landscape. Binay had filled his father in on their neighbourhood while having his morning tea. The head office of the company in which he worked as an engineer had recently shifted here and it was only a matter of time before the locality would be bustling with many more residential blocks and amenities. The children's school was close by; in a few years it'd be one of the best addresses in the town.

'Daughter,' the old man suddenly said, 'did I hear someone knock at the door?'

Suni gave a start. Her attention had been on the cooking and she hadn't noticed her father-in-law hovering at the kitchen door. For a brief moment she wondered who he was and was so bewildered that she nearly let the frying pan slide off the gas ring. Why should anyone knock at the door instead of ringing the bell, she thought as she hurried to the front door.

There was no one at the door. When she hurried back, a trifle irritated, she found the old man stirring the pan.

'Who was it?' he asked, not looking up at her. 'Or did my ears play a trick on me?'

Suni felt a stab of panic. Who said this man was normal?

'There was no one at the door,' she said. 'Father, please leave the cooking to me. You don't have to see to it. Go and sit on the balcony or lie down on your bed.'

He spun around with a strange laugh, which made her close her eyes in fright. 'No one at the door? Was I hallucinating, then?'

As soon as he was out of the kitchen, Suni wiped the beads of perspiration from her neck and face, wondering if she shouldn't lock the kitchen door. She tiptoed to the doorway and peered out. The old man was sitting quietly, and the sight was as reassuring as it was disquieting. What was he? A human being of flesh and blood or just a shadow? Why was there such an air of unreality about him? How could she stay under the same roof with someone who made everything seem unreal to her?

She bolted the door, gulped down some water and, fighting back her tears, hurried through the cooking.

But she felt no better even when she went back to the bedroom and stood under the fan; her cold sweat wouldn't dry under the oppressive anxiety. The silence was unnerving. It was difficult to believe there was another soul in the house. She felt a chilling numbness within. Why was he so quiet? His silence had suddenly blurred the line between life and death. Couldn't he at least clear his throat, make some human sound, walk about, do something to show he was alive?

She tiptoed to the door and opened it a crack. The old man sat grinning at someone; the newspaper had fallen from his hands.

Presently he raised his hands as if he was clasping someone, someone tiny and dear, to his breast; his lips curved to assume the shape of a kiss and he seemed to caress the invisible being. The sight was disturbing. What was the old man up to? Was he actually holding someone she couldn't see? How could anyone think this man was normal? She wondered for the hundredth time, as a feeling of helplessness came over her. Should she run away from home, have a fight with Binay, tell him to take the old man back to the village? Never before in her life had she felt so vulnerable. She took a bottle of cold water from the refrigerator, washed her face and neck, and drank a few gulps. Then she switched on the television, wondering if she should keep the kitchen knife or Jim's cricket bat at hand as a weapon.

During lunch with his son, the old man suddenly turned talkative. 'Binay, have you noticed the jamun tree on the side of the road? I saw a sight I can't forget under it this morning. A young mother was suckling her child with such joy that I could feel the vibrations. Not even owning the house she was working hard to build would have given her greater happiness. You should have seen how she was caressing and kissing her little one.'

Binay and Suni weren't impressed. After all, a mother's love for her child was only normal, and they had witnessed such scenes before. But Suni could now fathom, with a sudden sense of relief, the gestures the old man had made earlier.

'Father,' she said. 'Remember the movements you were making this morning when you sat out on the balcony?'

'Making movements? Was I? Really?'

'You seemed to be hugging and kissing a baby. Your face radiated joy and you seemed lost to everything.'

'Was I?' He sounded not ashamed but pleased with himself. 'These days I forget things so fast. Sometimes I can't recall what I've done or seen or said even a moment earlier. Yes, sometimes I do catch myself making movements and gestures. Watching that fond mother—oh, yes, now it's coming back to me—I thought I, too, was holding a little child. So what's his name? I began to think. Binay, Suni, Jim, Rosie? How I wished I had had a real little thing in my arms, a baby that'd have made me forget the world, have made me feel I was greater than God Almighty Himself!' His eyes welled up with tears.

Binay and Suni were amazed. Father had never been so openly emotional.

The next day was a Sunday and the whole family was at home. The old man, after breakfast, was sitting out on the balcony, the expressions on his face changing like a kaleidoscope. Drained of blood, his face paled and twitched, lips trembled, and then finally tears came streaming down. From time to time he dabbed at his eyes, unaware he was being watched by his son and daughter-in-law.

'Father!'

The old man gave a start.

'You're crying!'

'Am I?' he wiped his sunken eyes. 'You're right.' He looked away and gazed down at the road. 'Can you see the funeral procession on its way to the cremation grounds? And can you see the grief-stricken young man following behind? I first imagined him to be Binay at his mother's funeral. Then I thought why should his mother be dead. It's I, his father. Imagining myself dead and laid out on the bier didn't sadden or scare me in the least. All I was thinking was how horrible it would be for my grieving son, how it'd break his heart to light my pyre.'

Binay and Suni were stunned. How cool, how collected, how normal Father seemed! How quiet his tone!

That afternoon around five something unforeseen happened. No one had noticed when the old man had slipped away from the balcony and gone down to the road where a fierce quarrel was in progress. The sound of his commanding voice above the din brought Binay and Suni scurrying out.

Egged on by onlookers, someone was mercilessly beating a woman, and the woman was trying to return a few blows. They no longer looked human but like fiery balls of beastliness and violence.

'Have you all ceased to be human?' the short, thin, white-haired old man seemed like a flame surrounded by darkness. 'Instead of breaking it up, you're enjoying it!'

No one paid any heed to his words. The beating, the howling, the exchange of vile curses continued unabated. Undaunted, the old man elbowed his way through the throng to the centre.

'Away with you, you old fool!' The wife beater gave him a violent push, sending him crashing to the ground. His lip split, his knees and elbows skinned, and a lump on his forehead.

After being seen by a doctor, the old man was taken home and made to lie on his bed. Though dejected and defeated, he gnashed his toothless gums.

'What on earth made you go there?' a distraught Suni demanded. 'Did you imagine you'd bring the brute to his senses?'

'I don't know what came over me. The thought that the man and the woman could be my Binay and Suni was more than I could bear. The earth, water and air seemed to whirl around me, and I don't remember what I did afterwards.' He paused. 'But I'm such a silly fool. Why should I have imagined the quarrelling couple to be my son and daughter-in-law? Something's wrong with me. Of late I seem to be at the epicentre of things—everything that's happening is happening to me; my family and I are the entire world; we're the ones who are being born and dying, loving and loathing, being loved and despised, grieving and being grieved for. I have never felt like this before. You know I'm basically a quiet old fellow, not given to displays of emotion.'

The old man looked devastated, as if he had set in motion something that had spun out of control, something that would cause irreparable damage.

'Binay.'

'Yes, Father.'

'Shall we go see a doctor?'

'But we saw a doctor only minutes ago,' Binay said, as if to reassure him. 'He gave you a shot and some medicine. Remember?'

'I was thinking of a psychiatrist.' A sigh. A tremor of hesitation. 'Maybe he'll know whether I've gone mad.'

A tremor passed through Suni. 'Father,' she said. 'Forget psychiatrists. You aren't mad. There's nothing wrong with you. The truth is you're turning over a new leaf, becoming a finer human being, a more evolved soul. Nothing of this kind ever happens without God's grace! It takes arduous penance to reach this state.'

LONGING FOR RAMAKANTA RATH
NRUSINGHA TRIPATHY

Hemalata is gone; she died early this morning, at around six, and has been cremated. I was present until only her ashes remained.

She had cancer of the uterus and had been in horrible pain for over a year. But mercifully and, miraculously, her pain let up—disappeared virtually—on the last day of her life. When she passed away she was profoundly at peace.

I had been by her bedside since returning from Cuttack last morning. Her husband, Lalatendu, whom I know from our college days, was with her too, but in a stupor. He would run his hand over his wife's body every now and then to check if she was still alive. All I did in those last twenty-four hours was read aloud from Ramakanta Rath's latest book of verse, *Sri Palataka*. I had met Rath in Bhubaneswar a couple of days earlier, and he gave me an inscribed copy for Hemalata. Could there have been a better parting gift, tangible or intangible, for a dying woman?

As soon as I began reading the poems her face, until then distorted with pain, became serene with self-realization. As if she had finally understood herself as never before, as if she was completely at peace, with no expectations. The poems seemed to have been written especially for her, giving expression to her innermost thoughts: an easy and uncomplicated surrender to a Supreme Being—God, Nature, what you will—who created life and death, interspersed with a childlike revolt.

Did her excruciating pain cease the moment I began reading Rath's poems? I'll never know, but her breathing became gentler, slower. Sometimes she seemed to forget to breathe. Either that, or, like the expert yogis, she could live without breathing. For she seemed to be doing what only great yogis can do—taking leave of her body and slipping back into it at will! And yet I know for a fact she had had no time for yoga or anything even remotely religious. All the idols and images of gods in their house belonged to her husband; she had nothing to do with them. She didn't get along with them, was what she claimed. Neither saint nor sinner, she never visited ashrams or temples. Could listening to Rath's poems have suddenly transported her to an inexplicable yogic state of mind? Not only I, but even Lalatendu wasn't prepared to believe anything of the kind.

What mattered in the end was that Hemalata died at peace; that was enough for me because I loved her, and I loved her more than her husband did. I had caught a glimpse of her soul, which Lalatendu never had; he was never one for subtleties. The difference showed in our responses to her death: it filled me with enormous relief, while it drove him over the edge.

Fifteen years ago Lalatendu and I were studying at Gangadhar Meher College in Sambalpur. He was studying science and I, history. Though we shared a room in the hostel for two years, we weren't great friends. We had little in common. I was happy-go-lucky with no great interest in my studies, content to scrape by; I knew I wouldn't be looking for a job after I finished college, since moves were already afoot to take me into the family business. I was bent upon enjoying life to the full until then. I wheedled a large amount of money out of my family and blew it on cigarettes, movies and eating out with friends. Things became worse when I decided to run for president of the students' union. I was free with my money, and our room became a hub of activities. Lalatendu hated the racket and would walk out in protest. A fiend for discipline, he was always up early, exercised regularly, ate sprouted gram and other healthy food, never touched fish or meat, never missed a class, and went to bed early after a light dinner. He wore a dhoti and kurta in those days and grew a beard. He disliked me and my friends for smoking, drinking mugs of tea, and debating the most frivolous of issues late into the night. Often he'd press his towel to his nose to keep out the cigarette smoke and leave the room, but not before making me angry with his remarks: 'Not only do you stuff your body with poison but you're dragging this bunch of fools down with you!' Only once did I retort: 'Your beard isn't worth all this poison.' To this day I don't know what I meant by that, it was such a stupid remark; I don't know what came over me to pick on his silly beard of all things. Obviously it stayed in his mind, and when we ran into each other ten years after we had left college he winced at the cigarette in my hand and remarked: 'So this poison is still worth more than my beard?' I, like a fool, shouted: 'Yes.' Hemalata was with him.

Although we hadn't met after college, news of him would reach me from time to time. He had gone on to do his masters in physics, teaching at several colleges, both private and government, and was last heard of when he was in Baripada. And of course he had married Hemalata.

She was two years our junior at college and, being a science student, had often sought Lalatendu out for notes. Tall, slim, fair complexioned—somehow her face was fairer than the rest of her body—she stood out from the rest of the college beauties. She had sparkling eyes, which were as eloquent as they were hesitant, and a tiny black birthmark just below her nose. I had my eye on her; so did many others. Whenever she was on stage for college functions, most often as part of a chorus, my eyes would remain riveted on her. But never once did I speak to her.

She became a schoolteacher after she graduated, and when Lalatendu proposed she accepted. After their marriage they lived and worked all over north Odisha until they came back to Sambalpur. I ran into them when they were looking for a house to rent.

As for me, as soon as I left college I was drafted into the family business. Considered a wastrel and a spendthrift, I was given the Baragarh bookshop to run, under the strict supervision of my older brother, and married off shortly afterwards. Years passed. Our business grew. Contrary to expectations, I didn't do too badly, and when a branch opened in Sambalpur I was put in charge. We built a house on the land we had at the foot of Budharaja Hills. It had two identical halves, an apartment for me and another for my brother, connected by a door. Since my brother stayed on in Baragarh, we let out his portion. Meanwhile my father had retired and come home from Jamshedpur to help my mother and brother in Baragarh. Of course it was my mother who held the family together. It was she who decided that I would spend the weekends at our Baragarh home, where my wife lived and where my children went to school. The arrangements were fine by me; I got used to this life. In addition to looking after the business I became a correspondent for a daily newspaper.

A month before Lalatendu and Hemalata arrived in Sambalpur the rented half of the house fell vacant, so I made them an offer they found hard to refuse. When they came to see the place one evening, Hemalata fell in love with it right away. The sun was going down behind the hill and the shadows were creeping up. There was a gentle breeze and the ashoka tree by the fence was murmuring. Hemalata turned to her husband and said in a sing-song voice:

> Journeying across shaded foothills
> You arrive
> Like the soothing caress of the breeze.

Lalatendu snorted in scorn: 'What madness!' It was only long afterwards, after we got to know each other well and she read out to me poems from *Saptam Ritu*, that I realized that she had been quoting a line from Rath.

They took the apartment. Not because it was well appointed or convenient—from their point of view, it was anything but—but because it had magically brought alive a line of Rath's poetry for Hemalata.

After they moved in we became close. Lalatendu had retained the orderliness and discipline of his student days. He took long morning walks, topping them off with yoga, stayed off fish and meat, went to and returned from college at fixed hours, exercised in the evening before giving tuition to a few students, ate only fruit and sprouted gram for dinner and went to bed early. He continued to wear a dhoti and kurta too. The only discernible change was that his beard had started greying in tufts. Their seven-year-old sofa, which looked as good as new, epitomized his high standards of cleanliness and orderliness. Their toilet and bathroom, which he cleaned himself, were so spic and span they seemed not to have ever been used.

Hemalata, however, was supremely indifferent to housekeeping. She did nothing according to schedule—eating, bathing, or sleeping. Lalatendu would remind her from time to time about her neglect of their daughter and the household duties, but to no effect. She continued to be as unmindful as ever, and, muttering under his breath, Lalatendu would do all the chores—wash his wife's clothes, put them out in the sun and fold them when they were dry, do the shopping, bathe and feed their daughter and get her ready for school, drop her at school and bring her home. Hemalata's hours of teaching were from morning to twelve noon, and all she would do by way of cooking was put the rice and dal on to boil before she left; the rest was done by Lalatendu.

When she came home I would hear her putter about the house all afternoon, pacing from the sitting room to the kitchen to the bedroom back again to the sitting room, in one unending movement. It was obvious she didn't take a siesta in the long afternoons. Sometimes I would come out to the front veranda shared by both apartments and stroll from one end to the other, trying to peep into their sitting room.

'Aren't you bored?' I'd ask if I saw her.

She would open their door and invite me in. I was always trying to turn our conversation towards beginning an affair, but she took no notice. As soon as I arrived she would reach eagerly for a book of poems and start reading aloud. I would be transfixed—not by her passionate reading but by her; my eyes riveted on her the whole time. Sometimes when her sari slipped off her shoulders, a quick glance at her bosom would set my heart racing.

'What beautiful lines!' she'd gush, closing the book. 'I've never read better poetry! I wish I could meet him.'

'Meet whom?'

'Ramakanta Rath. Haven't you heard of him? You're in the book business and you haven't heard of him? How strange!'

What was she gabbing about? 'Look, I sell textbooks. Not poetry. Who buys poetry?'

She would make tea. She would invite me to join her for a walk around the garden. She'd stop by the lemonwood tree, pluck some of its dazzling white flowers and, quoting lines of poetry, throw them into the air. Sometimes a flower or two would fall on me and provoke me into fantasizing about my chances with this woman.

I was so besotted with her that I cut down on the time in the shop so I could be home in the afternoons when Lalatendu and their daughter were not around. Sometimes, when all of us were together, I would take perverse delight in praising Hemalata for her taste and run down Lalatendu for his cut-and-dried life of empty ideals.

After a year had passed since they became my tenants—the wheel of life turning as much as before—three things became all too apparent. One, husband and wife, poles apart in temperament, had no great love for each other; if anything, he felt scorn for her, while she was totally indifferent towards him. Two, the wife was crazy about Ramakanta Rath's poetry. She had all his books and placed them prominently in their sitting room, giving the impression that she valued them more than the holy books. (Noticing how taken she was with Ramakanta Rath, I, like a sly operator, had once tried to lead her on. 'I often go to Cuttack and Bhubaneswar to buy books,' I said. 'Why don't you come with me? I can take you to meet Ramakanta Rath.' But she laughed it off: 'I can't be bothered. If we were destined to meet, he'd come here.') Three, ignored by her husband, she was liable to be vulnerable and therefore might eventually succumb to my overtures. What else could explain why she let her sari slip, why she threw flowers on me? Her obsession with Rath's poetry was fine by me. She could admire it all she wanted as long as she had a fine little affair with me on the side. Sometimes I thought she was quite right not to take me up on my offer and come with me to Bhubaneswar. There was no point in getting a bad name. Whatever we could do in Bhubaneswar we could do right here; all she needed to do was take the latch off the connecting door and we'd have whole afternoons to ourselves.

I had long ago moved the almirah from in front of the connecting door, hoping she would seize the chance. Or, was she waiting for me, timid as I am, to take the initiative? Just looking at the connecting door would give me goose pimples, and I'd go so dry in the mouth that I'd have to drink several glasses of water.

One Sunday afternoon Lalatendu was home alone and I invited him for tea. Instead of tea, he opted for a cup of Horlicks. We began to chat.

'Who's this Ramakanta Rath?' he suddenly asked. 'Do you know him? Where does he live?'

'Search me!' I said. 'I first heard about him from your wife. But if you want I'll make enquiries the next time I go to Cuttack.'

'Too late,' he said in anger. 'The horrible fellow has already cast a spell over my wife. My life's ruined.'

'What's happened?' My curiosity was aroused.

The picture Lalatendu painted was of an affair between Hemalata and Ramakanta Rath. She had discovered Rath in college, where she began to read and write poetry, and had devoured his books ever since. His poems had addled her poor brain, and she'd more or less gone off her hinges. 'They must be writing to each other,' he sighed. 'She must be using her school address. And all those trips she makes to Cuttack for office work are merely a facade. She must be meeting her lover.' Nothing else could explain her total indifference to her husband.

Total indifference? Why, that was a heartening piece of news as far as I was concerned. The coast was clear. I kicked myself for having taken so long to catch on.

All I needed was to be a little bolder. A little courage is all you need, I reminded myself, if you hope to have an affair. I had always been a coward, a slowcoach, when it came to women, and there had been quite a few instances of that. Once a lady lecturer from a local college had dropped in at the shop to buy books, and we had sat chatting for more than hour. Twice she brushed her legs against mine and said 'sorry' with such an inviting smile that I should have taken the hint. Then there was the schoolteacher who used to place large orders with us. I always gave her a good discount. She gave me her address and invited me over several times. No fewer than a hundred times I must have set out for her place, but my legs would refuse to round the corner to her house. If I hoped to succeed with Hemalata, I needed to show more courage.

That night I fantasized so much I didn't sleep well.

The next day was Monday, and all afternoon I waited with bated breath, pricking up my ears at the smallest sound on their side. Hemalata came home, opened the door, walked across the sitting room to her bedroom, switched on the fan, and then to the kitchen to get her lunch, which she carried back to the bedroom to eat on the bed. I heard her put the plates in the kitchen sink, go back to the bedroom and flop down on the bed.

Now's the time, a voice prompted me from within. Get going.

I knocked on the connecting door.

Hemalata opened it.

'Oh, good!' she said. 'I'm glad you knocked. I was about to do that myself.'

Congratulating myself on my courage, I sat at the foot of her bed. She put a pillow against the headboard and lay back.

'I seem to be in luck today,' I said. 'Today could be the day of my tryst with destiny.'

'Destiny?' She closed her eyes. Her sari had slipped down from her shoulder. Should I put it back? I was debating with myself when she opened her eyes. 'Speaking of destiny, do you know what is in our destiny?' Her voice was so low and soft I nearly blurted out: 'Love!' She picked up a book from the bedside table and leafed through it. 'Listen to this. About destiny.' She read out as if she were reading from the holy scriptures:

> Remorse is our destiny
> It joins me to the hills, to the sky,
> To trees and to the wind.
> It wanders from year to year,
> from aeon to aeon...
>
> I had met it long ago,
> in a dream.
> It looked like a mendicant
> Dressed in rags...

All I could make out of all this was that poor Hemalata had had the bad luck of tying herself to a man as dull as a hill and was full of remorse. But who was the man in tattered rags like a sanyasi—Lalatendu? I couldn't agree more. 'You're bang on,' I said. 'One doesn't get to enjoy the company of a woman like you unless it's in one's destiny. By God's grace.'

'God?' Hemalata winced. 'Why bring in God? What has He got to do with it? Has anyone seen Him?'

Unwittingly, I had ruffled her feathers. 'Or call it luck,' I mollified her. 'Whatever it is, I'm sure our relationship will remain true the rest of our lives.'

She smiled enigmatically, rifled through the pages and recited:

> Yes, it's all counterfeit.
> I live a counterfeit life,
> smile a counterfeit smile and
> weep counterfeit tears,
> My face is a paper mache mask
> daubed with miscellaneous paints by
> a scatterbrained painter...

She seemed to have memorized the whole book. 'Whether God is a lie or not,' she said, 'what's important to find out is whether or not we are lies.'

'Oh, we're not,' I said. 'You and I—we aren't lies. Besides, we'll continue to remain as true to each other as we are today.'

'Pramod,' she laughed, rubbing her eyes. 'Ages and ages have gone by. Millions of men and women have been born. They have lived and they have died. They have lived their brittle lives, made love, had their hopes and dreams. What has happened to them? Where have they all gone? What has happened to their dreams? What has happened to their suffering?'

Damned if I know, I thought to myself. The discussion had gone off on a tangent. All this meaning of life—no, not my cup of tea. Who the hell is interested in such useless, never-ending discussions! So I asked her for some water, and when she got me a glass I made sure my fingers lingered on hers a few long moments. She seemed oblivious to it. Don't expect more, I reminded myself. You can't expect her to go all the way right at first. It takes time to get over shyness. Give it time, and she'll be yours.

It was already late in the afternoon, and Lalatendu was expected any time. What if he turned up earlier? I felt a little jittery and wanted to call it a day, but Hemalata hadn't finished. She proposed we go for a walk and out into the garden we went.

We walked in the shade to the lemonwood tree. She stopped beside it, caressed it lovingly, picked a handful of flowers and threw them into the air, and, with what I thought was a love-struck glance at me, recited:

> Stay here,
> among these stars and these flowers.
> Keep, if it pleases you,
> a fragment of our shared bad luck...

The lines as usual went over my head. Was Hemalata talking in code? What was all that about the company of the stars and the flowers? What about the fragment of shared bad luck? Surely she meant good luck! Never mind a bit of obscure poetry, I sighed. As long as I make progress with the object of my desire.

We slowly walked back to the veranda and sat next to each other. I concentrated on touching her hand as often as possible, while, oblivious to my little game, she spouted lines of poetry.

'You know, Pramod,' she said suddenly, staring off into the sky, 'the most painful thing in life is childbirth.'

I understand, I replied in silence, but you needn't worry, your worst fears won't come true. I wish you'd come out with it when we were in the bedroom. I could've shown you I had come prepared. Pregnancy and childbirth? Don't worry, Hemalata. Aren't you one dimwit!

'The pain the child feels slipping out of the mother's womb is as great as the mother's,' Hemalata explained. 'God, if at all He is there, has made it that way. And it is said that at the height of pain or pleasure a human being catches a momentary glimpse of the mystery of his life and death, of his past and future, of the meaning of creation. It seems that's what happens to both the child and the mother. Both have that vision, but just for a split second. The next moment their senses take over and they forget everything. But when my daughter was born I was so indifferent to everything I had no such vision.'

My irritation was spiralling. What was all this hogwash about labour, pain, childbirth and vision? I had come prepared and that was the end of the problem.

'I assure you,' I said, plucking up my courage, 'you won't have to go through the pain of childbirth again.'

'Oh, it's not my pain I've been talking about,' she said. 'I'm talking about Ramakanta Rath's pain.'

'His pain?' I wondered aloud.

'Yes,' she said gravely. 'His pain of giving birth.'

'Don't be silly,' I laughed. 'How can a man ever experience the pain of childbirth?'

'Who knows?' she said. 'He might have experienced it. His *Saptam Ritu* poems must have been born of such pain.'

I saw her eyes were closed.

Why did she have to bring up that blasted poet? I was getting fed up. But when I took another look at her serene face my first impulse was not to slap it but to caress it. How I'd have loved to do that! But her husband was expected at any moment, and I rose. She did too and, leaning close to me, removed the dry stem of a lemonwood flower from my hair, flicking it down the veranda. It was such an endearing gesture that my hopes started to soar once again.

Two months had passed since this incident, and I was ready to expire from my all-consuming desire for Hemalata. We had met no fewer than ten or twelve times already, mostly in the long afternoons when no one was around, and in the utter privacy of her bedroom too, but bedding her remained a distant dream. I felt in limbo, in suspended animation of some kind, incapable of going forward or back.

Then one day when Lalatendu left suddenly for Bhawanipatna to see his ailing mother, I decided to seize the chance. That night I went over to their apartment on the usual pretext of having a chat. As usual, she held forth for an hour or so on poetry I neither understood nor wanted to understand. Then I invited her to my apartment. She got up without a fuss. Her daughter was already asleep, and she bolted the door to her bedroom. I couldn't help but admire her presence of mind. It would not be good if the little girl awoke in the middle of the night and surprised us in bed.

In the middle of the conversation she continued in my bedroom, she said how grateful she was that I understood her better than her husband did. I needed no more encouragement. Nestling close to her, I held her hand and began caressing it. She did not pull it away, she did not protest. On the contrary, she playfully pinched my cheek, ran her hand through my hair, and came out with a fragment of a poem I suspected was no one else's but that Rath's.

> This body is a beggar.
> It stops at all the doors
> on its route
> and asks for alms...
> My soul is a postman
> Seeking itself
> at addresses made over to it.

She held both my hands. 'Didn't I once tell you it takes the mother only a moment to forget the all-searing, all-revealing vision of creation brought on by the terrible pain of childbirth?'

I looked at her uncomprehendingly. What was she babbling on about again?

'Even if someone were to ask me like an abject beggar for this body of mine,' she said, 'I couldn't offer it to him.' She broke into a convulsive sob.

She cried bitterly all night long. I rocked her in my arms. That was when she told me, for the first time, that she had cancer of the uterus. She had known about it for over a year. Her days were numbered.

I felt a chill run through me. I felt abject and mortified. Every time I looked at her I was awash with pity. Poor Hemalata. Poor me.

All my desire for her drained out of me. Towards the early hours I washed her face with cold water. I had never felt such love for anyone else.

'Why have you kept it from Lalatendu?' I asked, as I was accompanying her to their door.

'What's the point?' she said. 'Why hasten his grief? Let it wait until the end.'

'Don't you have any wish, any desire, you want fulfilled?'

'No, none I can think of.' She paused and smiled. 'But I think a tiny little wish has germinated within me!'

'What is it?'

'How I wish I could unite with Ramakanta Rath in death.'

I was stunned.

In the last two years of her life I was around all the time, and in the final three months I even stopped going outside Sambalpur. My business suffered; eventually things were such that if I didn't replenish my stock my business would have gone under. So I was forced to leave Hemalata for a couple of days.

I took a bus to Cuttack. It was a very unpleasant ride. I read something in the papers which sickened me to the core. Two brothers from Puri had been to Bhubaneswar on an errand and were returning home in the evening. Somewhere near Pipili the younger one, the pillion rider, took out a knife and hacked at his brother, severing his head from his torso in two strokes. 'Oh mother!' the dying man was heard screaming. 'My own brother's killed me!' How ironic, I thought. On the one hand, there was Hemalata, who seemed to have been waiting for death ever since she was born, and on the other, there was this younger brother, who was so oblivious to the end that awaits us all that he murdered his own brother in cold blood. What an enigma life is!

In Cuttack my shopping took all morning, but I was free by the afternoon. So, when a publisher friend asked if I wanted to join him on a short trip to Bhubaneswar, I was game. I suddenly wanted to meet Ramakanta Rath. To this day, I don't know why this impulse came over me. It wasn't something Hemalata had ever even remotely hinted at.

It was almost evening when I reached Ramakanta Rath's house. Luckily, he was at home. Wearing a dhoti, with a white shawl around his shoulders, he was getting ready for his evening prayers. There had been a squall earlier on, and there was no electricity. In the dying light of the day Rath looked more like a century-old white dove waiting for death than a flesh-and-blood human being.

On a sudden impulse I began telling him all about Hemalata. It just came pouring out in a great gush, and took maybe upwards of an hour. When I finished and rose to leave, Rath said, 'Your Hemalata is the greatest honour I'll ever receive.' He gave me a signed copy of his latest book of poems, *Sri Palataka*, for her. Only after I had reached Cuttack did I open it. All Rath had written was: 'To Srimati Palataka, Madam Escapist, from Sri Palataka, Mr Escapist.'

The first thing I did on reaching Sambalpur was give Hemalata the book.

She opened it and was so stunned that her eyes became still. 'I knew,' she said in a faint voice. 'I knew we'd meet at the time of my death.'

I spent the whole day yesterday reading out the *Sri Palataka* poems again and again. Time and again she begged me to go over what seemed to be her favourite lines.

> The nearer she comes
> The more I am aware
> that life has not ended,
> that an eternity of joy
> has just become real and
> has just begun...

Towards the small hours of the night, when Lalatendu and I, both dog-tired, were just falling asleep, Hemalata shook us awake.

'Goodbye,' she said cheerfully. 'I'm leaving. Everything's fine.'

NEWS OF THE DAY

KANHEILAL DAS

10 May

I'm in bed reading the newspaper, with Prasanti fast asleep beside me. An irritating cacophony of mosquitoes surrounds us.

Transport Strike Paralyses Koraput

Jeypore: *A wildcat strike by transport department employees hit the bus service across the entire district hard yesterday. As soon as the strike was called, buses no longer plied the roads, seriously inconveniencing passengers. This being the wedding season, there were several instances of guests getting stuck in the brides' villages.*

Wildcat strikes were unheard of when my wedding took place. I remember we boarded an express bus and went to Prasanti's town, which seemed bathed in peace and tranquillity. Every house had a garden in front; they all looked the picture of prosperity. When I sat with Prasanti on the wedding platform reciting the mantras, beautiful young girls in colourful saris stood around cheering us. I was overcome with the inexplicable desire to reach out and pluck the flowers from their saris and weave them into garlands. Prasanti, I remember, entered my home with a garland around her neck. She grew a tiny garden in front of our house. The house prospered. There was plenty of food and clothes with flowers printed on them. A year later, when little Anand was born, Prasanti seemed to take on a glow. But she stayed up late into the night, fanning mosquitoes from the little child with the end of her sari. Gone are those days. Now all she does is sleep. Like a log.

Goods Train Derails at Raniganj

The striking transport employees removed fishplates from the railway tracks two miles before Raniganj, causing two wagons of a goods train carrying coal to derail. The police have been deployed at all major stations of the Eastern Railway to forestall further mishaps. The situation is reportedly under control.

Train rides were my greatest joy, my addiction. Before marriage, I'd jump onto any old passenger train whenever the whim overtook me and take off for places I'd never been to. I loved setting foot on unknown soil and meeting strangers. When Anand was only a few months old, I took him and Prasanti to Sundargarh to visit a cousin of hers. What a ride that turned out to be! As the train chugged along in the dark, I sat by a window, watching stations come and go. Little Anand had his head in my lap and his tiny, rosy dimpled feet in Prasanti's. Prasanti was dozing. From time to time I craned my neck towards her like a giraffe and silently blew her kisses. At one point, all of a sudden, the train picked up speed with a tremendous jolt. The wheels clanked and screeched, and the lights went out. We were tossed around in the compartment like so many sacks. The train had jumped the rails. I groped amid the clutter of boxes, suitcases, and hold-alls and found Prasanti at last, first her feet and then the rest of her. We were in the hospital for fifteen days. Prasanti was a changed person when she came home. She withdrew into a cocoon. She began to sleep like a log. She said she was tortured by the memories of her dead baby. She still is.

Price of Paddy Soars

Subhendu Mund reports that the hike in the paddy procurement prices at the beginning of the year is likely to cause widespread discontent. The increase does not seem to be in the farmers' interest either. Discussion centres around how people will cope with rising prices until the next harvest. Protest meetings are being planned in several places. The government would do well to take necessary steps before the matter gets out of hand.

Things were back to normal. Well, almost. But then prices began to jump. Like the tongues of a leaping flame. Prasanti began to waste away. The marrow of her bones seemed to melt. She would go into the kitchen and come out soaking with sweat. The slightest exertion would leave her panting. The corners of her eyes turned dark, the colour faded from her lips. Then, one day, she confided to me she was expecting again. I fussed over her, trying to make her get over the bitterness of Anand's passing. I had names for the unborn child: Sundar, if a boy; Kalpana, if a girl. Prasanti would stare at me blankly. I filled the almirah with tins of Amul milk powder from the black market. Occasionally Prasanti would emerge out of her cocoon and become her lively self again. Somehow she had a presentiment that she would have a daughter this time. In the afternoons, she would undo the plait in her hair and sit with outstretched legs, stitching tiny frocks. It was like the old days again, well almost. She chatted a lot, scratched my back, ran her fingers through the hair on my chest. But those days didn't last. Not long enough. These days she remains asleep, fast asleep.

Provident Fund Employees Demonstrate

Bhubaneswar: *In response to a call by the General Secretary of the staff union, the employees of the Provident Fund Office demonstrated in front of the Commissioner's office yesterday. An eight-point charter of demands, which includes an immediate DA hike and implementation of the new pay scale, was submitted. If the demands are not met within a month, a spokesman has warned, an all-India strike will follow.*

It was on the issue of the pay hike that the staff union in our office called a strike while Prasanti was in the hospital. I was pacing the corridor in front of the labour room, smoking one Charminar after another. Sundar, if a boy; Kalpana, if a girl. My nerves were strung tight. But then the world came crashing down around us. The nurse came for me. I went inside and put my hand on Prasanti's head to console her. Then I left and headed straight for the demonstration at the office. I shouted my lungs out. Kalpana was stillborn. That was the end of the road for Prasanti. Life ebbed out of her. She stopped talking. She ate very little, she swallowed pills of every kind and colour, and slept. Now she sleeps the whole time.

Suspect Arrested

Balasore: *In an unusual display of swift action, the ASI of the local police station has nabbed and sent to the lock-up one Ashok Maiti. The culprit was caught red-handed in the early hours of 8 May, while he was trying to burgle a house in Manikhamba. The man hails from Khankhola of Hooghly and is suspected of being involved in a string of burglaries. Investigations continue.*

After the tragedy I tried hard to give Prasanti whatever happiness I could. I borrowed large sums of money and bought her fancy saris and jewellery of the latest designs. But she never wore them; everything was unceremoniously stashed away in the almirah. One morning, when I awoke, I found Prasanti staring blankly ahead. The almirah was wide open. For the first few minutes I couldn't comprehend anything. Then

Prasanti pointed to the back door, which was wide open too. All the happiness I had bought her from the market was gone. The burglar was never caught. Prasanti had slept through the night as soundly as she always did.

Acute Scarcity of Foodgrains and Kerosene

Balasore: *In addition to the shortage of foodgrains, the scarcity of kerosene has severely hit this area. Rice sells for ₹2.50 a kilogram, as does flour. The price of semolina has shot up to ₹3 a kilogram and Dalda vegetable oil to ₹14. Kerosene has all but vanished from the market during the last two months and is not available even at ₹1.50 a litre. The majority of the inhabitants of the town, daily wage earners without any regular source of income, are facing starvation. The government must step in and open at least two or three fair-price outlets to ensure the public distribution of essential commodities.*

I shut the paper and throw it over my head. Must stop buying papers. The news is the same everyday—demonstrations, agitations, strikes, sabotage, burglaries, fires, suicides, price rises, starvation deaths... What's new?

Prasanti is scratching her neck. Perhaps a mosquito has bitten her. She looks as lifeless as a sheet of paper covered with bites.

She rolls on to her side, facing me. The top button of her blouse is undone. I feel the slow stirrings of desire.

A mosquito flies past my ear, I can hear its drone. I get up and fix the net.

I call Prasanti several times. She just moans a little, without waking. I switch off the light, crawl into bed beside her, lifting her thin hand and putting it across my waist. Her breath on my cheek is hot.

After a while I think there's not just one but several mosquitoes inside the net. They're buzzing about. I wave a hand at them and with the other undo the remaining buttons of Prasanti's blouse. I feel a mosquito settling on the back of my hand. Before it can sting me, I flail my hand about.

I call out to Prasanti again. But she's like a corpse. How I wish she'd wake up, put her hands around my neck, and coo the words of love we forgot a long time ago.

A mosquito brushes past my nose. I press my lips on Prasanti's cheek. How I wish she'd wake up and kiss me.

A mosquito stings me on the cheek. I slap at it. I get out of the bed and switch on the light.

There are mosquitoes inside the net, trying to hide in every fold and corner.

I sit still, my eyes riveted on Prasanti. Even if I were to cut her in two she'd not wake up. Not before sunrise.

I slowly undress her and turn her on her back.

A bloated mosquito flies past. I try to squish it with a clap, but end up hurting my own hands. The mosquito flies away and settles on Prasanti's breast. As soon as I lift my hand, it flies away again.

I feel a sharp pain in my back. Then I see a mosquito landing on Prasanti's chin. It looks like a birthmark.

As I watch quietly, I see hordes of mosquitoes landing on Prasanti's body—her face, breasts, belly, thighs and legs. What a sight.

Helpless, I get up to switch off the light. It's then I see Prasanti's body for what it really is—a sheet of newspaper. And in it, without the slightest difficulty, I can read the headlines: railway strike, labour unrest, demonstrations, agitations, price rise, fires, suicides, starvation deaths…

THE WHORE: A LOVE STORY
KAMALAKANTA MOHAPATRA

Ghana was besotted with the little whore, a beautiful young girl from the south, dark and smooth as ebony, who had hit town some seven or eight months back. He saved the little money he made on the side and cut down on cigarettes and paan so he could visit her at least once a week. A bit thick-skinned, and you can cadge a couple of cigarettes and paan from colleagues and visitors, Ghana would chuckle to himself, but free whores? Maybe in some bygone golden age. Sometimes, tickled by the idea, he'd ask an unsuspecting colleague out of the blue: 'So brother, when will the golden age return?' At the look of incomprehension on the colleague's face he would break into bouts of helpless laughter. 'You never know with that crackpot,' the man would remark later. 'Who can guess what strange thoughts are going through his head!'

Ghana had already taken two important decisions: one, never to let his whoring friends wise up to the existence of his darling; two, never to go to her in the evening, when there was a queue outside her hut and a dim, smoking kerosene lamp inside. He preferred to skip office and drop in during the afternoon, when there was no line, when a million arrows of dust-speckled sunlight, piercing through the holes in the thinning thatch of the hut, transformed the girl into a magical being.

'You're the only one who comes by during the daytime,' she noted.

'Your place is a hundred times better than my office,' he replied, dropping a ripe grape into her mouth. 'It's so much better to be with you. Makes me feel younger, healthier, wiser.'

'What do you sit on in your office? A chair, or the floor like here? Do you have mats?'

Lazily trailing his fingers over the uncluttered expanse of her naked body, he smiled. 'Remind me to take you to my office on a holiday so you can see for yourself.' He gently ran his fingers over the pink birthmark in the middle of her right cheek, something he always did. Not a bad idea, he thought to himself. Most relatives, especially those from villages, wanted to be given a tour of the town; in order of importance the office figured right after Lingaraj Temple and the Khandagiri and Udayagiri hills.

'Have one more,' he said, holding a grape inches above her half-parted lips. 'Have you any idea how much a quarter-kilo of these costs? Never mind, I'm keeping track mentally. The day it adds up to fifteen rupees you'll be mine for free.'

'But you eat half of them!'

'Do you think I like grapes? Hell, no! I need to eat a few to keep up my strength. So you could say I'm eating them for your benefit and pleasure, my dear.'

'Take me away from here.'

'Where to?' he smiled, stroking her well-oiled curly hair. 'To the office? It's a den of wolves. They'll take less than five minutes to tear you to pieces.'

'Is it any better here?'

He caressed her face.

'Tell me,' she said. 'Doesn't anyone make a comment when you slip out of the office and head here?'

Outside, a dog rushed past the hut, yelping as if its tail was on fire, followed by a woman whose juicy abuses and curses made him chuckle. A bird landed on the palm-leaf thatch. The whore waved lazily, ineffectually at the ceiling.

'For my colleagues it's the secretariat I'm visiting on these occasions. Who'd imagine that I'm headed for the sextariat instead?'

'Someday you'll be caught.'

'Pants down?'

The girl laughed. 'Don't worry. I'll hide you in a corner.'

'The day you save me I'll reward you with a pomegranate. Not a tiny, sickly home-grown pomegranate, but a big, juicy one, imported from Afghanistan. And I swear I'll not eat a single seed myself.'

'If you only watch me eating it, I'm sure I'll end up with a bellyache.'

'If my hungry eyes can give you a bellyache, how come you're still in one piece? Is there any part of your body I don't covet?'

She laughed.

He looked around. A garish calendar of Lakshmi, goddess of wealth, hung on the mud wall. Close to it was a bamboo stake driven into the wall, weighed down by clothes. An aluminium pot hung from the ceiling in a jute sling. A glance at it and Ghana smelt dried fish. His whore, generous in her nakedness, lay sprawled in the middle of the room, and he sat cross-legged like a devotee beside her. Near the mattress a soldierly line of black ants led to a dead beetle, and two flies sat eyeing a red bindi fallen on the floor.

There were heavy footfalls outside.

'The police?' he asked in a whisper.

'My uncle,' she laughed. 'He wears shoes two sizes too big with wads of paper stuffed into them.'

'Does the bugger give you a little pocket money sometimes?'

'Pocket money? Are you dreaming? He grumbles when he has to buy me oil, soap and talcum.'

'Your clients must give you tips.'

'Not everybody, and not always. But where can I hide the little I get? I tried the rafters, but that aunt of mine sniffed out my cache. To hell with that barren bitch!'

'Why don't you open an account in a bank?'

'A bank? Keep money in a bank?'

'I'll take care of your account for you.'

'Hey, hey, take me for a dimwit, do you? Want to give with one hand and take away with the other?'

Ghana laughed. 'Come, open your mouth. Here's the last grape.' He squeezed the overripe fruit between his fingers and smeared the juice on her lips. 'So you think I'm a con man?'

'Took it to heart, did you?'

The sound of dogs fighting came from far off.

'Sounds like our Tiger,' she said. 'He's always getting into fights.'

'His wound has healed?'

'It never will.'

Ghana wadded the empty paperbag into a ball. 'You should have a clock. Necessary for the clients.'

She snatched the ball from his hands. 'No one but you wants to know the time. You're the only one who comes during office hours.'

Ghana snatched the ball back.

'You know something?' she said. 'I confronted that bloody uncle of mine yesterday. I told him point-blank that if he ever lined up more than seven clients a night, he'd find me gone one fine morning. The bugger can sing the Lord's praises all he wants.'

'That must've pissed him off.'

'Of course it did. What does he think, that he and his bitch of a wife can live off me? I didn't come here to wear myself out!'

'Time we went to Puri on a little outing,' Ghana said, slowly caressing her quivering belly. 'Puri's a fine place by the sea. Abode of our Lord Jagannath. The good Lord won't mind us, I know.'

'Got anything else to eat?' she asked.

'I gave you all the grapes. What else do you want? Now you give me your two little grapes.' He ran his hand over her breasts, and her purple nipples, crinkled like raisins, came alive. She shivered.

Outside, a gust lifted the palm-fronds of the thatch. The silvery rows of light swayed. There was a fetid odour of drying shit and open sewerage. A train passed and the ground shook.

'No sweet paan?' she asked.

'What'll I do if you want one every time? You know I gave up paan and cigarettes to save money to come to you.' He laughed.

She joined in.

'Besides, I think you've already cadged paan worth several rupees. What I should do is keep accounts. I'd better tuck a piece of paper and a pencil in the thatch. Your aunt wouldn't be interested in them, would she?'

'First you feed my habit and then you become stingy. Wasn't it you who pressed sweet paan on me?'

'Did I have a choice? You were so heavily into smoking your vile, hand-rolled tobacco leaves that I could barely stand you.'

The snow-white cat with black polka dots jumped down the wall.

'Here it comes!' she laughed.

'Thank God he has the sense not to steal in the middle of our lovemaking like last time,' he laughed. 'You know something, I've a feeling he's a spy.' A gecko chirped as if in agreement.

'He's a she.'

'Female cats make better spies.'

She laughed. His hand moved over her body still rippling like gentle waves. He loved these quiet moments afterwards, and wondered at the luck that had brought this wonderful little woman so full of life into his otherwise drab existence. To think he could've easily missed her had he not stopped by the shop at the railway station to buy a paan a few months ago.

'Sir,' the shopkeeper had said, rolling him a paan to his specifications. 'There's a garden-fresh thing in Malisahi.'

'Since when?' Ghana enquired, scooping out a little lime with the stem of the betel leaf.

'Must be close to two weeks already.'

'Two weeks! Two weeks have passed and I haven't heard a thing!' He stared at the picture of a well-known film star, her breasts bursting out of her skimpy top, pasted on the wooden wall of the shop. 'Never mind. Who's the pimp?'

'Rangaya.'

'God, no! Don't mention that fellow's name. No way I'm going to his place. He boozes away all he earns and doesn't pay the police. Every second night there's a raid!'

From the wooden slats of the shop wall a plump cockroach darted out and sprinted across the actress's breasts.

'All that's history, sir,' the shopkeeper said. 'Nowadays it's his wife who runs the show. For one thing, she beats the hell out of the old boozer if he tipples more than half a bottle of toddy. For another, it was her bright idea to bring in fresh blood. And this one she's got this time is a traffic-stopper.'

Ghana looked at him, as interested as he was incredulous.

'Sir,' the shopkeeper added in the same breath, 'why has Cavenders given up on its sales promotion campaigns? You remember those sailors on stilts?'

'It's fallen on bad days. Better brands have flooded the market.'

'Right, sir. Capstan rules the market at the moment.'

'Two weeks, you say? Two weeks is a hell of a long time. They must have turned her inside out by now.'

'I tried three nights after she arrived and there were twelve men before me in line. It seems for an entire week there was no business in any other hut in the whole of Malisahi.'

Ghana sighed. 'Hey, what's happened to the Triple Five cigarette packet you had on the shelf?'

'Bugger my cousin's son, sir. He came here to see the chariot festival and wouldn't budge until I had given him the empty packet.'

'You want a few empty ones? The boss in our office smokes only foreign cigarettes. Gets them duty-free.'

'If you'd be kind enough to collect a few for me, sir. They'd add to the decor.'

'How's business?'

'So-so.'

'What's the going rate at Rangaya's?'

Rangaya gave Ghana a big, cheesy grin. 'Come in, sir, come right in. I've saved a wonderful dish for you.'

'And you'll ask the heavens for it, huh?'

'Not at all, sir. The rate is most reasonable. But I beg you, go scour the whole bloody town, from Khandagiri to Rasulgarh, from Station Square to Santrapur. If you find a girl half as delectable as this one, I'll refund your money fully.'

'Enough hype! You're never short of superlatives, are you?'

The pimp made a face. 'I touch my eyes and swear.'

'Stop at your eyes, for heaven's sake. I don't want you to touch any other part.'

Rangaya's wife came into the hut, chewing on a sprig of grass. Thin and emaciated after her prolonged illness, she looked like a witch. Her brisk career as a whore had come to an end too. She gave Ghana a smile. 'Fresh fruit, sir. Garden-fresh. All you need to pay upfront is two crisp ten-rupee notes.'

'For two crisp ten-rupee notes I can have a film actress,' Ghana said.

'Go fuck your film actress, then. The five-rupee days have been over in Malisahi since the war broke out.'

'Woman, the war hasn't reached Bhubaneswar, has it? East Pakistan is a million miles away.'

'Have you noticed how the prices of everything have shot up?'

'Wait until the refugee girls from East Pakistan flood the Bhubaneswar market. Whore prices have crashed in Calcutta already, let me tell you. It's just a matter of time.'

'That's still far-off.'

'That may be, but you still can't hike up the price from five rupees to twenty overnight. Certainly not in one go! Show me anything else whose price has skyrocketed like that. Tell me the right price, woman. Who wants to haggle? And remember, I'm an old client. Let's settle for ten rupees. Or ten fifty. Eleven. No? All right, twelve then. That's the limit. My God, how could you ask for twenty?'

Rangaya intervened. 'Make it fifteen, sir. You're an old customer after all.'

His wife shot daggers at him. 'Fifteen then,' she grunted.

'Explain to me how you arrived at fifteen, will you?' Ghana wouldn't give up. 'How many clients do you get in the afternoon? And how many are as loyal as I am? Haven't I given you a calendar every year? And remember the bunch of plastic flowers I brought you last year?' For days after Ghana had swiped them from the office on an impulse, the office superintendent had raised a hue and cry. What the hell, Ghana thought, just a bunch of pale pink plastic flowers. Roses, were they? Three thick green leaves attached to each. All splattered with blue ink at that. 'And you come from a place so near to mine. After all, Icchapur is only a stone's throw from Chikiti. And you speak Odia as well as I speak Telugu; what's mother tongue to you is aunt tongue to me. With such a lot in common, surely you won't charge me the market rate! No way. Now, let's inspect the goods. Hurry.'

'Here,' said Ghana. 'I'd completely forgotten. This is for you.' He fished out his pocket notebook and extracted a parrot feather he had picked up on the road two days before on his way back from the market. It was bright green with a hint of blue at the edges. A money-order receipt fell out and he tucked it back between the pages.

'Can I eat it?' she laughed, twirling the feather.

'It's better than food,' he said, taking it from her. 'It'll give you more pleasure. Let me show you how. In a moment you'll see not just one but all fourteen worlds.' He ran the feather slowly over her nose, lips, neck, breasts and belly. She trembled like a leaf in a high wind.

'How's that?' he asked.

'Ticklish.'

'Damn you.'

'I'm dying to pee.'

'You'll never change! You'll remain the sweet little fool you were when you first came here. Stupid thing, haven't you watched the rasleela scenes in your village? Radha lolling on a bed of kadamba flowers and Krishna running a peacock feather all over her?'

'Bring me a peacock feather, then. I love peacock feathers. They're so beautiful!'

'All right, I'll get you one.'

She stretched like a lazy snake. 'Never mind, give me the parrot feather. After all, you've brought it for me with so much love. I'll stick it in the wall, near the hole for the joss sticks. See if you can find me a red feather too.'

'There're no real red ones. Con men dye white feathers and palm them off as red. More often than not what you're left holding is a feather from a hen or a crane.'

'Talking of con men, did you hear what happened two days back? There was this young college boy who tried to palm off two fake ten-rupee notes to a sister. Not only was he beaten black and blue, he was stripped to the skin and sent back to his hostel.'

'Really?' Ghana was surprised. He had always dreamed of resorting to the same trick. 'Not pulling a fast one on me, are you?'

'Pulling a fast one on you?'

'That's some story!' He took a red plastic comb from his shirt pocket and ran it through his thinning hair. 'Let's call it a day. That son of a pig, the office superintendent, must be frantically looking for me.'

'Stay a while longer.'

'Shall I ask you for something? Will you say yes?'

'For what?'

'First say yes.'

'Tell me.'

'Swear that you'll not say no.'

'I swear.' She laughed. 'All right, yes, you can have me for free. Now. Any time.'

'I know I can have you for free if I can manage to slip past your aunt.'

'Cut the suspense. Out with it.'

'Let's go to a movie. A matinee.'

'Why, what's showing at the Talkie House?'

'*Devdas*. Dilip Kumar, Vyjayanthimala and Suchitra Sen.'

'They're good, are they? Is the flick full of songs and dances? Plenty of fight scenes?'

'Plenty,' Ghana laughed, remembering the tear-jerking melodrama he had seen last week; a young colleague had paid for the tickets.

'But swear you'll not sneak your hand inside my blouse and fondle my breasts all through the show. Remember last time?'

'Don't worry. This film will have you in tears right from the first reel. You'll be soaking wet by the time it's over.'

There were sounds in the next room—people walking in, talking in low voices, the door being shut, a mat being rolled out. The mud wall was thin enough for the two of them to hear clearly. Someone cleared his throat, spat a jet of betel juice.

'Don't tell me people have taken a leaf out of my book and started coming here in broad daylight!' Ghana whispered with a low chuckle.

The whore chuckled too. She flung the paper ball up into the air and caught it before it could hit the floor. Her breasts bounced. Ghana caressed them gently. The visiting cat tensed and with a solitary mew of irritation jumped onto the low wall and left.

'I should be able to unplug these two delicious things of yours and take them with me. I'd plug them back in when I come next week.'

'Oh, take them. Take them away, do,' she said. 'They cause me no end of trouble. Everyone except you paws them as though they're mounds of dough or something. Believe me, some nights, after I'm through with the last client, my breasts feel like bruised brinjals.'

'The bastards should have their hands cut off.'

'Gently!'

They could hear a woman's voice from the next room. Ghana smiled. Someone began to groan.

'He groans like our office superintendent,' Ghana said.

'For all you know that's who it might be,' she laughed.

'How I'd love to catch him in the act.'

The whore turned on her belly. Her back bore the imprint of the reed mat. She had an inch-long scar right below her right buttock.

Ghana realized he had never asked her about it. Her spine looked like a swift-running mountain stream, falling into a deep gorge between the sculpted hills of her bottom. On the left cheek of her rump she had a unique birthmark: a shocking pink mole the size of a rupee fringed with pale straw-coloured hair.

'The golden island!' Ghana said, drawing a line around it with his fingers.

All of a sudden the whore struck up a conversation in Telugu with the girl in the next room. 'Why're you complaining so loudly, sister? Is your client a man or a buffalo?'

'A middle-aged Odia,' her friend replied. 'I need to shout out once in a while to make him feel he's getting his money's worth.'

Ghana's mouth widened in silent laughter. 'Do you also,' he asked his whore, 'take me for a ride? I'm just as much of a middle-aged Odia.'

She turned on her back and put a finger on her Adam's apple to indicate she'd never dream of it. 'What kind of a fellow is he, sister?' she carried on her conversation. 'A good client?'

'Good?' her friend replied. 'When it comes to humping, he straddles me as if he's a one-tonne turtle, but does it ever occur to him to leave a tip?'

'Why don't you ask for it? So what does this turtle look like?'

'Like anyone else. Short. Dark.'

Ghana smiled and whispered, 'Ask her if he has a moustache.'

Once the whore had relayed the question the reply came back: 'He has.'

'Thick or thin?'

'Neither thick nor thin.'

'What about his hair, black or grey?'

'Sister, bugger me if I have an answer to this. Bald as an egg, this one.'

'I think I know him,' whispered Ghana. 'Just ask if his front tooth is chipped.'

'Can't see it right now,' came the reply. 'He humps with his mouth shut.'

'Why?'

'What why? Do you know something, sister? This man rinses out his rubber and uses it more than once. I told him I'm clean. But he wouldn't forget the rubber.'

'If he's so scared of getting the clap, why does he come to Malisahi? You can't live in the water and not make friends with the crab!' The whore shook her head. Ghana ran a finger across her breasts. She gently pushed his hand away. 'Don't. I feel terribly ticklish.'

'Here I am gabbing away bang in the middle of it all,' the girl next room spoke up, 'but does he mind? Not at all. A hole in the ground would do for him.'

Ghana pursed his lips. The girl looked askance at him. He motioned to her to bring her ear close to his lips.

'I'm sure,' he said, 'that man is our office superintendent.'

'Is your office superintendent short and dark?'

'No. Not really. Ask your friend if the fellow has hair sticking out of his ears.'

'Your office superintendent does?'

'No.'

The girl next door began to giggle hysterically.

'What's up?' Ghana's whore enquired. 'His rocket went off too fast?'

'I've pushed one of his shoes behind the door. It'll be fun to watch the bugger look for it.'

'Good idea, sister. Tell him it might have been taken away by a dog or a cat.'

Ghana shook with suppressed laughter. 'The dog,' he whispered, 'might take it and put it under the table of the office superintendent of the state civil supply department.'

'Is that where you work?'

'No.'

'Do you really think that man could be your office superintendent?'

'Who knows? He might have come in disguise.'

'Will a tall man look short, or a fair one dark even in disguise?'

'Why not?'

'You want me to barge into the room next door and check him out?'

'Forget it.'

'Why?'

'His disguise must be as good as mine. No one can make us out.'

'What do you really look like, if this is your disguise?'

'In real life, my dear, I look like our office superintendent.'

She winked at him. 'You clown!'

'Not a clown. A buffoon more likely.' He rose to his feet and began to put on his clothes. While slipping his shirt over his head, he made faces at her as if she were a child easy to scare. His hair became tousled and he took out his comb and ran it through several times. He cleaned the comb by running its teeth briskly against his overgrown thumbnail before putting it back in his pocket. A lovely afternoon was over. Outside, the gentle November sun had paled and a strange golden light was streaming in through the wooden slats of the door. The mosquitoes had woken up and were flying about; one got into his ear but escaped before it could be slapped to death. The tingling sensation continued for a long moment.

His darling whore twisted like a boa constrictor that had gobbled a deer.

'So long, waterfowl,' he said.

'Wait a moment,' she said, getting up. 'I've something for you.' She went to the clothes hanging from the peg and began to rummage. From somewhere she fished out a packet of cigarettes. 'Here,' she said, offering it to him. 'The tobacco's strong, but...'

Ghana examined it: an old Cavenders packet, crumpled up.

'I tried one this morning,' she continued. 'My head spun so much I couldn't stand up straight.'

Ghana opened the packet. The protective foil was missing and there were half a dozen assorted cigarettes—Cavenders, Capstans, Charminars and a Gold Flake, the Charminars more bent and crooked than the rest.

'Last night,' she said, 'there was an old boozer of a client, drunk as a pig. I flicked the packet off him.'

A boozer who visited whores and collected different kinds of cigarettes? Tears came to Ghana's eyes. He wanted to make a wisecrack, but let it go. With a gentle pat on her head, he opened the door and stepped out.

APPENDIX

REBATI

FAKIR MOHAN SENAPATI

(*The First Modern Odia Short Story, 1898*)

> But oft some shining April morn
> Is darkened in an hour,
> And blackest griefs o'er joyous home,
> Alas! unseen may lower.
>
> —Rev. J. H. Gurney

'*Rebati! Rebi! You fire that turns all to ashes.*'

Patapur—a sleepy little village in Hariharpur subdivision, district of Cuttack. At one end stood Shyambandhu Mohanty's house: two rows of rooms, front and back, with an inner courtyard centring around a well, and a shed for husking rice behind the house, along with a vegetable patch, and a garden in front. It was in the outer room that visitors and farmers waiting to pay their taxes gathered and made themselves comfortable. Shyambandhu Mohanty, the zamindar's accountant, was responsible for collecting taxes. His salary was two rupees a month, but he could earn a little more by adjusting rent receipts and land records; all told, this added up to at least four rupees. With this he could make ends meet. And not just barely; no, to tell the truth, he was quite comfortable. His family never complained of wanting for anything. They had all they needed: two drumstick trees in the backyard, and a patch of land always full of greens and vegetables; two cows, which never went dry at the same time, so there was always a little curd and milk in the pails. Mohanty's old mother made fuel cakes from cow dung and husks, so they rarely had to buy firewood. The zamindar had given him three and a half acres of rent-free land to cultivate, and it produced just about enough to meet their needs.

Shyambandhu was a straightforward person, and the tenants respected, even liked, him. He went from door to door cajoling and coaxing them to pay their taxes; he never demanded a paisa extra from anyone. On his own initiative and without their asking, he would slip four-finger-wide palm-leaf receipts into the underside thatch of their houses. He never let the zamindar's muscleman cast his shadow over the village; he'd pump the fellow's palm, fondle his chin, tuck two paise into the folds of his dhoti to buy a plug of tobacco, and see him off.

In his own home, Shyambandhu had four stomachs to fill—his own, his wife's, his old mother's, and his ten-year-old daughter's. The daughter's name was Rebati. In the evenings Shyambandhu would sit on his veranda and sing 'Krupasindhu Badan' and other prayer songs; at times he would light an oil lamp, place it on a wooden stand, and read aloud passages from the Bhagavata. Rebati always sat next to him, listening with rapt attention; soon she had learnt a few songs by heart. Her melodious voice lent them more appeal, and people would stop by to listen. There was one hymn which gave Shyambandhu the greatest joy, and every evening he would unfailingly ask Rebati to sing it:

> Whither shall I take my prayers, Lord,
> If Thou turnest a blind eye?
> Surely shall I be finished.
> Be it salvation or damnation,
> To Thee this life a dedication,
> To Thee, this soul laden.
> Empty, empty, all the three worlds
> When I am without Thee.
> True refreshment, when I thirst,
> Only Thy love can be.

Two years earlier, in the course of his visit to the countryside, the deputy inspector of schools had happened to spend a night at Patapur. At the request of the village elders he had written to the inspector of schools, Orissa Division, and an upper-primary school had been established in the village. The government paid the teacher's salary of four rupees a month, to which each student contributed an additional anna.

The teacher, Basudev, a young man of twenty, had attended the teacher-training course at Cuttack Normal School. Urbane and polite, he never took on superior airs. He had been orphaned at an early age and had been brought up by his uncle. True to his name, he was a fine human being. Charming and handsome—the indelible mark of a bottle's mouth on his forehead applied by his mother to treat diphtheria during childhood enhanced rather than marred his looks. He seemed to have been sculpted out of a single block.

From the time he arrived in the village, Shyambandhu had taken a fancy to him: they belonged to the same caste.

Occasionally, on the day of a full moon or a Thursday, when cakes and savouries were made at home, Shyambandhu would call at the school: 'Son, come to our place this evening; your aunt has invited you.' A bond of affection had naturally developed between them after these visits. Even Rebati's mother, filled with concern, would sometimes exclaim: 'Ah, the poor orphan! What does he eat, who looks after his meals?' As the visits became regular, with Basu dropping in practically every evening, Rebati would wait at the door to announce his arrival. As soon as she spotted him at a distance she would call out to her father, 'Here comes Basubhai, here he comes!' Then she would sit beside him and sing all the prayer songs she knew. To Basu's ears, the songs were fresh and ever new.

One day, as they chatted about this and that, Shyambandhu learnt from Basu there was a school at Cuttack where girls could study and also learn crafts; instantly, the desire to give Rebati an education welled up in his heart. When he confided this to Basu, the young teacher, who had already begun to look upon him as a father, answered: 'I was about to suggest that myself.'

Rebati listened to the conversation and rushed inside. 'I'm going to study,' she announced excitedly to her mother and grandmother. 'I'm going to learn to read.'

Her mother smiled. 'Go ahead,' she said, but her grandmother's reaction was sharp: 'What good will it do you? How does book learning help a girl? It's enough to know how to cook, bake, churn butter and make patterns on walls using rice paste.'

That night, when Shyambandhu sat down to dinner on a low wooden stool with Rebati beside him, the old lady sat opposite them, restive, and itching to speak her mind: 'Serve him a little more rice, daughter-in-law, give him a second helping of dal and a pinch of salt,' and so on. Then she brought up the topic: 'Shyam, is Rebi going to study? Why should she, son? What good is that for a girl?'

'Never mind, Ma,' said Shyambandhu. 'Let her study if she wants to. Haven't you heard Jhankar Pattanaik's daughters can read the Bhagavata and *Baidehisa Bilas*?'

Rebati was furious at her grandmother. 'You silly old fool!' she snorted. Turning to her father, she begged him, 'Father, I do want to study.'

'And so you will,' said Shyambandhu.

The matter was left there.

The following afternoon Basu brought Rebati a copy of Sitanath Babu's *First Lessons*. She was so overjoyed she leafed through the book from cover to cover. The pictures of elephants, houses and cows thrilled her no end. Kings could be happy to own elephants and horses, others perhaps derived joy from riding them, but for Rebati it was enough merely to gaze at their pictures. She could hardly wait to show them to her mother and grandmother.

The grandmother did not hide her irritation. 'Take that silly thing away from me,' she shouted.

'Silly you!' the girl retorted.

The auspicious day of Sri Panchami dawned. Rebati took an early bath, put on new clothes, and flitted in and out of the house, waiting impatiently for Basu. The usual pomp associated with beginning one's studies was played down out of fear of the grandmother. Six hours into the morning Basu arrived and taught her the alphabet: a, aa, e, ee, u, uu...

The lessons went on. Basu never missed a day.

Over the next two years Rebati studied a great deal. All the rhymes of Madhu Rao were on the tip of her tongue and she could reel them off without faltering.

At dinner one night, Shyambandhu asked his mother, as if rounding off a discussion they had been having, 'Well, Ma, what do you think?'

'Nothing could be better,' said the old lady. 'But are you certain what his caste is?'

'That's what I was trying to find out. He may be poor but he comes from a good family. And he's a pucca Karan to boot.'

'Good. Caste counts more than wealth. But will he agree to live with us?'

'Why not? After all, his only relatives are his uncle and aunt. He probably won't insist on living with them.'

What Rebati made of all this she alone knew, but a change certainly came over her. She became noticeably coy with Basu. In the evening she would hang around the front door, as though waiting for someone, which riled her grandmother no end, but when Basu arrived, she would hide inside the house. It took Basu quite an effort before she would come out for her studies. Blushing and smiling for no apparent reason, she would refuse to read her lessons aloud and would answer him in monosyllables. As soon as the day's lesson was done she would rush inside, struggling to stifle her giggles.

One Sri Panchami followed another, and two years passed. Providence's designs are strange and inscrutable; no two days are alike. One fine Phalguna day, like a bolt out of the blue, a cholera epidemic struck.

Early in the morning the news of Shyambandhu coming down with cholera spread through the village. As always, the immediate response was to bolt the doors and windows, and keep out of the path of the demonic deity, as though the evil old hag was out with her basket and broom sweeping up heads.

Shyambandhu's wife and mother were soon driven out of their minds by worry and anxiety. Rebati ran in and out of the house, crying for help. When the news reached Basu, he hurried from the school and, without fear for his own life, sat at the bedside, massaging Shyambandhu's hands and legs and forcing drops of water between his parched lips.

Three hours passed.

Suddenly, Shyambandhu looked up at Basu and stammered: 'Take care of my family, I leave them to you...'

Basu could not hold back his tears.

Shyambandhu passed away that evening.

The women wailed. Rebati rolled on the floor.

How could the two grief-stricken women and the inexperienced Basu make arrangements for the cremation? Bana Sethi, the village washerman, a veteran of fifty or sixty cremations, saved the day turning up with a towel around his waist and an axe on his shoulder. Bana was rather philosophical about it: cholera or not, if your time's up you've got to go, whether today or tomorrow, but why miss out on a set of new clothes? Shyambandhu's was the only Karan family in the village, and help was neither expected nor forthcoming; the two women and Basudev had to carry the body to the cremation grounds and perform the last rites.

The morning star was shining in the eastern sky by the time they were done. No sooner had they got home than Rebati's mother came down with cholera. By midday the news of her death had spread through the village.

Providence works in mysterious ways—while one man is blessed with a regal umbrella atop his palanquin, another receives lashes on his fettered hands. Within three months of Shyambandhu's demise, the zamindar expropriated Shyambandhu's cows—apparently he had not deposited the last tax collection. This was hard to believe, however. Shyambandhu had always regarded depositing the money as sacred and would not rest in peace until every paisa of the collection was in the zamindar's treasury. The truth was that for a long time the zamindar had had his eyes on the cows. He also took back the three and a half acres he had given Shyambandhu. There was no work for the farmhand, and he left on the full moon day of the Dola festival. The team of bullocks had already been sold off for seventeen and a half rupees; with what remained after the funeral expenses, the grandmother and Rebati hung on for a month. In the month following they began to pawn household items—a brass bowl one day, a plate the next.

Basu visited them every evening and stayed until bedtime. He offered them money, but they would not touch it. Once or twice he pressed some on them, but the coins lay idle on the shelf. He had no choice but to accept the couple of paise the old woman produced every eight or ten days to buy them provisions. The house was falling apart, the straw roof had worn thin, but try as he might Basu couldn't get it rethatched; the bales of hay he bought with two rupees of his own money rotted in the backyard.

The grandmother no longer cried day and night; she now confined her wailing to the evenings. But she put so much of herself into it that it left her slumped in a heap on the floor for the night. Rebati, convulsing in sobs, would lie down next to her. The old woman's vision had declined and she had a wild look about her. She no longer cried as much and took to heaping curses and abuse on Rebati: the wretched girl was at the root of all her misery and misfortune; her education had caused it all—first her son had died, then her daughter-in-law; the bullocks had been sold off; the farmhand had left; the cows had been taken by the zamindar; and now her eyes had gone bad. Rebati was the evil eye, the she-devil, the ill-omened.

The moment the curses started coming thick and fast, Rebati would shrink from her grandmother and hide in a corner of the house or the backyard, tears streaming down her cheeks.

The grandmother held Basu equally to blame. If he had not been so eager to teach the girl, she could not possibly have gone and taught herself! But the grandmother could not take Basu to task, because she couldn't do without him. The zamindar kept seeking flimsy clarifications, and almost every second day a messenger came asking for this account or that. Basu alone could fish them out from the clutter of papers Shyambandhu had left behind. Yet, behind Basu's back, the old woman sometimes gave vent to her feelings.

Rebati's presence no longer filled the house; gone were the days when she would be heard mourning loudly. Nobody heard her voice, nobody saw her out of doors. Her large brooding eyes, awash with silent tears, looked like blue lilies floating in water. Her heart and mind broken, day and night were alike to her. The sun brought her no light, the night no darkness; the world was an aching void. The memories of her parents overwhelmed her, their faces hung before her glazed eyes. She could not bring herself to believe they were truly dead and gone. Hunger no longer stirred her stomach; slumber no longer closed her eyes. She went through the pretence of eating only out of fear of her grandmother; she grew thin and emaciated, her skin hung loose on her bones, and she could barely lift herself off the floor where she lay day and night. The only time she revived a little was when Basu visited them. She would sit up and fasten her gaze on him, lowering her eyes with a sigh when their glances met. But the next moment she'd feverishly stare at him again. For those brief hours of the day when he was around, Basu completely possessed her eyes, her mind and her heart.

Roughly five months had passed. On a hot Jaistha Saturday afternoon, Basu knocked on their door. Never before had he ever called at such an unusual hour. The old woman was full of foreboding as she let him in.

'Grandmother,' said Basu. 'The deputy inspector of schools will be camping at the Hariharpur police station and giving the students an oral test. All the schools have been informed; I received the order today. Tomorrow morning I'll have to start off and be away for about five days.'

Listening to the conversation from behind the door, Rebati felt her legs give way. Her hold on the door was barely tight enough to stop herself from falling.

Basu bought them enough rice, oil, salt and vegetables for five days, and bade them goodbye.

'Son,' said the old woman with a sigh. 'Don't walk about in the sun for too long. Take care of yourself; eat your meals on time.'

Rebati could not take her eyes off him. Before, she would look away when their eyes met, but today she stared unblinkingly, unabashedly into his eyes. A change seemed to have come over Basu too. For a long time he had contented himself with stolen glances, but today he did not turn away. They stared deeply into each other's eyes.

Evening came; darkness filled the house and covered the earth. Rebati remained rooted to the ground until her grandmother's piercing screams jolted her to her senses. Basu had left much earlier.

Rebati counted the days.

On the morning of the sixth she even rushed a couple of times to the front door, which she had avoided since her parents' death. Six hours had passed when the schoolboys arrived back from Hariharpur, bringing the news of Basu's death. He had succumbed to cholera under the big banyan tree near Gopalpur on his return journey. The village folk mourned; the women and children shed copious tears. 'What a handsome fellow!' said one. 'So polite,' said another. 'Never hurt a fly,' remarked yet another.

The grandmother cried so much she choked. 'Poor boy!' she repeated between sobs. 'You only brought it on yourself!' Implying that he had perished in his prime because he had been foolish enough to want to teach Rebati.

Rebati sank to the floor and lay there without a whine or a whimper.

The grandmother woke up the following morning without Rebati beside her and shouted out in anger: 'Rebati! Rebi! You fire that turns all to ashes.' She worked herself into a froth, and passers-by heard these terrible words repeated all morning long.

Half-blind and angry, she groped her way through the entire house. When she finally found the girl, she was shocked. Rebati, burning with fever, was unconscious. Worry and fear gnawed at the old woman's heart. She couldn't decide what to do, who to turn to for help. Exasperated, out of breath, and without hope, she tartly commented: 'What medicine can there be for an illness of one's own making!' Rebati had brought the fever on herself by daring to study.

One, two, three, four, five days passed. Rebati remained glued to the ground, her eyes and lips shut. On the sixth morning she let out a whimper or two. The old woman ran her hand over the girl's body. It was cool to the touch; perhaps the fever had left. She called out to her, and Rebati mumbled a reply, then asked for water, stared wildly around, and broke into incoherent babble. One quick look and even a country doctor could have quoted from his text: 'Thirst, fever, delirium; of imminent collapse these are the symptoms.' But the poor grandmother was overcome with a sense of relief. The fever had left, the girl was able to open her eyes and speak two words, to ask for water. A little gruel was all she needed to regain her strength and get back on her feet.

'Don't get up,' the grandmother said. 'Stay where you are. I'm going to cook you a bit of food.' She left the room and rummaged in vain among the earthen pots for a handful of rice. Her head became clouded with despair and she sat down with a sigh. If only her eyesight had been better she would have realized the provisions meant for five days had already lasted for ten.

But there was a flicker of hope in her yet. She picked up the only object of value left—an old brass bowl with a hole in the bottom—and set out for Hari Sa's store. The so-called store was in Hari's residence, in the middle of the village, and he kept a paltry stock of rice, salt, lentils and oil to sell to travellers passing by.

Hari saw the old woman with the bowl. He understood immediately, but let her first make her plea. He then took the bowl and examined it minutely, turning it from side to side. 'There's no rice,' he said, handing it back. 'Who's going to give you anything for a bowl like this?' Of course, he had both rice and the inclination to sell it, but getting the brass bowl for a song was what interested him the most. The grandmother staggered at his words, as though lightning had hit her. What would she do if she didn't get any rice, what would she cook for Rebati, how would the girl fight her weakness? She sat there for hours, depressed and silent, still as a log, casting imploring glances at the shopkeeper.

The day wore on. Realizing she had left the sick girl alone for a long time, fear stirred her old heart. 'Time I got back home,' she mumbled to herself, picking up the bowl. 'God knows how that girl of mine is doing.'

'Never mind,' said Hari grudgingly. 'Give me the bowl. Let's see if I can scrape up a little something for you.' He gave her four measures of rice, half a measure of lentils, and a handful of salt. The old woman hobbled back home, resting every four steps or so to catch her breath. She hadn't even washed her face since morning, and her mind was in a whirl.

She reached home hoping Rebati was better. She thought she'd ask the girl to draw water from the well. The rice wouldn't take long to cook. She called out to Rebati once, twice, three times, but got no response. Then she yelled at the top of her voice: 'Rebati! Rebi! You fire that turns all to ashes.'

By now Rebati was sinking fast. Her body, already feeble from spasms of excruciating pain, had turned ice-cold. Her thirst was so terrible she felt as if her tongue was being sucked back into her throat. She found the room unbearably hot and crawled out to the inner courtyard. Even that brought no relief. She rolled out to the veranda at the back and propped herself up against the wall.

Dusk had fallen and a gentle breeze was blowing. A bunch of bananas hung from the plant her father had planted before his death. The guava sapling her mother had planted two years ago had grown to a considerable height and was covered with blossoms. Rebati remembered how she had drawn water from the well in a small jug and tended the sapling. This brought back a rush of memories of her mother. Her head was in a whirl, her thoughts jumbled, but the image of her mother clung to her.

Night slowly descended. Darkness stole out from the boughs of the trees and shrouded the garden. Rebati tilted her head back and watched the sky. The lone evening star was gleaming brightly. She could not take her eyes off it; and it grew and grew and grew, bigger and brighter, invading the whole sky, and behold! Her loving mother sat in the heart of it, her face glowing with love and kindness, her arms extended towards Rebati in invitation. Rebati was overwhelmed. Two shafts of light pierced her eyes and moved down to her heart. Her breathing, heavy and laboured, rose and fell, breaking the stillness of the night. She wheezed, choked and cried out to her mother twice. Then there was silence.

The grandmother crawled around the house, going from the living room to the courtyard to the rice-husking shed, but Rebati was nowhere to be found. Then it occurred to the old woman that with the fever abating the girl might be taking a stroll in the garden at the back.

'Rebati!' she screamed. 'Rebi! You fire that turns all to ashes.'

She crawled out to the narrow veranda, which was only one hand wide and two high, and bumped into the girl. 'Death to you!' she cried. 'Sitting here, are you?' She wanted to shake her up, but she could sense something was amiss.

She ran her hand over the length of the girl's body and then held a finger close to her nostrils. The night's silence was rent by her eerie wail. Two bodies fell from the veranda and thudded to the ground.

That was the end of Shyambandhu Mohanty's family.

The last words which had emanated from his house were: 'Rebati! Rebi! You fire that turns all to ashes.'

THE SANYASI

REBA RAY

(The First Modern Odia Short Story by a Woman Writer, 1899)

I

A destitute woman had recently taken shelter in Nityananda Patnaik's home in Jajpur, along with her six-year-old daughter. The widow of a zamindar, she was from the same caste as Nityananda. Three years earlier her husband had lost everything in a lawsuit and, consumed by the pangs of poverty, had chosen not to continue among the living. It had been a harrowing time for her, those three years. Finally, when she had nowhere else to go, Nityananda had offered her and her daughter, Parasamani, a place to live in his house.

Nityananda had worked in the treasury office in Cuttack and was now on a pension. He had also inherited a small zamindari, and lived quite comfortably. His was a small family—wife, Ushabati, and son, Siva Prasad. An only child, Siva Prasad had been born after prayers to Lord Siva over many years, and so it was appropriate he should have been named after the god. When the boy was thirteen, Nityananda had sent him off to stay with a friend in Cuttack, so he could get a decent education.

Nityananda's wife, Ushabati, was as proud, foul-mouthed and haughty as her husband was gentle, calm and collected. After moving in, Parasamani's mother attended to every chore around the house, but no amount of toiling like a slave seemed to satisfy Ushabati. On the contrary, the poor woman was frequently subjected to and singed by the raging flames of the mistress's anger. Even little Parasamani was not spared; she too had to put up with slaps, blows and pinching. God Almighty be praised that He has bestowed on the lowly and downtrodden enormous reserves of patience! What would have happened to these poor souls if they lacked forbearance? It was just as well that Parasamani's mother took every bit of humiliation without demur. Nityananda was blissfully unaware of all this—not that he would have been able to do a thing about it had he known.

Siva Prasad was delighted to have Parasamani around when he came home for Durga Puja. As a single child, he had been lonely for as long as he could remember. He was a quiet and kind boy, which made it easier for Parasamani to take to him.

One day, sitting beside Siva Prasad while he was studying, she blurted out—perhaps out of childish enthusiasm or from deep-seated desire—that she, too, wished to study.

Siva Prasad found a copy of *Barna Bodhak*, a primer, right away and began teaching her. Until he left for Cuttack at the end of the holidays, he guided her through her lessons every afternoon, encouraging her to read and to write the alphabet and words with chalk. In just about twenty days, Parasamani mastered nearly half of *Barna Bodhak*. But her studies were interrupted when Siva Prasad returned to Cuttack.

Six months passed. Siva Prasad was back home for the summer vacation. Parasamani's studies resumed, and after finishing *Barna Bodhak*, she started on *Bodhadayak*. One day, Ushabati chanced upon her son teaching the girl and hurled uncalled-for abuse on them. From then on, Parasamani did not seek Siva Prasad out; she studied by herself.

The girl grew up to be an unparalleled beauty, graceful and well mannered; everyone took to her at first sight. Nityananda never missed an opportunity to express his love and affection for her. Perhaps because he did not have a daughter of his own, or because he was naturally generous of heart, or because Parasamani's sweet innocent face was difficult to resist. But unfortunately, the girl failed to gain even the smallest place in Ushabati's heart.

II

Five years went by, with days good and bad, all ultimately drowned in the boundless depths of Time. Many, dragged out of dark despair, reached the blinding illumination of happiness, while others, deprived of joy, were submerged in a bottomless ocean of grief. Who could count the number of human beings Time sent, against their wishes, to their deaths, just as it showered blessings on a grieving world by bringing forth a bountiful crop of babies, as lovely as fresh flowers?

But, through good fortune or bad, not much changed in Nityananda's family. Among the good things, Siva Prasad passed his Intermediate Arts examination and returned home. Ushabati's fond wish now was to get her son married and she began to pester her husband about it day in and day out.

One day, Nityananda took her aside. 'Place your hand on my head and swear you'll not refuse my request.' She hesitated, but let herself be persuaded.

'When Parasamani was just two years old,' Nityananda confessed. 'I met her father on some business. One look at the child and I thought to myself: God willing, someday I'll get our son Siva Prasad married to her. So intense was my wish that I let her father in on it, and we both swore we'd not let it be otherwise, even if one of us were dead.'

It was as if Ushabati had been struck by lightning. 'Is that why you asked me to place my hand on your head and swear? What will people say if I accept Parasamani as my daughter-in-law? Aren't there other beautiful girls around? How can I settle for a girl whose mother doesn't have a coin to offer as dowry? You want me to give my son in marriage to a girl whose mother works as a servant in this house?' Protesting vehemently, she trotted out more arguments.

Nityananda listened in silence. 'I cannot go back on my word,' he said quietly. 'If you're unwilling, you may do as you wish. But you'll be on your own when it comes to your son's marriage.'

For the next eight or ten days, husband and wife did not talk to each other. Ushabati vented all her anger on Parasamani and her mother, who in the meanwhile had come to know of what had transpired.

In the end, with no other solution in sight, Ushabati gave her consent.

On an auspicious day, and at an auspicious hour, the holy union between Siva Prasad and Parasamani was solemnized. Nityananda was euphoric that he had been able to keep his word. Parasamani's mother was ecstatic that the best possible match had been found for her adorable daughter. The only person who was unhappy was Ushabati. What about the newlyweds—did they feel blessed and happy to have found each other?

III

After the wedding, Nityananda did not let Siva Prasad return to Cuttack to continue his studies despite the boy's fondest wishes. Siva Prasad also tried, not once but two or three times, to look for a job, but had to give up the idea because of his father's opposition. No one knew what arguments Nityananda marshalled in support of his stand.

Ushabati was an ill-tempered person by nature, and her ire against Parasamani increased after she became her daughter-in-law. Parasamani's slightest lapse provoked disproportionate outbursts; Ushabati could not get over her old habit of raising a hand on the girl. Once, Parasamani, dead tired, let her eyes close for a few seconds while preparing the evening meal and, instead of meting out the regulation beating, the solicitous mother-in-law simply poured a pitcher of cold water over her.

Parasamani's mother learnt to keep quiet even as she witnessed her daughter's misery. And Parasamani herself remained as silent as a deaf-mute, drowning her sorrows in her mother's affection and her husband's love. At the tender age of fourteen, she worked untiringly from dawn to two hours past dusk, attending to chores of all kinds, but in great fear of her mother-in-law's curses and beatings. The few words of love and solace she received from her husband before she offered herself up to a restful slumber at the end of the day made her feel like the luckiest woman alive.

His mother's ill-treatment of Parasamani did not escape Siva Prasad. Although he could not say a word to his mother, one day he said to his wife: 'I know how miserable and tormented you are, but it is my loving request to you not to take Mother's unkind words to heart.'

'How can one who has your love be bothered about anything?' Parasamani replied. 'Besides, sometimes I do make mistakes and deserve what comes to me.'

One day, Parasamani came down with a fever. She lay in bed in her mother's room. When, after five or six days, the fever showed no sign of abating, Nityananda called in a vaidya, who took her pulse and wrote out a prescription. Ushabati didn't step inside the room even once to see how her daughter-in-law was doing. Parasamani's mother used the short breaks between her own chores in the household to drop in to give her daughter some food—toasted rice flakes, ginger, salt and pureed puffed rice. Without telling his mother Siva Prasad, too, went some three or four times to see his wife. After Parasamani recovered, Ushabati confronted her son about it. God knows what she said but Siva Prasad felt deeply wounded.

Five or six days later he begged his father to let him visit Cuttack, saying how much he missed the town and how badly he needed to see it one more time. Nityananda finally agreed, but only to a short visit. An auspicious time for the boy's departure was decided: between next Tuesday night and dawn on Wednesday.

On the night before he was to leave, Siva Prasad begged his wife to take care of her health. She was with child. Husband and wife held each other a long time, crying silently. When morning came, Siva Prasad took leave of his parents and others and started on his journey.

He put up with a friend in Cuttack and wrote his father within a fortnight giving him the good news: he had landed a job with a monthly salary of fifty rupees. He took it and was in no hurry to return home. This was exactly what a doctor would have prescribed an ailing man.

Four months after Siva Prasad left home, Parasamani gave birth to a baby boy. Nityananda promptly wrote to Siva Prasad with the happy news. But his family was not destined to enjoy this joy and happiness for long: the newborn deserted his mother's lap while she was still confined to the labour room and returned to the fairyland from whence he had come, plunging the entire family into grief. Parasamani came down with a fever almost immediately, from which there was no remission for the next fifteen days.

When he received the sad news, Siva Prasad wanted to visit home but could not, since he did not want to apply for leave from the job he had only recently taken.

Nityananda called in vaidyas and doctors to treat his daughter-in-law, but to no avail.

One day, quite secretly, and with a lot of difficulty, Parasamani wrote her husband a letter.

Dearest,

Your poor one wants to see you once before breathing her last. Will you be kind enough to take the trouble of coming here and helping your servant fulfil her last wish—to take the dust from your feet on her head before dying?

Forever yours,
Parasamani

She entrusted the letter to her mother, asking her to place it in an envelope with a postage stamp and find a trustworthy woman to take it to the post office.

Parasamani's letter moved Siva Prasad so deeply he requested a week's leave and rushed home.

It was as if the flickering flame of Parasamani's life had been waiting for one last glimpse of her husband's face. For once, Siva Prasad, past caring about his mother's feelings, went straight to his wife the moment he reached home. The poor girl burst into convulsive sobs when she saw him.

She beckoned him to approach. When he did, she took his right hand and clamped it to her heart. 'How I had looked forward to placing your son in your lap! Not only did my wish not come true, it will remain forever unfulfilled. This is the last time we'll meet in this life, and I pray to God I may have you as my husband in my next.'

It took an enormous effort for Parasamani to speak these few words. Tears silently streamed from Siva Prasad's eyes and drenched his wife's hands. Parasamani's mother rushed to her daughter's bedside, crying bitterly. Hearing her, Nityananda and Ushabati, too, rushed in. Parasamani requested each of them to bless her with the dust from their feet. Then she looked at her husband longingly one last time and took her last breath.

Two months went by, with yet another bereavement: Parasamani's mother, grieving over the death of her only child, followed her into the other world. Was all this predestined, ordained by God? Could anyone have changed any of it?

Siva Prasad did not go back to Cuttack. He withdrew from everyone, keeping to himself. His parents wanted him to quickly remarry.

In a short time a suitable match was found. The girl was a rich man's daughter and, Ushabati, elated, saw this as the fulfilment of her true wishes—all the wishes that had eluded her when Siva Prasad had married Parasamani. Soon preparations were afoot for an early wedding the following month.

Parasamani might have died but Siva Prasad constantly felt her presence. She was always around, gently laughing, extending her hands towards him, begging for his love and affection. So when he learnt of the plans for his second marriage, he did not hesitate for a moment to tell his mother straight out: 'I'm not going to marry again. Don't you people even think of it.'

His mother was stunned, as if felled by a blow. 'Son, even men in their dotage get married two or three times. You're a young man, yet you refuse to remarry? What will happen to us if you don't? We'll simply perish.' She used all sorts of arguments—some harsh, some sweet.

But Siva Prasad was unmoved. 'I won't marry again.'

When the matter reached Nityananda's ears, he thought that these words had come from his son's lips, not his heart, and that the boy would come to terms with it once the marriage took place.

The wedding day dawned. It was already eight in the morning, but there was no sign Siva Prasad had woken up. Wondering why, someone went to his room. Not finding him there, he combed the whole house. When Nityananda was finally informed, he too started looking for his son in every nook and cranny, and sent out search teams. Ushabati's tears of joy soon turned into grief and anguish.

The people sent out to search all returned dejected. A joyous and festive day darkened into one of agony and despair.

Nityananda and Ushabati cursed and cried themselves hoarse. The light had gone out of their home.

Though Siva Prasad had expressed his unwillingness in no uncertain terms, he knew his parents would overrule him and go ahead with the second wedding. So, on the night before the wedding, after everyone had gone to bed, he put together a few clothes and a little money, and secretly left home. Undecided where to go, he first headed for Cuttack. But he didn't feel comfortable going there, aware his father would soon get wind of where he was. So he decided to go to Calcutta, and felt somewhat relieved when he reached there. Not immense, unalloyed relief, but relief nevertheless. His more immediate worry was how to face the future.

A month passed. His money ran out. He had not cultivated the acquaintance of anyone in the city who could help him out with a loan of ten or fifteen rupees to tide him over.

One day, tormented by worries and anxiety, his hands clasped across his heavy heart, he was sitting in his room when he overheard someone singing in the next room. He was so drawn to the music he went next door and sat beside the singer, plying him with requests to continue.

The last song was one of renunciation and non-attachment. It touched Siva Prasad to the core, changing his life in that instant. The song was like a beacon, showing him the direction his life should take.

The next morning Siva Prasad donned the robes of a mendicant and repeated the holy names of the Almighty; the All-Merciful; the Lord of eternal happiness, love, kindness and peace; the Great Father; the Eternal One. Seeking shelter in Him, he set out to roam the wide world and sing His praise.

It is difficult to explain to readers the great peace and joy that came over Siva Prasad, who did nothing but speak of God, at whose feet he had found refuge. He had at last installed God in his heart, to whose mercy creation owed all its limitless splendour and riches.

Epilogue

Our wish is not to bring the story to a close with the sad plight of Nityananda and Ushabati. But for all those curious to learn the couple's fate, here it is.

Shortly after Siva Prasad vanished, Ushabati died. Nityananda sold off his property and, keeping just a little for his upkeep, made an endowment for the temple services of Lord Jagannath. He moved to Puri, where he did not live for long; he soon left for the divine abode.

NOTES ON AUTHORS

AKHIL MOHAN PATTNAIK (1927–82) was a distinguished lawyer with a flourishing practice. His works include six collections of short stories, a travelogue, two plays, a book of poetry, and a novel. He received the 1981 Sahitya Akademi Award for his collection of stories—*O Andhagali*. For years he held informal meetings in his own house, encouraging writers to congregate for intellectual discourse. He generously fostered talented young writers, giving them breaks in *Samabesh*, a leading literary journal he edited from the time it was founded until his death.

BAMACHARAN MITRA (1915–70) was lauded by critics for his extraordinary depth and perception, and his diverse interests ranging from classical music to swimming to football and detective fiction. He published three novels and more than a hundred short stories, which have been collected in eight volumes.

BINAPANI MOHANTY (1936–) has published twenty-six collections of stories and two novels, a collection of one-act plays, in addition to her autobiography and several books of translation. She received the 1990 Sahitya Akademi Award and the 2010 Sarala Award. She is the founder-president of Odia Women Writers, an organization to promote and encourage women writing in Odia.

CHANDRASEKHAR RATH (1929–2018) was a novelist, short-story writer, amateur painter and sculptor, legendary teacher, and a highly-popular speaker on the public circuit. He published four novels, including *Yantrarudha*, whose English translation won the 2004 Hutch Crossword Translation Award, fifteen collections of short stories, ten volumes of essays, and a book of poetry. He received the Sarala Award, 1982, the Sahitya Akademi Award, 1997, and was awarded the Padma Shri, 2018.

CHAUDHURY HEMAKANTA MISRA (1935–2005) was a professor of English and a recluse, who shunned all public adulation for his unusual humour and sharp wit. He published twelve volumes of short stories, and was the recipient of Odisha Sahitya Akademi Award in 1986.

FAKIR MOHAN SENAPATI (1843–1918) is widely acknowledged as the father of modern Odia prose. He wrote four novels, including the iconic *Chha Mana Atha Guntha*, considered a foundational text of Indian literature, two collections of short stories, an autobiography and several essays, besides textbooks and a book of verse. He had earlier translated the Ramayana and the Mahabharata into Odia.

GODAVARIS MOHAPATRA (1899–1965) wrote seventy books in a literary career that began at the early age of fourteen. Besides writing poetry, short stories, novels, humorous and satirical writings, belles-lettres, one-act plays, children's literature, as well as journalistic pieces, he edited and published *Nianakhunta*, a widely-read satirical journal, from 1939 until his death in 1965. 'Maguni's Bullock Cart' has been adapted into an award-winning film.

GOPINATH MOHANTY (1914–91) was the winner of the inaugural Sahitya Akademi Award in 1955 and the Jnanpith Award in 1974. His novels include *Paraja*, *Danapani*, *Amrutara Santana*, *Laya Bilaya* and *Dadi Budha*, all of which have also been translated into English. He was also awarded the Padma Bhushan in 1991. His prodigious output in a literary career spanning almost half a century included twenty novels and sixteen collections of short stories, an incomplete autobiography in three volumes, and several translations, including Leo Tolstoy's *War and Peace* and Maxim Gorky's *My University*.

J. P. (JAGANNATH PRASAD) DAS (1936–) has authored eight collections of short stories, twelve volumes of poetry, five plays, including *Sundardas*, a historical novel, *Desha Kala Patra*, and four research works on the traditional painting of Odisha and palm-leaf miniaturists. Nearly all his works are available in English. He was awarded the Sahitya Akademi Award (which he refused), the Sarala Award and the Saraswati Samman in 2006.

K. K. (KAMALAKANTA) MOHAPATRA (1951–) has written three collections of short stories, a novel, a book of non-fiction and an autobiography. He has also translated into Odia selected stories by Isaac Bashevis Singer, Jean-Paul Sartre, Franz Kafka, as well as William Shakespeare's *King Lear*, and collaborated with Leelawati Mohapatra and Paul St-Pierre on numerous works of translation from Odia into English.

KANHEILAL DAS (1947–75) wrote over seventy-five stories, experimenting furiously and feverishly before his promising literary career was cut short by his untimely death at the age of twenty-eight. His complete stories have been collected in a single posthumous volume.

KISHORI CHARAN DAS (1924–2004) published sixteen collections of short stories, six novels, and several books of essays. He was the recipient of the Sahitya Akademi Award, 1976, and the Sarala Award, 1985. A translator himself, his stories have been translated, among others, by Phyllis Granoff.

In 1969, he led the Indian delegation of writers to the Adelaide Literature Festival. He is credited with giving voice to the angst-ridden upper-middle class of society, and his work is well known for its psychoanalytical nuances.

KRUSHNA PRASAD MISHRA (1933–94) was a short-story writer and novelist. He also taught philosophy and founded and edited *Manas*, an influential literary journal for over a decade in the 1970s. He published seven collections of short stories and three well-received novels, one of which has been made into a film.

MANOJ DAS (1934–) is a bilingual novelist, short-story writer, essayist and columnist, and a hugely popular public speaker. Manoj Das was a left-wing student leader in college and led a delegation to the first Afro-Asian Students Conference at Bandung, Indonesia, in 1956. He has received several literary awards: among them, the Sahitya Akademi Award in 1972, the Sarala Award in 1980, and the Saraswati Samman in 2000, to name a few. He was awarded the Padma Shri in 2001 and the Sahitya Akademi Fellowship in 2006. He has published ten novels, nineteen collections of short stories, six travelogues, five books of essays and commentaries on history and culture, a memoir, and two volumes of poetry.

MOHAPATRA NILAMONI SAHOO (1926–2016) was a short-story writer, novelist, essayist, teacher, and a much sought-after public speaker all his life. He received the Sarala Award in 1983 and the Sahitya Akademi Award in 1984, for his collection of stories, *Abhisapta Gandharba*. He wrote a popular weekly newspaper column on spiritual matters for over a decade, along with two novels, twenty collections of short stories, and two volumes of children's literature.

NRUSINGHA TRIPATHY (1945–) has published six collections of short stories and nine volumes of poetry, routinely spurning every literary award that has come his way. He has edited the literary journal *Nabalipi* for over three decades. As a social activist, he helped found a medical centre for the deprived and the disadvantaged.

PRATIBHA RAY (1944–) is a short-story writer and novelist. Her prodigious output includes twenty-one novels, among them *Yajnaseni* (also available in an eponymous English translation), which has had one hundred editions since its publication in 1984, twenty-two collections of stories, ten travelogues, two books of essays, and an autobiography. She has received many literary awards, among them, the Sarala Award in 1990, the Moorti Devi Award in 1991, the Sahitya Akademi Award in 2000, and the Jnanpith Award in 2011.

RABI PATNAIK (1935–91) wrote over two hundred and fifty short stories, which have been collected in seventeen volumes. He was a recipient of the Sarala Award in 1991 and the Sahitya Akademi Award in 1992 posthumously.

RAMACHANDRA BEHERA (1945–) has published thirteen novels and sixteen collections of short stories, besides several radio plays broadcast by All India Radio. He has received, among several distinguished honours, awards and prizes, the Sarala Award, 1991, and the Sahitya Akademi Award, 2005. He was also the president of the Odisha Sahitya Akademi between 2010 and 2013.

REBA RAY (1875–1957) founded, along with others, *Asha*, the first women's journal in Odia. Her story 'The Sanyasi', published in March 1899, six months after Fakir Mohan Senapati's 'Rebati', has the distinction of being the first modern Odia short story written by a woman. Her stories were collected in *Shakuntala* (1904). Later, she switched her loyalty to poetry and published several collections. Her writings are marked by her deep interest in women's issues, communal harmony and nationalism.

SANTANU KUMAR ACHARYA (1933–) is a novelist, short-story writer, and popular public speaker. He experimented with magical realism long before the term became popular and fashionable after the advent of Gabriel García Márquez on the world stage. He has published fifteen novels and twenty-two volumes of short stories, ten children's books, in addition to his autobiography. He has received, among many other prizes, the 1987 Sarala Award and the 1993 Sahitya Akademi Award. His novel *Nara Kinnara* is hailed as a pathbreaking work of art.

SATCHIDANANDA RAUTRAY (1916–2004) is considered to have ushered in the postmodern period of Odia poetry. He was the recipient of the 1964 Sahitya Akademi Award and the 1986 Jnanpith Award. All his short stories have been collected in five volumes. His 1934 picaresque novel, *Chitragriba*, is considered the first anti-novel in Odia literature. He was awarded the Padma Shri in 1962.

SURENDRA MOHANTY (1920–90) was a short-story writer, novelist, critic, biographer and journalist. His four novels include *Andha Diganta* and *Nila Shaila*, for which he received the Sahitya Akademi Award in 1970. He published eleven collections of short stories, a two-volume history of Odia literature, several critical works on Fakir Mohan Senapati, a two-volume biography of Madhusudan Das, the architect of modern Odisha, a travelogue and an autobiography. Engaged in active politics for over three decades, he was twice elected as MP to the lower house of the Indian parliament. He also edited the dailies *Kalinga* (1966–70) and *Sambad* (1988–90).

ACKNOWLEDGEMENTS

Time for all those who helped the anthology along to take a bow. They are too many to be mentioned individually; although to cite some would seem inevitably to be slighting others, not to single out Narendra Narayan Dash would be an act of betrayal we'd hate to bring on ourselves. Not only did he throw open the forbidden doors of his vast collection of books and journals to us, but he acted as a serious and sensitive sounding board when we were faced with the unenviable job of hammering out the list of 'greatest Odia stories' ever told. Then there is Asit Mohanty, who too acted as a second line of defence and who, in addition, helped us track down stories which have inexplicably dropped out of sight. His phenomenal memory was much to our advantage. Both helped with their sage—and sane—choices, leaving it to us to take the final call.

We thank all copyright holders of these stories for having been so helpful; they have been as kind as they have been prompt.

Then there are the people behind all good and fruitful ventures, who unfailingly prove to be unending sources of gentle encouragement and inspiration. We've had our fair share of them (most of them aren't even aware of how important they have been to us): Mini Krishnan, Ananta Mahapatra, Debabrata Madanray, Himansu Sekhar Mohapatra, Mauricio D. Aguilera Linde, Renuka Rath, Jatindra Kumar Nayak, Sivapada Swain, Prasanta Das, Siddhartha Patnaik, Sailen Routray, Manu Dash, Sampad Nayak, Gandharba Pradhan, Ajit Das, Kamal Lochan Das, Ghanashyam Sahu, Omkar Nath and Nivedita Mohanty, C. P. Ramaswamy, Kata Chandrahas, Asharafi Munir Mehsania, Manohar Lal, Prasana Kumar Dash, Baikuntha Nath Panda, Lipika and Utpaul Ghosh, Shukla and Sudhansu Mohanty, Kritika Krishnamurthy and Anoorup Omkar, Mitali Monalisha and Pankaj Mohapatra, Pallavi and Sushant Mohanty, Soumya Mohapatra, Suswagata and Dhruva Banerjee, Samarendra Vikram Mookerjee, Basant Kumar Tripathy, Debendra Dash, Dipti Ranjan Patnaik, to name just a few.

We owe one large dollop of heartfelt thanks to Simar Puneet, our editor at Aleph. Not only did she give us a free hand (and a long rope), but she refrained, angelically, from breathing down our necks. Such magical, elfin souls do not come in large numbers in the cruel and cut-throat world of publishing. She does not know what wonders her occasional notes and nudges did. And how can we not acknowledge the inputs of Simar's meticulous associate Isha Banerji? Her sound judgement served to smooth out the rough edges.

NOTE FROM THE TRANSLATORS

Grateful acknowledgement is made to the following copyright holders for permission to reprint copyrighted material in this volume. While every effort has been made to locate and contact copyright holders and obtain permission, this has not always been possible; any inadvertent omissions brought to our notice will be remedied in future editions.

'The Solution' by Gopinath Mohanty. Reprinted by permission of Omkar Nath Mohanty.

'The Holy Banyan' by Bamacharan Mitra. Reprinted by permission of Sanghamitra Ghosh.

'The Witness' by Satchinanda Rautray. Reprinted by permission of Sriharsha Rautroy.

'Ghania Celebrates Ganesh Chaturthi' by Surendra Mohanty. Reprinted by permission of Pushpamitra Mohanty.

'The Atheist' by Kishori Charan Das. Reprinted by permission of Kumaree Das.

'Mother India' by Mohapatra Nilamoni Sahoo. Reprinted by permission of Anusuya Mohapatra.

'A River Called Democracy' by Akhil Mohan Pattnaik. Reprinted by permission of Timir Baran Pattnaik.

'The Tale of the Snake Charmer' by Chandrasekhar Rath. Reprinted by permission of Sashibhushan Rath.

'Plus Minus Greater than Zero' by Santanu Kumar Acharya. Reprinted by permission of the author.

'Trojan Horse' by Krushna Prasad Mishra. Reprinted by permission of Siddhartha Mishra.

'Mrs Crocodile' by Manoj Das. Reprinted by permission of the author.

'Savitri' by Rabi Patnaik. Reprinted by permission of Bijaylaxmi Patnaik.

'Savara' by Chaudhury Hemakanta Misra. Reprinted by permission of Sahana Das.

'The Mantra' by Jagannath Prasad Das. Reprinted by permission of the author.

'Patadei' by Binapani Mohanty. Reprinted by permission of the author.

'Salvation' by Pratibha Ray. Reprinted by permission of the author.

'Anatomy of Madness' by Ramachandra Behera. Reprinted by permission of the author.

'Longing for Ramakanta Rath' by Nrusingha Tripathy. Reprinted by permission of the author.

'News of the Day' by Kanheilal Das. Reprinted by permission of Asit Mohanty.

'The Whore: A Love Story' by Kamalakanta Mohapatra. Reprinted by permission of the author.